I0688454

Also by Joanne E. Zienty

The Things We Save

CHILDREN
OF THE
REVOLUTION

joanne e. zienty

Shaherazade
Press

WHEATON, ILLINOIS

Copyright © 2020 by Joanne E. Zienty. All rights reserved.
Printed in the United States of America. No part of this book may be used
or reproduced in any manner whatsoever without written permission except
in the case of brief quotations embodied in critical articles or reviews.

This is a work of fiction. Names, characters, places, and incidents either are the
product of the author's imagination or are used fictitiously. Any resemblance
to actual persons, living or dead, events or locales is entirely coincidental.

FIRST EDITION

Designed by Cecily Pincsak

Library of Congress Cataloging-in-Publication Data has been applied for.

ISBN 9781733688123

This book is for my mother.

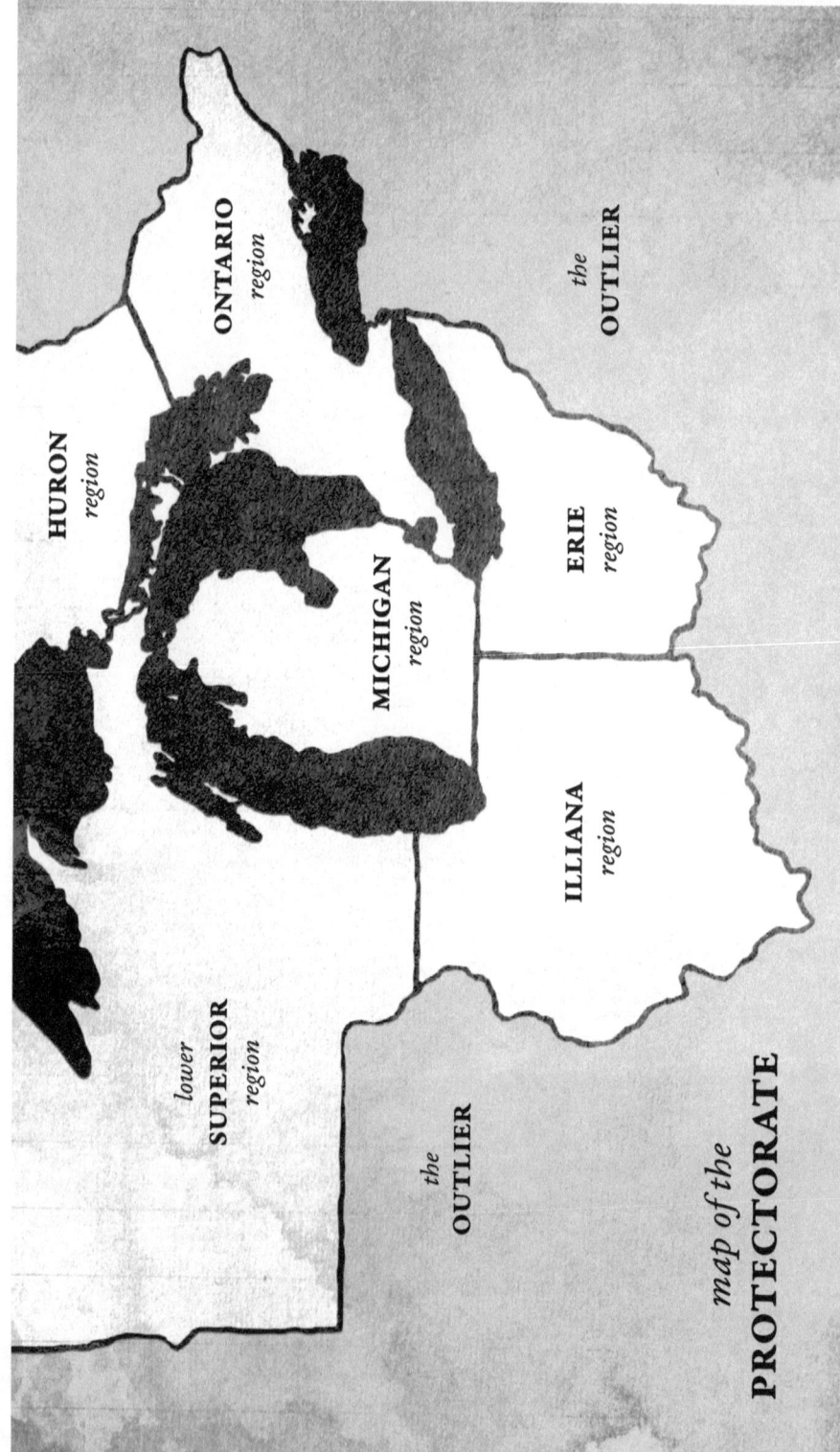

map of the
PROTECTORATE

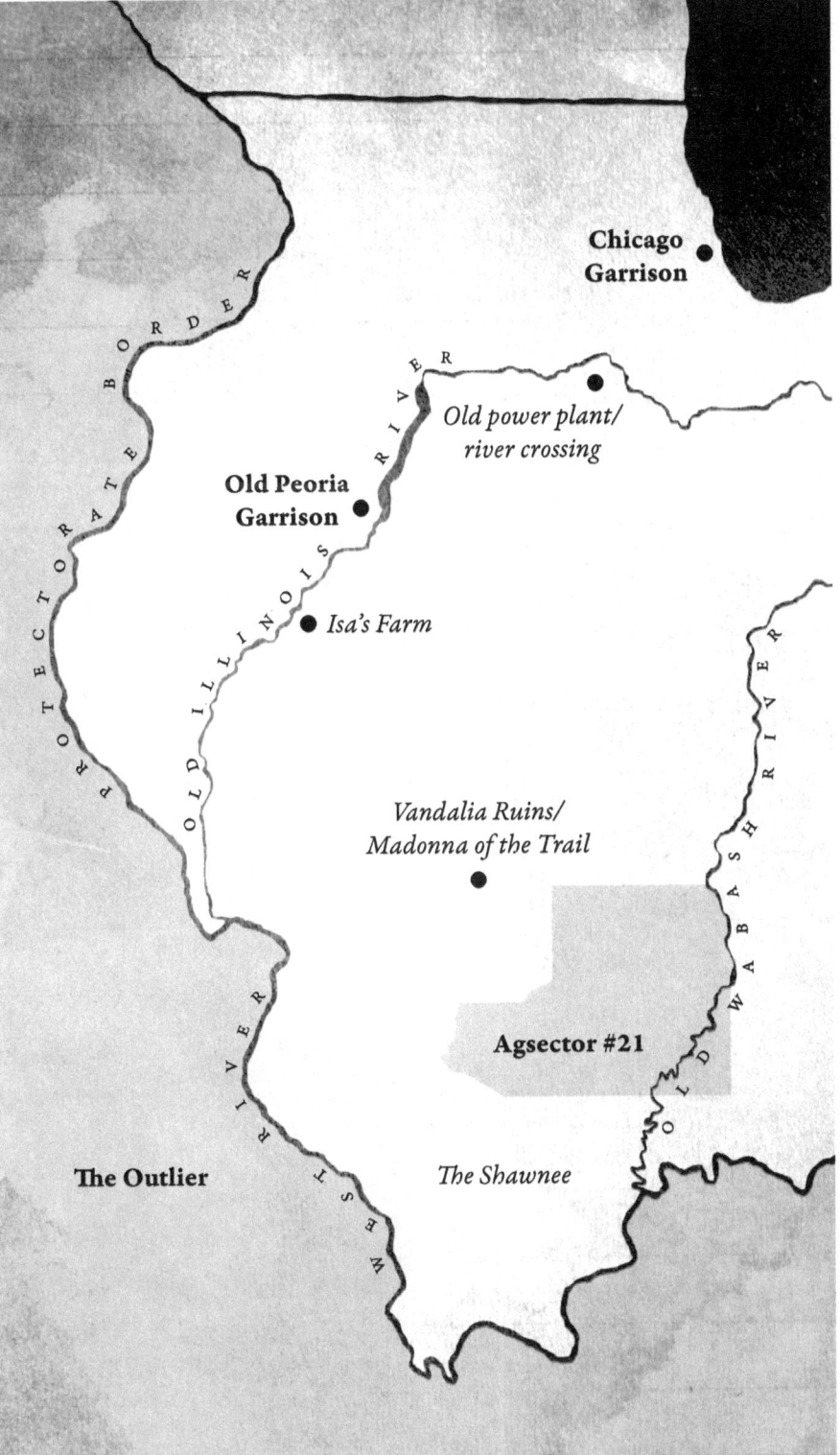

"The essential American soul is hard, isolate, stoic, and a killer. It has never yet melted."

D.H. Lawrence, *Studies in Classic American Literature*

Before you embark on a journey of revenge, dig two graves.

Misattributed to Confucius

Year 80 – December

SHE CAN'T REMEMBER. The recent past is a cold fog—thick, white, wet—through which she struggles to see. Are things mere inches from her face? Or miles away? Her efforts are fruitless, like a hand trying to swat mist away. It hangs there still. Heavy, dank, enveloping all in a chill embrace.

How many? How many are left?

She can't tell by the weight of the gun clenched in her fist. It feels as heavy now as it did the first time it was pressed into the sweat-soaked palm of her right hand and her fingers closed around its crosshatched grip. When she had hefted its black body then, lifting and straightening her arm, squinting down the barrel to draw a bead on the straw-stuffed head of the old man's useless scarecrow, she'd compared it to other things she carried that day. A ball-peen hammer. The canteen she'd sipped from moments before.

The old man had shoved a slim rectangle of black metal with a glimmer of brass up into the grip, pulled the slide back and let it go, chambering the first bullet. Then he'd pulled the clip out again and nestled one more cartridge atop the others.

"Thirteen. Yer lucky number," he'd said.

But now she can't remember. Does she have three left? Two? Just one? Questions crowd her mind, jostle for space, adding smoke to the fog. If two, which to take down first? The shave-head devil with the burning eyes, five yards to her right, with his own weapon trained on her head? Or the man five yards in front of her with the flummoxed, wide-eyed stare of one who hasn't given much thought to his own mortality. Until now.

And if only one?

She doesn't want to think about that.

And then she feels the soft roiling inside her, a kneading against the inner wall of her belly, a pressing down at her groin as if all of gravity has slipped inside and conspired to hold her to the earth.

It's time. To finish the thing.

PART ONE

A Day in the Life

Year 80 – July

For we... are as water spilt on the ground,
which cannot be gathered up again.

2 Samuel 14:14

1

Hymn to Water

THE WATERMAN BEGINS EACH DAY in the same way: seated before the massive bronze mural, contemplating. He imagines it depicts the origins of the world, the flow of all life from the rippling waves. He constructs this fable from the rising of the whale and the rising of the man-child, scenes which dominate the piece. Yet there is a confusion wrought in the metal—at one end of the sculpture, the whale, an ocean creature, arcs, huge head bent back over forked tailfin, while at the other, a horned bull lowers its mouth to drink from those same waters. In time, the waterman has come to terms with this weird juxtaposition. It is, after all, a hymn to water, as the sculptor, whose name is long lost, called it. So let land beasts drink from where sea creatures frolic. Let the humans wade amongst the fish and frogs, bearing baskets laden with the fruits of the land. Let the fish climb the tree-like torrent descending from a sun-burnished sky. Let the ancient one bend from the flow of clouds to lift the man-child from the roiling current. Or lower him in for a blessing.

It is his ritual, his liturgy, to sit and ponder here in this quiet space. To leave the small, but well-furnished rooms that constitute his home and step into this, his sanctuary. To feel small in its monumental space. To admire the patina of the mural, the finish that time has lent to the metal, the green-tinged verdigris that deepens its meaning. To give thanks for being a part of something greater than himself. He ends his meditation by raising his glass to the east, where the sun is rising from its watery bed, and sipping its gift of life.

If he were to construct a religion, it would be this.

Yet perhaps the favorite part of Chief Engineer Rivers' day is the moment before he pushes open the gun-metal slab of steel that is the door to the control room at Galt Calumet Number 1. The anticipation. The suspense. The question. What will he see today? Then in a bold, blue instant, the gray monolith is gone, replaced by the lake, sparkling before him, the morning sun winking diamonds in the waves.

It looks ever the same and yet always different. The vast expanse of blue is constant and yet constantly changing with the movement of sun and clouds. As a child, he'd learned the names of colors from its palette of shades. Aqua, the lovely blend of green and blue that tints its shallows under the glare of high noon. Prussian blue, the blackish hue of the deep waters, the color of a moonlit night sky. Lapis, the bright pure blue of the rising waves on a windy afternoon. Steel, the grey-blue of the water when moody under the shadow of a passing cloud. Teal, the sullen blue tinged with green and grey, the tint of an angry lake weighted with the storms of November. On this particular morning, it is a fine ultramarine. Soothing. Entrancing.

As a boy, in the long summers, he and his father had shared beach mornings, his father rousing him before sunrise to hike the mile down to the sandspit, carrying breakfast in the old red cooler. He'd spread a blanket and as the horizon bled pink to orange to gold, they'd eat his mother's melt-in-your-mouth blueberry muffins slathered with butter, his father winking as he spread another dollop. *"What we eat on the beach, stays on the beach. No Protectorate nanny here to remind us that one teaspoon is plenty."*

When the sun had risen, they'd amble along the shoreline in the sweet spot where the waves just kissed the sand, their bare feet delighting in the icy touch of the water and the rough caress of the sand. They'd search for feldspar, beach glass, and furnace glass, tiny, ancient remnants of the industrial behemoths that had once hugged the curve of the lake's southern shore like a necklace of toil and labor. Slag, his father called it, the leavings after iron ore is heated and the iron separates from the impurities in the ore.

"*Days long past,*" his father said. "*Before the Protectorate.*"

A daring thing to say. A thing to be said only on the beach and only between themselves.

"*Look at her, boy. Joined with her sister, Huron, she's the largest freshwater lake in the world. Three hundred seven miles long. One hundred eighteen miles wide. At her deepest, she goes down nine hundred twenty five feet. Back in the day, with her sister lakes, she held over twenty percent of all the freshwater on Earth. That percentage is probably higher now. Of the water that's still potable. Safe to drink.*"

His father would recline, closing his eyes for a last respite before the cares of the day began. He knew by the height of the sun in the sky when it was time to pack up and head for home so he could arrive in time to flip on his feedcom and catch the first broadcast, the second start to his day.

Gazing at the water now, from behind the thick glass window, Rivers still feels the hole in his life, gaping and raw as a fresh wound, and he looks away. A hard thing to lose a parent. To watch him board the bullet train. To watch that train quickly recede from view. And yet one tells oneself it is for the best. And so the waterman turns from the lake vista to the mundane yet essential work that it is his duty to perform: regulating the flow of water from this vast but not infinite bounty to the homes and workplaces of the people who shelter in the Illiana region of the Protectorate.

He smiles at the panel of buttons and switches that wink merrily in shades of green and blue, not unlike the lake to his back, and the mantra forms silently on his lips.

Galt provides.

A lesser man might have succumbed to feelings of self-aggrandizement, delusions of grandeur. Not Rivers. He understands the decisions are made far away. In fact, he's glad of that, thankful he's only an instrument, merely the hand that pushes a button or twists a knob, the fingers that punch in the passcodes. And so it is on this fine morning. A decision made. A decision implemented.

Galt provides.

Think of the Protectorate as a body. Corporate, *the Hive* as the rabble call it, is the brain, controlling all, envisioning the plan, setting the course, programming the actions. The lakes are the five-chambered heart from which the life blood flows. And the pipelines are the arteries, carrying precious fluid—water— to the tissues and limbs, the six Regions that fall within the Protectorate's walled, electrified and closely monitored border.

The pipes—concrete, steel and PVC—some so large in diameter that a pair of men, one atop the shoulders of the other, can stand comfortably inside, others barely wide enough to accommodate a child's fisted hand, extend for hundreds of miles to the north, south, east and west, forming an elaborate yet elegant grid. A vast circulatory system of veins and capillaries and vessels, transporting clean water, recycling waste water.

And the watermen are charged with keeping that heart beating and the lifeblood flowing. Perched in the aging towers of garrisons that were once great cities—Chicago, Detroit, Cleveland, Toronto—they monitor the system for signs of stress and disequilibrium. Finding an issue, they spring into action. An adjustment here and there, a recalculation, a finger-swipe on the smooth surface of a screen. Problem solved.

They are highly valued men, along with their co-workers

who serve in the new cities that have risen on the northern shores. Valued for their ability to anticipate weak spots and leaks. Prized for their steely-eyed cool under pressure, for the ice water in their veins. To be called a "waterman" is the highest of compliments and to be one is to be well-provided for. Elite. Dining on beef twice a month. And not the tough chuck and rump cuts that have to be cooked into submission. Selecting from the freshest vegetables in season. First pressed wines. Artisanal ciders and ales and cheeses and compotes. Living with embed in hand, rather than brain. With options for reproduction.

The good life of a swag.

2

The Dry Tap

WHEN MERIT TURNS THE KNOB on the pitted chrome faucet, a thin stream of water dribbles from the spout. Then the stream dies to a trickle. Then a drip.

Then nothing.

This is not a shock. Outages have been occurring all summer. An hour here, a half-day there. It's been nearly a year since the precious liquid flowed out regularly in a clear, quenching stream. It's the reason the bottles and jars are stacked in the basement, where the natural insulation of the earth keeps the air, and thus the water, cool, even on the hottest days of the endless summer.

But that water is reserved for drinking or cooking. Hand-washing only in extremis, Eben reminds. A little too often, making her chafe, reminding her of the bottles of hand sanitizer purloined from the clinic that sit on counters and tables and desks and bureaus in every room in the house, expiration dates long past, but still viable. Still effective. Or so Eben says. And he ought to know. As a medic, he emphasizes the crucial importance of hand-washing to ward off illness. Has drilled this into Merit's head since she was a toddler.

"There's nasty stuff out there. This is the easiest way to keep it from getting to you."

She sighs. As she turns the knob back to the off position,

she avoids her reflection in the cloudy medicine chest mirror. Fixes her eyes instead on the sage green wall of her bedroom, confronting the failures of her young life. All the tiny smiley faces, arranged in neat rows and columns, hundreds of them, most slashed through with thick black hashmarks. Their silent reproach speaks louder than any shout.

*Try as you may to be **that**... you are always **this** instead... a black mark across the face of the planet. Fail.*

Yet she takes up the pencil with its soft, waxy lead and draws another circle, adding two dots for eyes and a swooping curve for a mouth.

New day, new face, another chance.

"Find one thing to be grateful for," Eben would say.

I am grateful... that I took a shower last night.

She sighs again, squares her shoulders and draws her own lips into something between a smirk and a grimace.

3

The Hammer

THE TIRED TOWN SAGS at the base of the northern rise of the rolling Shawnee Hills, holed up like a ragged man too daunted to make the climb, looking as if one swift kick will send it toppling to the dust. Tanner has seen towns just like it all across the Protectorate. He's endured postings in every Region: from the lush Superior and Huron with their acres of high-yield farmland to the industrial triangle that is Ontario, from the waste pit of Michigan to the dying Erie, wracked by yearly floods. And now the near-corpse that is southern Illiana. He's hunkered here eight months, waiting, listening to his wife piss and moan for the first three, until he finally sent her back from whence she came. Sadly, that was no way to make the baby she desperately craved. But she'd made her bed and now she'd have to lie in it. Sort of like this place.

The sooner it's put out of its misery, the better.

"Eh, boy?" He scratches behind the cropped ears of the massive black pithound sitting beside him. The dog tilts its enormous wedge-shaped head, with its broad flat skull and wide, deep muzzle. Whines a little. "Place is uglier than you."

The Shawnee should have been tamed, too, decades ago, but it was left to fester wild, the decision, no doubt, of some bleeding heart enviro throwback, blathering on about ecological diversity.

The vast oak-hickory forests, the flourishing wetlands, the razor-back ridges. The swamplands of tupelo and cypress. The thin-soiled hill prairies and barrens where rare native wildflowers thrive.

A place into which the handful of wetbacks that manage to cross the river and elude the Border Patrol can disappear. Of course now the place was a tinderbox. All it needed was one well-flung match.

Tanner's fingers itch. He glances over at the low-slung cinderblock barracks where his eight-man squad idles, playing cards to pass the time. Waiting. Always waiting on the bureaucracy. On the other hand, it has made Tanner a more patient man.

And that is a virtue.

He is something of a legend, not quite a mythical figure but a man that few see, whose name alone is a threat, whether uttered by parents to their recalcitrant spawn—*Eat those peas or Tanner will get you!*—or shouted by taunting bullies to the weakest links in their social chain—*Dare ya! Scared? Wettin' yer pants? 'Fraid Tanner's goliaths'll come after ya?* His official title on the Corporate flowchart is Director of Special Services for the Illiana Region, Lower District, but those are just a lot of words that don't say much. That fail to impart the true essence of who he is and what he does. Rumor has it he started out as a guard at the breeder complex up north in Superior and bulled his way up the ladder until he was overseer of security for the entire facility. Talk says that, after some internal scandal, he'd been tapped by Corporate to take over command of protective services for the whole region. And then, during the Uprising, he'd been sent south to fix that problem in his own unique fashion. Because folks know what Tanner really is. The Corporate hammer. Powerful. Blunt. Brutal. Effective.

No one even agrees on what he looks like. Some say short and muscled, with pitch black eyes set deep in the folds of a fleshy face, with a strong resemblance to the pithounds that roam alongside him and his brute squads. Others swear he's a long, gaunt skeleton of a man, with strange, yellow-tinged eyes that glare from tight-skinned sockets. Many describe him as hairless, to the point of lacking eyebrows. There is some squabbling over whether this is due to disease or a sharp razor applied daily. But these are always third- and fourth-hand descriptions anyway. Stories that begin with "my friend knows someone whose neighbor once..." The way all legends begin.

Here and now, in one smooth movement, he swings his long leg over the seat of his overland and hops to the ground. Folds his arms across his chest and takes a hard look at the field before him, its sparse patches of spindly cornstalks withering in the stark glare of the summer sun. Tall, he is, but not gargantuan, as so many think. And muscular, but not in the tight-bound, twelve-pack, roided out way of the men who serve him. And, indeed, he has no hair to hide the contours of his skull, the egg shape of his head. But he does possess a lush growth of eyebrows, thick and black. They, along with his eyes, oddly colored with gold-ringed pupils gleaming in a blue iris, are hidden behind the lenses of his blackout shades.

He ponders the task ahead of him: achieving full eradication while keeping chaos to a minimum. Tanner loathes chaos and its siblings: noise, confusion, recklessness, panic. He is a man of neatness and order, of the tucked-in shirt, the polished boot. That extends to the severances that he oversees. He prides himself on maintaining calm, the aging migs and workers standing placidly in rows, some even smiling, in anticipation of better things. But calm, always calm, waiting like so many chess pieces to be moved at will. Like so much chaff to be winnowed. And move and winnow he does.

But this will be different. He's never supervised a severance of this magnitude before. Anticipation bubbles in his gut.

And a rare smile tugs at the corners of his thin pale lips.

4

The Non-Compliant Child

"Parents have always lied to their children. They lie to protect them. They lie to give easy answers to difficult questions. They lie to spare them the pain of the truth."

Say that to Merit as she watches the blue jay feed its nestlings in the dying oak tree outside her window, and she may, depending upon her mood and who you are, either laugh and call you batshit crazy or spit in your face and curse you as a fracking liar. But most likely she would just stare at you for a long moment. Two-toned eyes staring. Just staring. Hinting at something. Until you are gripped by the overwhelming urge to scream at her to just go ahead and say whatever it is she's thinking, hidden, but not really, behind that stare. Then, without a word, before you have the chance to open your mouth, she would have turned back to the bird.

The care the mother takes to fill each gaping beak with tender morsels wrestled from the uncooperative earth: *that* is how a parent nurtures its offspring. The calm she displays in the onslaught of their ceaseless chirping, until their protruding bellies are filled and they fall into a restless sleep born of the exhausting effort to survive: *that* is how a mother handles the responsibility of raising her young. And the father, doing his share of the hard work, does he ever sleep? Or is he wide awake even in the blackest part of the night, flared crest signaling aggression, fixing his steely black eyes for predators prowling above or below?

Of course, the argument could be made that these parents are just stubborn and stupid, attempting to raise offspring in an area grown ever more inhospitable over the last few years. That they should have moved on long ago.

After all, they have wings.

Escaping the heat of her bedroom, Merit heads downstairs to the kitchen. It's dark and noticeably cooler, the solar shades drawn against the insistent glare of the morning sun. She threads her way through a maze of bike parts at the bottom of the stairs, pedals and gears and handlebars. Eben has set a bowl of millet porridge at her place at the table, with the last of the mulberries arranged in a striking purple spiral above the bland beige, their juice seeping across the surface in blood red veins. Her grimace softens as she realizes that for the first time in weeks, since the heat of summer settled like an unwelcome blanket, food actually looks palatable. Not that Eben hasn't tried, sorting through the wilted, brown-fringed lettuce and the bruised cucumbers with their melting innards, offering her the best of the poor harvest and the lackluster provisions that have come down from Corporate. Not unlike the blue jays. *This is what a parent does.* Especially a mother bird—or a mother Bird. Merit lets the grimace ease to a grin, amused at her play on words and Eben's family name. Because in the year since Serafina's severance, Eben truly has made an effort to be both father and mother.

"Finally dragged yourself upright? And it's barely eight o'clock! Commendable. There's another bike to fix. I nearly killed myself trippin' over the project at the bottom of the stairs. And Mr. O was asking when you'd have his generator ready. You're leavin' your work unfinished again. Time and again—"

"I know, you've told me," Merit singsongs. "Never leave your work undone, lest it unravel like a thread unknotted. Couldn't you just say good morning?"

Eben, standing at the counter in his navy scrubs, finishes his nettle tea in one deep swallow and places the mug in the sink. He scrutinizes her. "I don't know. Is it?" He runs a fine-boned hand over his short bush of black curls. Each month the frost of gray seems to expand across his temples, a tide of age that never recedes.

When Merit doesn't reply, just slings her body down into her chair, he cracks a little curl of a smile. "Look, the man can't get by on just three hours of electricity."

Why's he run it at all in the summer? Yesterday, it was light 'til almost nine.

Merit means to keep it all in her head, but some slips out. "He's an old sweat. How late can he possibly stay up? What's he do with the extra light?"

"Yours is not to question. Yours is to fix the generator. And you'll enjoy the vouchers he'll pay. After you've finished the work. Besides, it's the neighborly thing. Keeps up morale."

Merit props her chin on her hand. "I bet he sits up making plans for after his severance. Almost 60, yeah?" She swings her feet up on Eben's chair and leans back, tilting her own. "Probably slumps in his easy chair, drooling into his mug of oblivion, picturing he'll hook up with some beautiful old ova on the train out."

"Merit." Eben's wide mouth is set in a curt slant that means a reprimand is on the way. "Don't make me regret I saved you the mulberries."

"It's true. I see the way he looks at—" The freshly drawn smiley face upstairs looms in her mind's eye and she bites the words back with a sigh, attempting to head off a lecture. "I'll finish it today. But I'm low on spare parts. Have to hit Bartertown."

Furrowed eyebrows. Downturned lips. Here it comes.

"You know I don't like you going there alone."

"You don't like me doing anything alone. Still." She leans forward, letting the chair thump down hard on all four legs again. "You treat me—"

He cuts her off. "If you go, make sure you wear your respy. Besides the dust, there's a nasty virus going 'round. And you left your talis hanging on the arm of the rocker. Again. Where's your head lately?"

Eben slips the fine silver chain over Merit's neck and tucks the tiny, plastic-encased circuit board that hangs upon it, barely the size of an apple seed, down the neck of her baggy yellow tunic.

"You know you need to wear it—"

"At all times! I know, you've told me a million times!"

And there it is, barely five minutes into her morning: another black line bisecting yet another smiling face.

Eben sighs wearily as he tugs up her sleeve. "Let's not fight. If you're going out—"

"I know, go early before the sun's at its height. Another thing you've told me—"

"A million times, yes, and a million more, if I have to." He swabs her upper arm with an anti-bac wipe. "And remember your hoodie. And your sunglasses."

Merit turns away to avoid seeing the needle, but she feels its prick. "Broken."

Eben shakes his head, anger narrowing his nut-brown eyes. "Again? You've burned through your allotment for the year already!" He closes those angry eyes. Huffs a breath in deep, blows it out slowly. "Stop. Breathe. Focus. Think." His mantra. He opens his eyes again, softer now, the anger dissipated. He drops the syringe into its sterilizer tube. "I'll see if I can scrounge some from the clinic. And before you start on the generator, finish your lessons. You forgot to login yesterday. And the day before. There was a feed scroll for me this morning, noting your noncompliance and questioning the quality of my parental supervision."

"Sounds like something Iris would say."

"It's exactly what Iris said."

"I forgot."

"You forget too many times. It's noticed."

Merit eyes her breakfast, growing cold in its bowl. Wait much longer and it will congeal into a sticky, unappealing pile of goo. But there is a point to be made. And with today's smiley already toast...

"It's boring—just watching and listening—or doing the tasks virtually on the swiper. Waste of time, tapping on that stupid screen. I want to be doing things—for real. Holding things, fixing things. Creating *new* things—"

"That's not the track you're on—"

"I know—I'm on Service track, not Innovation—and I also know I'm on the wrong track." She collapses into herself, hunching her shoulders, folding her arms.

"Service is a good track. There's always positions, especially in health care."

"Not following you down that path. Gonna walk my own."

Eben's lips are pursed in that way he has when he's biting down on something sour. "Well," he finally spits, "it's the path you were born to, and there's nothing to be done to change that. You can struggle against it for the rest of your life and be miserable—or move on and try to find some joy in it." Then he sighs. "We're out of flour. If you hit Bartertown, stop at the mart on your way home and pick up a bag. And just finish things, will you? You've gotten a rep for flitting from one project to another, leaving a mess, like a fly going from shitpile to shitpile, and that needs to change."

With a nod for emphasis and a glancing kiss on Merit's cheek, her father slips on his sunglasses and is out the back door, hurrying off down the street to catch the mobile to the Agsector #21 clinic.

Thanks for leaving me with that image. Shitpile, yeah. Buzz off, worker bee. Go and give the sweats their shots like a good little stinger. Then her eyes catch the ruby glint of the mulberries and she regrets her peevish thoughts.

You'll be one soon enough.

True. At the end of the year, in just five short months, she will turn seventeen. The age of taking the final assessments, of being assigned a vocation, of beginning an apprenticeship in the Galt Corporation. The age of becoming a worker.

A bee, a prole, a sweat...

"Angel, anything worth doing is worth doing well, with honor and pride. We are the backbone of the Protectorate. Without the workers, it all falls to pieces." Serafina's mantra, repeated whenever Merit scoffed at the men and women standing three-deep at the mobile stop, faces composed, tiny colored headsets curling like neon-colored, armored shrimp around their right ears, buds planted firmly inside, red for Service sector, green for Enviros and Agris, yellow for Energy and Tech, blue for Water workers, all of their gazes fixed on something in the distance only they could see.

"They look so vacant—like there's nothing going on behind their eyes."

"They're listening to the feed so they know what to expect from their work day. It requires focus. Believe me, querida, there's plenty going on behind their eyes."

Merit knew she shouldn't doubt. Serafina had been a worker and whip-smart; the one who'd taught her how to not only ride a bike, but fix one. The one who'd let her scrutinize her big callused hands, greenish veins writhing like worms under the bronze skin, as they tinkered with the odd appliances the neighbors brought for repair. Merit watched and absorbed until her own muscles were strong enough and her hands large enough to hold a wrench and she was ready to tinker herself. And then Serafina would marvel over Merit's long, tapering fingers, gripping them, murmuring, *"Angel, these hands will do great things. Wondrous things. In time."*

Serafina has been gone a year and Merit still can't get through a memory of her dry-eyed. She'd sworn that she would keep in touch. That she'd vox whenever she could. And then... nothing. Just a silence settling onto the days and weeks and months like the dust that settled over the windowsills and into the corners of the baseboards.

Baby, she curses, swiping roughly at the tears that dare to seep onto her cheeks. *Toughen up.* She rinses her bowl in the sink, peevishly splashing more water than she really needs out of the bottle that Eben has left on the counter. Scowling, she hefts her tool belt and slams out the back door to square off with Mr. Oceguera's generator.

5

Writ in Water

WATER SHAPES THE ROCK. It is excavator, sculptor, builder and destroyer. And the teller of stories, writing its tales in the geology of the land.

It begins in a shallow tropical sea, in waves of warm water, like gentle fingers caressing a barren shore. Strange and beautiful creatures lurk beneath its surface, an explosion of hard-shelled life crawling along the ocean floor. Trilobites in their flexible, shield-shaped armor. Brachiopods in their shells. Crinoids. Corals. And later, fish and giant cephalopods, the ancestors of squid.

And water gives birth to the land, with each layer of sediment it scatters. Sand that will become stone. In death, too, it is a creative force, as the water leaves behind billions of seashells, the calcium carbonate of mollusks transforming into the rock called limestone. And over time, water kneads the land like dough, bending and folding, punching it down, adding new layers. The Earth's crust sinks and rises and sinks again, in the shape of a broad, flat-bottomed bowl.

Water writes its story time out of mind. Things change. Evolve. Adapt. Where there was once a sea, there is now a muddy delta swamp. Trees tower a hundred feet above the thick, silty river winding through gloomy woodland. Animals that haunt our nightmares arise. Dragonflies with the wingspans of hawks.

Cockroaches the length of a yardstick. Poisonous centipedes the size of grown men.

And still the water shapes the rock, writing the story. Far to the east, mountains rise and rain sweeps sand, silt and clay down the raw slopes into rivers, the veins of the land, with the water ever seeking a way back to itself. The rivers carry sediment westward into the shallow inland sea. At the place where all the waters meet, the delta is vast. Fertile. Ever changing. It buries the ancient ocean rock.

Time and water destroy and build, excavate and sculpt, as powerful forces twist the land, folding and bending the rock, fracturing it. And the delta and its great forests pass on and are buried, layer by layer, and under this burden, this great pressure, the mud and the once-living matter unite to form shale and oil and coal. Even when the water leaves, it bends the rock to its will. The land, no longer swamp nor covered by ocean, is a land exposed to wind and weathering and erosion. When the cold settles and the snow falls and falls and never melts and turns instead to ice and the ice spreads and glaciers scour the land, rock is ground into gravel and gravel into sand and sand into silt and clay. Water, even frozen, will have its way and move where it will, and so the ice moves, leveling hills, filling valleys, and building anew, long, curved hills called moraines, the glaciers' icy fingers reaching, reaching, falling just short, leaving some of the ancient ocean rock exposed. Great beasts, the megafauna, hunt and are hunted: the mastodon, the saber-toothed cat, the giant ground sloth, the mammoth.

When the warmth finally returns and the glaciers begin to melt, the water continues to work its will, changing the course of great rivers, flooding the creation of lakes, cutting paths through ancient sandstone and limestone, carving out towering cliffs in the north and the south, leaving a flat rich land in the middle, as the tundra and spruce give way to oak woodlands and the endless prairie.

Tanner knows none of this. Only a handful do. In the Protectorate, history does not exist. There is no time before. Only waste and void and darkness and chaos, out of which Galt created a haven on Earth.

History and propaganda are written by the rulers.

But Tanner does not contemplate this as he scans the landscape before him. Rolling hills, dark, mysterious hollows, rocky bluffs, the curious formations that jut out from the sandstone pillars, resembling the faces of men, sullen, watchful. Nor is he thinking of its beauty. He's thinking logistics. It's why he's so good at his job. So highly valued. He anticipates problems. Works the angles beforehand. Plots the alternatives.

Though the gas mining operations have leveled much of the forest along its northern boundary, a vast, dim, brooding swath still remains, a dark mouth ready to swallow a runner. He knows he's likely to encounter a handful of those. Fear of the unknown. A basic human instinct. Sometimes they resist getting on board. And this time there will be no train.

Just the water.

The plan is not to his liking. It hardly constitutes a plan. But it's not his decision to make. Above his pay grade, as they say. His is only to enact. To ensure its success. Because he knows that if it fails, to whatever degree, it will be *his* failure. And if it succeeds—well, he can claim a modicum of responsibility.

And for this he anticipates being richly rewarded.

6

The Mart

THE STRUGGLE WITH THE GENERATOR is less battle than siege. The machine is a fossil, a crusty carbon-powered model modified at some point to run on biofuel. After ripping it apart and piecing it back together twice, invoking Eben's mantra—*stop, breathe, focus, think*—Merit decides the capacitor is dead. No replacement lurks in Serafina's old tool chest in the shed. She weighs telling Mr. O that *he* needs to find a new one—or heading to Bartertown to hunt down a spare and maybe earning an extra voucher for her resourcefulness.

The sun is higher than Eben would like. *Too bad.* She wipes her greasy hands on a ragged towel and grabs her respy from its hook at the front door, slipping the bands of the white mask over her head. She adjusts it over her broad-tipped nose and full-lipped mouth, catching a glimpse of herself in the long mirror, swiping a hand through her cropped brown hair, trying to suppress it into the required androg straight cut. But its waves and whorls tumble here and stick out there, as if to say they have a mind of their own and damn what Corporate decrees. It's getting harder and harder to pass, even with the loose, shapeless tunics that androgs are required to wear. Even with her strong, angular jaw. Do her eyes betray her, those hazel eyes, golden brown ringed with green, long-lashed, sharp and slanted above the fabric?

Look at that ravin'—thing, she taunts her reflection and its tall, lanky body, all willowy limbs and tight little muscles. Her length helps. And the careful regimen of diet and exercise. But a body grows the way it wants, the way it is destined to grow. And now there are things she must hide. Curves and swells that mark her as something other than what she is supposed to be. And the bright conspicuous yellow of the tunic draws the eye. And yet, even Eben does not appear to see that the shots he administers, prescribed by Corporate edict, are not really working. At least the monthly bleeding, so terrifying when it began a few years past, has ceased. The burden of keeping that secret lifted. Another secret that Eben and Serafina insisted she must never reveal. Just another thing that makes her special. Susceptible. Weak. Mocking her image, she sticks out her tongue under the mask. The tip of it brushes the fabric, tastes its staleness. She adjusts the respy again. The worn band snaps under the added tension.

Frack! She fingers the frayed edges of the elastic. If she folds it over and stitches a repair, the band will be too tight. If she hits the mart to pick up the flour and a new respy *before* she heads to Bartertown, she'll have to lug the bag around. *Frack.* She shrugs on her hoodie to hide her already tawny arms from the noon-time glare and tugs on her black knit gloves.

She wends her way down the rutted street, with its gauntlet of poorly patched potholes, through the curtain of dry heat, past the old homes with their fading, chipped paint and crumbling mortar. In its heyday, when the gas mines had been at peak and the agri fields still produced a lush bounty, the Galt Corporation's Quality Control had sent in the sweeps every fall to tidy up the place, to saw and hammer and paint and clean for the influx of swags who vacated the Chicago garrison and others situated inland or along Lake Michigan or Superior to winter along the Protectorate's southern border. A time when people still wanted to escape the ravages of winter. A time when there was still a winter to escape. Not that the swags ever stayed in town. It was strictly a waystation, a pass-through on their way to somewhere else. Some might have briefly lazed by the pools that dotted the estates in the Gates, the manses built for the engineers who oversaw the gas operations. They alighted from their personal transports, slumming it, tossing fistfuls of vouchers around like confetti, acting as if the entire place was a flea market to pick through, carrying off an antique bureau here or a hand-carved oak mantel there, because, after all, it all belonged to Corporate and they *were* Corporate. Deigning to take a quick meal at the Red Rooster Café, mocking its farm theme. Snickering at the carved wooden chickens that leered from the cross beams in the ceiling and the ancient hex signs writ in peeling paint. Hooting over the worn vinyl tablecloths, the red checked pattern faded to pink. The swags confined their jaunts to the two or three blocks that constituted the town center, marveling at the aged buildings with their staunch brick facades, their crenellations, strong and square like battlements. Wondered aloud why Corporate hadn't brought in the QC wrecking balls and 'dozers to demolish these relics.

But it's been years since the swags stopped coming through.

The Bottom is, as its name implies, the ass-end of town. Its sagging two-stories and tired ranch homes, some nearly swallowed up by strangler vines, haven't felt the slap of a paintbrush in years, not even in the high-rolling times. Swags have always avoided the Bottom like a contagious disease. The only time the QCs set foot there is after a severance. With the occupant gone, on the train out, only then will the house get a swath of paint: a huge red X from a spray can marking the spot where the 'dozers will come through and level it.

Merit was maybe five years old the first time Eben had taken her to watch a teardown. Scavengers—first the corporate-authorized men and then the independents—had swept through beforehand and picked the little frame cottage clean of anything worth recycling: windows, copper pipes, furnace parts, metal fixtures, faucets, doorknobs. In the bare bulb brightness of morning, what was left resembled the bleached bones of an animal carcass left to rot in the dirt. Then the 'dozer had rumbled in and flattened it with four passes of its massive blunt blade and enormous wheels.

"Why are they tearing it down?" she whined, fearful of the noise and violence.

Eben gripped her hand. *"No sense rehabbing old places. More economical to knock 'em down and build new houses, built to corporate standards."* He tousled her hair with a wink. *"Makes it a whole lot easier to keep an eye and an ear on the occupants when you control the wiring. Savvy?"*

But with the drought going on four years, no new homes have risen and the holes yawn deep and wide, even the weeds struggling to fill these gaping mouths in the earth.

The GaltMart sprawls on the edge of town, flat and boxy, a concrete slab punctured at intervals by large rectangular windows. Back in the day, folks could get anything there. Anything the Hive considered necessary and appropriate for the bees of southern Illiana. A reasonable selection of meats, dairy, vegetables, fruit and grain products. Modest, utilitarian clothing that suited their status and working lives, sturdy denims and twills, durable cotton/poly blends. Subdued colors. Gray, khaki, navy, drab green. Boots and shoes made for walking. Supplies to keep a home neat and tidy, ready for inspection at a moment's notice. If it wasn't in the GaltMart, you didn't need it, a fact memorialized in their slogan: *You need it, we have it.*

Even as a child, Merit could detect the subtle implication. *If it's not here, you don't need it.*

Over the last few years, the mart has changed. The once well-stocked shelves, arrayed in precise rows from one end of the cavernous building to the other, are now pitted with gaps, like a six-year-old's mouth. Some are shockingly empty. Now the mart is stocked with mutters and grumbling. Women clucking over poor cuts of tough meat—when meat is even available—and shaking their heads at the sad-looking vegetables, brown and melting around the edges. Complaining about the extra vouchers they have to fork over just to get the weekly Corporate-approved ration.

"Frackin' Hive mind. Takes too much for the swags, leaves too little for the rest, the grunts. And what they leave is just that. The leavings. Don't need 'em countin' calories for me. People can make up their own minds what's good for 'em."

Inevitably, in the middle of the aisle, some older bee will pipe up and staunchly avow that without the Hive, without Corporate, there'd be no Protectorate, and without the Protectorate, they'd all be on their own, in the midst of dog-eat-dog chaos.

"You accept Corporate protection, you accept Corporate rules. Live by Corporate rules. This wasn't—how did that old cliché go?— 'of the people, by the people, for the people.' Galt provides. If they say it's enough, it's enough. That's what made it all go to hell in the first place. People confusin' needs and wants. People thinkin' that there was no one right way, no absolute truths. Thinkin' that everyone could decide what was right and true for themselves. What a mess that made! Galt provides!"

Most shoppers avert their eyes from the spectacle. A few may half-heartedly salute the ranter. Join in with a rote *"Galt provides."* Because you never know what Corporate stooge is lurking. The eyes of CEO Blanche and his surrogates are always watching. Ears, listening.

"There's a fellow who knows a bit too much," Eben had once commented, watching a stoop-shouldered loudmouth shuffle away past the neatly stacked cans of corn and green beans. *"Of the people—"* But Serafina had quickly shushed him.

Back home, standing on the stool, helping Serafina slice vegetables for stew, Merit had tried to chop up an extra carrot or two to throw in the pot.

"No, Angel, only two."

"But I love carrots. Why can't I put in more?"

"Because the feed recipe says two is enough."

"You don't have to follow it."

"Yes, I do. We have our ration for the week. Using an extra carrot now means we'll have none for later."

"We'll just get more."

"There's only so much to go around, Angel. Growing crops is a tricky business; a combination of science and luck. Nature doesn't always cooperate. Plus, there's only so much food we need to be healthy."

"Says who?"

"The Protectorate, Angel, you know that. Galt Corporation has figured all that out for us, thanks to CQO Zinni and her metrics. Now stir the pot, please."

But had the slightest edge of sarcasm sharpened Serafina's voice?

Now, Merit presents herself before the entrance portal, under the watchful gaze of Chief Quality Officer Mora Zinni, who beams from the 'tronic billboard with her eyes the color of wet cement and her silvery helmet of hair and her ultra bright white teeth, each easily a foot tall. As a child, she'd thought the woman's name was Damora. The memory makes her smile a little, inside her head.

Playing at the park, listening to the men blow off steam on the hoopball courts as they fulfilled their daily fitness requirement. They played hard, running, leaping to block shots, driving to the net for a quick two pointer. If anyone tried to dog it, dribbling in place to catch his breath, his Metrics monitor would emit a high-pitched buzz that set the others to laughing.

"Ha, caught by the pulse patrol, get your butt back in gear, bro." The taunts were meant as jokes, but inevitably they morphed into muttered gripes. *Corporate owned every frackin' thing. A man didn't have a pot to piss in that he could call his own. Couldn't turn a corner without Corporate knowing he was taking the long way home. Now comes this Damora Zinni and her metrics. Can't skip a workout without getting a "what for" on the feed. Workers weren't workers; they were slaves. Damora! Damora!*

Asking him about it later—who's Damora—Merit caught Eben's quizzical, sideways stare until he put two and two together and laughed. *"Not Damora. Just Mora. The men were just bein' a little, uhm, doin' a little embellishing. Of her name."*

"Swearing?"

Eben had shrugged. *"People always whine about something. It's not in human nature to be content. Think about it, Merit. A man can't even play a simple pick-up game without being monitored. They're wondering why the Chief Quality Officer is sticking her sharp nose in their sweaty armpits. Metaphorically speaking."*

"Yuck! But it's really for their own good, Pop. Metrics help them stay healthy. That's what Corporate says. Healthy workers are quality workers."

"Ah, Merit, you're learning your lessons too well. Might even grow up to be a fine little Corporate player one day. Just like CQO Zinni. Imagine that. Rising from worker bee to queen."

Now the sensor pings, registering her digital presence and recording the embed that marks her as a legal inhabitant of the Protectorate. Its pinpoint light changes from yellow to blue. The steel and armored glass door glides open with a muffled hum. A gust of refrigerated air envelopes her as she steps over the threshold. This artificial relief from the ever-present heat makes the trip worth it, even if lugging the chunky bag of flour will be a hassle later. As she enters, a drift of shoppers eases toward the exit, ambling, transferring parcels and totes from one hand to the other, pausing to adjust their posture, arch their backs, not in a hurry to trade the chill for the heat. As they draw near the door, the sensor makes a read and the portal slides on its guide bar.

The boy is quick, stealthy, slithery, snaking his way in through the out door, under the cover of the others as they exit. About her own age and scrawny. The ragged Damn Otis t-shirt slips around his shoulders, bones jutting, stretching the surface of his bronze skin. Cargo shorts barely cling to his hips. He has the hairs-on-edge look of a fox about to spring.

I've seen you. Slinking along the edges of Bartertown. Skulking in the mobile station. I've seen your hands slip where they shouldn't. Thief.

The boy's eyes meet Merit's and he can't suppress a cocky little grin. Maybe he's not even trying. And is it just the glare from the overhead arc lights or are his eyes truly mismatched, the right, amber, the left, brown?

Merit hurries on, skirting the voucher station, heading purposefully to Aisle 10, where the grain dry goods are stocked. The pickings are sparse. Several shelves of barley, another of quinoa, a barren stretch of gray metal where the rice should be, then several ragged sacks of wheat flour. She inspects each, checking for tears. Selects the package that appears least likely to split open and tucks it under her arm. She heads ten rows down to the med supplies. Turning into the aisle, she sees the boy enter from the other end, averts her gaze, keeps her focus on the near-empty shelf. The white surface is dinged and dented from years of use, wear and tear that remained hidden in better times, when it groaned under the weight of its bounty. Now all is exposed.

One respy remains, hanging dispiritedly from its hook, the cardboard backing of its package dog-eared, the color faded, bled out at the soft edges. The one that's always fronted the display. The one shoppers paw, turn to and fro, as they decide if it will fit the shapes of their faces: broad, narrow, round, oval, square. The one they never buy because they want the fresh one—the one nobody's touched—from the back of the hook.

Merit normally wouldn't take it either, preferring one without a residue of other people's filth and germs. But that's not an option. So she reaches for the respy and her gloved hand brushes up against the boy's, who is suddenly by her side, reaching, his hand bare and grasping. Her fingers close around the package first, but release it immediately, as if it's white-hot to the touch.

"Nope, it's yers." The boy pulls his hand back, gives it a little twirl in front of a funny half-bow. "Easy to ken that you needs it more than me. To hide that face."

She grabs the respy off the hook with a jerk that rips through the top of the hanger hole. Turns on her heel. Aches to stomp but strolls instead, swift but in control, cursing him in her wheeling mind. Hears the patter of his steps behind her, beside her. The boy is a walking smirk, his trainer shoes outlandishly oversized, ragged as his shirt, their original hideous lime color muted now amidst stains of dirt and grass and grease. They plop and splat against the tile.

"You took that wrong. I ken that. What I mean was, you wasn't born to be a 'drog. That ain't really your—mold—izzit?"

She ignores him, but he persists, clinging to her side, like snot.

"I take you for one of them pleasure girls."

She jabs with her elbow, a good swift one intended for his ribs. But given the boy's lack of height, she hits higher, an ineffectual glancing blow to his upper arm.

"Piss off!" she hisses.

"Yes, yer swagness. From yer lips to my ears, it be done." He peels away at the end cap, turning left as she turns right.

The absolute fracking cojones!

At the voucher station, she fumes, foot tapping, behind a rumpled man with bloodshot eyes and a hunch to his shoulders, a burnt smell wafting with his every movement. Inducing a headache as she strains to check her peripheral vision. The boy has disappeared into the vastness of the mart. And then it is her turn to swipe the v-cards. Green for dry foods. Red for meds. To grab up her purchases and get the hell out. She pauses only to rip open the respy pack, affix the mask over her nose and mouth and toss the waste in the recycler. Throwing a last look over her shoulder, she catches a glimpse of the boy in the grain aisle, slipping a packet of barley into his pants.

7

Bartertown

IF A VISIT TO THE GALTMART is like a lap swim in a carefully regulated pool—cool, calm, predictable, ordered, antiseptic—then a trip to Bartertown is a wade through the thick waters of a river delta. A swampy confluence clogged with things washed in from other places. Rich with sediment and filth. And fear. A crazy, walk-on-the-wild-side blackmarket with no sensors on the doors to read your embed when you enter. Half the time, there are no doors at all. Galt periodically sends a brute squad of goliaths to clean it out, but it keeps popping back up in different locations, like a carnival whack-a-mole. This month it crouches on the far side of the dry creek bed that runs along the western edge of town, amidst the rubble of a dilapidated asphalt trail and a crumbling overpass, where hungry-eyed men and women squat under tattered tarpaulins or beckon from behind battered folding tables laden with flotsam and jetsam, someone's trash that might prove a treasure.

With Eben, a trip to Bartertown is quick, to the point. Get in, get what you need, get out. Don't touch, barely breathe. *Remember you're susceptible.* Germs, bacteria, and who knows what lurk on the unwashed surfaces and in the mucous membranes of this rabble. Even in the Protectorate there exists an unsavory element to avoid.

"How are they allowed to stay?" Merit had once asked.

"Most are legals. The others keeping moving. Even Galt can't keep track of everyone all the time. Much as they'd like to."

Now, without a chaperone to prod her, Merit lingers at the tables, fingering baubles that might once have dangled from the ears or wrists of some swag's daughter, pretty but useless: an earring missing a third of its rhinestones, a bracelet of silver from which the jewels have been pried, the prongs yawning empty, dark as the eye sockets of a skeleton. Further on, she sorts through batteries of all shapes and sizes.

"Guaranteed fresh!" squawks the vendor, a gaunt, pale man with an angry red cluster of mosquito bites running up his neck and a trickle of sweat running down.

Merit shakes her head and moves on to the next table.

"Don't try 'n get a word outta it, Rennie. Agua Quieta never speaks, least not in the public eye. 'Just walks in beauty, like the night.' Doc does all the talkin'. Yo, golden eyes, where's your keeper?"

The bike man, his waxy skin stretched tight over the wide bones of his face, winks from under the brim of his ragged cap. Another old sweat who has no business eyeing her that way.

"Just in—a clutch of Galt Rally 'raillers and crank sets. Or got some old-school Shimanos, if that's yer thing. Mint condition, just out the box." He waggles the gears, hands encased in the well-worn canvas work gloves that he always wears.

Tempting. They look almost new. "What'll ya take?"

"It speaks! ¡Tres palabras! I heard 'em," he guffaws, then drops to a whispery rasp. "Them pain meds, the pink ones."

Merit frowns behind her respy, shaking her head.

"What? Out? But you could get some, your keeper has 'em. No? Then what about the lethe juice? Pure or cut, don't care."

She lets her fierce eyes do the talking.

The man takes his cap off and mops beads of sweat from his

forehead with a filthy, grease-streaked rag. He settles the cap, once perhaps a vivid scarlet, now faded to a sad blotchy pink, back on his scab-covered scalp. The cap's embroidered logo is missing letters, the threads worn away ages ago. "I take it they're watchin' the clinic. Fine, water vees then, two per."

"These ain't new," Merit scoffs, tossing the gear back on the table. It lands on the bike man's left hand sheathed in its filthy glove. The tough old bird doesn't even flinch. "Flip it. Two 'raillers and a crank set for one voucher."

"A speech, that was! Quite the hard bargainer, Stillwater. Two 'raillers for one voucher—and a peek at that face. Like to see what side you lean to." He winks again. "I got my ideas."

"No deal, Mr. Cain. And my name's not Stillwater, so piss off." She turns away and stalks off to find a capacitor.

"Frackin' newbies and yer 'tudes. No respect for yer elders," the man rails bitterly to her retreating back, then sighs. "All right, Mx.—Bird. Two 'raillers and a crank set for a water vee. And here's hoping they get them spigots flowing again soon."

Returning to the table, she nods curtly, lifting her head to avoid breathing in the mildewed odor and bacteria emanating from his t-shirt while she slaps at the vicious black flies swarming under the threadbare canopy.

"Need some new skeeter netting," he mutters, wrapping her parts in a threadbare pillowcase, the navy fabric faded to gray in the spots where someone has laid his head for year upon year. But he keeps the parcel in his grip until she produces the blue swipe card from her backpack. He flips it several times, eyeing the date embossed on the back.

"Ever cheated you?" Merit snarls, eyes narrowing.

"Looks too new for a card issued a year ago."

"Never used."

"Why's that?"

"Dead men don't drink water."

Merit slings the pillowcase over her shoulder and turns away.

"Ah, now there's a slogan. Here's another. 'All that's best of dark and bright meets in her aspect and her eyes.'"

The lilting phrase stops her in mid-stride, and she feels the question hovering on her lips, but bites it back.

"Wanna know what it is, dontcha? Cuz you know I din't make that up—me, smelly old lout of a bike man. Used to work for Corporate swags. In maintenance, workin' the gardens. Lady of the manse would sit all day, drawing her finger cross her swiper, readin', flippin' her 'tronic pages. She 'specially liked that poem. Would say it aloud, like she knew it by heart." He taps his chest with a gloved fist. "Til I had the words all up inside me too, from hearing it so much. But I din't mind listenin' to her. Had a lovely, soothing voice, husky and deep in the throat for such a tiny creature. A voice that oozes through your ears, soft-like. Velvet persuasion. Like yours. You should talk more, Miss Stillwater. Agua quieta."

She doesn't turn around. "Don't you worry a goliath'll get you, lettin' fly with forbidden words?" As she finally glances over her shoulder, the mask may conceal the smile on her lips, but not the spark in her eyes.

The old man eyes her cockily. "What? Español? Huh, I say what I want, when I want, how I want. B-squaders can bite me. Wanna know why I call you that? Agua quieta? Still water?" He pauses, tilts his head back, as if awaiting a reply but knowing he won't get one. "Nother story for you. Traveler's trying to cross a river. Maybe like that one down on the border. No bridge, no boat. Sounds it up and down to find where it'd be easiest to ford. Testing it, he gets the old a-ha. Where the water makes the most noise, burbling and crashing, raising a scare, it's actually way shallow and easy to cross, cuz the stones that raise the ruckus are easy to see. But where the river runs smooth and flows quiet, that's where it's deep and there's no easy path to follow."

Rennie, the battery man, who's been listening, hoots. "There he goes, preachin' again. Preach, preacher man."

Cain ignores him, winks an oozy, bloodshot eye. "Sure, that's what they used to call a parable. Still waters, you ken? Man has to wonder what's going on behind those almond eyes." His voice drops, barely audible, just a bare exhalation of breath. His eyes flick in the direction of a pair of androgs browsing at a table ten paces away, skinny and wan in their yellow tunics, brown hair lank under a sheen of sweat, in need of a cropping. "Because we both know yer not like them."

8

The Happy Warrior

"HE GIVIN' YOU PROBLEMS?"

The voice, incongruously cheerful, rings out from behind Merit's shoulder. The bike man's lips clamp shut and he sits back in his folding chair, pulling the brim of his cap down over his eyes, shrinking into himself, tucking his hands under his pits, a pack wolf cowed by the sudden appearance of the alpha. Merit turns, her head instinctively tilting up to avoid staring into the broad chest of Mars Lund.

"No, no problems at all. Just an old man—"

"Who likes to get up in everyone's business."

"Bikes. Likes to talk bikes. Diarrhea of the mouth on that topic. Right, Mr. Cain?"

Cain flicks at a fly investigating the seeping welts on his forearm, nods. "And now our bizness—and chat—is over."

"Well, then, Mx. Bird, may I walk you home?" Mars asks, taking her elbow and guiding her into the path between vendors.

"You didn't have to do that," Merit hisses under her breath as they step away. "He's harmless. Just another old sweat tryin' to keep his grip on the bar."

Mars smiles that maddening, ever-present smile, broad and open, teeth white and even. His is a carefully sculpted face, with a long, narrow nose and flat cheekbones and fine skin that is pale in his quieter moments, but flames ruddy with every gust of laughter that escapes him. "Just doin' my job."

"It's not your job yet. When'd you get back?"

"Yesterday. And today I got the summons. Two more days. Not even." He glances at the Metrics monitor on the inside of his wrist. "Thirty hours. Report to Agsector #21 barracks at 1800 hours tomorrow. And life really begins." He blows a long puffing breath. "Sometimes I think I can't wait. And then other times, I think I can... wait. Like I'm not sure I want it to actually happen. For the time to get here, you know?"

Since March, Mars has been away at boot camp, the last step on the Protective Services track before permanent assignment. The security spectrum is broad. He may end up as a specialized local officer, or a border ranger, as Eben had once been, or even a brute squad goliath. Merit can't—won't—wrap her head around that last possibility. Mars—happy, forever smiling, never angry—not once!—or frustrated or even the slightest shade of brooding. Mars, the vegetarian farm boy who can barely bring himself to kill a tick, who eats the flesh of animals only as required to build his body to the mass and size dictated by Corporate standards.

"You could just *not* do it," she'd once told him. "Take a stand and say no."

He'd stared at her as if the concept of disobedience was beyond the realm of his understanding, as if the word did not exist in his vocabulary. "You don't say no to Corporate," he'd finally sputtered. Then that fabulous grin cracked his face, slightly goofy in the moment. "Oh, I get it. Ha! That was a joke. Hey, yeah, you know I'm just a bit slow on the uptake." How could this manchild possibly be cut out for life as a corporate hammer ready to bash heads in a feedcom second?

She lets him guide her down the aisle before she replies. "So this is your placement? Here?"

"No, just orientation. I could wind up anywhere. Hoping for Superior. Cooler summers. Psyched for that."

"So shouldn't you be on the farm packing instead of skulking around B-town?"

"Still packed from boot camp. Don't let you bring much. And hey, this gives me a chance to hang with you." He gives her a playful nudge with his shoulder.

Mars was the first child she'd met after the Birds had been relocated to the agsector almost ten years ago. Other children her age or thereabouts were scarce, so it was a bit of a shock when Mars had shown up at their front door in a drenching rainstorm, a sturdily-built boy who towered a good five inches over her, offering to help tote their boxes inside. His wet hair gleamed like a golden helmet. Merit had shrunk away and run to grab her respy, but Eben had reassured her that it was a neighborly thing and asked him to stay for supper. Afterwards, they played chess in what Eben called the way of the ancients, with actual pieces on an actual board. Mars never threw a fit when he lost, the way Merit often did, sweeping her hand across the board, sending pieces flying. Mars just smiled and suggested they play another. Sweet and languid, a molasses boy, always a step behind her, the slow-rolling rumble of thunder to her lightning flash. They'd been tight ever since.

Though, in the past year, things had gotten a little awkward. A little static-filled. Sparky. Joltish. And then this spring. That... thing. Fueled by the home-brewed oblivion. A thing of blood and flesh and the commingling of each. That thing she doesn't like to think about. Won't think about.

Mars nudges her again now. "Plus, we need some spark plugs. A tractor's down." His eyes scan the tables as they walk.

"You're looking for 'em here? Don't the Corporate Agris keep you supplied?"

He shakes his head. "Something's up with that. Supervisor

says they're not sending anything anytime soon. Wouldn't say why." He sighs, taking off his cap, wiping the slick of sweat from his forehead with his shirtsleeve. "Not sure it matters. Nothin' to harvest. Corporate stopped letting Pop divert water in May. Ain't rained since the middle of March. Ground's so dried out it's like trying to cut stone. What did come up from the spring planting is long dead." He runs a hand over his short razor cut, before replacing his cap, adjusting the visor. "Four years now and this is the worst. There's gonna be nothin' to bring in, Mer."

"And yet you smile and smile. Sometimes I wish I could be like you, Mars. Just go with the flow."

The boy shrugs. "Can't change the weather. Not on Engineering track. Got to trust the brainiacs in the Hive will come up with some way to make it rain when Corporate wants it to. They control everything else, right? Why not the weather?"

"And if they don't?" Merit persists.

Mars grins and points his finger. "Then I guess you'll all be migrating north."

"Mars! Let's go!" The deep voice rings out over the buzz of Bartertown. Mars' father waves from the edge of the encampment. He is a short man with barely enough meat on his bones to keep the faded jeans hanging on his hips. His t-shirt looks a couple of sizes too large for his wasted frame. He glares with the twitchy eyes of a man who wants to be somewhere else quick.

"I'm gonna walk Merit around!" Mars shouts back, jerking his thumb at her.

The older man frowns. "I should think it knows its way around here."

Merit, her eyes on the ground, doesn't catch the look that passes between them.

Mars' father sighs. "Make it quick. I don't keep an eye on those dirtpicking migs, they'll be snoozing all afternoon."

Mars waves his massive hand in reply, then turns back to

Merit. "As if there's anything else for 'em to do," he says under his breath. Then, louder, "Done here?"

"You don't have to do this, you know. Go. I can take care of myself."

Mars shakes his head. "He's just got a lot of fear in him. Fear and worry. Glad I'm not like that."

"Nope, you are a happy warrior."

"Soon-to-be." He flexes his biceps, that goofy grin splitting his face. "So, done?"

"Not yet. Need a part for my neighbor's generator."

"Ah, yes, Mx. Fix-it."

With a shrug of her slim shoulders, Merit moves on and Mars follows, roaming from table to table, swatting the ever-present flies, until they find a trader with the capacitor she needs. She swaps two spools of copper wire and another water voucher.

"Alright then, let's blow this waste pit," Mars huffs, adjusting his cap again. "Hey, how come you're never on the vox anymore. I miss the night chats."

"Don't like the idea of Corporate trackin' everything I say."

Mars shrugs. "Don't matter. We never say anything worth their time listenin'."

"It's the idea that they can."

"What? You just realized that now?"

"No, but it just started bothering me—now."

"Well, I miss it. Miss you."

A hand on her shoulder. A finger brushing up under the hair at her neck, the static crackle of skin on skin. She rounds on him to dislodge it.

"You want to talk to me, do it like this. Face to face." Merit yanks her respy down, letting it hang limply around her neck.

Mars nods, the grin crinkling the corners of his eyes, which shine like shallow water under a summer sun. "I can handle that." He leans in, folds his huge hand around hers, hooking her thumb with his. Then, just as suddenly, he catches himself, eyes cutting to the side, as if to gauge who is observing them. He keeps hold of her hand, turns it palm up, raises it as if examining its surface. Rubs his thumb along the web of flesh that flares from the base of her thumb to her index finger. "Healed just fine, didn't it," he murmurs before letting her hand go. Shakes his head and shrugs. "Well, maybe it's just me. Training's been so intense. Sometimes I wonder whether I've really got the stuff for Security track."

Merit forces a laugh and punches the bulging tricep that strains against the fabric of his shirt sleeve. Mars flexes his arm. "Oh, I've got that stuff." He taps his forehead. "I'm talkin' up here. The trainers are just animals. Relentless. Lately, my head, you know, it just—hurts."

"Too much thinkin'."

"I wish. No, it's weird. Like something's inside, something that shifts or expands or—I don't know—grows and takes hold. And when it does, I don't feel right. Not like myself." His voice breaks a little, lowers to a confidential tone. "I almost punched a wall this morning. All of a sudden." His eyes shift, scanning the periphery. "The old man said something and I just—I don't even know what to call it."

"Anger?" Merit teases. "Welcome to my world. Sounds like every day to me."

"But that's just it. It's not *my* every day."

She frowns. "Stress. You're stressed out. You're not used to it. But look at the bright side. At least you get to actually do—what you do. Not just virtually. Not just interacting with a fracking roboteach on a screen."

Mars slings an arm around her shoulder again. "That's my Mer. Always wanting to be doing something—for real. Okay, so let's do a ride. For real. While I'm still here. Maybe head to the Shawnee before they outlaw climbing the rocks."

"Mars, light a fire under it! Dust's kickin' up and we need to get back." His father waves a hand as he glowers from the height of the creek bank, where two bikes are chained to a spindly tree of heaven.

"Okay, well, guess I should go." He hesitates, then, under the harsh stare of the older man, lets his arm slide off and away. "Let's do that ride, though." He turns, breaking into a trot. "Soon!" he calls over his shoulder.

Merit watches him go, his head towering over the crowd, a giant amidst a race of dwarves. But for all his size, he shuffles along with his shoulders hunched, the walk of a man who maybe hopes to never get where he is going.

9

Em

"Guapa!"

Another voice calls from behind and again Merit knows its owner by the lilting tone. Only one person ever calls her by *that* nickname. She turns. Sure enough, Em is standing in the scanty shade of a spindly hickory.

"¿Como está?" The small, fine-boned girl flashes crooked teeth in a wide smile with a sly edge. The smile a cat might wear when toying with a mouse.

"No habla español. ¿Habla ingles?" Merit replies, with a quick shake of her head.

"Oh, you're no fun," Em whines, beckoning Merit to join her under the narrow canopy of the tree.

"No fun, maybe, but smart enough to know even the trees have ears."

A frown chases the smile from Em's heart-shaped face, with its sharp chin and broad forehead. She flicks a loose strand of hair our of her eyes and then whips the band from around her chaotic ponytail, shaking out her full, black mane. "Then let them hear this! Frack you, Galt! ¡Vete al infierno!"

"Shhhh! I don't know about you, but I'm in enough trouble already."

"¿Por qué?"

"Stop."

"Okay, okay!" Em shrugs. "It just slips out. So?" She swoops her hair back up into a smooth tail and secures it with the blue band, revealing the silvery shimmer of six fishhooks impaling the curve of her left ear.

Merit pokes one of the metal shafts. "Another hook?"

"Another year, another hook. Six years caught with that bruja."

"It's not so bad, is it? Could be worse."

Em swats her hand as if shooing a fly. "Tell me your problems, mujer. Make me feel better."

"The usual stuff. Lessons. Eben." Merit flicks her own hand dismissively. "We don't need to go there."

"Oh, such *big* problems," Em whines again, rolling her eyes. "I don't wanna fix the widget their way, I wanna fix it my way," she moans. "I don't wanna touch this swiper, I wanna be touching—" She jams her hands on her nonexistent hips. "Just what is it that you wanna be touching? I saw you chattin' up that hulk, whatshisname, the future goliath. And with your respy down! Don't seem 'fraid of catching his germs."

Is it the rising heat of the day or are Merit's cheeks suddenly flaming? She tosses her head as if tossing the very idea. "Mars is a friend. Like you're a friend. And he's not necessarily going to join a b-squad. There's lots of Security jobs."

Em's wide brown eyes, deep-set, flash and narrow. "Yeah, he's got lots of possibilities. Unlike some people."

Em is not one of the *walking grinbees,* as she and Merit call the other kids. Not permanently sunny like Mars. Her twelve-year-old temper changes like the sunlight amidst swiftly passing clouds: one minute bright and hot, the next cool and dim, the next hazy and somewhere in between. Maybe this is what bonds them, that shared strain of orneriness that transforms them from silly to sullen and back again in the time it takes to inhale and exhale one long breath. That feeling that they are always walking in the opposite direction of the crowd, struggling against the prevailing current, the tide of smiles.

"How's life in the big house?" Merit asks with a snarky grin. "How many pecks of peppers did you pickle this week?"

Most of the migs spend the day in the sun's angry eye, backs bent for hour upon hour, inhaling dust, fingers callused to the bone from the constant picking and rubbing of rough stems. Em's one of the lucky few who labor in the artisan house, where the duties—making the hand-crafted cheeses and breads and jams and compotes and pestos that the swags crave—are considerably softer on the body, even if carried out under the watchful eye of the Agri foreman's wife.

"A batch of peppered okra and some jalapeño blackberry jam, baby. Make no mistake, this be a spicetastic week. The gringos better have mucha leche in the fridge." She toes a pebble and kicks it, stirring up a cloud of dust. "And they also better make it last," she adds, "because there's not more where that came from."

"There's always more where that came from for the swags."

Em shakes her head. "Not this year. Not from here. Some migs who were hauled over from Ag 29 brought a rumor 'bout killer dust storms that turn day into night. It's bad, Merita, and it's getting worse. Galt provides? Yeah? How's that gonna happen? Where's the food gonna come from? And this morning, no water again. You got water?"

Merit shakes her head. She has noticed the haze softening the sharp edges of the sunlight. The grit that lodges in her nose and throat after a deep breath of air. She eyes the horizon, obscured by ragged trees. "Maybe the other sectors haven't had it as bad."

"Maybe." Em frowns. "I've heard those rumors, too. We might be movin'. The bruja's been rumbling like thunder, says there'll be no more overstock to trade at B-town. Says Mr. Espino might be transferred, says we might be headed north."

A bead of sweat trickles down Merit's spine, like a lazy,

wandering finger. "Mars said that, too, but he was joking."

"Maybe not. It's nothing to joke about. Kids s'posed to get bigger as they grow up, fill out their jeans, not get skinnier, so last year's jeans are hangin' off their butts." She lifts her shirt to reveal the length of twine she uses as a belt to hold up her pants. She kicks another pebble. Her face darkens as she notices an older woman gesturing to her from under a canvas awning on the edge of the row. Mrs. Espino looks pinched and weathered, shriveled like a fruit left too long in the sun.

"¿Qué chingados?" Em rolls her eyes and gives Merit a long, flamboyant hug. "Whatever. Now I'll get an earful. No touching! Like its some disease you can catch. Androgobia. Hasta la vista, Merita. Hop on that bike of yours and come see me. I'll pierce your ears." She winks and puckers her plum-colored lips, blowing a noisy kiss.

"Against the rules for 'drogs. And too painful."

"Why have a rule unless to break it? And pain, it's mi amigo. It's a reminder, you know? That I'm still breathin.'"

"Take care, pequeñita." Merit watches her friend wink and then dodge a clout from the wizened woman and disappear around the edge of the canvas.

Rather than weave back through the mass of unwashed bodies and their stench, Merit strolls the Bartertown perimeter, pausing on the shoulder of the two-lane, sidestepping the carcass of a blue jay teeming with ants. Is it one of the parents from the nest outside her window? *Skeeter virus season.* She tugs the sleeves of her hoodie down to cover her wrists. Shuddering, she hurries on, ducking her head to avoid eye contact with CEO Blanche, head of the Galt Corporation, who smiles with casual violence from an enormous 'tronic billboard under a boldfaced banner emblazoned with the symbols "G-A-L-T-P-R-O-V-I-D-E-S." Pale skin unlined and smooth as the surface of a candle, black hair slicked back, immaculate, blue eyes dead cold behind his wire-framed glasses. Merit's movements trip the board's motion sensor. Through the hidden speakers, a deep uber-masculine voice pronounces the message of the day.

"To make a better future, abandon the past and give your all to the present. Galt provides."

Two minutes later she is turning down her street, squinting in the sharp sunlight that glitters and winks off the solar panels on the rooftops. She slips through the dust-caked picket fence, striding toward the wide porch of the two-story brick and stone house that Eben had once confided was over three hundred years old and had welcomed travelers on trails of dirt and iron, in a time well before the Protectorate was ever born.

"This house has memories in it... snow, ice, floods. It remembers. It's a place I think I can settle into." Then he had laughed and added, *"Galt willin' and the creek don't rise."* Serafina had shushed him and shook her head, but a smile was tugging at the corner of her lips, too. But the smile was on the sad side and the laughter seemed ragged and a little harsh, as if the taste of it was bitter in Eben's mouth. And they wouldn't explain, just went back to whatever they were doing, keeping their little secrets.

Merit shakes off the memory with her hoodie and gets back to her work.

10

The Lesson

MERIT, having coaxed the generator back to life, has actually finished a task, and is rewarding herself with a smidgen of homemade bread daubed with the last scrapings of blackberry jam, when Eben's irate voice barks over the com-link.

"Merit, what did I tell you to do first?" Without waiting for a reply, he sputters on. "I'll refresh your memory—your lessons. Repeat: your lessons. Have you done those? No. I checked Edulink and you haven't even logged in—and here it is, five hours later. Hustle your bottom into the screen room, login—now—and get it done—now! This is old, Merit. Time and again, what have I said? Finish what you start. Tie the knot!"

Even the sign-off beep sounds tinged with fury.

Frack!

Her fingers, purple-tinged and sticky, leave grainy streaks as she angrily swipes the pad of her index finger over the print reader and taps her login code on the virtual keyboard. She'll clean it later, after she's cooled down.

Or maybe not.

The lesson involves following a sequence of detailed verbal instructions to construct a virtual widget. Merit has blown it twice already: once because she had been daydreaming and put parts together out of order and once because she'd spotted a way to improve the widget's design, but had been stymied by Iris' insistence that she do the work according to instructions. Iris, the virtual teacher, intones each step in her meticulously cadenced voice, which retains only the slightest trace of its computer-generated origin, like the hint of an accent that clings to an immigrant decades after she first sets foot in her new land. In Iris' case, it is the lack of contractions and the absence of "uhmms" that mark her as something other than human.

"The program requires you to follow the sequence of instructions for a given task, whatever it may be. You are neither expected nor allowed to make changes to the task."

"But what if I see a better way? What if—"

"Mx. Bird, there is no 'but,' no 'what if,' and no 'better way.' You are required to complete the task as it is presented to you."

"And if I don't?"

"Students who prove unsuited to the conditions of the corporate environment or unable to fulfill the requirements of employment have the option of early severance."

"Sounds better than making these stupid widgets. How can I make that happen?"

"That question is above my programming. But I have made a note of your refusal to follow instructions. You will have one more opportunity to complete the lesson. Disconnecting now."

Merit has avoided logging in while she mulls her options and the two sides of her brain duke it out. *Just do it. Follow the instructions and get it over with.* The left—cool, analytical, linear. *It's stupid! I have a better way and I should have a chance to use it. I can see the bigger picture!* The right—spontaneous and creative.

It's not about your brilliant ideas. It's about doing what you're told—perfectly.

But I know a better way!

Then find out what program level deals with early severance and make plans to take your better way and go.

That thought shut the right side up quick.

Severance. A word Eben rarely speaks, and if he does, it's with a slight rasp, as if the syllables are something jagged lodged in his throat. On the other hand, Mr. O rolls the word around his mouth like it's a rare fine chocolate melting on his tongue. He's spent the past four years counting down the months, weeks, and now days, until he boards the bullet train out.

"245," he had chirped as he dropped off the generator, his round moon face set with a cagey grin. "When I start countin' the hours, you'll be the first to know."

But the specifics—*the where, the what, the how*— are enveloped in a vague haze, like the distant hills are obscured by fog rising off the warm earth on chilly autumn mornings. When questioned, Eben is never more than brisk and concise, Corporate-speak issuing from his taut mouth: "It's the time when people stop working for Galt. So it also means they have to leave the Protectorate. The only people allowed here are those who contribute to the Protectorate's existence and well-being: corporate execs, workers and—" Here he will smile. "Future workers."

"Where do they go? After severance? I thought the Outlier was a dead zone, full of—"

"What? Zombies? Boogeymen? That's the sort of thing children whisper to each other in the twilight. There are other occupied areas out there. Some are like the Protectorate, some are... different. Some are set aside for the released. Galt promotes it as a better place for them. As for me, I'm happy enough here, with you. I can wait."

That was as far as Eben would go. Ask about the 'different' places and he would just shrug and be maddeningly logical. "I can't describe something I've never seen."

And once, when Merit had pressed, asking, "Then how do you know they even exist?" he leveled her with a hard, no-nonsense stare.

"Simple economics. We sell them water." Then he softened his face with a smile, but it was lopsided, as if some uncomfortable emotion was tugging down on one corner of his mouth, and he had turned back to chopping vegetables for soup.

Now the lesson is before her on the screen—her final opportunity to follow the instructions, construct the widget as requested, and finish the task. Tie the knot.

"Are you ready to begin, Mx. Bird?"

Roboteach sounds especially animated and life-like this afternoon, as if joyously anticipating the failure of her most difficult pupil.

"Almost," Merit mumbles, turning away from the blue slate with its annoyingly large, exuberantly green start button, her eyes searching the screen room for a life jacket of any kind, something to cling to before she takes the plunge.

Eben keeps the room sparsely furnished. *"Stream-cam goes both ways, like the feed. Never know when it might be looking or listening. They don't need to know every little thing about us in our own home."* The white shelves lining the wall are empty; the biblios they may have once held long since reduced to ash and pulp. In the corner leans the battle-scarred black hard-shell case in which Eben's guitar rests. In the years before Serafina's severance, he'd pull it out and perch on the stool in front of the screen. Serafina would sit beside him and wink, murmuring, *"If they want a show, we'll give 'em one."* Then Eben would strum and they would sing at the top of their lungs, old, old, old songs that had been handed down through the generations, since way before the Protectorate had existed. They always finished with a rendition of a folk song that he started slow, in a whisper and she ended with a frantic, raw wail: *"some are wonderin', if this land's still made for you and me."*

The digipix frame sits on the desk beside the screen. Merit flicks the power button and hears the purr of the drive coming to life. The first image is always Serafina. Eben often switches it to a portrait of the three of them from a few years back, grinning on the shore of the little pond on a sunny summer afternoon. Merit hates that shot: her idiotic grin full of big white teeth, her skinny arms and legs as gawky as those of the herons that wade in the background, her untamed hair, longer then, kinking around her head like a halo. So she always programs it back to the image of Serafina in the dress she called her "best," the fabric splashed with flamboyant peonies, huge and pink, her face, round and pug-nosed, semi-smiling, semi-serious, and completely beautiful.

After that final song, she'd wink again, but her voice would be low and somber as she whispered in Merit's ear, *"Angel, don't you ever forget that. This land is your land, querida. Don't you ever forget. Time will come... time will come. But in between now and then, sometimes you got to play along."*

"Mx. Bird? I am waiting for you to press the start button."

"Sorry, Iris, daydreaming again."

"Are you sure you want to attempt this today?"

"Yeah, let's get it over with."

"That is not an appropriate attitude, Mx. Bird."

Merit presses her still-sticky finger to the green oval in the center of the screen and then pulls it away, leaving a grayish, boogery fingerprint.

"Attitude adjusted, Iris. I'm ready to follow your instructions."

11

Orders from Above

CHIEF ENGINEER RIVERS dabs his moist lips with the white linen napkin, then folds it neatly onto his crumb-strewn plate. He's partial to the mild white flesh of the silver carp and looks forward to the days it's served for lunch. Now he sits back in his plush velvet chair and gazes out the floor-to-ceiling windows of the dining room. Its location on the uppermost floor of the tower offers a panoramic view of the lake, the garrison and the ruins beyond.

"Must have been beautiful in its day."

Rivers has been thinking that very thought, though he knows it wouldn't be prudent to admit it. He subtly adjusts his gaze to the east, where the water looks churlish under the looming thunderheads that have billowed up in the heat of the morning.

"I find the lake has a calming effect," he replies to the tall slender man who has slid into the chair across the round table. "I do enjoy sitting for a moment after lunch, just pondering it. The view never gets old."

Garrison Director Daniels nods. With his bald pate, narrow face, wide set eyes and jutting down-turned lips, he bears a striking resemblance to the fish that Rivers has just consumed. Rivers blinks to rid himself of that unsettling image and takes a sip of ice water, a delicious palate cleanser with its pure lack of flavor.

He prides himself on that lack of taste, being something of a water connoisseur, having traveled the regions and sampled all five of the lakes. Here there is no distinctly earthy, almost moldy taste, which plagues the Erie system, with its unfortunate algal blooms that spoil the flavor every spring. No metallic or salty undertones and never the rotten egg smell that signals bacteria or hydrogen sulfide. No chlorine bouquet, for he is a stickler for using the absolute minimum amount of chemicals necessary for the purification process: chlorine to disinfect, alum and polymer to promote coagulation to settle impurities, blended polyphosphate to coat the oldest of the pipes and prevent lead leaching, fluoride to help fight cavities in children's teeth, and, of course, activated carbon to remove unpleasant tastes and odors. The total volume needed to treat one hundred gallons of water is about a teaspoon full, just fifteen parts chemical to one million parts water. The water takes a monumental journey, from the intake cribs far out in the lake to the treatment plant on the shore just to the north, through the underground pipes that carry it in all directions, to reach taps all over Illiana. As a professional and a devotee, he's made his pilgrimages. And he's satisfied that there is nothing to taste but the clean, light, pure absence of flavor.

Rivers pushes back his chair and prepares to excuse himself as the black-clad server quickly and quietly places the director's lunch on the table. Another plate of the silver carp with a colorful side of root vegetables, the magentas and oranges a happy contrast to the white of the fish. He nods, then pauses, remembering the question he needs to clarify.

"Sir, with regard to Lower Illiana. The order came down for an outage, which I put into effect this morning at oh-seven hundred. However, the action did not give an end time, as it normally would. Was something possibly garbled or dropped in the transmission? The feed quality is sometimes affected by storms to the north."

Director Daniels tucks into his lunch with gusto, hefting a heaping portion of fish into his mouth. He chews and swallows before he replies. "No end time was given because there is none."

Rivers nods. He knows better than to ask the whys and wherefores. In his linear, detail-oriented brain, he is already calculating the trillions of gallons of water that will remain in his lake as a result of this action.

It is an issue. With the unrelenting drought, the lower regions are obviously worse than the others. Erie, alternately flooded and parched. Illiana, especially the southern district, just parched, the bleached bones of a once beautiful animal. The recent downpours in the north will help, but overall, with the lack of substantial summer rain and winter snow, the levels of all the lakes are down, way down. Corporate has twice slashed the number of gallons to which each voucher entitles the bearer. Causing grumbling.

On his inspection tours, Rivers makes a point to get out into the communities. He stands on the piers of the small enclaves that hug the curve at the bottom of the lake, watching the men prepare to fish for those huge silver carp, readying their snagging gear and their fishing bows. He listens to the muttering.

"*Lookit the pilings. You can see the high water mark, the old level of the lake. Look how far below it is now. But are they cuttin' what they're tradin' to the Outliers? No, we're the ones who take the hit. Their own people.*"

"*We're not 'their people.' Just another somethin' they own.*"

"*They don't own me.*"

"*Just keep tellin' yourself that, you old sweat.*"

"*You wait, day'll come when you'll be choosin' between a shower or yer drinkin' water.*"

"*Or we'll be drinkin' our shower water!*"

"*Or yer toilet water!*"

"*Oh, yer laughin' now but wait...*"

The men had pushed off and taken their argument out in the boat with them. But he'd heard the same from others, in other places. Bellyaching, and plenty of it.

But that's not his problem. Those are headaches for the ones who hand down the decisions from above.

As he makes his way to the elevator, he glances out the windows again. The lake has vanished, obscured by the clouds and mist that envelope the uppermost floors of the tower. The rain has begun and for a moment, he wishes he were a child again, standing out in the downpour, face turned to the sky.

12

Map of the World

WITH THE VIRTUAL WIDGET CONSTRUCTED and one real bicycle repaired, Merit faces off with a relic that somehow plays music from small, shiny discs. Or so its owner claims. Ms. Salinas brags that it dates back to the year 2000 BC, when it had belonged to a relative of the great-great-great variety twice removed. The woman had rattled off the entire history of the slim black metal box before setting it in Merit's hands, proclaiming it had survived terrorism, plague, chaos, famine, flood, government coups, climate change, and rebellion with only the slightest scratches marring its smooth surface.

"It's more than an antique, it's something to help us remember. If we don't get it working again, thousands of voices will be permanently silenced, gone forever," the crank had lamented with dramatic gusto. "I won't rest easy 'til it's back in my hands."

Later, Merit had rolled her eyes. "What a meme, goin' on and on 'bout back in the day this and that. What's this 2000 BC crap? It's Year 80."

Eben had bristled. "BC. Before Corporate. And as a matter of fact, she *is* a knowledge keeper—and a good one, struggling to preserve what's been lost—or deleted."

"That's against the rules. Talkin' about the past."

Eben's rapid blinking had signaled his unease. "Well, yes, for now. But that may change. The Protectorate may realize that we can learn from the past. From its mistakes and its successes. And knowledge keepers will be ready to help."

"How many are there?"

"Don't know. *They* probably don't even know. It's all on the down low. And it stays that way. Forget BC, there is no BC. Zip your lips and give the thing your best effort."

Another secret to keep. But Merit is used to that. What she's not used to is feeling flummoxed by a machine. How can she possibly fix something she's never seen before? There is a drive motor, and a tracking arm, and some sort of lens system with tiny mirrors, and colored wires snaking in and out amongst green chips and black cylinders. Where to start? She spins the machine around and glances at it from the back, hoping a different perspective will spark an idea. Minute letters and symbols, smudged, fragmented and barely white, linger on the black casing. *Must have belonged to a swag back in the day. Maybe she should ask one of them to fix it.* Then her eyes catch a grouping of letters that seem familiar: M-A-L-A-Y-S-I-A.

MALAYSIA. She's seen that before. But where? Closing her eyes, she pictures the letters, those straight lines and angles with the curve thrown in, black against a blue background, just to the side of a green landform that resembles the neck and head of a slithering snake.

"Look at all the islands, Pop!"

"Yes, it was a nation of islands—Indonesia. The fancy name for that is archipelago. But this one here is different. This is a peninsula. Malaysia."

When she was little, they would sit for hours, pouring over the bound artifact Eben called an atlas. He taught her landforms and the old ways that he had learned from his father and his father before: the way of the compass rose, the meaning of topography, longitude and latitude, the breadth of the world that used to be.

"Is it still there, Pop?"

"We don't know. The world has changed and we don't even know how much. The oceans rose and swallowed up whole nations. And in other places, once-fertile land just dried up and became a desert."

When she asked why, he would simply put his finger to his lips and then take her hand and guide it over the map. He led her hand up, up and to the left, in a diagonal over the blue and green and tan, until her fingers rested between the markings in bold black: NORTH AMERICA.

"Be thankful that by an accident of birth you live in the middle of an enormous continent. And not on a small island."

Tracing the borders of the Protectorate, his fingers followed the curves of the five blue lakes, each larger than the one before. *"To remember their names, think HOMES: Huron, Ontario, Michigan, Erie, Superior. Our home. Control the water, you control the people."* Then he would tuck the biblio away in its hiding place under a pair of loose floorboards in the back of his bedroom closet.

"Why do we have to hide it?"

"The Protectorate outlawed books a long time ago. To get rid of misinformation and rumor. Wiped all the memory clean, too. Of the cloud, the machines... and the people. This is something that has to be a secret. Something we never talk about. Can I trust you with that?"

She'd nodded, her mouth set in a solemn line, but a little thrill ran up her spine.

She still loves to drag the decrepit biblio out of its hidey-hole and imagine herself traveling to this place and that, seeing with her own eyes what exists out beyond the boundaries. *They say the land is dead in the Outlier, but how can so much land be dead?* These are not questions to ask out loud, only to ponder, questions in which to lose track of time. And so when Eben comes home, he finds her lying on the floor of his bedroom in a pool of late afternoon sun, a half-drunk bottle of water by her side, running her fingers over the fragile, yellowed paper and carefully turning the dog-eared pages as she breathes in their rich, moldy odor.

"From the looks of the disc player on the kitchen table, I'd say you're not finished with it," he says, pulling the red headset from around his ear, flicking the power button on his feedcom and tossing it on the bed.

"Started on it. Looked at it. Left that shitpile for another."

Eben scowls. "Finish anything?"

"My lesson. Mr. O. A bike."

"Good. After dinner, I need you to help me tote some of the bottles up. Not everyone's put some away and the tap's still dry."

"That's their problem. Why should we—" The look he throws stops her lips from forming the words. "Fine," she huffs. "What's for supper? There's nothing but sesame butter in the pantry."

"Then sesame sammies it is."

"Again?"

"You were at the mart. Did you see meat? No, you did not. And barely veggies. The ration transports haven't delivered anything all week. Even if they had, I spent the last voucher on a gift for Astra. She and her husband received their baby yesterday. Gave him the once-over this morning. Cute little boy."

Merit sweeps her fingers one last time along the jagged blue line of a river that meanders north over a smooth field of green until it reaches the craggy brown peaks of a mountain range. "That's a waste, giving them a gift. You said they were transferring out." She catches Eben's frown. "What they name it?" she asks, adjusting her tone, her index finger circling the letters that sprawl across the page.

"Win."

"Stupid," she snorts. "Who came up with that? Astra or her suck-up mate?"

"Hush. They found it on the list of approved names. It's a fine name, strong, aspiring."

"Since when does Corporate have a list of approved names?"

"Been like that for awhile, baby girl. How d'ya think you wound up Merit? Coulda been worse, though. We might've called you Obedience." Eben nudges the atlas with the toe of his clog. "Make sure you put that back in its place, Obie."

Frack.

13

A Man of Character

"FOUR HUNDRED SEVENTY EIGHT BOTTLES."

"And sixty five men, women and children." Eben squinches up his eyes, doing the math in his head. "Seven to each, yes? That's four hundred fifty five, leaving—"

"Just twenty three for us."

"Just? That's more than plenty," Eben asserts.

Merit is not so sure. The outage is going on twelve hours now, longer than ever before. The feedcom has been mute, offering no reassurances that the WQs are working on the issue, that service will be restored momentarily. Eben's inquiries on the vox have been met with a similar unusual silence.

"What if this goes on for another day?"

Eben smiles, though his eyes reveal an exhaustion his voice hides. The hollows underneath are the grayish purple of an old bruise. The lids sag as if it takes all his strength just to keep them open. "Well, then this place'll reek to the skies and everywhere between. Maybe the Hive'll catch a whiff up in their glass castle and get it through their collective brain that hey, we need to get the water back on down in Asswipe so they can drag a wet rag under their armpits and other unmentionable places."

"It's not funny, Eben. You told me about the Rule of Threes. You can live three minutes without air. In extreme cold or heat, you can last about three hours without shelter. Three weeks without food. Without water, you're down to three *days*."

"As a general rule, yes. So we still have, what? Sixty hours? Oh wait, that time clock starts when you *actually* run out of water. Which hasn't happened."

"Yet."

He takes her chin in his hand and tilts it up to his. "It won't. And we're not going to cause needless panic in these people. We're going to calmly hand them their seven bottles of water and send them on their way with a smile and a cheery *no worries, there's more where that came from and don't drink it all in one place*. Savvy?"

He eyes her with a look that brooks no further discussion and then gives her a smacking kiss on the forehead. "Because in the immortal words of someone whose name has been lost, er, deleted, this could be our finest hour. Now, let's get to work."

The basement is dim, dank, musty-smelling, a place Merit rarely ventures on her own. Too many spiders and other many-legged critters lurk in its shadowy corners. The containers of water are stacked in a haphazard collection of wood and plastic crates. They line the outer edge of what Eben calls the safe room, a small-ish metal-framed enclosure screened in fine copper mesh that stretches from the far wall to the middle of the basement. To Merit's mind, it resembles a cage, a very large cage to be sure, but a cage nonetheless. When Eben built it, of course she had asked why.

"*Treehouse I never had*," was his gruff, uncharacteristically short answer. "*Indoor all-weather treehouse*."

"*But there's no tree.*"

"*Use your imagination.*"

Inside, four beat-up folding chairs, always in danger of collapsing, cluster around a tiny, nicked end table. And they do indeed sometimes play in it. Chess, checkers, rummy, liars' poker. But mostly it is reserved for the times when they talk about serious matters. A place where Eben brings others to talk, as well. No prying eyes or ears, here.

Merit hefts a crate packed with containers of all shapes and sizes and varieties. Plastic, glass, stainless steel. Gallon, quart, pint. Containers they have been scavenging over the years for just this purpose. Her back aches as she lugs it up the stairs. As she reaches the top step, a sharp knife of pain slices from her buttock to the calf of her right leg and she staggers. Eben grabs her elbow to steady her.

"Okay?"

She nods and shakes him off. "Yeah, yeah, just put a foot wrong." But she is huffing, her cheeks pink from the exertion.

"I'll get the rest."

"No, I can—"

"No," says Eben firmly. "You stay up here and start sorting them. Efficiency. That's always been Lesson One, yes?"

As he descends the stairs, Merit finds her hand slipping down to her abdomen, sliding over the gentle slope that swells there under her tunic. Her body feels loose, shaky, not entirely hers. In this moment, she longs for Serafina's firm embrace and feels the liquid heat welling in her eyes. But by the time Eben reappears with another crate, she is lining up bottles on two long folding tables he has set up on the back porch.

The people come in dribs and drabs, worry settled in the hollows of their faces, thirst in the corners of their mouths, the salty musk of their bodies weighing down the air. Eben gives each a smile along with the water, a handshake to the men and a hug to the women who need one, his very presence calming the waves of fear like oil cast on stormy water, until a wiry man elbows his way through the clusters and plants himself at the bottom of the porch steps, arms tight across his chest.

"Oh sure, you got it in there. Yer their man." The voice was a raw rasp. "Yer tap's runnin', ain't it, you Corporate sack a shit."

Merit recognizes the malcontent as a Bartertown regular. An Agri about Eben's age with a still in his basement, local source of a particularly wicked home-brew.

Eben's voice is low, patient. "I guarentee you, Cal, my taps are dry as those fields up the road. Just like yours." He descends the steps slowly, holding a gallon jug. "We're all hurtin' here."

The sinews in the man's scrawny arms flex. "Most are hurtin' more'n others, you frackin' swag." He thumps Eben's chest with a pointed finger.

Eben's bark of a laugh cuts the man short. "I imagine if the Hive were listenin' in on this conversation they'd be rolling by now, just havin' a big ol' hoot. That's three times you've elevated me way above my place. Ten years I've been here, tryin' my best to serve this community. As one of you, not above you. Tryin' to show by my actions where my heart lies. Ever given you a reason to doubt me? Cal, man, you're cuttin' me to the quick."

"Oh, now yer denying yer Corporate, Eben?"

A long pause. Eben's eyes drift upwards, parsing his words, as if the right ones are written in the sky. His vocal rhythm, usually clipped and precise, has fallen into the angry man's cadence and speech pattern, the regional drawl, as Eben uses the personal touch that never fails him.

"One can be in the world and not of it." He extends the jug. "Take it. And however many more you can tote."

The man hesitates, cocks his head, scrutinizes. "You know it's comin' back on, dontcha? Otherwise you wouldn't be handin' this to me. You know. That's why come you can stand there, Iceman. But you won't say, willya?" He grabs the container, but Eben holds tight to the handle.

"Just tell me you'll share it with someone. Maybe someone you love."

The man snorts. "Eben, that sounds like old-time preacher talk. Got rid of 'em when we was kids. Better watch 'fore

Corporate gets a whiff and puts you on early severance. Or izzat what yer aimin' for? At this rate, I'd take my chances in the Outlier. Hell yeah."

"I'm already on that list. Aging out. Time's comin' soon." Eben releases his hold on the jug.

A slow nod. "Me too." The man twists the cap off, lifts the jug midway to his mouth, then hesitates. "Ever hear from Fina?"

Eben shakes his head. "You, from Gilly?"

"Naw, been a year now." He tips the jug to his mouth and takes a long swallow. "Bet they got water. Must be a paradise so frackin' wonderful they can't find time to send a vox, eh? Or the Outlier can't let people know 'bout it cuz then we'd all be clawin' to get out."

After a moment, Eben shrugs. "That's what I'm thinkin'."

"Well then, bring on the train." He takes another long slug of water and then shoves the jug back at Eben. "S'all I needed."

"No, Cal, keep it. Like I said, share it."

The man taps his forehead. "Like *I* said, you know somethin', damn bushwazee." The man staggers away from the porch, a little unsteady on his feet, like he's been swilling oblivion instead of water, the jug slung on his shoulder."

"I'll plan on a shower in the mornin'," he croaks.

"We'll all thank you for that."

But the jollity is forced, Merit can tell. After the man shambles away down the street, she hears Eben's deep, shaky sigh, the low whistle of air through his teeth.

The evening drifts along with the sector folk. Merit sneaks glances over her respy as she bends to a sweet old-school cruiser with a flat tire and a busted chain, digesting her sesame butter sandwich even as her stomach growls for another, making repairs, hands black with grease. She spies the scrawny boy from the GaltMart lurking at the edge of the picket fence, eyes shifting from the rapidly diminishing rows of containers to the folks hauling theirs away in totes and baskets. Gauging. She is about to alert Eben to this up-to-no-good interloper when Eben gives a hearty wave, beckoning the youth up the steps.

"Suraj!"

When he brushes past her, Merit smells both the fear sweat and the bracing scent of antiseptic wafting from the boy. His wrist and calf are wrapped in gauze, starkly white against his skin.

"Nothin' to carry 'em in? Here, take a crate." Eben hefts one into the boy's arms. "How's the arm and leg?"

"Flesh wounds, sir. Think I'll live," the boy answers in the boastful tone of one who probably puled like a kitten in the actual moment of distress, but has conveniently forgotten all about that now.

"Good man, all right then. Onto the next."

They bump fists and the boy clambers down the steps, clutching his precious cargo.

Merit tries to catch Eben's eye with a raise of her eyebrows, but he has already reached out to shake the hand of a slump-shouldered mig with the gutted look of a man who hasn't had a decent meal in days. She bends back to the bicycle, gasping as a twinge arcs through her lower back, pondering the secrets that each of them carry. A pair of tattered shoes invades her view. Hideous green.

"If you'da kenned I knew him, you'da been sweeter to me at the mart."

She doesn't even bother to look up, just gives the bolt a good hard twist with her wrench. But the tool slips from her sweaty grip and lands on the edge of the old pie pan that corrals her washers, nuts and bolts, upturning it and sending the pieces flying.

"Frack!" Her thought spouting from his lips.

She sits back on her heels, scanning the ground, but the pieces could be anywhere. Scattered in the dead grass, hiding in the gloom under the porch, blending in with the soil of the barren flower bed.

"No worries, fem." The boy sets his crate on the stoop, fishes in his drooping pocket and pulls out a small u-shaped magnet. He squats and wafts it around, snagging a few washers immediately.

"Where'dya steal that?"

"Salvaged, fem. I salvaged it."

"Like those shoes? And that ridiculous t-shirt."

"Shoes were a dumpster find, yeah. Shirt I got legit." He shrugs at the downward curve of her lips. "Rockin' show. That's right, I seen 'em. Live and in person. Tour two years past. Up near Chicago garrison. Oops, forgot, they don't *tour*, they're just always on the lam. Wanted: dead or alive."

A thief AND a liar.

Nobody ever actually saw that band. Because it didn't exist. Merit stares at the print emblazoned across the front of the boy's gray t-shirt, the letters of the name forming the silhouette of a battered black guitar. Damn Otis was just samples of songs that bled through over the student feed or suddenly sliced into the audio tracks of movies on the screen cam. Music that pulsed anger in every drumbeat and scorn in every ringing guitar chord and contempt in the biting lyrics that the singer spat or wailed or hissed. Damn Otis was someone who knew how to hack the system, for brief moments in time. Someone playing jokes on the Corporate feed.

Most of the fasteners are back in the pan when the boy heaves a sigh. On his belly, he's rooting around, an arm through a hole in the lattice of the porch skirting.

"Can't reach this one." He wriggles back to a squat, shoves the magnet at Merit. "Here, you got longer arms, maybe you can fish it out."

Merit has no intention of sticking her hand into the murk under the porch. But when she hesitates, she sees amusement glinting in the boy's mismatched eyes, amber mockery, brown derision. She grabs the magnet, flattens herself to the ground and maneuvers her right arm through the lattice hole. The angle of the setting sun slips a sliver of light under the porch. At its edge is a glint that might be the bolt. She stretches. Not quite far enough. Jiggles the magnet. Not quite there. Scoots right up against the skirting, straining. Still no luck. Relaxes her muscles, resting a moment before another try. For this final push, in straining, she squeezes her eyes shut, reaching, reaching, sliding the magnet just a wee bit farther, farther, exhaling when she hears the slightest metallic clink. When her eyes fallen open in triumph and relief, she discovers eight beady black ones staring back at her in the midst of a fanged face.

The shriek may be actual, escaping her throat, raw and blatant. Or it may just be the sensation of her skin scraping over the bone-dry splintered wood of the lattice. But in the instant, she's dropped the magnet and is batting at her face where she's sure the wolf spider's hairy legs are scrabbling for purchase, even as, out the corner of her eye, she sees it dart back through the porch skirting into the gloom, fear driving its own hasty retreat.

The boy calmly picks up the magnet, detaches the bolt from its tip and tosses it in the pan. He bends to retrieve his crate of bottles. Winks his amber eye at her.

"Well, fem, I'd say you need to grow a pair. But I don't think the he-she shots will help with that."

He hoists the crate to his shoulder and saunters off down the broken sidewalk.

14

Children of the Revolution

AFTER THE LAST STRAGGLERS DEPART, bottles clenched to chests, nodding their thanks, hustling to make it home before curfew, Merit joins Eben on the porch. In the indigo gloom where the heat curtain of the day still hangs thick and heavy, they are silent. The electric lights in all the houses along the street go out in that instant, like a row of candles extinguished by a great, huffing breath. Next door, Mr. Oceguera's generator sputters to life with a growl and his lights flicker back on. Across the road, the subdued wavering glow of tapers and votives warm the windows of several homes, like glimmers of hope rising in dark, forlorn eyes. The scent of lavender is already wafting from the home-made candles.

"You know he's a thief?" She slurs the last, so it sounds midway between a statement and a question.

"Who?"

"That boy. The one you called Suraj. You bandage him up?"

"Of course. Last I checked, I am a medic. And he was injured."

"Probably thieving."

"Actually, he was doing some work for me and got hurt in the process."

"What work?"

"Well, ain't we full o' questions tonight. What if I said it was nunnayerbizness."

"I'd say since when."

Eben doesn't respond immediately, just gazes out at the settling dusk. Sighs. "Reminds me of me, when I was his age."

"You were a thief?" Snark thickens her voice.

"When I needed to be."

"You never told me that."

"Lots of things I never told you."

"So, tell me. Or is it something for the safe room?"

Eben glances around. "Last time I looked they had an eye in the sky, but not an ear—yet."

"So?"

Eben takes his sweet time, wiping a trickle of sweat from his temple, pulling his t-shirt away from his chest, flicking at a black fly that lands on his hand. "When I was fifteen, I walked with giants, ran with wolves, marched with rebels." His fingers trace the arc of the scar across his right cheek. "Got this."

"You said you got it in a fight."

"I did. It was."

Merit grabs a leftover water bottle from the table, cracks it open and takes a long swallow. Eben is a paradox. Sometimes he is nothing but diarrhea of the mouth, going on and on about some trivial thing that barely amounted to squat, and other times his lips are shut tight as a river clam and she's got to pry him open to gouge out the sketchiest bit of detail.

"Walked with giants? Like that José and the beanstalk bedtime story that Serafina used to tell me? These giants have names?"

"Joachim Debs." He says it quietly, almost under his breath, but with emphasis, like the name is supposed to mean something to her.

"Wak-who?"

"Joachim."

"Yeah, so? Who's that?"

"Who's that?" With a shake of his head, Eben sits down heavily in his favorite chair, one he'd carved from an ancient oak that had once stretched its limbs across the front lawn like the mightiest of goliaths. After lightning had felled it in the middle of a thunderstorm, Merit had been totally in awe of the enormous trunk sprawled across the lawn like a slain giant. Eben had taken her hand in his and helped her count the rings, explaining that the tree had lived nearly one hundred years. Impressing on her that this was one way of knowing there was a time *before*, of which she was not a part, but which formed the world in which she lived. Something called *history*.

"Who's Debs?" Eben repeats with a sigh. "One of the reasons Galt Corporation would have you believe there is no past here in the Protectorate—only the present and the foreseeable future." He smiles bitterly at her blank stare, flat and impassive, like a sheer rock face he is attempting to scale. "Joachim Debs. The Son of the Mississippi." He thrust a finger at her water bottle. "An engineering genius who helped design the water systems that keep us alive. A pioneering scientist who was working on a purification process to reclaim the poisoned aquifers here and in the Outlier. Joachim Debs, the leader of the Handed, the visionary who inspired the first uprising against the Protectorate. A man of many, many talents. And you don't even recognize his name."

"Cuz he failed?" Merit's voice is as flippant and dismissive as a shrug.

"Yes, the rebellion failed," Eben growls. "And he and his band of guevaras went into exile. But that's not the point. The point is before this minute you had never even heard of him. Because history is left untold—or rather, it's been moved to trash."

"What's 'the Handed'?'" Merit asks.

Eben stretches out his left hand, with its purplish veins snaking just under the brown skin, knuckles furred with dark hairs. "In the early years of the Protectorate, when Corporate first had the notion of embeds to keep track of people, the surgeons placed them in the hands."

"Like the swags have, for easy in and out?"

"Yes and no. They embedded them in the left hand, but not just below the skin like swags have now. Deeper, under and, eventually, as the hand grew, entwined with the muscle and bone, so there was no way to remove the embed without permanently mangling the hand. So, if anyone wanted to fade into the blur, you can guess what needed to be done."

"The guevaras chopped off their own hands?" Horror and a spark of morbid fascination lights her eyes. "That's hardcore." A tingle radiates through her hand and she flexes it automatically. "How d'you know all this?"

"Marched with him through the streets of Chicago, the day we seized the water plant. I was a fifteen-year-old boy trying hard to be a man, wearing the red bandanna. Earned my badge." He turns his cheek to show the scar.

"What was it all about?"

"We wanted to free the water. Crazy idea, huh? That water, clean water, is a right, not a commodity."

"What happened?"

"Mass murder. Security forces moved in and slaughtered anyone in the crosshairs of their guns. Same thing happened in garrisons all around the waters: Chicago, Detroit, Cleveland, Toronto, Duluth. Thousands of guevaras, men and women, mostly unarmed, who thought they'd get a chance to plead their case, to negotiate." A bark of derisive laughter escapes him. "What were we thinking? Galt doesn't negotiate—with anyone—ever. *Swift. Brutal. Thorough.* That's when the brute squads got their motto."

"But they didn't get you. What about this Debs?"

"Plenty escaped in the chaos. We re-grouped, but Debs was pretty shaken up. His science was a threat to Corporate profits, maybe even its very existence. As the face and the voice of the rebellion, he was a wanted man with nowhere to hide from the eye in the sky, so he decided to make a run for the Outlier and his inner circle was determined to go with him. They knew they were all targeted for elimination. That's when they became the Handed. One legend says they laid the hands, a hundred or so, at the base of a Galt Protects sign, middle fingers extended. Another has it they boxed 'em up in twos and threes and sent them via the parcel service to the regional offices. Supposedly drove security crazy because they were picking up readings on the embeds moving all over the place. Then, boom, one morning, picture the swags sitting in their clean, bright offices in their cushy chairs behind their grand mahogany desks getting the grisliest surprise of their lives!" Another bark of laughter.

"You didn't follow him." Merit nod at Eben's hands, fine and whole.

He shakes his head. "Wanted to. Would've, but he asked me and the others, plenty of others, to stay. We were all very young. He said we weren't in danger. Galt couldn't afford to get rid of us and lose a generation of sweats. Told us to stay and work the inside game. Called us the INS. Infiltrators and Subversives. *Lay low, bide your time. The heel will keep grinding down on the neck of the people until the day comes when they are ready to throw it off. They just need the right words and the right voice to speak to them.* I pled guilty to a moment of youthful stupidity, gave up some nonvital info about the guevara cadre and got with the program right quick. Took up my apprenticeship in Security like a good bee. Did what the feed told me, knowing the eye was on me extra close." He scans the darkening sky as if searching for the telltale blinking path of the zoom. "When I showed skills as a medic during some skirmishes at the border, I got the opportunity to train. And when one of the swags from the Hive had the idiotic hubris to come down to inspect the border and took a couple of bullets to the chest, instead of letting him die, as I should've—as a guevara would've—I saved his sorry ass. Earned the cushy posting at the Breeder Islands as my reward." A tight smile stretches his lips. "And there our stories intersect when you were assigned into my life."

Merit's face is taut with fascination. "Anyone know where Debs is now? If he's still alive?"

"He was, as of last fall. He was born elite and after the rebellion his family disowned him. Self-preservation trumps blood ties, most of the time. But his younger sister was secretly sympathetic to the cause and appears to remain so. She's in Comm Tech up in Superior, mid-level but high enough so's a message occasionally slips through. The Handed have been known to hack the feed, now and then. But those who stayed are scattered far and wide. Communication's haphazard. And dangerous."

"Where's he holed up?"

"Rumored to be just across the West River. What used to be the Mississippi. I've pointed it out on the atlas. The river that splits the land and runs south to the ocean."

Merit nods, picturing the long meandering blue line. "He's never tried to come back?"

"He's an old man now, maybe seventy-five or so. Older than anyone in the Protectorate. There's not many guevaras left who are old enough to even remember that rebellion. In a few years, all the legals who were in their teens then will hit sixty and be severanced. Just like there's not one person alive, not one, who was here before the Protectorate was formed. That's how the memory, the human memory, is lost." Eben sweeps a hand across the porch rail. "And the next generation is a blank slate on which the rules are written. Because if you have no shared memory of the prior world, you can't possibly compare the new system with the old, can you? So the new system becomes the natural order of things."

"That wouldn't happen if they pass the story on to their children."

"Not many bees are approved for raising children. You can bet the swags won't pass it on to theirs." Eben stands and slings an arm around her shoulders. "But enough of my yappin' about ancient history. Let's talk about the here and now, like good Protectorites. A quiz for the worker-bee-to-be."

Merit sighs.

"Indulge me, my fine androg." His voice is playful, and yet there's an edge to it. He grabs a small water bottle and twists the cap off, downing half in one long gulp. "To assure me that you are a compliant bee." He winks, but something's kindling in his eyes.

She shrugs, playing along.

"Ever ask why all the lights go out at once?"

"It's the rule."

"Ever wonder why and whether it's right?"

"Saves energy."

"Who decides these... decisions?"

"Corporate. For the good of the Protectorate."

"Fair enough," replies Eben, his voice lower now, his mouth inches from Merit's ear. "Shall I advocate for the devil? Let's follow that line of thinking, shall we? Who learns to read?"

"Swags."

"Tsk, tsk."

"I mean, the upper echelon."

"Better. Now, why only them? Why not workers?"

"Bees get what they need to know from the feed."

"Ah. And who decides what they need to know?"

"Corporate. For the good of—"

"The Protectorate." Eben finishes her sentence in a terrible hiss. "And do you ever ask why there are no old people around and so few children?"

They've played this game before but the stakes have never seemed so high. His anger is electric, its thrum scorching her skin.

"There's a balance of life for sustainability. They only need so many workers. And only those who can actively contribute to the Protectorate can stay."

"And who decides that?"

Merit grips the porch railing, grinding the tips of her fingers against the unyielding wood. "You know the answer!"

"I do, but I need to know that my little bee knows it."

"Corporate for the good of the Protectorate." She bends and presses her forehead into the corner post, the painted surface coolly soothing. Her back throbs.

"We could stand here all night and recite that mantra, couldn't we? From the water you're allowed to drink. To the amount of food that's on your table. To the job you're given. To the place you live. The person you marry. The child you are or are not allowed to create or raise. To the day of your severance. To the very name by which you are called. All the answers would be same, wouldn't they?"

She's never seen him like this. The raw heat of the fury that grips him cracks the cool, smooth calm of his surface, the flames here and there licking up through the ice. And then he takes a breath, holds it and blows it slowly out and just like that, the flames are doused.

"Now, tell me what a queen bee would say, but softly, softly, in just the softest whisper of a buzz."

From the moment he taught her the words, he warned her never to say them outside the safe room. That they were words to be thought, not spoken. So she hesitates.

"If she were queen..." she mumbles.

"*When* she is queen," he corrects.

"There is another way to live, a way to truly live and not just exist, as a child of the revolution."

Pah-pa-rah. From the 'tronic billboard, the bright metallic blasts of trumpets sound the opening notes of the vespers fanfare. And inside every home, the music blares as well, calling all to attention for the evening statement. Then the trumpets subside, the drums throb low and the resounding voice of CEO Blanche booms.

"Workers of the Protectorate, good evening. As you end this day that Galt has provided, ponder this. That the last thought of your evening, every evening, should be a question. And that question should be: What have I done to aid my fellow men and women, to assist the Protectorate in its mission to create a safe and sustainable future for all, and to live by the Corporate Way? And the first thought when you rise in the morning should also be a question. And that question must be: What can I do to know my place within the mission of Galt Corporation and to have the humility to accept that place." A pause for effect and then the baritone voice goes on, placing a stronger emphasis on the words. "I repeat, to *accept* that place—*without question*—so that I may help preserve the Protectorate as a sanctuary for all who live within its boundaries and abide by its rules? Workers of the Protectorate, let these thoughts guide your life at all times." Again, a pause and then the benediction. "Galt provides."

The voice of Chanel, light as spun-sugar and tinged with its burnt sweetness, launches into the Corporate hymn. *"In the moment, in this moment, you must ask yourself..."*

"Yes, question only yourself." Eben spits into the gray dirt where clumps of daylilies had once blossomed, as if the words are bitter on his tongue. "Do not question authority."

Merit feels her shoulders tense, fighting even as she senses her resistance slipping away, being pulled into the flow of his righteous anger, through row upon row of slashed-out smiley faces. *Because it's my anger, too.*

Eben presses his fist, the skin glowing purplish under the solar light, to his chest. "To remake the world."

It is the catechism he has taught her, but, again, one only to be used in the privacy of the safe room, not out here, under the twilight sky.

How strange and awkward it feels, as her own hand closes tight and rises to her heart. Yet the words come willingly to her lips, as if they are always hovering there, just beyond the tip of her tongue.

"To remake the world."

She has barely uttered them when the burden they accept settles like a woolen cloak on her shoulders. Heavy. Itchy. Enveloping.

15

Nessun Dorma

MERIT SOLVES THE PUZZLE of the disc player in that time of night that Serafina called the small hours. She is, and always has been, a night owl, according to Eben, which makes little sense to her. There are no day owls, after all. They are creatures of the night. Nocturnal, Eben says.

By the flickering light of the beeswax candles, with only their lavender scent and dancing shadows for company, she discovers a strand of wire that has come loose from its moorings. Could it be something as simple as this? The exposed ends are dull, but when she slits the green plastic coating and strips away a tiny chunk, the fresh wires glimmer a bright copper. With nimble fingers, she reattaches the wire to its node and then sits back, fretful, eager. Waiting until morning when the electricity kicks on will be interminable. But Eben frowns on using the solar generator for anything other than emergencies. A quick scan of its battery shows a full charge. And how much energy can this little trinket actually suck up?

She'll only try it for a minute. Just to see. To reward herself for persevering, for finishing. For sticking with the shitpile.

When she plugs it into the adapter and presses the power button, the display glows a warm amber. She presses random buttons until the tray with its circular cut out slides open. She returns the shiny prismatic disc to where she found it hours ago and nudges the edge of the tray with the tip of her finger. Nothing happens. She tries the buttons again. The tray withdraws and she hears a low whir from the bowels of the machine. Numbers appear on the display. 14. 1:09:29. When she presses the arrow button, the machine purrs again and she hears music and then a voice.

She doesn't understand the words. They are a language she's never heard before, but it doesn't matter. She can somehow sense, if not the meaning, then the feeling they are trying to convey. The voice starts on the earth. Warm, full, with a masculine sweetness, honey in her ear. A yearning in the tone, but confidence, too, smooth as polished wood. An instrumental interlude ensues and then a chorus of women, subdued, as if from somewhere in the distance, sing a hushed lament. And then the voice returns, commanding, resonant, no longer earthbound, but reaching for the sky, soaring to the stars, with a gleaming brilliance. And she feels her own intake of breath, lifting her head, closing her eyes, rising, rising on the wings of the voice. She senses a stirring inside, the fluttering of some small winged thing.

Breathless at this beauty in her midst.

Tanner can't sleep. He is given to tossing and turning in the nights leading up to an action, his mind racing from one thought to another, running through scenarios, configuring and reconfiguring responses to problems, visualizing the process, perseverating on the what-ifs, endeavoring to know the unknown unknowns. He refuses to consider lethe juice to settle his mind and body. That would be a sign of weakness.

So he walks. The press of the darkness and the still, warm air feels good, like an enveloping womb. With each footfall, his breath comes easier. He navigates the shadowy streets, lit only by the violet glow from the solar lights, with a predator's ease. He's walked here before, in the days after parting with his wife. When he couldn't stand the hollow manse, its silence. He doesn't like to think about that time. Not one of his better performances. Too much emotion. Fraught. He refused to blame the oblivion, but afterwards he put the bottle down. Kept his hands busy with other things.

The lack of scent in the night air signals the lifelessness of the land. Where there should be the rich odors of loam and manure, of ripening life, there is an arid nothingness. It gets up inside his nose and he turns down an old strip of asphalt that leads to no place in particular. The white brick of the structure at the road's end is eerily luminescent. The medic's home. Far too big for one man and his androg. Should have been torn down years ago. But the semi-swag has pull, given the status of his profession. Which raises the question of why he would want to practice in this waste pit when he could have his pick of assignments.

Someone's awake. An open window on the lower level casts a light both flickering and steady. Music seeps out, a melody familiar in a far off and long ago way. He turns in at the path leading to the front door, treading lightly over the stepping stones through a small patch of herbs that have wilted in the intense heat, crushing them underfoot. Ah, now their fragrance enlivens the air. The pungent lemony scent of coriander. The sweet tang of basil. The brisk aroma of lavender.

Burning candles ring the kitchen table, while a flashlight hangs by a length of twine from the simple wrought iron chandelier. A slim figure sits at the table, back to the window. Likely the androg, which Tanner realizes he's never seen. Strange, that, but a man can't know every beast of burden in his territory. Although, like the music, there is something familiar about the back of the head. The whorls of hair. Its weave of colors, caramel to auburn to brunette. The body shifts, the neck inclining. A glint there, at the nape. Of a fine chain, perhaps? Odd, to feel a sense of knowing this unknown thing.

The singer's voice expands and rises, a wave swelling and rolling, curving and folding and encompassing everything in its path. For a moment, just a moment, Tanner pictures that wave breaking against him, engulfing him. Then the song ends with a swell of applause, shouts of "bravo." The androg reaches out a hand to touch the sound box. Do its fingers tremble?

A crawling sensation along her neck. But when she reaches a hand back to swat, there's nothing. No gnat or mosquito, no six or eight-legged critter to claw from her skin. No loose thread or stray hair.

Still, she feels something, vaguely itchy, the feeling she gets when the eyes follow her through Bartertown. But when she cranes her head around, slowly, uneasily, to look out the window, there's nothing there but the night.

PART TWO

Water on the Parched Land

For I will pour water upon him that is thirsty,
and floods upon the dry ground:
I will pour my spirit upon thy seed,
and my blessing upon thine offspring.

Isaiah 44:3

16

The Hundredth Hour

THE PEBBLE IN EM'S MOUTH, tucked up against the inside of her cheek, has long since ceased to work its magic. Dust she is. Desiccated. The moisture wrung out of her. Cracked and gray as the soil in the barren fields that stretch to the horizon. Dry and shriveled as a husk from a wasted ear of corn. When she touches the skin of her face, she hears the rasp, like sandpaper scraping over wood.

They gulped when they should have sipped. But in the heat, who could blame them? The outage couldn't last, could it? On the first day, the second, and the third, they were ordered to keep working. But there was nothing to be done but sweep the dust from porches and windows. They'd dug out the canning jars of tomatoes that the bruja had put up from the last decent crop, the jars hidden under the false floor so they could swap them at B-town. They'd slurped those down. And the pickles, too. Though that was a mistake for the brine just left them thirstier.

A mob of migs had taken sledgehammers to the front window of the padlocked GaltMart, only to find the shelves nearly bare. Just dry goods. Sacks of flour. Boxes of pasta. Cannisters of millet.

Em can't remember the last time she peed. Within the cage of her ribs, her heart thrums and her breaths comes fast and shallow, like they do when she's been running. But she's standing still.

She scratches and swats at invisible ants that crawl up her legs and arms. She knows she's crying as she leans against the cinderblock, trying to find a cool place, but her eyes are as dry as the dust.

Merit sweeps, pushing the dust toward the edge of the porch with her broom. It's been her daily chore for a couple of years now, sweeping the silt every morning, fighting against the wind that lifts the soil from its rightful place in the fields and drives it head-long to places it shouldn't be. The porch, the roof, the panes of the wide windows. A useless fight on the best of days. And to persist in it now, with the outage going on close to a week, is sheer folly. This morning, slurping the sticky juice of canned peaches, she lacked the energy to roll her eyes when Eben reminded her.

"What's the point?" she murmured.

He had grabbed her arm and turned her to face him. His eyes were sunken in his flesh, the folds and wrinkles surrounding them deeper, but they were fierce and flashed fire. "We do not give in to it. Never. Today, of all days," he said cryptically, minutes after the feed had come through, heralding a visit from some Galt lackey. Who, Eben refused to say.

And so she sweeps. It's not such a bad task. There is a quality to its repetitious rhythm that sets the dehydrated mind free. Two short pushes and then a long one. Brush, brush, sweeeeep. A task to get lost in. But today she can't lose herself in the familiar motions. Something gnaws at her, like a hound worrying a bone. So when Suraj comes stumbling down the front walk like a man under the influence, swaying, clutching his ribs, she's almost glad for the distraction.

He pants his words. "There's water at the barracks." Without waiting for a response, he staggers up the steps. Plunges through the door like it's his to open.

This isn't a conversation she wants to hear second-hand. She slips through the door and flattens herself against the wall just outside the kitchen, where Eben has sat the boy down and given him what's close to the last bottle of water.

"We mob it. Round up our own brute squad, tear the frackin' fence down and—"

"No, that's—"

"How can they stop us? We all do this together and—"

"No, it would be a slaughter," Eben says. "And we don't even know the intent here. For all you know, the squad could be at the Ag passing out bottles as we speak."

"Right," scoffs the boy. "How likely izzat? Not—that's how likely."

Silence from Eben.

"Then I'll go alone," the boy huffs, pushing back from the table. "Not sittin' here while there's water for the takin'."

"Suraj, wait—"

But the boy is out the door, brushing past Merit without a glance.

A sigh from Eben in the kitchen. "Stop. Breathe. Focus. Think. Can't get him to do that," he mutters to himself.

Merit waits a beat. For Eben to come striding through the doorway. For him to go after the impetuous boy. But he doesn't. Where's the man of action now? The man goading her on the porch?

"You just gonna sit there?" She steps around the doorframe, hands on her hips. "What happened to the big talk? 'Never give in. Remake the world.' That's it? Just talk?"

Eben is slumped in his chair, elbows on the table, shrunken. "Merit, keep your voice down. There's a time and a place." His own voice is a rasp, dry and brittle.

"Maybe the time is now."

His back is to her and he makes no move to look her way. So she turns and strides down the hall, grabbing her backpack from its hook before she steps out the front door. She takes the porch stairs two at a time, breaking into a lope to catch up with the boy, who is halfway down the street. Falling into a quickstep beside him, dizzy after her dash, feeling the earth sway under her feet, she doesn't need to say a word. And for once, the boy has no wisecrack for her, just a nod. And she nods in return.

The hike to the b-squad compound crosses scrub land bordering the fallow fields, an uneven land of low hillocks and shallow dales. At the top of a rise, Suraj stops and points. The low-slung building mars the earth like a concrete carbuncle.

"Squad supply house. There's the water."

Two pallets sit on the ground just to the side under an overhang. The building looks deserted, but something about its quiet façade makes Merit's skin itch.

"How you know it's empty?"

"Seen 'em leave with another pallet on the back of a transport."

"All?"

"All."

When she doesn't respond, he waves his arms around. "See any hulks lumberin' by? Nine of 'em left here on the transport. Even the gate house is empty. So we've got a one hundred percent chance to rip it. I'm goin' in."

The barrier fence enclosing the depot is tall, thick steel chain-link topped with coils of razor wire, sensor eyes studded in the posts. Armor without a chink.

The boy must read the skepticism on her face. The unspoken question. His answer is also unspoken. A nod at the tree.

Maybe it had been the builder's decision to leave the ancient oak standing just outside the enclosure. Or maybe the first squad leader who presided over the compound was some secret enviro who enjoyed the greens of its boughs in the summer and the scarlets in autumn. Maybe someone had gotten a thrill at the thought of something so old still hanging around, something from back in the day. Whoever it was had made a sentimental mistake, because the tree had continued to grow, as trees will, and it stretches a few of its thick branches over the top of the fence.

Merit eyeballs it, folding her arms across her chest.

"I know what yer thinkin'. Easy climb up this side. Long drop from that branch over there. How we s'posed to get back up? Got it covered, fem." Suraj says.

She doesn't even try to blink the scorn from her eyes.

"Uh-yeah, why you think I'm totin' this?" He pulls a coil of thick rope out of his backpack and slings it over his shoulder. Shifts on the balls of his feet.

Her mind is skittering around like her eyes, thoughts caroming like the steel balls in the ancient pinball machine in the back room of the Red Rooster Café.

I can't do this. Why am I trying to do this? I can take things apart. Ask me to fix something and I'll try and sometimes I'll even finish the job. But this? I can't even come face to face with a fracking spider without losing it. What happens when the goliaths come back? What happens to people who do these things... Bad things? Crimes.

Yet she already knows. People disappear. Just disappear. Not like a severance, the public boarding of the bullet train. Just gone. Without a why or a where. Just... gone.

All your life you've been butting heads with instructions, with the need to follow instructions. There are no instructions. Just do it.

But if some trap is lurking there, watching behind the windows, then it's over. And then it's all unknown territory.

"Lose the tunic. It's a giveaway. Put this on." Suraj tosses her a black stocking from the backpack he's shouldering. He tugs a second one over his head. He's fashioned it into a mask with ragged eyeholes. He pulls the rope from his shoulder and begins to tie simple knots at intervals along its length. "We get in there and goliaths show up, run like a rabbit. Someone's chasin' you, zig and zag. Throws 'em off."

Merit stares at the makeshift mask. "What's the point? One

click of an embed reader will give us away."

"Just wear it." The boy shrugs. "Or don't. Look, if yer scareful, wait here. I can ride this thing solo."

Oh, that would be the easy path. Plant myself under this tree, like I'm rooted with it, and let this crackwise get himself hauled in by the traps. He got himself into this by being a braggart as well as a thief. Let him join the ranks of the disappeared!

Eben's face looms before her, smiling grimly, nodding as she had uttered that curious phrase and pressed her fist to her chest. *You made a promise. To—what? And when the time came for action, he couldn't move.*

"Going with you," she mutters, tugging the stocking over her head, balling up the tunic and stuffing it into her backpack. She stumbles over an enormous root as she makes her way to the trunk, teeth clenched as she grabs hold of the lowest branch and tries to swing her leg up. She doesn't quite make it and peels bark off the trunk with a crackle as her foot slides back down.

Without a word, Suraj thrusts out his hands, fingers entwined. With the surprisingly strong boost from his twig-thin arms, Merit straddles the thick branch. She scrambles up to the overhanging limb, Suraj close behind.

"Keep your feet up. Not sure how high the sensor reads."

They inch forward on the branch, tucked into themselves like jockeys on horseback, passing over the thick twists of barbed wire. A couple of feet beyond, Suraj ties one end of the rope around the branch and tosses the rest down. The end dangles just above the ground. He grabs hold and slides down, the soles of his shoes making a soft thud on ground. Without waiting, he heads for the depot, crouched low, a dark figure zigzagging across the dirt.

The rope, rough and fibrous, leaves a stinging burn on Merit's palms as she slides down its length.

The pallets are stacked with slender bottles of water labeled with the Galt logo, the bold mouth of the G swallowing the rest of the letters. Suraj splits the webbing that holds the containers in place with two slashes of his pocket knife.

We can't carry much. Better to get others to help. But she starts grabbing the bottles and shoving them into her backpack.

Suraj twists open a cap and flings it away, pushes the stocking mask above his mouth and guzzles, water spilling out the corners of his lips, dribbling down his neck to soak the front of his t-shirt.

A weak hiss. Just beyond the pallets, a pile of dust-crusted crates leans against the building, inches from toppling. Another hiss. From behind the slats of the bottom crate, a pair of green eyes glower.

The resident rat-catcher.

Merit crouches and extends her hand. "Kitty?" she ventures uncertainly, wiggling her fingers.

"Leave it be," Suraj orders. "Prob'ly chomp you. Rabid, what?"

Ignoring him, she waggles her fingers again and the calico slinks out of its shelter. Under its coat of dust rise swaths of matted white and orange and black fur. Its tongue lolls, its eyes are sunken, ribs ladder-like. Merit glances around. Neither dish nor bowl in sight. Then she spies a dustpan on the front stoop of the barracks. Upturned, its three raised edges will hold water. She wipes away the entrenched dust as best she can with the bottom of her shirt, grabs a bottle and pours the water into the pan.

"Water, kitty?" she murmurs, wiggling her fingers over the improvised bowl.

The cat regards her, mews with a note of feline suspicion, then wobbles forward. Sniffs, sniffs again, then lowers its muzzle and begins to lap, delicately, hesitantly at first, then methodically.

"That's a waste," Suraj mutters. By now his backpack bulges with its load, the zipper resisting his efforts to close it. "Wonder what other goodies is here. Inside." He steps up to the lone window, pressing his forehead against the wire-reinforced glass.

"No room for anything else," Merit says, stuffing bottles into her pack, calculating the likelihood that she'll be able to haul herself up that rope. Only then does she take a bottle from the pallet, crack it open, push up her own mask, and quaff a long swallow. So good, the liquid blankness of it. Lukewarm in her mouth, silky and flavorless on her tongue.

They should be taking flight, but Suraj takes his time, acting as if they have all kinds of it. Reconning the outer walls of the depot. Tugging at padlocks. Twisting knobs. Shoving window jambs. When he disappears around the far corner, in that instant aloneness, the hairs on Merit's arms prickle and she hastens after him.

When they turn the last corner and are back at the pallets, Suraj grabs another bottle. "One for the road," he sighs, lifting it in a salute.

And then she spies the cat.

Merit lunges, her arm reaching Suraj just in time to slap the bottle out of his hand before it reaches his lips. The bottle plummets end over end, spraying an arc of water.

"What's yer loco?!" the boy sputters, his shoes freckled with droplets.

She points a finger.

Dead. There is no doubt. No need to probe the still flanks or squint at the shallow place where haunch meets ribcage to seek the telltale rise and fall. Her eyes trace a path from the cat to Suraj to the bottle on the ground, seeping liquid into the thirsty earth, to the bottle she still clutches in her hand.

Waiting. Calculating.

He drank an entire bottle. The cat mere sips. Yet he is so much larger, weighs so much more. If they get back to Eben in time, is there a chance... for what?

Then her eye catches it. The label. The Galt logo. The colors. Some are green. Some yellow.

The bottle next to the dustpan. The one she poured for the cat. The enormous G is an eye-popping acid yellow, the one in her hand a deep forest green. The one she batted out of Suraj's grasp is yellow.

"Where's the first bottle?"

Suraj shrugs, glances around. "Tossed it, somewhere."

"Find it!"

"What—"

"The labels. They're different. Some must be poisoned. Which did you drink?"

The boy just stands there, dumb-eyed as a cow. So she takes off down the length of the supply depot. There. Just before the corner. She nudges it with her toe.

Big G.

Green.

Relief jolts her body, like a crackling, hissing jagged arc of lightning. But, like the shuddering boom of thunder, dread quickly follows. A plume of dust billows, obscuring the black body of the transport as it crests the rise and rumbles to a stop in front of the gate. A black clad man, face hidden under his visor, lurches down from the cab and thumbs at the 'tronic box on its metal post.

Might be a lifetime. Might be a millisecond. What she hears may be the sudden gust of wind as it sweeps through the pines at the far side of the compound, setting the needles to whispering. Or her own quick intake of breath. Or the mechanical gasp of the 'tronic gate as it slides open. And the blood burns in her veins now, skin on fire, except for where the icy sweat has begun to seep, in the places where cold fear and hot adrenalin meet.

Go!

And still she hesitates, in a trapped animal crouch, listening to the wind and the pounding in her temples.

Words are forming on the goliath's lips. She can see his jaw now, as he advances. And she thinks she recognizes the hunch of his shoulders. And that walk. Or is it her imagination? Wishful thinking? Because if a goliath were to catch them, wouldn't that be the best-case scenario? Is that his walk? That walk of a man—no, a boy—a boy who doesn't really want to arrive at where he's headed.

Though the goliath's eyes are hidden, she can sense the astonishment gathering at the corners. "What are you—"

That's all she hears of the low-pitched murmur, for then she is off, flying, running under the unbridled light of the noon sun. Like a deer she is—no, a bird—for she swears her feet never touch the ground. Suraj's advice rattles around her skull and she rabbits, veering one way, then another, bounding crazily, but with a method to her madness.

Until she hits the low-lying patch of loose gravel. She skids and slides, footing gone, as if some wicked, grasping hand has yanked the world out from under her feet. Far ahead, she sees Suraj nearing the tree. Behind her comes the trap, closing fast.

He's going to hit this, too. Or take the long way 'round.

She scrambles up, losing a shoe. She takes off again, leaping past the edge of the gravel, on solid ground again, breath ragged in her throat. Awkward and off-balanced, she jerks to a stop and tugs off her other shoe, flinging it at the goliath's knees. He stumbles, avoiding it, but going down hard. Quickly recovering, rising on an elbow, reaching toward the utility belt at his waist.

Don't look back. She plunges forward. The tree is less than twenty yards away. *Don't look back.*

Ten yards.

Don't look back. I've never climbed a rope. A leap and her hands close on the coarse fiber in a fierce grip.

"Pinch it with yer feet! Anchor on a knot, then reach higher!" Suraj's voice is a ragged, panting croak from above.

"Don't wait! Go!" She cries, while her inner voice screams. *Wait, please wait!*

"Ain't leavin' the rope. He's down. C'mon, use yer frackin' arms!"

I can loosen the tightest screw. Why am I so weak now?

Arms aching under the ungainly weight of the backpack, legs cramping, hands flaming, she pulls and draws her knees up to her chest, shinnying up the rope, feeling the bulky knots, rough and welcome, on the soles of her feet.

"Frack all! He's right there!"

A water bottle sails past her head toward the goliath. Then another.

Then the limb is within her grasp and she swings her leg up and over as Suraj works with frantic fingers to haul the rope up and undo the knot.

"Bail! Now!" he hisses, stuffing the rope into his backpack. Scrabbling across the limb, he swoops to the ground in one wild, ape-like swing.

"Not going to shoot, don't have orders for that. But you can't run far." The goliath, panting below, his face obscured by the shroud of hanging leaves, sounds strangely calm. "We've got the focus on you."

The voice strips away Merit's uncertainty. *Don't look back. Don't say a word.* Whatever she'd like to say, a plea or rebuttal bubbling up from deep in her gut, she bites down hard before it can leave her mouth. A bitter taste then. And sad.

But Suraj cannot resist a taunt. "However far I run'll be enough, cuz yer eye is blind!"

Always the talk, the mouth running.

But it distracts the goliath long enough for her to scuttle across the branch, swing down on the other side of the fence and light out after Suraj, already just a rustling of dry leaves in the thicket of shrubs ahead.

They rip the masks from their heads and sprint through the trees, avoiding the road that runs alongside the scrub, a road lit by the unforgiving sun and down which they are sure the brute squad is speeding. Beyond the rasp of their labored breathing, the huffs and wheezes, they hear the crackle and snap of twigs, as they dodge and juke like ballers in a gladiator game.

On the edge of town, they should slow to a stroll. As a clever thief who can blend into the background, Suraj knows this. A runner attracts attention. But something keeps him running just the same. To the medic's house. Up ahead looms the porch. The door. Until he hears her shout-whisper.

"Stop! Someone's coming up the street."

He pulls up sharply and doubles back, following her lead around the corner of the house, pressing his body along its flanks, feeling the rough, splintered surface of the wood siding scrape the skin along the length of his arms.

"Wait here," she orders and he obeys, watching her jettison the backpack and slip around the corner. He hears the thump of her feet on the steps up to the porch. Then a rasping sound, rhythmic. Gentle. Sees a gray cloud billow past the edge of the house.

The low hum of a personal transport. A mechanical purr of an engine being cut. The tick of metal cooling. A slam of doors. A creak of wood protesting the weight of feet.

17

The Bureaucrat

"IT DOESN'T LOOK LIKE THE OTHERS."

The child, loud-mouthed, plump, skin moist and pinchable, as only the offspring of a corporate bushwazee can be, notices immediately. "It has bumps, like Mommy."

The boy, perhaps five or six, hair white-gold as the strands of silk that cling to an ear of corn, frowns up at her as he circles around, his mini-drone hovering just above his shoulder, picking his way, nose wrinkled, as if inspecting a large smelly pile of dung. Well on his way to becoming a proper swag.

His father, the regional manager just down from the Springfield garrison, gives a cursory glance. With his dark, darting eyes and whiskered jowls, he has the look of a boar, stout and shifty at once. He puts a guiding hand on the boy's shoulder, directing him toward the front door where Eben waits, his left eyelid twitching.

The man frowns at Merit. "Where's your tunic? And your shoes." Disgust puckers his face. To the boy, he smiles reassuringly. "It happens sometimes, Kors. Nothing a hormone adjustment won't fix. Although, at this point, it really doesn't matter."

The screen door slams with a clatter and then the black steel door to the house closes, shutting out the mid-day heat. Leaving Merit alone, the echo of the words ricocheting inside her head.

At this point, it doesn't really matter.

She darts around the corner of the house. Suraj is gone. She slips through the backdoor, leaving it ajar. Moving through the kitchen, she creeps on the balls of her feet, skirting the creaks in the boards. Eases into the long windowless hall that runs the length of the first floor, dim and cool. Presses herself against the wall, ears alert.

"Decision's been made, Dr. Bird. Lower Illiana is no longer viable."

"No longer—viable?"

"Yes, well, it's a strain on the system and has been for several years. This sector hasn't produced enough food to sustain itself, much less provide support to other Regions. The gas wells are, for all intents and purposes, spent. And the process has left those areas uninhabitable. Seismographs have recorded quakes of increasing magnitude. Groundwater has been undrinkable for decades. The entire region is a drain on resources without showing a return in goods and services. The time has come to right-size the district."

"That sounds straight off the feed, Mr. Walsh. But I'm sure the strain has lessened. We've been without water for nearly a week."

"Yes, well, we had hoped to begin the removal process before that, but circumstances, as always, arise."

"As always. What removal process are you talking about?"

"Yes, well, all inhabitants of the region will be removed— effective immediately."

"Removed to where? Another location—or are we talking severance?"

"I don't get into the details of that process. Director Tanner handles that. I'm just here to offer you a transfer to the Lower Superior Region, specifically the Duluth Garrison. You've done decent work here, maintaining a healthy population under some admittedly trying circumstances. It's a chance for you to get out of the backwater and enjoy the delights of an urban existence. It's an excellent posting, Dr. Bird. It's where I'm headed. I'm afraid your androg can't make the move with you, however. It's nearly of age, so it goes wherever the personnel directors decide, of course."

"And if I say no?"

A long pause. "No? Dr. Bird, this really isn't a matter of choice."

"I want to know where these people are going. And when you're going to get some water down here."

"Dr. Bird, as I said, I don't make the decisions about the who, what and where of removal. And it shouldn't be your concern either, although it reflects well on you to have a certain level of passion for your patients'—ah—former patients'—well-being. As far as water, I believe Tanner's squads are distributing some as we speak, to ease what will be an admittedly painful process. But it's all for the ultimate good of the Protectorate. And what's good for the Protectorate is good for the people."

With a whir, the tiny drone suddenly swoops around the corner into the hall. The boy follows and stands there, regarding Merit keenly for a moment. He glances over his shoulder into the living room, and then sidles up to her, beckoning with a plump finger. She bends cautiously, bringing her face closer to his.

"You're a fem," he hisses in her ear. "I can tell."

She brings her finger to her lips. "You're very skilled," she whispers back. "It's quite a talent to see an androg's origin."

"You've just got the haircut to look like one." His high-pitched voice is rising.

Merit shakes her head. "No, it's you. Your ability to..."

Think fast!

She forces herself to shrug, as if defeated. "All right, I admit it." Drops her voice even lower. "It's my special secret. I'm a spy from Corporate doing important investigative work." She stares deep into his widening blue eyes. "You can help me. Be my spy brother."

He nods eagerly.

Ah, for the gullibility of children.

"Good," she says. Her mouth is so parched and his face looks so juicy and smooth and round, like a ripe nectarine. She resists the urge to sink her teeth into his pink cheek and turns her focus back to the conversation in the living room.

"This is all happening too fast, without any warning," Eben is protesting.

"What's the point of a warning? In the end, that sort of thing just causes unrest and makes the process far more difficult. When the board makes a decision, it is made and executed. This Region has been declared uninhabitable. These workers are movable and, frankly, expendable."

A tug on her wrist. The blue eyes in the pudgy face signal an eagerness to share. "I have a spy secret, too," the boy whispers.

"I'm not leaving these people, not until I know where they're going," Eben states flatly.

"Dr. Bird, I don't have that information. I am not the master player. I don't move the chess pieces. I, like you, am just a piece myself."

"Yeah, a real piece of shit."

Merit nods impatiently. She's tired of humoring the brat, but she forces sugar onto her words. "Oh, really? Share it with a sister spy?"

The boy's eyes give sidelong glances to his left and right, canvassing for enemies and eavesdroppers. He crooks a finger. She bends her ear to his lips again.

"It's in the water."

Merit squints into the boy's round face, but before she has a chance to formulate a question, the manager calls from the living room and the child obediently turns and hustles back through the entryway, his drone buzzing after him.

"I sincerely hope you change your mind, Dr. Bird. But be advised you don't have a lot of time to reflect. This area will be decommissioned and cleared before the end of the day. I hope to see you in Duluth, sir. If not, good luck to you in your severance."

Edging back into the kitchen, Merit watches through the window until the manager's mobile rolls quietly down the street and turns the corner. When she whirls to run to the living room, she is startled to see Eben already standing in the doorway, ashen-faced.

"It's zero hour, Merit. You heard?"

She nods. The wheels are spinning, his eyes scanning the corners of the room.

"All the things I haven't told you. Taught you. Thought I had all the time in the world. Stupid! Stupid!" His fist strikes the casing of the doorway. "Always waiting for the opportune moment. When there is no opportune moment."

"You won't go to Duluth?"

"Not if it means leaving you behind to..." His voice trails off.

"Severance?"

Did he flinch at that? "To whatever. Whatever they have planned. It's—it's not—"

"There's poison in the water," she says, cutting him off. "At the barracks, there was a cat." The story tumbles out in fragments, just nouns and verbs. "And that stupid boy, the manager's piglet," Merit growls. "He said something. *They put something in the water—or it's in the water.* I was in the hall, listening and he came in with his piss-ant drone and—"

"*As far as water, I believe Tanner's squads are distributing some as we speak...*"

Her next thought is of Em.

"We've got to warn them!"

"Merit, wait!" shouts Eben.

But in two strides, she's slipped into her sandals and out the door. In another two, she grabs her bike from where it leans against the porch rail, straddles it and careens through the front gate.

18

Rose Red

PEDALING THROUGH MUD. That's what it feels like, her thighs and calves protesting each push and pull. Like in a dream, trying to run as fast as you can, but feeling like you're running in place, on the tips of your toes, going nowhere, blocked by some invisible wall.

From a half mile away, she spots the dust billowing in the air like a gray curtain and hears the rumbling thrum of heavy machinery. Ditching the bike in a thicket of stunted trees of heaven, she scuttles down the dry gully that runs alongside the two-lane. Jogs the last quarter mile along a path baked so hard even the weeds have given up trying to penetrate it.

The path ends at a low fence that forms the perimeter of Ag-sector #21. Layers of wind-blown soil have settled on the once-white rails, staining them a chalky gray. A hundred yards beyond the fence stands the supervisor's residence, a sprawling L-shaped structure built of red brick that is now, like the fence, encrusted with dust. Next door squats the artisan house, a long, narrow, shed-like building with small glass blocks embedded the length of it, just under the roof line. The mig barracks stand another two hundred yards or so away, at the end of a gravel lane. Black transports idle there, three in a row. Two are the kind used by border security: huge, rugged, with massive tires and smoked glass windows that obscure the interior. The third is an armored truck, a gigantic black cab towing an open flatbed. When the transports turn and trundle down the gravel drive straight towards Merit, she ducks back into the gully and scoots inside the metal culvert under the roadway. When the huge beasts rumble overhead, she cranes her head around the edge of the pipe. A dozen or so men clad in the black b-squad uniform hunker on the flatbed, some sitting with their legs hanging over the edge. Visors flipped skyward, their faces are a revelation. They look barely old enough to have taken their final assessments, but they have a hard set to the jaw, the grim visage of veterans. In the midst of these, Merit thinks she spies a familiar face. Pale, with a long narrow nose and flat cheekbones. It has to be him. Even here amongst the boys bred for size and brute strength, his head rises above the rest. But the truck speeds away, and in the momentary glimpse, again she can't be sure. Something is different. Missing. And then she realizes, in all the years she's known him, for the first time, Mars Lund isn't smiling.

A curious twinge, an itch flares on the palm of her right hand, a crawling sensation along the base of her thumb. She stares at the skin curving there, sees the blade and the blood, and the hand that dwarfed hers. *"A blood covenant, Mer. Unbreakable."* Blinks and shakes the memory away.

She crouches in the pipe until the roar of the engines dulls to a distant grumble. Plunges out and scrambles up the slope, ignoring the throb in her lower back. With each footfall that brings her closer to the barracks, a fist clenches her guts, relentless even as she tries to reassure herself.

They're on those transports. They are. Behind those smoked-out windows. Asses and necks cradled in the cushioned comfort of high-backed seats. Arms at rest. Hands fingering the caps of their water bottles, pressing the chill sweating curves to their foreheads, luxuriating in the hotcold trickle of condensation. Peering through the

clear, distorted, liquid beauty within. Bringing the bottles to their
mouths. Drinking deeply.

She wants to wake from the dream now, before it becomes a
nightmare, but she can't stop herself from moving forward. Her
tongue running along the inside of her mouth feels like sandpaper. And when she pinches the flesh of her forearm, it hurts.

Just beyond the corner of the first building, a body comes
into view. And then another. And then a dozen in haphazard
rows. On their backs, on their bellies, slumped to their sides,
curled up, knees to chest. They still wear nightclothes. And yes,
some could be asleep, eyes shut. One has an arm flung over his
face, as if warding off the morning sun. She walks among them
with light feet, as if afraid of waking them. Empty water bottles
lie in the dust. Some are still cradled in hands.

She knows few of these people by name, but their faces are
familiar, from the GaltMart aisles, from Bartertown, from the
hoopball courts in the park, from the Harvest Festivals of years
past. They are people she has passed in the streets or brushed
elbows with standing in line for the live acts when they swept
through once a year. She's felt their life pulsing beside her in all
its nasty, brutish, amazing beauty. Smelt the stink of garlic and
onion on their breath, the citric tang of their sweat. Seen the way
the blood pulsed in their veins just below the skin of their wrists
and their temples, the way their lips could bend just as easily
into a smile as a frown. The bright light that, even in the worst of
times, had flickered in their eyes.

All dead.

But the one she seeks is not among them.

Treading carefully, Merit makes her way back to the gravel lane and then to the stone path that leads to the supervisor's
house. The back door yawns. She steps over the threshold into
the dim interior of the kitchen. Mr. and Mrs. Espino are at the
table, as if in the midst of breakfast. But Mrs. Espino is face down

on the polished oak surface, loose strands of her brown hair blending with the grain of the wood. Her husband is slouched in his chair, head tilted back and to the side, as if he has just nodded off, as if a chortling snore will momentarily erupt from his nose and mouth. A half-empty water bottle stands on the table between them. But Em, who should be in her chair, is not.

Hope swells within Merit's chest. It burbles and wafts, scratches her inner wall like something itching to get out.

"Em?" Did the sound actually leave her lips or is she just imagining herself uttering it in a dust-choked rasp?

Again. "Em?" Surely not loud enough for the girl to hear, wherever she is hiding. And so again. "Em?"

The artisan house.

Ignoring the rapid thumping of her heart and the double shot of adrenaline that urges her to run, she moves cautiously down the path, pausing under the bare beams of the pergola, where ivy once stretched its emerald vines. The front door to the workroom hangs open. As she steps up to it, she opens her mouth to call out again, but the sight before her strangles the name on her tongue.

Some enormous force has rolled through the room, upending everything in its path. As if a tornado has whirled through or some giant's child has grown tired of playing with her dollhouse and knocked things aside with a petulant sweep of her hand. The long worktables are lying on their sides, stools are strewn about the floor in the midst of smashed crockery and shattered glass. Bits crunch under her sandals as she tiptoes through the debris.

"Em?" Barely a breath, much less a whisper.

The ragdoll lies in the corner, wedged between the open back door and the wall, a toy flung there carelessly, ruthlessly. A red rose blossoms across her small body.

She almost made it out.

The blood that has seeped to the far edges of the girl's

nightgown is already drying in the heat, the crimson turning to rust, as the vibrance of life ebbs, browning like wilted petals crushed under the heel of a boot. Instinctively, Merit knows there is no need to take the fragile wrist in her hand, to press her fingers to the skin and feel for a thrum. But she does it anyway. Her legs give way and she is sinking, sinking, sinking, a soft body meeting the hard floor, curling herself around the broken rose, gathering its limp petals to her chest, pressing her burning cheek to the cool white tile, and her nose into the brown hair that smells of sweat and lavender, letting the tears that she has held onto so tightly finally flow, mingling with Em's blood on her cheek, tasting the salt of each as it pools at the corner of her lip.

But what should have been a torrent is barely a trickle.

19

The Promise of Living

TANNER LETS THE CORNERS OF HIS MOUTH relax just a tad. You wouldn't call it a smile, much less a grin, but it's not the tight mask he has worn since before dawn. The morning has gone as well as might be expected. Oh, there have been a few minor snags. A couple of non-conforming types at the Sanitation facility asking questions instead of following directions. The smart-mouthed old lout rousted out of his tarp tent in the dregs of Bartertown, buying just enough time with his rap about having Corporate connections to escape from the pair of newbies tasked with clearing that shithole. Damn the new ones. There's always issues until the chemicals get balanced.

And the mess with the little bitch over at Agsector #21.

But all in all, it was a smooth action, the bulk of it complete. The hard work, the brain work. Disposal takes nothing but brawn. So only the wrapping up left. The tying of the inevitable loose ends. One of which is the medic. *"Recalcitrant"* as the district manager phrased it. Walsh has an apparent misunderstanding of what Tanner's job is.

"Convince him it's in his best interest to take the Duluth position," the bloated bureaucrat had said before boarding the transport to his posting, along with his piglet child and sow of a wife, jiggling in her glee at finally moving on from this wasteland.

This is not within Tanner's purview, this convincing. What does it signify anyway, this need to be convinced? There is a choice, yes, but it is a stark choice, an obvious one. Accept the job you are assigned or accept severance. No options exist beyond that.

It is the medic's decision to make.

When Suraj finds Merit, she is still cradling Em's lifeless body.

"Come on, got to get back home. Let her go. There's no time."

She doesn't have the strength to resist. Her arms are reeds, bending to the wind of his will. He is curiously gentle, lifting the dead girl from Merit's lap, laying her carefully on the floor, taking the time to pull her nightgown over her knees, to brush a strand of blood-matted hair from her pale cheek. He is much rougher, less patient with the living, digging his hands under Merit's armpits, hefting her to her feet. But when she totters, shaky as a newborn foal, he slips an arm around her waist.

"C'mon, fem, you can do this."

"All dead," she mumbles. Her mouth feels stuffed with pebbles.

He's not sure if it's a question or a statement. "It's like that all over. They got to 'em before we could. Maybe some didn't drink, though, eh? Maybe some figgered it out? Like you. And got away." Does she need that hope to move, to trot down the path, to get on the bike, to ride back to where Eben waits? If so, he's willing to feed it to her, though he doesn't really believe it himself.

It is Suraj's first time in the basement. When Eben ushers them into the safe room and pulls the hidden sliding panel closed, the boy gives a long, low whistle.

"These old houses, long may they stand." Eben pats a support beam that rises from the cement floor. "It's the foundation, the thickness of the cinderblock. Neither the zoom nor the feed can penetrate it."

Suraj jerks a thumb at the bronze-colored mesh stretched across the boarded up window and nailed as a canopy to the beams. "Quite the stash of copper. It's not just the foundation keepin' the zoom out. You built a frackin' faraday cage, yeah?"

"Kudos. Where'd you learn about faradays?"

"Pick up a lot skulkin' around Bartertown. Where'd you score the copper mesh? That stuff's—"

"Illegal for workers, yes. You're not the only one who knows his way around B-town."

"Bartertown's gone," Merit finally whispers. "And this room kept no one safe, did it? They're all dead."

Eben puts a hand on her shoulder. "It'll keep us safe, for now. While we make some decisions."

"They're all dead," she repeats.

"You're alive." Eben grips her arm. "We will grieve, in time, but now we need to focus. They'll do an embed sweep and discover there's at least two bodies missing. Mine and yours."

Merit eyes Suraj. "Three."

Suraj shakes his head. "Not me. Born in the blur, live in the blur." He shrugs at Merit's narrowed eyes. "Believe it, fem. No embed. Totally clean. Never had one. Never will."

"I knew you were a river jumper," she says.

"Nope, born here," the boy insists.

"How—"

Eben cuts her off. "Now's not the time. Ask him to tell you the heartwarming story later. You'll be spending a lot of time together on the road."

"I don't—"

"Look, Merit, we've got to get you out of here."

"I know, but where will we go?"

"I can't go with you. One sweep of the zoom and they've got me in their sights."

"Eben, you're not making sense. So he doesn't have an

embed," Merit says, flinging her hand toward Suraj. "But what's the point of me running, when the focus will pick up my signal, same as yours. They must already know I hit the b-squad depot. And the agsector."

Eben and Suraj exchange a look. Finally, Eben sighs.

"You don't have an embed either." He digs his fingers under the neckline of her t-shirt, grabbing the talis hanging around her neck. He yanks and the silver chain breaks, nipping the skin of her nape.

"Your talis," he says, glaring at the miniscule chip that glitters as it swings in the space between their faces. "My first daughter's embed. You don't have one."

Merit stares at the talis as if mesmerized.

"I don't—" she stutters. "What're you—you told me—"

"I told you that you must wear it at all times."

"Yeah, to keep me healthy, you said it was a monitoring system—"

"Safe. I said it would keep you safe. And it is a monitoring system, so that's not—"

"A lie." Anger slithers inside her guts like a snake, while a cold sweat beads on her forehead.

"Fine, call it that. Doesn't matter. I did what I had to do to keep you safe." Guilt and defiance, resignation and resolve color a shifting mosaic on Eben's face.

Suraj keeps his eyes downcast, as if embarrassed to witness this drama. Merit glares at him. "Okay, he was born in the blur. What's my story? Corporate doesn't let anyone raise more than one child. How'd you get two? And where's the first?"

Eben collapses into the chair beside Merit and folds his arms tightly to his chest. "Serafina and I waited six years for a baby. Psych testing went well, we were physically healthy, but we kept being deferred. Only so many babies come out of the breeder program each year, and competition is fierce to get one. I was assigned to the Breeder Facility back then, and to be in the midst of all this... fertility, all this life, and be denied a chance. It was very painful." He rubs a hand across his face, as if brushing the memory away. "Then, suddenly, the feed came through from the assignment bureau. We'd be getting our baby in less than a month."

The hard set of his jaw softens. "She was a sweet little thing, our dark-haired, dark-eyed June bug. But no sooner did we settle her in the cradle, she turned sickly and weak. We couldn't share our joy with friends, because I was so damn worried she'd pick up some infection or get bitten by something, a tick, a mosquito, a flea. And we didn't dare report the problems because I was sure Quality Control would take her and we'd have blown our chance. It was so damn frustrating. Here I am a medic and nothing I did seemed to help, my infant was failing to thrive." His jaw hardens again. "But, working at the clinic, I could forge her health updates. So I did."

"What was her name?"

A flinch wrinkles the corners of his eyes and lips, as if he's been kicked. "Merit."

It's like a sudden blow to her stomach. "What happened?" she demands, choking on the words even as she spits them out.

"We should have reported it, I know that, but we were terrified—for her, for us. And then—" His voice quits on him and he looks away, to the corner of the safe room, or maybe to somewhere beyond the place where the walls meet, far beyond. Something settles in him, like a feather floating to the floor, and he turns back to her and reaches out a hand to touch her cheek. Merit pulls away as if stung.

"I found you."

Before she can speak, he puts a finger to her lips. "Corporate's never built a bridge to those islands in Lake Superior, still relies on a ferry. Security." He shrugs. "But when you're a facility medic, you have certain privileges. Piloting your own boat back and forth, having a special slip to dock in. So I'll never really know whether it was pure chance or... something else.

"One evening I was getting ready to cast off and head for home. I was unfastening a line and I heard it, just barely, the slightest mewling. Seemed like it was coming from a stack of crates sitting on the dock waiting for the supply barge. There was a basket there, off to the side. Wasn't a freight container, it was one of the storage baskets that the women have in their rooms. I go over and give it a lift and it feels heavy. Then I hear this little cry again, like an animal of some sort is trapped inside. I'm a little nervous prying open the lid, worried that something—rat, cat, I don't know—is going to leap out and claw me. But when I peek in, I see a baby, a newborn, still bloody, all swaddled up in a towel, just its squashed little face peering out. And tucked in a fold is a piece of fabric with words scrawled across it. Like they were written by someone who knew her time was running out. And I panicked. None of the women I was treating were due to give birth. I don't really know why but I put the lid back on and carried the basket to my boat. Then I remember the security camera. But the one scanning that part of the dock was mounted low, under the overhang of the shed. And someone's draped a towel over it. A towel stiff with dried blood."

Again, a wince narrows Eben's eyes. "So I brought you home to Serafina and the medic in me took over. Removed the umbilical cord. Checked your vitals. Cleaned you up. Fed you. How you howled through the process; a good, strong, full-throated cry. I guessed you were only a few hours old and once we finally got you to sleep, nestled in the crib next to Merit, two little dark heads on the white sheet, we sat down and tried to puzzle it out. What to do? Turn you over to the assignment bureau? That would have been the proper thing to do, the Corporate thing to do. You belonged to Corporate. You were obviously meant to be assigned to a set of parents. Whether you're an elite or a breeder, no birth happens without Corporate approval."

Suraj lets out a snort that draws a tight smile across Eben's lips and a nod in his direction. "Unless it happens in the blur."

The snake of anger inside Merit has morphed into something else, something fluttery and fearful with wings. "You didn't do the right thing."

The heat of Eben's hand as it closes over her own startles her. "Oh, I believe we did. We knew we'd never be assigned another child if something happened to that first baby. There are no second chances. You were so healthy! And we weren't thinking with our heads. We were running on pure emotion those first few weeks we sheltered you. We had no plan for what we'd do if you both survived. How could we keep you secret? In some ways, it might have been easy. We knew your mother must somehow have given birth in secret and hid you before the techs got a chance to implant your embed. So you weren't on record anywhere. But what kind of a life would you have, off the record? It's one thing to split a three-way ration of food four ways. But you couldn't register for lessons, couldn't take the aptitudes. Couldn't get a feedcom and join the workforce. You would have been, for all intents and purposes, trapped inside these walls."

The winged creature is frantic now, beating, clawing, straining to tear its way out. "Where's the other—baby?"

"One morning I found her barely breathing and unresponsive in the cradle. And I—let her go." Eben bites down on his lower lip, draws it in, before he continues. "And then I took a scalpel from my kit and found the place at the back of her head where they had inserted the chip, just near the foramen magnum, the hole in the bottom of the skull where the spinal cord passes to connect to the brain. The tiny scar was still visible. And her hair was so soft and fine, it felt like the wind slipping through my fingers."

Eben stares at his hands, resting on his knees, for a long time before he continues. "There's a wilderness up in the Superior called the Chequamegon. We buried her there. Took her deep into the forest. It was October and the leaves were finally starting to turn. It had rained so the soil was easy to dig. I picked a pine tree, so the fallen needles would cover her like a blanket. And when we came home, you were Merit. It was an easy deception. Yes, she was pale-skinned and you were darker. But so few people had seen her and babies change so quickly. For the sensors and the focus, you wore the embed hidden on a chain. And it became your talis." He takes Merit's hand and gently places the tiny square in her palm and folds her fingers over it. "And we never told a soul."

No air—there's no air left to breathe in the basement, so with the creature still battering away at her insides, Merit slams the embed down on the table and takes flight. Up from the chair, sending it tipping backward to the concrete floor with a clattering screech. Out of the safe room and up the stairs, the soles of her shoes pounding a drumbeat on the wooden treads. Through the hall to the kitchen and out the back door into the indigo gloom. Flinging her body to the porch railing, leaning over to vomit up the beast that is tormenting her.

Her breath is still coming in great, ragged gasps when she hears the screen door creak open and slam shut again. The hand on her back feels large, warm, and, to her annoyance, strangely comforting.

"Don't punish me for doing what I thought was right."

Merit shrugs the hand off and steps to the side. "Kids get punished all the time for doing something they think is right, but adults say is wrong. What's the difference?"

Eben sighs. "That's childish talk. It's time to start thinking like an adult."

"Why? So I can call something black when it's really white,

or say up is down, or two plus two equals five?"

"Merit—"

She spins to face him, fists clenched. "It's all been lies! Everything I've ever heard from your lips! *'You have a weak immune system, susceptible to everything under the sun.'* Lie! *'The talis keeps you healthy, must wear it always, next to your skin.'* Lie! *'You were born a service track androg. Accept it.'* Lie!"

A new critter stirs in her stomach, so she quickly sucks in a deep breath, holding it for a five-count before slowly expelling it through her lips.

Eben stares at her. "Parents have always lied to their children. They lie to protect them. To give easy answers to difficult questions. To spare them the pain of the truth."

That sits between them for a moment like an insurmountable wall. "Come back inside. There's much to do and very little time," he finally says.

She resists the hand on her shoulder, his trying to bend her to his will.

"You don't realize how special you are."

"That's all I've ever been told! I'm special!" Merit explodes, her voice a savage lilt. "But not in a good way. I'm sick to death of it. And now I find out I'm not. Not in the way you said, the way you were constantly warning me about. You never really gave me the shots, did you? The androg meds. What have you been doing this whole time? Just pricking my skin with needles? Telling me, just look away, it'll hurt less." Her voice drops. "But that one's on me, yeah. Because I've known the truth about that lie for a long time now." She brings her fist down hard on the railing, wincing at the pain that jolts through her wrist and up her arm. *Pain to drown out the pain.*

"Merit, you're untraceable. You know what that means? To be untraceable, here in the Protectorate?"

"Means I'm trapped, pretending to be someone I'm not."

Eben grabs hold of her shoulders, turning her to face him. "It means you're free, free to be whoever you want to be."

She twists out of his grasp. "You're just a lyin', crazy old sweat. Free? I couldn't even walk into the GaltMart to pick up the week's rations. You need an embed for that."

"And you have one to use, when you need it. When you don't, you can go anywhere you like, without anyone knowing where you are or where you're headed, without your every step being traced. That's freedom."

An image seeps in amidst the anger. A pool of sunshine on the floor, the atlas opened, the map of the world cool and smooth under her fingers.

That's just whack, a girl afraid of creepy-crawlies and every last germ that wafts in the air or seeps through blood and snot, that girl heading off into the unknown... In her mind, an unseen hand slams the atlas shut with a resounding thud. But then another thought springs forth. *This is why Serafina never called me by my given name... why I was always Angel or Querida to her.*

The solar light wired to the porch winks to life and casts a cool blue-white glow that deepens the lines and shadows on Eben's face, turns his scar a pale silver.

"You saved that Corporate man, down at the border, but you didn't save your daughter."

"I made the decision—"

"Like Corporate made the decision, here. What they did here. Today."

"Don't compare this with that. She was weak. You were, are strong. I had to choose and I did. In my mind, it was a revolutionary act."

Words, words, words. She is drowning in them. It's too exhausting for the girl who has been groomed to prefer silence. What did the bike man call her? Miss Stillwater. All too new and tiring, like the time she'd tried to swim across the little inland lake where she and Serafina fished and she miscalculated the distance and was only midway when her smooth strokes degenerated into hapless flails and her rhythmic breaths to spasmodic gasps. Only Serafina's strong arms had saved her from drowning. *But she's not here. And I'm going under. Nothing to cling to.*

In the raw silence between them, an image comes. *A woman, not much more than a girl perhaps, shivering in pain and terror, squatting in some dim corner, catching her slimy, bloody newborn before it hits the floor.*

"What happened to her—my birth mother?"

Eben is silent for a long moment before answering. "Breeders have one purpose. And one doesn't just lose a baby at the facility without evidence. I still can't fathom how she managed to give birth in secret. But she did. Then she disappeared. Speculation was that she drowned in Superior. But, as far as I know, security never recovered a body."

"You know who she was."

"Come." He gestures toward the door.

"Tell me."

"I can show you." He holds out his hand, but she keeps hers firmly on the railing. "Merit, please, come with me to the safe room. We have so much to do. And time is racing away. You have the rest of your life to hate me, if you must. But trust me now."

20

Zero Hour

SHE HAS HER MOTHER'S EYES. The picture, small as it is, a rectangle no longer than her thumb, reveals the many similarities they share. The eyes, striking green ringing the inner brown, wide set in the oval face. The broad-tipped nose. The swell of the lower lip. The high forehead. But her mother's skin is darker, her hair black.

"She was beautiful," Suraj says, peering over Merit's shoulder.

Is beautiful. She could still be alive, somewhere out there in the blur. Breeders don't have embeds, Eben said. Interferes with fertility. So she could be out there. Somewhere. Maybe.

"Brave. She was brave. That's what's most important," Eben retorts, beckoning Merit to the battered cabinet shoved into the far corner of the safe room. Its dingy white paint is crackled and peeling, the surface of the wood scarred with gouges and scratches that resemble some forgotten hieroglyphics, the story of its life written in a language no human can decipher. This is the first time she's ever seen it open, the bolt of the ancient padlock that kept its secrets hanging unlocked. As a young girl, when she'd begged to know what lurked behind those doors, Eben had always chuckled, *"When the time is right. When the time is right."* Now she quails and hangs back, the shock of the day overwhelming her curiosity.

Inside, hanging from a rod, are necessities of harsher winters long past: bulky, hooded parkas, pairs of snow pants, long woolen scarves twined and draped like black snakes on their hangers. A pair of black backpacks bulge on the bottom of the cabinet underneath the winter gear. Eben gropes along the shelf above the rod. When he withdraws his hand, it holds a small swatch of white fabric. The soft cotton square looks like a remnant torn from a bed sheet or a shirt. He offers it to her.

Without asking, Merit knows. Her fingers trace the letters scratched across in dull brown-red.

"And that's one reason we vowed to teach you to read, no matter the risk."

Her thumb brushes the symbols again. *Her blood? My blood?*

ANGEL, THERE IS A FATE WORSE THAN DEATH.

The world sways until Eben catches her and folds her into a chair. And then it is all just dry sobbing. A hushed, stuttering ebb and flow of breath punctuated by a soft moan, a phantom type of mourning, a ghost lament.

Eben takes hold of her hand that hangs useless between her knees and folds it around a canteen. "Drink." He runs his fingers through her tangled mat of hair, smoothing it back from her forehead. "Stay with me now. Hold it together."

But it's falling apart, slipping away. And the tighter she clenches her fists, the faster it all seems to be escaping. The things she knows to be true. The very world she knows. Going, going, gone. Everything just a racing, tumbling, blur-filled jumble. Askew. Sideways. Backwards. Upside down. The realization that nothing will ever be the same again.

The weight of Eben's hand is a comfort and an irritant, something to ease into, something to shake off. But before she can do either, the hand is gone and Eben has crossed back to the cabinet. From behind the winter gear, he withdraws a piece of apparel that looks both odd and familiar: a vest of mottled camouflage, dull greens and browns and grays, with straps that wrap around the sides.

"My armored vest, a souvenir Corporate should never have let me keep. But when a man owes you his life and thinks you're a good Corporate soldier, a bee to your depths, rules get bent, overlooked." He holds it before her. "I want you to wear this at all times."

Merit run her fingers over the thin fabric, tracing the outline of the hard, super slim plate encased within its soft surface. The hook and loop patches snap and sizzle as he rips them apart and slips the vest over her head before she can resist. But when he starts to tighten the straps, she pushes his hands away and works them on her own. It fits surprisingly well once she gets the straps adjusted, the stretchy fabric molding to her body, the plates over her torso and back rock-hard but amazingly light, accommodating the slight swelling of her belly. It will be completely inconspicuous under her tunic.

"Got another one?" Suraj asks

A crisp shake of the head from Eben. "Sorry."

"No problem. I'll just juke and dodge any bullets that come my way."

With a grim smile, Eben reaches back into the cabinet. When his hand re-emerges, a black band about 3 inches wide dangles from his fingers.

"Feedcom armband. First-gen models were hand-helds. This was how you went hands-free." But from the streamlined pouch, Eben draws not a slim feedcom, but a chunky black handful of obsolete technology.

"A vocoder?" Suraj scoffs. "That's a dusty bit, for sure. Probably older than—"

"Me?" Eben nods. "Yeah, just about. Came and went in a

nanosecond. Corporate engineers worked 24/7 on the first-gen feedcom, so this little baby went into recycle."

Merit is mute, but her eyes ask the question.

"Listen to it."

She takes the vocoder from Eben's outstretched hand and unwinds the ear pieces from around its rectangular body. Warily, she fits the black buds in her ears and after a moment's hesitation, presses the power button. The mini-screen lights up with a soft blue glow and a circling arrow. A broad-boned, sharp-jawed face fills the screen and a lilting, low-pitched voice fills her ears.

Serafina.

"Angel, if you're listening to this, then it must be time."

The strangest thoughts carom through her mind. *Spin around—she's right behind you. Turn around quick enough, you'll catch a glimpse before she disappears.*

"It also means I'm not there to help you get ready for what's coming."

She grinds her thumb down onto the power button to silence the voice. It is all too much and too horrible and too quick and too soon. She turns away from Eben to hide her eyes, afraid of what he will say, more afraid of what she might say in return.

No hay lágrimas en la Revolución. There are no tears in the revolution. Serafina's mantra.

So she sucks it up good and tight, slowly removing the buds from her ears. Winding the cords around the vocoder with meticulous care. Tucking it into a side pocket of her cargo pants, before finally turning back to face him.

Eben waits. When the question doesn't come, he answers anyway. "She gave me that just before she was severanced. Said she'd failed her task. That she hadn't told you enough. Because there are some things that only she could tell." Eben pauses, waiting for a response. When none comes, he takes a firm hold of Merit's shoulders, as if to shake one out of her. But his fine-boned hands just grip her tightly, fingers digging down to the bone.

"She was a knowledge keeper, a meme, and a damned good one and she was in the process of passing it along to you. Had been doing that since the day you came into our lives. But time slips by. You think you have so much more of it than you really do. Maybe she was betting things would have changed before her time was up. But she lost that bet. What she knew wasn't a finite amount, something you can measure. She must have realized recording it was dangerous, too—if the device slipped into the wrong hands." Eben's grin was humorless. "Danger. She never sweated it. Sometimes I think she courted it. Used to joke it was her middle name."

There it was, the substance of her childhood laid bare. The way Serafina had always kept her close, explaining the how and the why. Never letting a question go unanswered or dismissed with a "because I said so." Anticipating the questions that Merit never opened her mouth to ask. And yet she could have said so much more.

Sometimes we lie when we speak and sometimes we lie when we are silent.

"Did you listen?" she finally asks, her voice barely a whisper.

Eben shakes his head. "Not my burden to bear. But you have many miles to go. Maybe she meant to keep you company on your journey." He holds out the arm band. "Though at the time, she couldn't be sure where you'd be going."

Where am I going?

She's not aware of having said it out loud, but Eben doesn't hesitate. "North. I'll accept the Duluth posting. I'm assuming it's not too late since the goliaths haven't shown up on our doorstep with their water. But I'm not letting them haul you off. You'll make your way to Duluth on your own. In the blur."

Excitement flashes in Suraj's eyes. "I'm there, Eben," he says, an edge of glee sharpening his voice.

Eben keeps his focus on Merit. "I won't send you out blind. We've raised you with the skills to do this. Because it was always in the backs of our minds. There are more of you out there. The untraceable. I know it in more than just my gut. There are cells, safe houses. Others that will help you."

Seconds tick by, precious time she is wasting, sitting hunched on the battered folding chair, head in her hands, hair hanging limp over her face, hiding the confusion there. He shouldn't be asking this of her. He should be patting her back, folding her in his arms to comfort her, letting the horror of the day wash over them together. His voice should be soft and soulful. Doesn't he, too, feel pierced to the core?

"We'll make our way back to each other," he murmurs, as if reading her thoughts. "This was unthinkable. I can't even fathom what drives a human being to do this. But it's not the first time. And it won't be the last. So now we have to split up. I'll go to Duluth. I'll tell them you ran off. It's on them to figure out why you're not showing up on the zoom. They'll put some heat on me, but I can take it. The word will spread. That was Corporate's mistake, so long ago, not removing all the guevaras when they had the chance. We're still out there. There'll be people to shelter you. There's ways of getting messages through."

"How?" she demands. "How do you get your info? Pass the words between your—cells? You can't use the vox. That's monitored."

"Oh, we can. We do. In ways primitive and sophisticated. Coded phrases." He glances at Suraj. "We go face to face. Person to person. It's not easy and it's not efficient, but you do what you have to do." He clasps her hands. "Merit, you have to do this. You can face a life of slipping from Bartertown to Bartertown, in the blur, or you can try to make a better one, for yourself and for others. This is the first step on that journey. Serafina and I prepared you. I know you can do this. Now you have to believe it."

Minutes are sliding away, as the memories rise, slowly at first and then in a rippling wave.

"A quick learner, this one, my Angel." Serafina cooing praise as Merit takes to the orienteering compass like a bird to flight: casually, like she was born to explore.

"See this red and white arrow? That's the compass needle. Red part always points towards Earth's magnetic north pole. Got that?" Serafina tapped on the fluid-filled housing. "These two straight lines? That's the north alignment arrow. Get the red part of the needle within those two lines under the N and you've hit north."

"To find your direction, turn the dial until the North mark and the north alignment arrow are lined up with the North end of the needle. Kinda looks like a shed, right? So remember you always want 'red in the shed.'"

"Red in the shed," Merit giggled.

In the here and now, Eben squats beside her, brushing the wild hair back from her face, tucking the strands behind her ears, his hands gentle but his eyes radiating a cool intensity.

"If you can do this," Merit asks, her voice a croak, "get messages in and out, get the down low on old guevaras and the Handed, why not on Serafina? She swore—"

"Serafina's dead."

And there it was, stark and bleached white as the bones of a carcass under a blinding sun at noon.

"Just like all the others who've ever been severanced."

A piercingly hot afternoon, its white glare sharp and serrated as the blade of a hunting knife. Serafina's clumsy joke anticipating the cool interior of the mobile transport behind the blackout glass. If it occurs to Merit to question why they aren't allowed to accompany Serafina to the bullet train station, she never says it out loud.

Of course not.

Serafina slips a fine silver chain over her head. At the end hangs an oval gemstone, of a brownish-red and orange hue banded with thin white and yellow veins in a squarish symmetry. "Lake Superior agate," she whispers, "in a fortification pattern. The red comes from the iron in the land. Angel, I am a woman of rationality, of reason, by temperament and training. And yet there are more things in heaven and earth than are dreamt of in philosophy."

Serafina smiles at the girl's quizzical expression. "A great man, an author, wrote those words hundreds of years ago. About things we can't explain. Things that call for faith. In ancient times, warriors wore breastplates encrusted with agates to give them strength and make them victorious in battle. Who am I to question? And so, another talis." She taps the amulet with her long, strong-boned finger. "For protection, for strength, for courage. I will see you in my heart, until I see you with my eyes. Hasta siempre." She draws Merit into a quick tight hug, then releases her and turns away. She strides up the steps and into the blue murk of the mobile's interior, never turning back for one last glance, the better to miss the tears streaking down her daughter's cheeks. No háy lagrimas.

Merit, sullen and hurt at Serafina's lack of communication, stopped wearing the stone months ago. It sits in the top drawer of her dresser, buried under a pile of ratty, mismatched socks that she rarely has occasion to wear. But suddenly she yearns for its gentle weight hanging from her neck.

"Shit! The one thing I should have put here long ago. Maybe it was my way of warding off ever having to use these things." The voice sounds far away. "Merit," Eben snaps his fingers in her face. "Get the atlas."

21

The Ghost

HER HEART IS AN ALIEN CREATURE burrowed beneath her skin, ready to emerge, struggling to break out, fists pounding the walls that contain it. She knows this house, every inch of it, even under the black veil of deepest night. Yet now it seems a foreign place, wild, dangerous. A place to be navigated with fear, where each footfall may be a wrong step and each corner a wrong turn. To retrieve the atlas from its hidey hole, she has to climb two flights of stairs, each with its own peculiar squeaks, sighs and groans. Her path will lead her past windows in the kitchen and on the stair landing and in Eben's bedroom. Do goliaths lurk outside, night goggles fixed, scanning for movement?

No, they'd be kicking the door in.

Still, she crouches low and crab-walks, scuttling over the cool tile in the kitchen, around the corner of the entryway and into the blessedly windowless hall. She pauses, presses her hand to her chest, an attempt to quell the battering. She's made up her mind to retrieve the agate.

No time. No time for this.

Holding her ragged breath, she listens. Just the rush of blood in her veins. The air is still thick with the day's leftover heat, yet the hairs on her arms prickle. She senses that she is not really alone.

I can't do this.

Yes, you can. Suck it up.

She needs to climb the stairs to the second floor, but her feet are weighted, as if her sandals have transformed into boots of cement.

Move!

Still she hesitates, crouching on the bottom step, one hand to her chest, the other flat against the riser.

No one's in here. Just keep telling yourself that. Until you have a heart inside your body instead of a critter trying to beat you to a bloody pulp from inside out.

Then she feels it. At first she thinks it's just the hair on her arms standing on end in the barest wisp of a breeze wafting through the open window on the landing. But it's not static, like an itch. The sensation moves, a tickle on the skin of the back of her hand, crawling slowly up and around toward the crease of her wrist. Something she doesn't want to see, but she can't help looking down. In the black well of the stairs, the creature is hidden, but she can picture it all the same, its flat, segmented body and the many, many fast-moving legs. And she screeches, just barely, not loudly, not really, frantically batting the centipede off her arm, scrabbling around, jamming her knee into the edge of a stair tread, her head rocked by a firework flash of pain. Bolting up, she forgets to duck as she sprints past the window.

He stalks the empty streets that are beginning to smell of death. A sweet rotten odor the flesh gives off as the process of decay begins. He breathes it in deeply. Appreciatively. It's the scent of power. Of a force greater than life.

He wishes the stars that glitter overhead held a fascination so that he might pass these restless hours staring up, noting the patterns they create or the movement of the brightest across the sky, wondering why some are travelers and others not, and why the moon has a pock-marked face. Instead he is intrigued by the inherent stupidity of the human race, its gullibility, its capacity to believe a lie, its hopeless hope.

He appreciates these qualities. After all, they are what made the action flow so smoothly. But they leave a rank taste in his mouth. It was too easy. He would have preferred to see a little fight. One man with the cojones to resist. Or ask questions.

The girl at the farm squat hardly counts.

He finds himself at the end of the asphalt lane, gazing up at the medic's white house, gray under the subdued light of a half moon. Tonight the place is dark. No music seeps from the kitchen window.

He'd had to tussle with the sector KM dweeb to get the file on the medic. Knowledge management, his ass. It was a problem he had with Corporate. Its ideas about the creation of knowledge. The spread of knowledge. Its use. The who, what, when, where, why and how of knowing. Who gets to have his finger on the send button. Call him a guevara, but a man couldn't do his job without knowing things, so it was a little degrading to have to ask for the file from such a pathetic excuse for a life form.

Yet though his was righteous anger, he had gone to some lengths to make it look like a natural death. The irony was that the file held scant useful information.

EBEN BIRD

BORN:	Year 22
PARENTS:	(NATURAL) Roland and Megan Bird
BIRTHPLACE:	Rock Island Agri Sector #1
	Illiana Region North
EMBED:	235711131719
TRACK:	(INITIAL) Security
	(CURRENT) Service – Medical
APP TEST SCORE:	95 (SECURITY)

INCIDENT REPORT

YEAR 32: (AGE 10) Refusal of lessons, summer in
retrenchment camp. Sufficient progress to
return home.

YEAR 37: (AGE 15) Embed registers in Chicago garrison
during uprising led by Joachim Debs. Arrested.
Denies participation. Stated presence was
"out of curiosity and duty as a future
security track worker." Provided minor
details regarding insurrectionist activities.
Released but remanded to youth home for
security track adolescents.

YEAR 40: Passed security app test; initial posting to
Border Patrol - Erie Region

YEAR 42: Commendation for saving life of [redacted]
during border skirmish

YEAR 43: Enter medic training program

YEAR 46: Posted to Breeder Facility - Superior Region

YEAR 50: Approval to marry Serafina Cruz

YEAR 52: Applied for child-rearing privileges
(initial denial)

YEAR 64: Approval of child-rearing privileges;
assigned Embed #717379838997, an androg
of female origin

YEAR 66: Requests transfer, posted to Columbus,
Erie Region

YEAR 68: Requests transfer, posted to AgSector #120,
Michigan Region Central

YEAR 70: Requests transfer, posted to AgSector #21,
Illiana Region South

Embed reads at garrisons, large and small, all along the eastern, southern and western border. Pittsburgh. Cincinnati. Evansville. More along the West River in Illiana.

Nothing that stands out. Other than the unfortunate escapade in his youth, the medic has been a model Corporate bee. In fact, if that blemish did not exist, he might have risen into the elite, considering his promotion.

But Tanner knows better. Once a traitor, always a traitor. So it did not surprise him when the embeds of the medic and his androg did not register during the scan of the removed. The dead. Nor did it faze him when the focus failed to pick up a reading on them anywhere. He knows exactly where they are. He's a man who knows his way around a Faraday cage.

So when he sees the flit of movement behind the glass of the second story window, a ghost movement, barely there, like the flexing of air itself, he allows himself the briefest twitch of a lip, a ghost of a smile. And here that fabled patience comes into play, that ability to delay gratification.

Because he's also a man who prefers to work in the harsh light of day.

22

The River Road

EBEN RIPS PAGES OUT OF THE ATLAS. When a keening moan of protest slips from Merit's mouth, he fixes her with a steely eye. "Can't lug this around. You'll be traveling close to the bone. Maps were made for use. Since you're off the feed and in the blur and can't get directions streamed to you, let's be thankful that someone had the foresight to keep this out of Corporate hands or else it would be tenth gen toilet paper right now."

He lays the sheets out on the table, side by side, matching where they had met up in the binding of the biblio. It is the geography of the old, when there were such things as states. Maps of northern and southern Illinois. Sinuous red lines crisscross the sprawling landmass like narrow veins coursing with blood. Eben points out the old main roads that are still in use, the ones marked with numbered blue badges.

"You could take the regional routes, it'd be the fastest way, but the pipelines run along some, so they're patrolled and while the focus can't read you, the human eye can. Safer alternative is to follow the rivers." His fingers trace the light blue squiggle of the waterway that forms the border. "The West, the old Mississippi."

"That'll put us in the sights of border traps the whole way!" Suraj blurts.

"Yes and no. There's viewcatchers everywhere, but not

necessarily manpower. This whole sector," Eben flicks his fingers across the map as if brushing away crumbs. "It's all agri. Word is the drought hasn't been as severe up there. Migrants are always moving between sector farms. You two look the part. That said, don't go out of your way to get face to face with a squad. Get off the road when you can."

A hundred miles a day was the goal, biking along the old routes hugging the river, starting in the green stretches on the map that marked the old forest, the Shawnee.

"Can't be sure it's all still forest. Plenty's been cleared. The flat land, anyhow. Acres may have been lost to beetles and the fungus. And now, the drought. It'll be like tinder. But there's rocky land there, too, that's no good for farming and that wasn't plundered with gas mining. Terrain's too rugged. Good places to lose yourself."

At the river, they'd skirt the St. Louis garrison and head north. He taps the small yellow square that outlines a town on the map. "Used to be called Rock Island. That's where I was born and raised."

Eben lays another page over the first map. His finger continues to trace the blue meandering of the old Mississippi north. Then it draws an imaginary circle around the western-most section of the lake labeled Superior. It's curiously shaped like a fist with a single accusatory pointing finger. He taps the paper again, right at the tip of that blue finger.

"Duluth. And the Hive. The destination. Where we'll rendezvous." Eben folds the maps and shoves them into the inner pocket of Merit's black backpack.

Too fast. Too fast. Happening too fast.

But she can't find the words, summon the voice to tell him to stop.

The bikes have seen plenty of miles. And that's putting it nicely.

"Forget gettin' to the river, crap like this won't get us outta town," mutters Suraj, frowning as he examines a long, deep scratch in the fork of his roadrunner.

"They'll do. Tires are newer. That's what counts. Beaters like these won't attract a lot of attention," counters Eben.

Merit nods. She ought to know. She's the one who refurbished them.

"Provisions are in the saddlebags. You've got vacuum packs of protein, mainly silver carp. Pouches of dried fruit. Carb bars. Main thing is to keep yourself hydrated. Water'll be an issue." Eben points to the bulky backpacks, the go-bags he's pulled from the cabinet. "These'll help you make it through the day. Got a reservoir that stores a gallon of water. And a UV light filter that'll purify it. But only draw from clear, running streams. Nothing stagnant. That'll be hard to find down here, but further north, where the rains have hit, you'll find it. Down here, there might still be some places, old migrant worker squats mainly, that never got hooked to the pipeline, still drawing from wells. Most are probably dry. Even if they're not, don't draw from 'em. The filter won't clear the poison from the chemical leaching. That said, there are a few clean ones still around. They're labeled."

Eben grabs a marks-all and sketches a tiny symbol on the underside of one of the pack's straps. "Look for this. Signifies it's safe, whether it's a well or a house. A place where you might find some help."

A clenched fist enclosed within the outline of a heart.

"What kind of help?" Suraj asks, a tinge of suspicion in his voice.

"Food and a place to sleep for a start. After that, it's up to you." Eben glances at Merit. "This one's been taught to keep her lips zipped, when she manages to hold that anger in. Silence often leads people to want to fill in the conversational gap. Ever notice that? And when they open their mouths, sometimes interesting things come out."

Miss Stillwater.

Suraj slings his pack over his back and snaps the harness in place. "Where'd you pick these up?"

"Old school tech rescued from a security storage bunker." Eben winks. "Helps to have friends in low places."

"You *have* been planning this for years," Suraj says, with a hint of admiration.

Eben shakes his head. "Preparing, not planning. Merit, you've got the tent. Medi-kits are in your backpacks along with the rest of your gear. Things you want to keep handy, store in your pockets."

From his look, Merit knows he means the pair of hunting knives he pulled from the old cabinet. Lethal-looking, each has two blades that fold neatly into the grip, one smooth and spear-tipped, the other serrated with a gut hook. Each blade flares opens with a tap on its release catch.

Eben helps Merit adjust a pack onto her shoulders, tugs the fabric of her tunic out from where it bunches under the straps. His voice buzzes low in her ear. "No fear. Stop. Breathe. Focus. Think." He continues, louder, bringing Suraj into the conversation. "Got maybe a three-day ride til you reach the Mississippi 5 garrison. From there, it's north. And what're you lookin' for along the way?"

They stare at him blankly. He sighs, brings his clenched hand up to thump his chest.

"The fisted heart," says Suraj, pounding his own fist over the place where his thrums. "And the people will know us by our words."

To remake the world.

"Safe water, safe houses," Eben nods. "When you reach Duluth—and you will reach it," he asserts, nodding his reassurance, "it's a much larger garrison. There'll be several clinics. Just keep going 'til you find me. I'll try to get word through to the cells along your river route, but that's hit or miss. You'll reach me. You will."

His voice trails off and he stands there, hands shoved in his pockets, fingering his keys, looking a little lost. Is it that there is nothing left to do? Or too much left to do, but no time in which to do it?

In that moment of silence, they hear it. The drawn-out protest of a floorboard sagging under the weight of a body. Someone is above, in the kitchen.

A prickling of flesh. And a wet fear suddenly welling on temples and under armpits and in the small of the back. Did Eben lock the door to the basement from the inside? And would it really make a difference? Just a minor obstacle strewn in the path of—who? What?

He doesn't speak, merely gestures towards the door that leads to the outside and the six concrete steps up to freedom.

Unless the house is surrounded.

It's a chance they have to take. Merit and Suraj roll the bikes while Eben heads in the opposite direction, toward the stairs that rise to the main floor. She pauses at the door, waiting for Suraj to swing his bike around so he can carry it up and out. Craning her head around, her last sight of Eben is of his calves and feet, his brown clogs ascending in the open space between the stair treads and the ceiling beams. Then he's gone.

23

As Sheep in the Midst of Wolves

TANNER KNOWS HE HAS A CRUEL STREAK beyond the parameters required to perform his duties to Corporate expectations and to his own exacting standards. He is not necessarily proud of this. Views it as a character flaw. Knows it springs from a weakness inside him. Prides himself for his self-awareness. At the same time, he makes no effort to change. Because there are some things that a man can't change. Why waste time trying? Particularly when the flaw contains within it the seeds of so much pleasure.

Waiting in the kitchen, as the black of night fades into the moody indigo of pre-dawn, he fully comprehends the unseemly relish he takes in the anticipation. Hearing each crunch of the wood as feet climb the stairs that lie behind the closed door, he feels the spark that ignites somewhere in his pelvis and travels up through his innards, from guts to stomach to heart. When the door opens and he thumbs his flashlight to bright, hot life, the way the medic squints and jerks his head to the side, away from the glare, excites him, even as he recognizes that this giddiness is inappropriate. And yet.

"It always surprises me when people don't take advantage of every beneficial situation placed before them," Tanner says.

The medic blinks again. Bats his hand as if to swat the light away from his face, but Tanner keeps it fixed on him. When the medic makes no reply, Tanner shakes his head. "The question sits on the tip of my tongue. Why? But then I remind myself that it just doesn't matter. Knowing the answer wouldn't change the outcome. Not one bit."

The medic is adjusting to the harsh light. His hands relax. Drop to his sides. "Actually," he says, voice brittle, "I've changed my mind. I'll accept the Superior posting. So I guess in this case, the outcome will change."

Tanner shakes his head. "Nope. 'Fraid not. You opted to stay with your patients. Your... people. Well, now your patients are no longer in need of a medic."

The first bullet misses when the medic, anticipating, dodges to the left. But the second hits its mark, a clean kill through the temple. Quick. Painless, they say. Although how would they, the nameless they, really know?

The act itself brings no thrill. It's just something to be done. A task.

All in a day's work.

One sharp crack splits the murky blue velvet quiet. Then a second.

The sounds knock Merit's feet off the pedals and whip her head around. The house is already out of sight beyond the curve of the bike path. But she knows without seeing. The bike wobbles, threatens to slide out from under her, along with the rest of the world, leaving her falling through some black void, grappling with nothing, hanging on to nothing, because everything is gone, everything is nothing, there is nothing, until Suraj, riding just to her left, grabs the handlebars and steadies the bike.

But not her. He senses that. She's too used to having things, not having things taken away. The fem will slow him down. Not just a fem, but a squeamish fem—squawking 'bout that itty bitty critter under the porch. Frack, having to pair up with anyone would slow him down. Fem. Dude. Didn't matter. *He travels the fastest who travels alone...*

Mum's words. Admitted she stole 'em from a biblio. She'd had two thick, dusty, leather-bound ones she hauled with her as they bounced from place to place. Reading him the poems of one and the epic, crazy-wild tales from the other. Like the story of Manu, the first man and how he saved a fish and survived a great flood. And the hero, Arjuna, who walked with Krishna and won a great battle on the field of Kurukshetra. Though Mum said in the end it was no victory, for the war destroyed the world that he knew, and the emptiness colored the rest of Arjuna's life. Then she would say *"Pity the poor boys who only have the feed, who know nothing of the mistakes of the past, who know nothing of heroes and great causes."*

As he got older, he decided the quote—that's what she called it—fit him like his favorite pair of jeans and he adopted it as his brand. *He travels the fastest who travels alone.* He would like to let it fly now, like Arjuna letting fly with an arrow, but instead Suraj sucks in his lips and bites down to keep his snark and his motto inside his mouth.

Like Arjuna, the fem has just lost everything she's ever known.

Steady, fem. Miles to go before we sleep.

Another one of Mum's.

Promises to keep and miles to go...

Tanner doesn't know the secrets of the basement stairs, the proper placement of feet on the treads to keep them silent. They creak under his soles. But he has a keen eye for finding other hidden things. He runs a large hand down a seam of one of the wood panels, pressing tentatively until it pops loose with a click. He pushes it to the side to reveal the safe room. The copper mesh glimmers in the beam of his flashlight. As he sweeps it through the gloom, the beam catches another glint on the battered table.

A chain of delicate metal links. He picks it up, letting it dangle before his face. It sways, a pendulum with a bob no bigger than a grain of rice. It doesn't come to him immediately. Has to ponder awhile. Put the proverbial two and two together. It's a circuit chip, of that he's certain. An embed, most likely. But not embedded.

And then his gut knows the truth even as his mind rebels against it. Glints of silver against bronze skin. When gold would have looked so much better.

The first five miles are a wet, gasping heart-in-mouth blur. *Stop. Breathe. Focus. Think.*

Eben's mantra comes to Suraj unbidden, like a calming hand on his shoulder.

The bike path meandering along the old road is a pockmarked gray ribbon of asphalt. Deep in his gut, dread prickles. This is the wrong way to go. He wants to have his feet on the ground, wants to be under the cover of trees. And it's not just his gut working overtime. He can hear a low grumble coming from some distance behind them, out of the east with the violent light of the rising sun.

Suraj slows, dropping back alongside Merit. "Need to get off the road," he calls.

The girl, clutched in shock, in screensaver auto-mode, only pedals faster.

He has no patience for this. Churning his legs, he draws even with her again. "We really need to get off this road!" he shouts, braking hard.

A derelict shed slouches at the edge of a long abandoned fueling station. The bike bumps along the broken, pitted concrete. He skids to a stop, tires kicking up a swirl of grit. The shed's door sags halfway off its hinges, but it's secure enough to hide the interior from view. Skirting the edge of the door, he wheels the bike inside. Merit follows him in, but leaves her ride outside.

He flips his kickstand down, makes a quick dash out and drags her cruiser into the murk.

The fem stands mute, eyes barely focused.

The grumble has grown to a growl, the distinctive sound of b-squad overlands. Instinctively, he ducks into a crouch, though the shed is windowless. Reaches up and grabs Merit's hand, yanking her down alongside him.

Thoughts bead up like the sweat on the boy's forehead.

Did their tires leave visible tracks in the dirt or was the ground too hard-packed to leave such a trace? If a goliath approaches, swings the door open to peer inside, can he move quickly enough?

His fingers trace the smooth curve of the button that secures the flap of the pocket of his cargoes. Feels the grooved handle of the knife under the fabric and eases the button through its hole.

A sharp line of light slices the shed's rotting floor. Leaning to his left, the boy can see through the gap between the door and its jamb. He nudges the fem with his knee, tilts his head and eases back so she can crane her head and get a look.

The overlands cluster at the crossroads, engines at a low purr. From a distance, the black-clad and helmeted riders meld with their machines, impossible to tell where one ends and the other begins. Which of those blackout visors hides Mars Lund's now-grim face? And was the man who rode at the rear, helmet-less, bald head gleaming, eyes hidden behind his shades, the one called Tanner?

Recognition. A feeling like her insides are icing over with a brittle frost. Merit has never seen him before and yet senses that she has. Somehow. Something itches in her belly, tapping at the glaze of fear, trying to crack it. Her fingers seek Serafina's gift under the curving neckline of her tunic and close over the agate, cool against her skin.

The man sits, head bowed, as if listening. Pushes the shades to the top of his skull and brings a scope up to his eyes. Scans left, scans right. Tucks the scope away. Readjusts his shades, then trundles his ride to the head of the pack. He gestures right and then left. He's splitting the squad.

In that moment, Merit realizes the boy is right.

We need to stay off the roads.

Although the squad can travel just as easily over the fields as the roads, the pack will stick to the asphalt in the early stages of the hunt. At least, that's what she wants to believe, what she has to believe, in order to break the paralysis that has turned her legs to stone.

No fear. Stop. Breathe. Focus. Think.

And what she believes is true, for now. Four of the squad veer left and head down the two lane that runs south, all the way to the border river. The other five continue straight, heading west. The boy and girl stay crouched until the guttural moan of the engines is swallowed by time and distance.

"Shit," the boy mutters. "That was frackin' close. We should sit tight for a bit. They might double back and we'll run right smack into a pair of steel bracelets. Though I doubt they'll be arresting us."

"No roads," Merit says as she rises, feeling the anger burning in the muscles of her thighs.

Suraj nods. "Yeah, at least until we—"

"No roads. Ever. Until..." Her voice trails off.

Until. There is no until. Until is gone.

She longs to lie down, to let her body join the rot that is slowly consuming this structure, to let that rot consume her, too. But she feels the boy's hand under her arm, steadying her, and she shakes that desire off along with his hand, shifting and setting her shoulders as she resettles her backpack.

"We'll go back country." Suraj states. "Hoofin' it'll take longer and it's not a sure thing. Them rigs ain't called overlands for nothin'. But they can't move through the woods like us. They still need some kinda trail. We don't. And we can blend in."

Speculation is clear in his eyes as he stares, measuring her. His gaze holds on her chest. "Well, me, maybe," he continues. "You, not so much. Spot you a mile away."

She stares back at him.

The boy thumps his chest. "I can fade this way 'n that, slip through the trees." He grabs the yellow sleeve of her tunic. "Yer screamin' *come'n get me* in this thing. Ditch it."

Her shoulders slump as she realizes he's right. She hesitates, then lets her backpack slide off. She tugs the fabric up and over her head, shrugging it to the floor, and stands before him in her gray t-shirt and the camouflage vest.

He nods. "Now you got a chance to blend. Slip into the blur."

24

Human Quarry

USING THE PITHOUNDS appeals to the old-school, analog hunter in him. Raises his game. Harkens back to his days as a young border patrol officer tracking jumpers and eels who thought they could evade the eye in the sky. Thought they could live in the blur, unnoticed, sucking at the Protectorate teat. Hunting humans—if you could call the illegals that—is much more thrilling than hunting dumb beasts. Stalking with the knowledge there is something more than just the flight-or-fight response working inside the quarry's brain. The human prey know they are going to die.

So after the first fruitless day using the scanners, Tanner heads back to the medic's house and picks a gray t-shirt out of the laundry basket in the androg's room. He stares, head cocked, at the little stick figure faces drawn on the far wall, all those little curving smiles slashed through.

He never could understand the rationale for the he-shes in the first place. *Build a better worker bee devoid of all the undesirable traits of either sex. Eliminate the volitility that seethes at the core of both the masculine and the feminine. The toxicity.*

A Corporate experiment gone wrong, in Tanner's estimation, producing nothing but weakness and a certain devious passivity, without the promised benefits of productivity. But the Hive mind couldn't admit the fail. Just kept culling and injecting, tweaking the hormone formula, doing the same thing over and over and expecting different results. The definition of madness.

Tanner hawks up a wad of phlegm and spits.

Creating a herd of misbegotten freaks.

He stares again at the slashed smilies.

Then again, this 'drog may be a bit of a challenge.

He balls up the fabric and holds it to the dog's wet nose and slobbery muzzle.

"This is the one we want, boy."

Each step crackles as they tread the edge of the forest. Some of the trees are already shedding leaves and those that droop from the branches are yellow and brown-tinged. Sad and withered, the edges curling in. Crisp, yet listless in their lack of purpose.

The girl and boy stutter and dodge through the thickets, avoiding the ragged, furry, red-tinged vines that snake up some of the tree trunks, the poison ivy that grows like crazy in the heat, shooting out trios of still-glossy emerald leaves, pretty to the eye and smooth to the fingers, but so painful after. The consequence of beauty.

Merit senses more than sees the road as it curves around and she plunges deeper into the woods, ignoring the sting as a whip-thin branch slashes the corner of her mouth. The taste of blood only drives her harder.

Finally, it's Suraj who gasps, "Slow down!" when they've pushed so far into the wilderness that all they see are the trunks of trees and billowing shrubs of undergrowth in every direction. She ducks her head to avoid another slap in the face from the aggressive branches of a jack pine. The light here is muted, cooler and green-tinged under the forest canopy. Even the air smells different. Earthy, yes. But sweet and pungent, too. Thick with something like possibilities.

Suraj sinks onto an immense rotting log. Fishes a curious metal object out of a small pocket of his cargoes. It is round, but flattish and fits comfortably in his palm. An image is etched into its surface, something that harkens to an ancestor of a bullet train. He flicks his finger and the gold disc pops open like a river clamshell. Glances down.

"Couple past noon. I'm starved." He snaps the cover shut. Moves to tuck the object in his pocket. Catches the question in her eyes. Waggles the piece. "Watch."

Merit squints, expectant. When nothing happens, she sighs. "Watch what?"

Suraj arches a bushy black eyebrow. "A watch." He flips it open again and taps a finger on its transparent surface, avoiding the hairline crack that divides it. "What it's called. Tells time. Well, they used to tell time. This one still does." He offers it and she warily steps closer.

Bold black numbers ring the face under the glass. "Ancients used to carry 'em on a chain. Others you'd wear on yer wrist. S'posedly when the first feedcoms came out, they were synched to focus time and people 'ventually stopped using these. Clocks, too. Same idea, but bigger. Had 'em in their houses. Some swags collect 'em. Sometimes you'll see a swag wearing a wristwatch, to be all retro and 'ronic."

Merit doesn't grasp his meaning, so she says the first thing that comes to mind. "You stole that."

Suraj shrugs. "Puttin' it to use. Why should it sit on a shelf just gatherin' dust for the housekeep to brush away? Swag I took it from don't need it. Got his tenth-gen feedcom to tell him the time of day down to the millisecond."

Curiosity overcomes her scruples. "How's it work?"

Suraj points to two thin black strips of metal that extend from the center of the face like arms. "Shorty points to the hour, long, the minute. Each hash around the edge marks a minute. So you've got five minutes per number. Right now it's—"

"Twelve fifteen."

"Props." He holds out his fist for a bump, but Merit ignores it. With a shrug and a nod, he snaps the case shut and slips it back into his pocket. "Here endeth the lesson."

She scowls at him.

"Somethin' my mum used to say. And she got it from her mum and she got it from her mum and so on. Time out of mind. That, too."

This sense of his, of knowing the history of things, of having an attachment to it himself, is disconcerting. It's a narrow bridge between them. He, too, has had his moments of being pulled close, of being told things that others have not been told. They are the sharers of secrets.

He pulls a protein bar from his backpack and wolfs it, washing it down with gulping swigs from his vitajuice bottle, then wipes his mouth on the back of his hand and looks around, as if wanting more and somehow expecting to find it on the forest floor.

He is the lowest puke on the squad, the omega wolf suffering abuse at the teeth and claws of the rest of the pack. The jester mocked by the king and his court, yet always willing to instigate a joke. Acting the fool. Fawning for favor. And paying for it with a piercing, pulsating ache in his head.

He has not earned their trust yet. He knows this. And like any good grunt, Mars Lund is determined to prove his worth. First awake, before the barest hint of dawn softens the edges of the night sky. First to have his gear loaded and ready to go. Last to quit at shift's end, volunteering for scanner duties, hawk-eyed for the presence and movement of embeds where there should be none. Manning a remote border cam, trolling for jumpers.

This morning, at roll call, when her image filled the screen, he had betrayed nothing. Or so he thinks. The tremor passed invisibly through his body, a secret quake felt by him and him alone. The twinge in his hand, a ghost pang.

Those eyes. Those lips. And then the pain had seized him like the razor talons of some fierce winged creature. Bright white with the heat of a thousand suns. And then it was just the face of another androg. One that needs to be put down.

"The drone's out of commission right now. Of course," Tanner had added, the sour disdain of the secret technophobe flavoring his speech. "We've sent out a call for a replacement, but we're not waiting around 'til it arrives. Drones can't do what we need to do anyway. They're just eyes. So we'll be hunting with the hounds. Boots on the ground," Tanner had said, shutting down the projector, the androg's image vanishing in an instant.

They assigned Mars the worst of the hounds, the one they called Verruckt, a black devil with mismatched eyes who snaps at imaginary flies and real fingers, even with his jaws strapped tight in the muzzle. Now the beast peers intently through the leather straps, straining at the harness that binds his massive body, keeps him tethered, in semi-control. The pair of them have been set down at the crossroads with a piece of torn shirt and instructions to retrace some paths, pick up the scent. But before offering the fabric for the dog to sniff, he brings it to his own nose and inhales, a deep hit of her unique smell. A lingering of crushed lavender. Hints of bike grease. The tang of metal. The sourness of fear.

Merit.

The odor of her triggers the memory. The acute slice of pain. The slick of scarlet. The ache of wound on wound. The movement of bodies. The sharp ping of rain on a metal roof. Skin of their cheeks slick from standing, faces turned to the deluge. The way the straw was soft, yet pricked the flesh of his thighs. The resistance and the yielding. Wet hair clinging to her forehead.

The dog meanders to and fro, snuffling the cloth, snuffling

the asphalt, snuffling the air. Whining low in its throat, slob-
bering, snapping, pawing. They crisscross the cracked and pitted concrete slab of the decrepit fueling station before the beast
picks up on something at the far edge. He strains at the harness,
lifts his head, gives a short, strangled bay. Leans forward.

Mars gives him a short lead. The dog barrels toward a dilapidated utility shed at the far edge of the property. Up close, Mars
sees that a single determined shove would topple it. White froth
bubbles at the hound's jaws as they reach the shed's sagging door.

*"Let's not play Corporate games and pretty up the language on
this one," Tanner had said. "Terminate. With extreme prejudice."*

So why does his hand hesitate, even for the barest blink of
time, before he draws his burner?

But when he yanks the door aside, with such brute force that
it comes off its last hinge and crashes to the ground, nothing's
there but a pair of banged up cruiser bikes leaning in the shadows amidst the rusted body parts of archaic personal transports.

And something stark in the gloom. A quick sidelong glance
might mistake it for a spill of paint, pooled deep and fresh. But
he recognizes it before he even stoops to pick it up with fingers
that, curiously, are trembling.

Balled up in the corner rests a bright yellow tunic.

25

I am Poured Out Like Water

THEY TRUDGE ALONG THE ROCK-STREWN BOTTOM of a dry creek bed, ignoring the protests of their sore muscles, the sleeves of their jackets pulled down and hoods draped over their heads, even in the midst of the murderous heat. Towards evening, the creek curves around a bend to reveal a tiny clearing with a ramshackle hut, a sad excuse for shelter. Merit is startled. She's been here before. And she realizes she's crossing a threshold.

This is the farthest she's ever been from home.

They'd come here when she was little, just she and Serafina, to visit a weathered woman, cropped red hair shot through with silver, whose green-gray eyes seemed to pierce Merit's skin and see all the way to her throbbing heart. A woman who stirred a shiver in her gut even when she smiled, the crinkles radiating from the corners of her eyes like a warning. The two women would sit and chat for hours, lounging on a couple of battered folding chairs, heads leaning in close, while Merit played on the bank of the creek, constructing towers with a set of interlocking blocks, the colors of which, reds and blues, yellows and whites, were muted with grime.

Then the visits had stopped. Serafina said the woman had been severanced. A knowledge keeper. Merit understands that now. She had been passing along the depth and breadth of what she knew to Serafina. And, in a way, to Merit.

She realizes now that this had not been the meme's home. Just a hidden place for their clandestine meetings. And then she remembers the water pump and its gush of liquid that bled from rust to clear. She'd hesitated to drink the first time until Serafina cupped her own hands under the spigot and took a deep swallow.

"This is safe, querida."

The water had tasted like a mouthful of nails. She'd give anything for a swallow of it right now.

"Izzat yer stomach rumblin' or a 'dozer gearing up for a teardown? Rest here?" Suraj asks, with a nod toward the shack.

They hunker on a slab of rock, watching the setting sun's deep orange rays flicker behind the trees, leaves glowing amber and red in the bending light. A few songbirds flit from branch to branch far above, their muted trills weaving melodies sweet and sad.

Suraj wipes the sweat from his face with the bottom of his t-shirt, lifts an arm and takes a whiff of his pit. "Sorry, fem, don't mind the reek, but I'm thinkin' it'll only get worse before it gets better." He sucks from his backpack reservoir. "Frack, near drained. Need a refill, like five minutes ago."

Merit dips her head as she stands and beckons him to follow. She leads him down a narrow overgrown path round the far side of the hut, their footsteps muffled by the spongy carpet of dead pine needles. In a small clearing choked with dead and dying weeds, she points to a worn iron standpipe rising out of a clump of thistle and ragweed.

"Been here before. It was safe to drink then. Though that was a long time ago." She tramps down the weeds, which crackle and sigh, to reveal a crumbling concrete slab. Crouches low. Squints. Sure enough. A tiny greenish fist enclosed within a reddish heart, the paint on the hex sign faded and flaking, but still distinguishable. She grabs the pipe's curved handle and pumps it up and down, tentatively.

Nothing but the screech of rust and decay.

She tries again, more vigorously. Her muscles ache before a gurgle of rusty brown fluid finally trickles out. Suraj waves her away and takes over. As he pumps, the trickle becomes a spray and finally a clear gush. They fill their reservoirs.

"I'm gonna clean up a bit," she says and he nods.

"Tent? Shack?" he asks.

She shrugs and watches as he disappears back down the trail to what will be their campsite for the night. Stifles a sudden, strange impulse to cry out. *Don't leave me here all alone. In the gathering gloom. With whatever is out here.*

Swallowing that, she swats at a pair of black flies dive-bombing her head.

Stink. Not stink. Crap. Either way I'm still gonna stink. Just maybe a little less.

She unstraps the vest from around her chest and strips off her shirt and cargoes, draping them over the pump. Inspects her legs carefully for tiny, noxious, burrowing blood-suckers. Her gaze moves to her torso. A thin reddish line bisects her abdomen where the edge of the armored plate has dug into her flesh.

By the end of this, it'll be permanent. Like a brand.

She washes the mental image from her mind like she washes the dirt from her neck. With a cold, smacking cascade of water to her head.

Suraj offers to stand the first watch, but Merit shakes him off. The thought of sleeping in the tent with only a thin layer of fabric separating her from all manner of creepers and crawlers is like a dose of caffeine mixed with a shot of adrenaline—just the thing to keep her eyes wide open and her hearing attuned to the faintest sigh or rustle in the brush.

She sits in the crisp-soft needles strewn at the foot of a towering pine, knees to chest, hands clasped tight around them.

Something is missing in the settling of the dark, but she can't quite get a sense of what it is. She tries mentally ticking off a list.

Solar lights. The hum of Mr. O's generator. The flickering light of candles.

And then the realization seeps in. For the first night in her life, she hasn't heard the booming voice of Galt intoning vespers. Nor the quiet murmur of Eben saying goodnight. Flinches at that, pushes the thought away, denies it, buries it under the twinge in her thigh and the spasm that clutches at her ribcage as she shifts her body.

I'll hear him again. Soon. When we reach Duluth.

As the long twilight finally fades to black, her eyes are on the sky, counting the satellites as they troll their paths, the Corporate eyes that never sleep. She fingers the agate, idly runs it across her lips, smooth, hard, calm. Still, it has been a punishing day, and she finds her head doing the bob-and-jerk. To stay awake, she whispers the names of the creatures she loathes—*wasp, black widow spider, cockroach, earwig, brown recluse, centipede, skeeter, black fly, yellow jacket, fire ant, silverfish, termite, stinkbug, bunch beetle, june bug, hornet, fruit fly, deer tick—*

"Yer gonna have to get over it—quick."

The voice startles her out of her insect reverie.

"Didn't hear me comin', didja? That's right. My brand. Silent but deadly."

A stark beam in her face leaves her temporarily blind. Shielding her eyes from the painful brilliance of the minilight, Merit squints up at her shadowy tormentor. "Yeah, I been tryin' to figure out what you remind me of. And it's definitely a smelly fart."

"Very funny. I'm here to relieve your swagness."

"Just don't relieve yourself *on* me."

"Whoa, that was comicallastical. Knew you could dish it if you tried."

Merit shoves the flashlight out of her face and scuttles

into the tent. She wraps herself in the cocoon of her sleeping bag, where she lays awake in the enveloping dark, body on hyper-alert, tensing for the slightest tingle on her skin, listening for the whisper-soft scritch-scratch of movement across the nylon surface. Flips and squirms, itching and scratching bugs and bites real and imagined, shifting from left side to right, from back to stomach, trying to find the sweet spot that will bring sleep.

When she was little and found herself suddenly bolt upright in bed in the middle of the night, pursued by a demon nightmare, she would skitter down the hall to her parents' room. Moving from one side of their bed to the other, she would nudge their shoulders and poke their arms until one or the other woke. Eben would mumble for her to go back to bed.

"Just a dream. Go back to sleep."

As if it was that easy.

But Serafina would climb out of bed and shamble back to Merit's room, holding her hand. She'd tuck her back in and sit down on the floor beside the bed, her head resting on the edge of the mattress. Merit's fingers would twirl the wild tufts of Serafina's bedhead hair, while the woman's voice would ease her back to sleep, sometimes with a story, sometimes with the multiplication tables, sometimes with a murmuring recitation of all the edible wild plants and fungi that she knew.

"If you're ever stuck out in the middle of nowhere with nothin', here's what you can scrounge: amaranth, asparagus, boletes, burdock, cattail, chanterelles, chickory, chickweed, clover, dandelion, field pennycress, fireweed, garlic mustard, gooseberries, hackberries, jewel weed, milkweed, morels, mulberries, plantain, pokeweed, purslane, rosehips, russulas, salsify, thimbleberries, wood sorrel..."

But now, reciting the list in her head doesn't do the trick. The real sleeping potion had been Serafina's voice. *Her voice...*

Reaching out in the dark, she finds her backpack. Easing the vocoder from the small inner pocket, she feels a shiver of anticipation. Fits the buds in her ears and runs her thumb over the case until it finds the power button. Her fingers glow blue in the light cast by the tiny screen. And suddenly she has Serafina's face and voice to keep her company in the night.

"I'm sure you've heard it from Eben by now. Maybe you even guessed it, cuz you're my whip-smart little bird. But I owe it to you to tell you myself. Angel, I'm a knowledge-keeper and the plan is for you to carry that on. It's an honor, but it's a burden, too. Carrying the things we need to save and pass along. History, ways of thinking and living and doing. How we know who we were and are and what we can be. What we want to be. Things that don't come through the feed."

A heavy sigh, a pause. *"Oh damn, I've already messed this up. It'd be so much easier to say this to your face, your lovely face—but in case that doesn't happen, well, this is it. And just let me start."*

A pause. A low chuckle. *"I'm no good at this. Okay, here goes."*

Another pause, longer. Then her voice again, changed. Somber. Formal. *"The ancients would call upon a muse—a goddess— to help them tell their tales. There were nine, all born of the same mother, a goddess with a memory as long as her black, flowing hair. One cared for poetry and another for music. One sister inspired comedy and her twin brought forth tragedy. Another loved dance and one loved to gaze at the stars and protected astronomers, the men and women who studied them. One gave life to hymns of worship and another sang the epics, the deeds of great heroes. And then there was the muse of history who most resembled her mother, the muse who kept the knowledge eternal. So speak through me, Muse, that I may tell the story that needs to be told, for a people who no longer remember the ways of the past have lost their history and their souls."*

26

Glory in the Dust

"IT BEGINS WITH THE LAND, *from which we come, to which we return. We know its worth. It's in our bones, harbors in their very marrow; it's in our blood, seething in every cell. We know the rhythm and chords and melody of its song as if it was in tune with the very beating of our hearts. But sometimes we forget.*

"*In the time of kings, when the world was a much larger place, green and rich with promise, the people believed in the idea of a higher power and called it God, though it had many names: El, and Yahweh and Elohim and 'ilah and Elaha and Allah and a thousand more. And this God was unseen and unknowable, yet there were many who saw its hand everywhere and in everything, even in the fall of the tiniest chirping bird. Men built special places to honor God and called them churches and cathedrals and temples and mosques, breaking their backs hauling the cut stone, piling it higher and higher, until the spires soared into the sky, pointing to the place where men thought God lived. From the lowliest sweat tilling the soil to the most exalted monarch, they all went down on their knees to pray to God. They prayed for small favors—a crust of bread to eat at the end of the day. They prayed for success in the largest enterprise, the building of a castle or the making of war, in hopes of crushing their enemies... all in the name of God.*

"*As you may guess, men, in their foolishness, always believed*

God favored their own cause. It is enough for me to tell you that more wars have been fought and more blood spilled in the cause of honoring God than over land and precious metal combined. And many died for the right to worship God as they saw fit. Martyrs, they were called, willing to die for their faith.

"So when word spread of a New Land beyond the waters, some were willing to flee the devil they knew to face whatever lurked in the unknown. They risked the tempest, taking only what they could carry. Some came to follow their God. Some came to escape the corruption they saw in their homelands. Some came to seek the riches promised by explorers who blazed the trails. Some came to make a name for themselves; others to be free of poverty and degradation or a life in chains, which is no life at all. Some came simply for the adventure, the shock of the new, the electric charge of the blood racing through the body in that moment of discovery and wonder. Many reasons, but one word. Freedom.

"Problem was—yes, there always is a problem—this land was already inhabited, by people who called themselves Wampanoag and Anishinaabe and Diné, the first people. And these people, these original people, held the land sacred. In their minds, no man owned a piece of earth. To them, the world was swayed by many spirits, not just one. And man shared a kinship with plants and animals and trees.

"Freedom for one man can mean death for another when different ways of life collide. And many of the people—most of the first people—died. By war, by massacre, by disease. Many came to say this was the first plague upon the land.

"And yet in taking the land and making it their own, the elites were woefully unprepared. Conquest is the easy part. Building a new world requires back-breaking labor. And so they made a fateful decision. They needed a workforce. A class of bees that wouldn't challenge their authority. So they turned to slavery. The buying and selling of human beings. Of keeping your fellow human being in bondage. *In chains. Many came to say this was the second plague upon the land.*

"And the people sweated and prospered. A free man could take pride in the land he owned, and raise a family as he saw fit, and pocket or spend the coin he earned as he decided. But the people weren't content to be tied to the old world, bound by old allegiances and subject to the whim and will of another power, a government in which they had no say. They might ask the question, are we truly free? Is there freedom for a man who lives under the rule of a king— or the protection of a corporation?

"When empires clash, it is the common man, the bee, the sweat, who pays the ultimate price in blood and treasure. They pay it willingly if they believe in the cause—and see a benefit for themselves. But if they pay the price and are then thwarted in their aspirations? If the boot heel grinds down harder on the neck and the grasping hand reaches deeper into the pocket? What then?

"There rose a race of giants at this time, though some say they were no taller than the average man, but it was their minds that made them so. Renowned for their intellect, praised for their bravery, they banded together as brothers to free the land and the people from the shackles of the old world. Though their names are lost to us, their deeds are not. And some of their words remain, passed on through time. For this became their rallying cry to the people. 'You who dare oppose tyranny and the tyrant, rise! Even the dirt of the old world is blighted by oppression. But not the soil of this new land. In other places, freedom has been hunted down. Driven to the ends of the Earth. But we can receive the fugitives. For we are the fugitives. So let us build a safe house for mankind and freedom. Shout it with me—give me liberty or give me death!'

"And the people heeded the call and answered to one name— American. They took up arms against the tyrant and the struggle was long and bloody."

27

The Art of Manliness

MARS IS ON FOOT NOW, having abandoned the overland a half mile in from the old fueling station. Maneuvering the vehicle's bulk through the close-standing trees proved impossible, too thick a thread to slip the eye of this particular needle.

After a half dozen fits and starts, nosing the earth, its nostrils flaring with each waffling intake of breath, the pithound seems to have settled on a tracer trail. The invisible path leads up a rise and follows the ridgeline south and to the west. As he and the beast bob and weave among the oaks and hickories, Mars marvels that this wilderness still exists. That it wasn't clear-cut decades ago.

Why is she heading south, into its maw? Does she have a plan? Is she making for the river border? Is this just some desperate flight response? Movement driven by terror and adrenaline?

Out the corner of his right eye, light, a white flash, a yellow shimmer. Needle-like pricks migrate up his right arm, from fingers to shoulder. He knows the pain that will come after. It's too loud now, it's all too loud. The rise and fall of the forest's breath, the low thrum of its beating heart.

He'll do anything to make it go away.

After a day and a half of hiking, Merit's feet are aching. The original plan had been to bike, thus the lightweight trainers.

She tugs them off and peels the low cut socks from her feet. Two blisters, white and watery, throb on each heel. They'd be killers when they broke. She digs out the medi-pac and considers using two of the bandages as cushioning, then decides against it. There were a precious few. Better to save them for a real wound. Tucking the case away, she pulls out an extra pair of socks, easing them on over the first.

"Walk much?" Suraj snipes. Then, "Talk much?" He shifts back and forth, weight on one foot, then the other. "Just a joke, yeah."

He extends a hand to help her to her feet. She ignores it and stays perched on the rotting log, even as she realizes she's neglected to inspect it for critters. She shrugs, pulls out a baggie of walnuts and eats them one at a time, chewing slowly, savoring their oily, soothing richness and the complex flavors on her tongue. Earthy, bitter, fruity, tart. She takes small sips of water after each nut as she senses the light dimming between the trees. The setting of the sun. All her life, the part she can remember anyway, she's lived where she could see the sinking of the orange orb through a vast expanse of sky and mark its progression, the settling movement as it slips below the edge of the known earth. She's always had the panorama, the union of sky and land. She feels lost without it in this horizonless world.

A clicking chitchat punctures her reverie. The squirrel considers her, tail enormously bushy, curved, flicking with every complaint. Its black bead of an eye regards her with what seems a mix of astonishment and disdain. A skittering. The sound of sharp claws scraping over dry bark. Scritches and rustles. Out the corner of her eye, she catches movement, the slightest wavering. The cottontail blends with the gray of the tree trunks, except for the delicate pink lining of its ears. It sits erect, head forward and alert, ears turning, one forward, the other twisting to the side.

"Game trail," Suraj whispers, his eyes on a narrow line tramped between the roots of the trees, roots that resemble gnarled knuckles clawing the soil.

"I'd fancy a bit of fresh critter for breakfast."

Merit feels her eyebrows lift and her nose wrinkle.

"What?" Suraj snaps, though it's not really a question. "Only ever get your meat from the GaltMart?"

The rabbit startles, then darts away, zigzagging through the brush.

Merit allows her eyes to roll, and lets him see it, too.

"Doubt my skills? You'll see. And you'll be begging me for a bit of the meat come breakfast."

Of course she does not reply. But she observes. Out the corner of her eye. Behind a wave of hair. He roots around in his go-bag and takes out a roll of fishing line, breaking off a length. It is near invisible in his fingers. He folds an end back onto itself and ties an overhand knot to secure a loop, then runs the other end of the line through the loop to form a noose. A quick scan of the ground. He grabs one stick, then shuffles through the fallen leaves and pine needles, kicking aside debris until he finds another that suits his purpose. He contemplates the Y-shaped sticks, each just shy of a foot long, then carefully stakes one into the ground. He has to work at it awhile, the dry soil unyielding. But he finally gets it in, standing upright.

He catches her watching. Points to a scattering of round brown pellets, the size of pebbles, in the midst of the leaves. "Rabbit scat. Guessin' they come through regular."

He ties the noose to the other Y-shaped stick. Grabbing the slender trunk of a sapling, he pulls, bending it over the game trail. He cuts off another length of fishing line and ties one end to the tip of the sapling and the other to the stick with the noose. He fits the Y-shaped sticks together, the one branch nestling securely into the notch of the other. The tension from the bent sapling straining to reach skyward keeps the snare in place.

It's a marvel of construction. Of innovation.

It's nothing she would ever have thought of. Or been able to create. *Maybe Iris and the Hive mind were right.* She feels a grimace-smile tug the corner of her mouth. *As if it matters now... and yet.*

She grabs up a thin branch from the ground and snaps it into several smaller twigs. As Suraj watches, she props up sections of the noose in place.

So that it becomes easier for an animal to blunder in.

She sees the realization on the boy's face as he comes over and pats her shoulder awkwardly.

"You got the mind of a hunter. And hunger is a good teacher. At least it forces you to try. I'll show you how. Let you build the next."

It's almost a question.

She blinks. Nods. Just an almost imperceptible lift and lowering of her chin.

He grins.

Another night watch passes with Serafina's voice in her ear.

"The first shots were fired as the sun was rising and from then on the battles raged. Six years they fought, these men who called themselves Patriots and the Sons of Liberty, through all seasons and manner of weather, during summers that saw the rivers run with blood and the bitterest of winters in which many perished from disease and starvation. They were farmers and store owners and woodworkers and they were poorly equipped and ill-fed and badly clothed, but fighting against the world's greatest power, they managed not only to hold off disaster, but to gain ground. Because they believed. And they were willing to fight and die for those beliefs. Independence. Freedom. Angel, they forged a country, a nation, with sweat and blood and the bones of their dead comrades. And we, their descendants, no longer know what those words mean. But out of the furnace of struggle strong things are forged. And a new nation was born through the work of many.

"The War of the Revolution was over but the Revolution itself went on with the hard-won knowledge that freedom, however won,

is never assured, never static, must always be fought for. As free men and women established themselves in a free nation, they moved west. At first, they came in a thin trickle, through the old mountains of Appalachia, hacking out a road through the wilderness. Then the trickle swelled to a stream and then to a river in flood. Oh, they were an independent people, willing to be bound only so much, and they held tightly to their independent ways as they pushed across the continent through the tall-grass prairies of the Great Plains to the new jagged mountains of the West and over the peaks and through the passes to the far ocean called the Pacific.

"But there was a thoughtlessness to it. A carelessness and a cruelty in pushing aside those who had lived on the land for generations before. Blood and tears were ploughed into the soil along with the prairie grass. Blood and tears fired with the clay that made the bricks. Blood and tears on hands and cheeks, dried into the very foundation of this thing they called a nation.

"Angel, the nation had its roots in the land. But commerce and industry took hold and grew like sturdy trees. Factories arose. Cities grew, spreading their influence deeper and deeper into the farmland. History and geography were on our side, Angel, in a land separated from its enemies by oceans. We flourished without fear, without interference.

"And yet, we were not perfected. Not while slavery still existed in the land. The more we triumphed in bringing land into our nation, the more we disagreed about what to do with it. The industrial North was free territory, the South, the rural land of cotton, held slaves and defended this savagery as the price of success. But the West, the new West. Should it be free or shackled? But the deeper question, Angel, was how could a nation survive half slave and half free, so very divided?

"While those who specialize in talk—yes, Angel, there have always been people like that—while they debated how to rid the country of slavery, the doers, as always, were taking up the dangerous

work of smuggling slaves to freedom along escape routes that flowed from south to north. It was a railroad without tracks and trains. A railroad of trails and safe houses and signals hidden in plain sight. Hidden in the patterns of hand-made quilts and the lyrics of songs. And the refugees traveled in the black of night, with the North Star to guide them, risking everything for the freedom that had been promised to all but given only to some.

"And so the nation, still so new, broke apart. And a second war bloodied the land, a war that pitted families against each other, brother against brother and father against son. And the people sought for giants to aid them and a few did rise again. One came out of the hardscrabble frontier, a giant who rose out of ignorance and poverty, shook the dirt off his coat and crossed the land with mammoth strides to take command. Again, the names are lost but we can speak of their actions—on the battlefield and in the halls of government—all the places where men did the bloody deeds that had to be done, turning from the whispers of their better angels and answering the call of a more fiery gospel writ in burnished swords, terrible and swift, killing and dying so that others may live and be free, and that a country itself would not perish. And we can echo the few words that are left to us, of a government of the people, by the people and for the people. That is gone, Angel, but know that it did exist once—and that you can be a force in bringing it to life again, reborn like a phoenix, the bird that burned and rose again from its ashes."

28

The Feral Child

THE CHOW'S BEEN DOWNED, the mess cleared and the new puke hasn't returned to the barracks. Radio silence since the one cryptic message sent mid-afternoon—*following a trail.* Tanner appreciates a dogged man. But he wonders. Thoughts do cross his mind.

Daggett's out there, too, checking in every hour, logging in seemingly every last beech and maple, woodrat and timber rattler he spies.

Tanner doesn't appreciate extremes.

He taps his embed scanner screen, calling up the eye in the sky, entering the coordinates. The dots appear, two scarlet pinpoints in a field of green. They are in line, approximately. Could very well be following the same trajectory, the same trail of scent and effluvia left behind by a neophyte not used to covering her tracks.

Daggett is in the lead by several miles.

In his belly, an ache, and not from the swill they'd had for supper. He'd barely touched his. Prefers to hunt on an empty stomach. No, this is a different ache. One he knows well.

He wants this one for himself.

They are perched at the base of a massive gray sandstone cliff, a place where water and wind have taken turns sculpting the rock, carving their names across its face, notching the passing of time in millennia along its shoulders, scouring the rock of vegetation, except in the narrow protected cracks where emerald green moss and golden lichen blaze like gaudy jewels against the somber backdrop.

"Up top we'll get the lay of the land. See what we're gettin' into," Suraj says.

Merit frowns. It's a risk they don't need to take. But she's curious, too. Eager to know what lies beyond. Eager to see the forest, not just the trees.

The path ends at a ledge where a natural staircase, or part of one, begins. Slabs of stone jut from the rock wall, slabs just wide enough to hold a foot. Suraj scrambles up like a squirrel scuttling across a tree trunk, his backpack swaying from side to side as he ascends. At the top of the outcropping, he stands poised, hands on his hips, staring down, lips twisted in what Merit interprets as a sneer.

Sooner we get this over with, the sooner I'll wipe that smirk off his face...

And yet. Is it thirty feet she must climb? Fifty?

Merit plants each foot deliberately, digging her fingers into the ridges, determined not to make a misstep under his challenging gaze. *Don't you dare say hurry it up.* Midway her shoe slips on a loose pebble and her shin skids along the sharp edge of a boulder, ripping the thin fabric of her cargoes, scraping a raw red line along her skin.

Stop. Breathe. Focus. Think.

On the next foothold, she sweeps the sole of her shoe along the narrow slab to clear any rock debris before letting her foot land.

"Faster you go, easier it is," Suraj chirps from above. "No shit. Sometimes it's best to just do and not think so much."

Gravity is her enemy, the pull of the earth, the weight of her backpack, the sensation in her own body, the desire to stay firmly grounded. A moment to pause, to catch a thin breath. A quick upward glance. The boy's face is gone. But she can still hear him, though the mockery has drained from his voice, replaced by what sounds like amazement.

"Frackin' unbelievable."

She's only three or four feet from the top. And maybe that makes her hurry. Lose focus. Because one second her foot is firm on the sliver of ledge, her hand jammed tight in a fissure, and the next, she's dangling, feet scrabbling for purchase, finding none.

And the earth is waiting to reclaim her, like a prize.

Maybe she screamed. She's not sure. Maybe it was just her arms, the muscles stretched, tendons straining. They're not screaming now. It's more a whisper, a whine.

Life is pain. Nothing but pain. So just let go.

Another voice cuts through. "Hold on! Dig in!"

But she can't. Sweat slicks her palms and the creases between her fingers. She's slipping, the rock unforgiving. And then the rock lurches back from her desperate embrace and she's free falling.

Except she's not. She's defied gravity. Defied the earth.

The straps of her backpack cut into the skin of her armpits as she feels the tug upward.

"Grab the ledge!" A sharp bark.

A moment when her body hesitates. *Life is nothing but pain. And deceit.*

"Grab it!" The bark is now a wheeze.

The gasp of a boy burdened beyond his measure. A boy about to break.

And so her hand shoots up, again defying the earth's pull and its siren song. The tips of her fingers brush the smooth, solid edge and grip it. In an instant, another jolt of pain shoots down her arm as the talon grip of the boy's hand closes around her wrist and gives a yank.

"Dig in! Don't struggle, I've got you. There's a foothold! There! Find it. Calm-like now. It's there."

And then, it is. She feels the solid under her toe and eases her foot along until she pushes upward off it and he's pulling. Push and pull until her head tops the ledge and then her shoulders and she's over it with another pushpull and her face is pressed to the sandstone, warm under her cheek.

They sit back to back on the ledge, eyes scanning the horizons to the north, south, east and west. From the summit, they can see what they have been wandering through. Colors lay across the earth like a tattered shawl. Browns and greys where greens should flourish. To the east, the fracked landscape of the gas mines stretches to the darkening sky, a web of well pads, abandoned access roads and pipelines, scabs and scars and gouges. To the north lay the dry forest and far in the distance, the gray-green flat of a barren agri sector. Beauty and devastation.

Suraj shifts and settles again. Merit feels his bones slide under his skin, a sensation oddly comforting.

"So, what's your story?" she finds herself asking.

He is silent for a moment, shoulder bones shifting again. "What d'ya mean?"

"How'd you wind up without an embed?"

She feels his shrug. "Wasn't s'posed to be born."

For once he seems reluctant to talk. But Merit waits, knowing he won't be able to resist filling the gap.

"Mum was a swag. From up in the Huron. Medic. My dad, too. Or so she said. Swags who got the okay to make their own spawn. Me."

A pause. She resists prodding. He resumes. "So them tests they do before babies are born. Mum called them pre-natals. Them tests claimed I'd be born with something wrong with my heart, something serious. And something wrong with my mouth. Don't remember 'zactly what she called it. Cleft whatever. But it's bad. And Corporate decreed she had to terminate it. Terminate me. Cuz Corporate don't waste time or money on that kind of thing. Not even for swags. Why fix damaged goods when you can just order up another? She said my dad agreed with it. That I was something to be gotten rid of. But Mum couldn't stomach that. She fled with me in her belly."

"Where'd she go? Couldn't they track her?"

"Naw, she was in the blur. When swags get the okay to make a baby, they take the embed out short time. Something about the embed gums up the works. So they take it out. Swags have 'em in their hands. Easy in, easy out. She stayed with a medic friend of hers who was willing to help, even if it meant going against the Hive."

Merit scoots around to look him in the face. The scar is just a pale fold of skin in the space between the boy's nose and his lips, barely noticeable in the dimming light, but Merit's eyes are drawn to it. Funny how she hadn't noticed it before. Now she can't help but focus on it and Suraj wilts a little under her gaze. A conscious act or not, his hand moves to cover his mouth.

"She fixed your outside. What about your inside?"

Suraj shrugs. Thumps his chest. "It's beating. S'all that matters."

There it is again.

A howl from somewhere deep in a throat. A baying that rises from low to high in a crescendo cruel and mournful at once.

Suraj shrugs it off. "Coyote."

Merit isn't so sure. This is a fuller call than the shrill wail punctuated by yips, yelps and barks, the distinctive banshee vocalization of the coyote.

Pithound. Maybe.

The boy cocks his head. "Miles away, whatever it is. Hear how the sound bends?"

She defers to him, against her better judgment. Because, after all, who has done up most of the snares, the successful ones,

and skinned the rabbits that haplessly wandered into them? Who
has roasted them on improvised spits fashioned from green sapling twigs and offered her a kebab of fresh meat for breakfast?

"Who taught you all this?" she ventures between mouthfuls.

"Mum was a fantasterrific cook. Chefed her way around the
lakes, from gobble-n-gos to posh three coursers with gigs at private swagettes in between. Put something tasty in front of 'em
and wash their dishes, too, and swags'll choose their gullets over
Corporate rules any time. A bee without an embed is just one
less voucher report they have to file. With me along to do the
odd jobs, they got two for the price of zero."

"And the hunting? She taught you that, too?"

He dismisses that notion with a scathing arrow of a look and
a flick of his fingers. "Learned this on my own. She never had to
wild it."

It's hard to place the tone of his voice. Pride, mostly. But is
there a tinge, just the barest hint of scorn, too, the disdain of a
wounded child, bereft?

Silence, except for their chewing, which has eased from ravenous to almost contemplative.

Finally. "What happened to her?"

"Life," the boy snarls, mid-chew. "Life in this shit-hole."

Silence again. Even the chewing has ceased. But she feels a
need to know. To ask. To rile the still water.

"How?"

He's up then, using his foot to scrape soil over the ashes and
dying embers of their cooking fire. Sloshes a little of their precious supply of water from his canteen onto the fire ring. Squats
and stirs, checking for the glow and spark of living heat and flame.

"Took her," he mutters. "Came back to the manse where
we'd been hanging for six months, squatting out in the guest
house, they called it. Yeah, they were high enough to have two
frackin' houses on their property. Thought we was safe. Swags

were all that, but seemed on the level. Liked their meals, yeah. But they handed her over. And would've handed me over, too, but I saw it in the little swag's eyes. Little frackers can't keep a secret, can they?" A dark grimace. "So I grabbed our go-bag and dubbed it out of there. Been floatin' ever since."

Another grimace. Feral teeth. *Something Serafina once said. More than once. What was it? Something... red... red... in tooth and claw.*

"But I got 'em back, but good."

And she knew he'd spill without her ever opening her mouth. The water riled.

It was just a mutter, vague, low in his mouth, as if intended only for himself.

"I know my way around a match."

29

In the Clearing

MAYBE THE BOY IS RIGHT, with his feral instincts. The howls that seemed to be drifting ever closer to them have ceased, giving way to bird calls, the banter and repartee of the field and forest. The harsh rejoinders of jays, the jibber jabber of tiny sparrows, flocking and decamping from the underbrush enmass at their approach. The forest breathes around them, clouds of gnats shimmer and hum. She muses that she can hear the trees growing or dying. The snaps and crackles, the whispers and creaks. Morning gives way to noon and beyond before they pause in wonder. Before them is a slice of crystalline light, pure and piercing, so different from the mellow syrupy light in the thick of the woods. The trees have been cleared in this rectangular patch just beyond the dribble of a creek. An attempt at a garden struggles to assert its dominion over the land.

Someone lives out here. Someone who could be watching us even now.

She grabs the boy's arm and tugs him back a step or two before he shakes her off.

"I'm getting me one or two of those cukes, pitiful as they look. There's melons there, too. Look," he says, pointing out a few undersized spheres.

She should latch onto him again, but the thought of a cool, juicy cucumber, even a shriveled, half-hearted one past its prime, makes her mouth tingle. The meat from this morning is a distant memory. Her belly yawns with hunger, her throat creaks with thirst. He won't listen to her anyway. Will go where he chooses no matter how she may admonish. So she says nothing and watches him crouch low and skitter along the edge of the clearing. He eases himself up to the vines lolling over and around cages improvised from sticks and chicken wire. He stretches his shirt tail out, harvesting quickly, piling his bounty in his makeshift basket.

Suddenly there's a black blur, a shadow that's not a shadow, leaping from the trees on the far side of the clearing. Without so much as a snarl, the beast bears down on the boy. The vegetables tumble back to the soil from whence they sprang as Suraj spins to make a run for it. But a second black blur, another shadow that is not, looms just behind the pithound. The dog rears and brings its huge front paws down on the boy's back. Then he's on the ground and the dog's teeth, wetly gleaming, are inches from his ear with the heat and thick smell of its breath up in his nostrils, mingling there with the scent of the turned earth.

Merit can't heed the voice inside shrieking at her to run. She is frozen, compelled to watch, as if invisible hands grip her shoulders. As the goliath calls the hound to heel. As he grabs the boy under the armpits and hauls him to his feet. As the dog whines and circles and drops its nose to the ground.

It knows.

"Where's the androg?"

Suraj is speechless, the shock freezing his mouth in a gaping O. The dog whines again. Raises its massive, hideous head.

It knows.

"Where's the androg? Your traveling companion," the brute repeats.

"I don't—"

A clout whips the boy's head to the right.

"Where's the androg?"

The dog licks slobber from its muzzle. Turns its head. Stares, locks onto something.

The boy mumbles through a mouth full of blood and teeth. Another swift movement of the mammoth arm and then there's a brief fountain spray of red. The boy slumps down and to the left. One shudder. Another. Then he's quite still. Only the blood moves, seeping down the front of his Damn Otis t-shirt.

The hound's eyes are locked in her direction. And Merit's limbs are locked, too, preventing her escape, while the pulse in her gut warns that it would useless anyway.

A feathery whisper cuts the stillness, a whiz, a whir, a sound not quite of the natural world. The dog yelps, staggers. Another quiet rush of artificial wind and the hound is on the ground on its side, two sticks jutting up from its shuddering flanks.

The goliath utters a curse and takes off in the direction from which the arrows flew, squatting low, darting and dodging, stutter stepping when he rises. Then, in the barest blink of time and crackle of sound, he's hanging upside down, his ankles confounded, torso twisting, arms flailing. Something glints in his right hand. He's struggling, but he's strong, so very strong. He can bend and pull his upper body up, lift his arms, stretch to reach the snare that binds his ankles.

A tree moves. Crossing swiftly and from behind the snared man. Another glint. Another fountain of red. Another body that shudders once, twice, then goes still. Another stream of blood seeping.

Merit is flying then. Fleeing. Or trying to. But her feet betray her. Why won't they leave the ground? Why is it so difficult, like she's running through a gushing flood, instead of the dry, leaf-strewn floor of the forest? And then her feet do leave the ground, swept up by cruel claws that dig into the flesh of her ankles, gnawing down to the bone. The straps of her backpack strain at her armpits, slipping, dragging toward the earth, which is now where the sky should be as her cheeks and temples pulse with the thick sudden rush of blood to her head.

A random thought as she dangles. *Strange how the trunks of trees look the same. Upside down.*

A singular moment of stillness before she's flailing. But the movement only tightens the snare's grip, sharpens its throttling teeth. And she can't breath. The vest, strapped tight, constricts her now, binds her heaving chest, killing her slowly. Heart pounding, big to bursting, and that whispery clawing in her belly. *Why fight it?* After being ignorant of death for so long, and now having it shoved up in her face... What could be the way forward? Why go forward?

The memory of Serafina's whisper in her ear. *Hasta siempre. Until I see you with my eyes.*

A rasp. A croak. A sound coming from an instrument not much used. Could be a growl. Could be the word—girl?

"Girl." The growl again. "Stop strugglin'. I mean you no harm. Providin' you mean no harm to me."

The tree moves as it speaks. Now it is standing before her.

Legs clad in very worn brown cargoes, the knees patched thrice over with fabric in different shades. A putty-colored shirt, half-tucked, tail flopping over a sagging tool belt, the leather creased. A pair of hiking boots that have traveled many, many miles.

She cranes her neck.

The tree has a face as weathered as the bark of the dying oak that grew outside her window, a thousand miles and years ago, it seems. Rough-skinned. Lined. Grey. The most wrinkled face she's ever seen. A face she senses is very, very old. The hand that moves in front of her eyes and over and around her head is black-gloved, holding a black chunk of something.

"What're you?" Another rasp from the man-tree.

Not who. What.

"Where you from?"

He thumbs a switch on the side of the black chunk, some sort of 'tronic device, and then sweeps it over and around her, shaking his head.

"Brute bastard was pingin' for a day and a half, twenty miles away. You—nothin'." He runs a hand roughly through her hair, bending to examine her scalp.

"Where they stashin' 'em now?" Another growl.

The closures of the vest protest as he rips the straps apart, shoving the device underneath, scanning her chest and back.

"Where's yer frackin' embed?" He squats to stare into her face. His silver hair is caught back in a tail that hangs lankly over his shoulder. His eyes, deep-set amidst the sagging flesh of his lids, are blue gray, changeable, like water under sun and cloud. Questions settle into the finely-etched lines that radiate from their corners, like the course of rivers stretching over a map.

He repeats the question. Then sighs. "¿Habla ingles?" Smoothly rolling off his tongue, as if he's singing.

She stares dumbly at his knees, the patches. Her head has too much blood. Full of blood, throbbing with blood. It must explode soon from all the blood. She needs to answer before it does.

"Find your voice, girl, before death takes it away."

Say something!

"Don't—have—one." Merely a breath squeezed out of her chest and mouth. She marvels that he even hears, but from the way he cocks his head, she knows he has.

"Don't have what?" He cocks his head to the other side now, gauging with those calculating, changeable eyes. "Answer me, girl."

She forces it out. "Embed." Her head is too heavy, it will burst now, like a melon under the weight of a sledgehammer.

"But you know what that is?"

She nods, feeling, seeing the edges of the world growing dim.

"Girl, I'll set you loose, but you best not run. If you do, I'll have to kill you. Make no mistake, I will." He gestures to the strange object slung over his shoulder, a curving shaft of smooth wood strung at either end with wire.

"What's your intent?" He waits.

It's twilight now, the edges of her visual world veering toward full dark.

"Answer, girl."

"Won't—run."

The man-tree shuffles around, out of her swiftly blurring line of sight. She senses him behind her, somewhere in the dark. She closes her eyes, braces for a jarring return to earth. Which never comes. First, the weight of the backpack is gone. Then the vest. She feels the brush of his hands along her outer thighs, down her legs. He has her knife out of its pocket in one swift motion. Then there's a slow sense of easing. Her head and neck and shoulders. Her back and thighs. Her feet.

"Don't try to sit up. Let the blood settle."

She follows his instructions, resting in the crisp carpet of leaves, grinding her cheek into the soft prickle of dry pine needles, breathing in their scent, the smell of burnt sadness. The darkness eases. The blue of dawn seeps in, the quiet light of the woods. Her head no longer pulses. Her hands creep along the curve of her belly.

He misses nothing. Pulls her wrists behind her, not in a rough way, and secures them with something cool and steel that makes a glittering sound when she shifts. His hands under her arms, he guides her into an upright position. And then he is sitting cross-legged before her, but looking coiled, ready to spring at the least provocation. But his eyes are not zeroed in on her face. They are focused on her middle, the swelling under her t-shirt. Then they slowly travel upwards and lock onto hers.

"You an ova?" Regards her mute stare. "A breeder?"

Still she stares.

"How'd that baby come to be in your belly?"

30

The Manse

IT WAS THE FIRST RAIN IN MONTHS, *that early March storm.*
And it was the last, too. A huge rumbler that gushed so much water
so quickly, all that moisture had nowhere to go. The packed ground
was too hardened to accept it. So it sat.

Em must've reminded me to wipe my feet half a dozen times
before we reached the front stoop. Swags had a huge tan mat, too
fancy considering its purpose, stenciled with lattice vines and an
enormous bushwazee T in the center. I had no business being there,
but Em begged me to tag along.

"Come on, chica. Cece is sick in bed and I don't want to go to la cabro-
na's house by myself. You don't have to lift a finger. Just keep me company."

Twice a month, Em cleaned house for the tall, willowy blonde
esposa of the Director. But it seemed to be on the down-low. She
never saw the Director. Not once since the couple had arrived in
the gloom of late December. And she got paid in things—food, cast-
off clothing, trinkets from the jewelry box—rather than traceable
vouchers. Like the mujer was keeping it a secret. From somebody.

I'd scoffed. Ridiculous. He could just do an embed scan. Probably
did one every day. He's the frackin' head of security, the goliath of all
goliaths. He'd know who's been in his own house. Em just flashed that
smirk she kept for times she was down with info nobody else knew.
But then her eyes slid away, as if she recognized her oops, and started

rattling on about the mujer this and that, distracting with too much information. Mujer despised agsector life. Even with a crib in the Gates. Too many vacant manses. Too isolated, even for a swag. Too much dust. Em overheard her bitching to someone on the vox.

The mujer and her hairless bastard were gone as usual this weekend. She'd seen their personal transport heading out, sleek and black with its smoked out windows.

"When he does his sweep what's my excuse for being here?"

Em shrugged. "If he does—and he won't—but if he does— which he won't—Cece is sick. You're helping me. Mujer can't expect me to clean this manse all by myself."

She hooted when I showed up wearing my knit cap with the silly canine ears and white-ringed eyes, Serafina's handiwork, pulled low over my forehead. "¡La loba!"

"It's cold," I muttered from behind my respy, knowing I looked wonky.

I'd been in a vacant manse once or twice before. Under Em's devious influence. We hit 'em to rip out whatever was left. Copper pipe. Chrome. Nickel. Fixture wiring. Furnace parts. Fodder for Bartertown. Scavenging. It was Em's hustler mantra: you leave it, I'll heave it. But stepping foot over the threshold of an occupied manse? Not once that I could remember. Though the desire was there, a niggling itch somewhere just beyond reach, annoying, prodding.

We had a snicker over the white tile and carpet.

"These people think they're all that, putting white under their feet," Em snorted.

Oh, but it was beautiful. In a strange, sterile, exquisitely fragile way. And in the milky light of late afternoon it looked like it would all splinter into a million pieces if I rested a hand on it. Or just cut my eyes at it the wrong way. I had no names for the fabrics that covered the immense sofa and chairs sprawling throughout the hearth room, fabrics I only dared brush with a single pinkie finger. I just knew they were the softest I'd ever touched.

31

Body Bag

SHE EMBRACES THE TREE like a loved one, arms wrapped around its slender trunk, cheek pressed against the smooth bark, but it's a forced embrace, compelled by the chain that binds her wrists. The old man is busy making Suraj, the goliath, and his pithound disappear. Strangely, the grave, a deep hole dug at the far edge of the garden, had been ready. As he chained her, he must have seen the puzzlement on her face, however fleeting, before it faded to a blank stare. Then, of course, he had to tell her.

"Dug it two days ago, when the pings started coming regular."

He's stripped the brute's corpse of items he's deemed useful—boots and socks, utility belt—and now he struggles to fold the massive body into a large black duffel bag, but the brute won't fit alongside his beast. He can't zip the bag, so he slices one end open and lets the stiffening legs hang out, sealing the gaps with duct tape. Glancing over, he catches her speculation before she can hide it. Again, he fills the silence.

"Not just any old duffel. This one's special. Magic." His eyes fairly twinkle, ice blue, grey blue. "Blocks the focus from reading the embed. They'll never find him."

She blinks. She refuses to let him think she's some gullible child. Or worse, a fool. So she takes the bait, even as she curses herself.

"Faraday cage," she murmurs, low but not at all tentative.

That stops his labors. Brings a stare. "Heard of 'em?"

She just returns the stare.

With a grunt, he rolls the duffel over the edge of the hole. The feet, enormous and pale-skinned, tumble after, first one, then the other. He turns his attention to Suraj. The threadbare clothing is beyond salvaging. But when he shoves a hand into the boy's pants pocket and removes the timekeeper, he cocks his head in appreciation and then tucks it in the back pocket of his jeans. Merit makes a mental note to get it back.

He lowers the boy's body into the grave with a slowness that suggests a gentle regard even as Merit's stomach roils at the thought of the three bodies lying so intimately together, of good and evil cheek to jowl. Then he's shoveling. As the clods of dirt hit the bag, their thuds are punctuated only by the old man's huffs and snuffles when he pauses to catch his breath. When the hole is filled and the ground leveled, he rakes leaves and pine needles and withered corn stalks and husks over it. The ground still looks disturbed. But no more so than the rest of the garden plot.

He gulps from a steel canteen. Wipes sweat from his forehead and neck with a ragged bandanna that was perhaps once red, a very long time and many washings ago. Squats and unlocks one of the steel bracelets. Eases her arm from around the trunk. Snaps the cuff back on her wrist. Folds his long legs and sits before her.

"Now, girl, time to tell me who you are."

Minutes later, in the face of her silence, he turns to her backpack for answers. He arranges the contents in neat rows, grouped by category. Her water containers and the purification straw system. The cooking kit with its metal pot, plate and cup. The security grade heat sheet and poncho tent. The fire steel. The medi-kit. The multi-tool. The flashlights. The duct tape, fishing line, respy. The compass. The vocoder.

"First rate EVAC bag. What we used to call a Battle Box. Whoever put this together knows his—" A sidelong glance at her impassive face. "Or her—stuff. Just missing the sustenance. Guessin' you ran outta that quick. When's last time you ate?" A significant nod at her belly. "Even on the inside, a baby's got to be fed." A trickle. "This morning." And then a torrent. "If you're gonna kill me, then just go on! Stop toying around! They're gone. Gone. So just do it and put me down like you done the brute and the hound. If that's severance, I'll welcome it."

It had only been meant as an internal monologue, those defiant thoughts. What she has been so good at for so long when in the company of strangers, sucking it up good and tight, holding the anger in. But now the words and the fury slip between her lips.

A tightening of the skin around the old man's mouth. "Mighty cavalier about throwing away something precious." He squints, realizes she doesn't understand the meaning of the word. "*Cavalier.* Dismissive. Contemptuous. Just don't give a damn." He stands and hitches up his jeans around his skinny waist, tightening the rope he uses for a belt. "Hell, ain't that always been the way. But I'm not so cavalier about taking an innocent life. And I'm not referring to you."

"I've done nothing!" Merit cries. "Nobody—not one of us did anything! We were just livin' the best we could, obeyin' the frackin' rules, followin' the program, sendin' it all north. And then the drought hit and we were still doin' our best, tryin' to meet the quotas. And they just took and took and took and left nothin'. And nature turned a blind, dry eye. And they kept takin' and expectin' more 'til there was nothin' left to give. Cuz we're nothin' without water. Then they took that away, too. And when they gave it back, instead bringin' life, it brought death. She was innocent. They were all innocent. And they killed them all! Killed—"

Eben.

And there it was, the last shred of hope, fed on denial. Gone. It spills out. Words. Tears. Guttural, hiccuping sobs. Gusts of rage and fear heaving her chest, her shoulders, fists clenching, ragged bitten nails scraping the skin of her palms, as she hugs tight to herself, the only thing she has left to hold.

He sits, wearing his own game face, letting the tumult roar until it's spent. She swipes savagely at her eyes with the backs of her hands, struggles onto her knees, straightens her spine and squares her shoulders. Feels the agate thud against her breastbone as she shifts her weight, gains her balance. Lifts her head, tips it back, baring her neck, her long neck, vulnerable, pulsing with the dregs of her emotion, with life.

"Go on, do it."

The trees rise and converge. A tunnel, narrowing to the yellow-white light, unforgiving as always. Until she closes her eyes. The sunlight washes red through the delicate filter of her skin. She's ready for the single slice of pain and the release the knife will bring. But instead of pain, there is the lightest sensation on the skin at the base of her throat. A scritching whisper of soft leather as the weight of the agate is lifted.

"Where'd you come by this?"

She has said too much already. A heavy exhalation of breath, the sound of air escaping its container. She tenses, then wills herself to relax, breathing out, letting her shoulders drop, unclenching her jaw, even as the weight of her back-flung head strains her muscles and she sways as disorientation creeps in behind her still-closed eyes.

"Open your eyes." His gloved hands press her shoulders, steadying her. "It's safe to say you're far more interesting alive than dead. But if you have a death wish, I'll gladly accommodate it. But only after you've told me what I want to know. On the other hand, if, in your secret heart of hearts, you desire to live, you need to start answering my questions."

Pressure on the back of her head, tilting it forward. When she opens her eyes, his, red-veined, deep-set among the wrinkles, are inches from hers. She blinks. Considers.

"That makes no sense. Either way I have to talk."

"Bit of a paradox, I'll admit. Back in the day, we called it a win-win situation. Either way, we both get what we want." He waves a gloved hand in her face. The leather has the worn-soft look of time and use. "I'll qualify that. *To a certain extent,* we both get what we want. Now come on, our stomachs are starting a chorus and it's not what I'd call a happy tune."

He takes hold of her upper arm and pulls her to her feet. Not roughly. With an economy of motion, he unlocks the cuffs that bind her wrists, slips her arms through her backpack straps, adjusts it on her shoulders and binds her again. He gestures to the golden glow that suffuses the woods. "Crib's a fair hike. Best be movin' if we want to make it before dark."

"So I'm your prisoner." He's got the height of a goliath and she has to crane her head to look him in the eye.

"My guest."

She raises her bound wrists in his face. "If this is how treat your guests, then I'd hate to see how you treat your prisoners."

"Well, here's the thing." He inclines his head in the direction of the field. In the direction of the newly-filled grave. "I don't take prisoners."

32

Nom de Guerre

THEY HIKE FOR SEVERAL MILES, first taking a seemingly random route through the trees, but then meeting up with a more obvious trail, beaten earth bending around oaks and hickories, thick-trunked and thin. They tread the low ground through the woods to the outcroppings of a bluff. Here the trail forks, one path meandering on through the trees, the other hugging the rock face.

"Follow the rockwall," he orders.

As they walk, the bluff rears up, its layers revealing the secret history of time and the earth. Lightish bands of sandstone fold over into darker bands of shale. Blooms and drifts of red and orange indicate the presence of iron in narrow veins. At times the rock curves above to shelter them. At other times it leans in menacingly, at seemingly impossible angles. The path skirts clots of small boulders that have separated from the bluff and collapsed. In places, the rock is pockmarked and scarred, in others it is smooth and fine-chiseled, like a hand wielding a sculptor's knife has cut and scraped away its imperfections.

Twilight settles a murky cloak over the woods as they pass a towering vertical wall. Merit senses the damp. Her fingers are drawn to its cool, rough, impenetrable face, armor without a chink. Except water has found a way to pierce it. She feels its slime marking a slender trail. Like the rock has shed tears.

Another bend and the bluff is striated again, moss tumbling over its ridged bands, like a thick green syrup oozing down a stack of pancakes. Her stomach roils. Hunger. And that whispery, scratching sensation. The other living thing inhabiting her body.

And then she sees it. A black mouth gaping in the rock face, easily thirty feet wide. Stops short, feels the jostle as the old man bumps into her pack from behind.

"Go on," he nudges. Sighs. "You got the incommunicado down, but you've got to work on your game face, girl. Even in the gloaming, I can see the question there. 'A cave? You live in a cave?'"

And indeed, the question hovers, just behind her closed lips.

"I stay here from time to time. When I'm in this neck of the woods and need a place to crash. And no, it's not technically a cave. More of a rock shelter."

"Go on," he nudges her again and she steps under the overhang.

The single lantern throws just enough light to illuminate the sunken ring in the rock floor where Merit sits. It's a place where water has pooled and, over the arc of time, carved the surface to form this shallow pit. She hasn't uttered a syllable since they entered the cavern and the old man unshackled her wrists, while he's been talking non-stop, though not in complete sentences, just words and phrases gushing like water through a broken dam. He is performing either a magic trick or a science experiment.

"Old MREs," he says, brandishing the brown foil packets he's retrieved from a duffel bag stashed in a crevice at the far edge of the rock shelter. "Meals Ready to Eat. Security squad rations. Keep forever. Easy to tote."

He slips each packet into green polybags that hold a white pad about the size of a deck of cards. Adds dribbles of water from his canteen to both.

"Magnesium mixed with salt and a little iron dust. Oxidation of the metal generates heat. Instantly. No flame required."

What looks like a white flume of steam rises from the bags. He quickly folds the tops over and slides the bags back into their original cartons.

"I spy your lack of faith." He bends over the duffel again, paws through it and pulls out a pair of sporks.

A few minutes later, when he hands her one of the foil packets, she's astonished at the heat that seeps through the package's skin.

"Caution. Contents will be hot," he chuckles, tossing her a chunk from a small round of flat bread he's pulled from his backpack. "Says so right on the bag. Idiots. As if we need the warning."

The chicken and noodles are surprisingly tasty. Or maybe it's just that she's ravenous.

"So, I can ask questions and you can respond, or you can just talk in any order you choose. Tell me what you think I want to know and if you leave anything out, I'll take it from there."

"Already told you," she mumbles around a chunk of chicken.

"Yeah, about the agsector and your immediate past, but I've the mind of a scientist. Always wanting to know more."

She ignores that. Takes another forkful of the mush. Chews slowly. *There is a time to be silent. And a time to talk. You have nothing left to lose. Absolutely nothing.*

"When were you a scientist?" she ventures, to distract him.

"Nope, not your turn. That comes later." He eyes her, tilts his head back, drains his canteen. "Maybe. First, I need to know how you come to be here in the depth of the Shawnee with a bugout bag on your back and no embed under your skin."

"I told you—"

"Not enough. Not yet." Those changeable eyes, the hard grey of concrete now.

Nothing left to lose. So she spills it. The mystery of her birth, of the basket and the baby girls, of the talis on its chain, the story that Eben told her. It provokes a raising of the old man's white eyebrows, feathery and wild. He ambles over to the duffel, roots around inside, comes back, a biblio in his hand, thick, black, leather-bound. The cover is crisscrossed with creases, soft at the edges, the spine cracked, separating from the pages, threads and glue giving way under use and time. The pages look as fragile and translucent as the skin of an onion, and crackle as he thumbs them with care.

"Exodus, Chapter Two. *'But when she could no longer hide him, she took a papyrus basket, and put the child therein, and she laid it in the reeds on the bank of the river. Then Pharoah's daughter came down to bathe in the Nile. Noticing the basket among the reeds, she sent her handmaiden to fetch it. Upon opening it, she looked and there was a child crying. She was moved with pity...'*" He snaps the biblio shut. The sound echoes off the rock. "A lovely story, no? And now, the truth."

Merit shrugs. "It's what I was told. It's all I know."

He taps a finger on the biblio. "For we walk by faith, not by sight."

"I could make up some other story, if you want."

He holds up his hand. They sit in silence. It stretches and stretches, past the circle of dim light, out into the dark corners of the cavern and beyond, into the night, where the staccato hoot of an owl punctures its enveloping skin. But the hole closes quickly again, and it's almost comfortable, like they are long-time companions beyond the need for words.

"How'd you do that?" she finally asks, in little more than a whisper.

He cocks his head at her. "What?"

"Kill that man."

"You saw, girl. Finish your stew."

"But—"

"In this life, you can be the hunter or the hunted. It's a choice that comes early."

"But you can't choose—"

"You have to choose. And then follow through. And be prepared to pay the price for your choice, whatever it is."

Silence again. Expanding, filling space like an encompassing bubble until she breaks it again.

"Would you... help me?"

He doesn't look up from his pouch. Chews for a bit. Swallows. "With what?"

"Following through."

He keeps his eyes lowered. "Never been good at riddles. Speak plain."

"I want to be the hunter." A pause. And then, "There are... men... I want to kill."

And as the words leave her lips, she realizes they are true.

"There's your first problem." He finally looks up, his icy stare fixed on her face. "There's a difference between a want and a need."

"I... need... to kill these... men."

"And what's the price you'd pay to do it?

She stares, astonished. *I've already paid the price. It's time for the brutes to pay.*

He shakes his head. "See, there's the sticking point. The unwillingness to sacrifice. To do what's necessary, no matter the cost. Because there's a price to pay for taking vengeance. It'll gnaw at your heart until it's a bloody pulp—"

"Don't talk to me about sacrifices and paying the price," she snarls. "I've already sacrificed. They killed my family. My friends, my people."

"Killing won't bring your people back."

"I know that. But those who did it deserve to die."

The old man forks more stew into his mouth. "Who's 'they'?"

"A brute squad."

"Ah, so one day they just decided to kill off these people?"

"No. They were following orders," Merit says, growing impatient.

He points his fork at her. "And where did the orders come from?"

"I don't know. The Hive, I guess. Where else? But what does that matter—"

"It matters. Because you can chop off the hand, but that won't destroy the body, the heart, the brain." He lifts his left arm. With his right hand, he tugs off the black glove that covers the left.

It is beautiful. Hideous. Cruel. Fierce. The digits glint in the shaft of lantern light. Bones wrought in dull metal, cleverly jointed and hinged. Forged out of a grim necessity.

"I am living proof of that."

He could be any of them, but Merit knows with some uncanny certainty who the man sitting across from her is. It is a certainty that comes from the bowels. A belief that starts in the gut and seeps north and south, into the veins, coursing through them to the meeting place, thrumming in time with trepidation and excitement. *Because he would be a man to stay rather than flee.* The recognition washes over her face though she quickly tries to conceal it. But she's not quick enough.

"You've heard the story." He shoves the last of the bread toward her. "From?"

"The man who raised me."

"Where'd he hear it?"

"He lived it. Said he knew you."

"Knew me? And who am I, then?"

"The Son of the Mississippi. Debs. Joachim Debs."

A sigh. A tiny twitch tugging at the corner of his mouth. "Been awhile, a long while, since I heard that name."

"*Your* name."

His smirk neither denies nor confirms. "The man who raised you? What name did he go by?"

"Eben Bird."

If the name sparks a memory in the old man, his face does

not reveal it. "But then a name is just a name," he muses. "Not the thing itself. Not the person."

Merit would like to doubt. This man looks so very old. With skin so thin, sagging and folded. With the hollow-boned frailty of a bird. A tremor running through his fingers. Yet at one time, with his great height, he must have cut quite the figure. Must have strode the earth like the giants of Serafina's story.

"Perhaps this man you call Eben, perhaps he marched under a nom de guerre." He grins at her confusion. "War name. A pseudonym. A false name you take so you can do the deeds that must be done." He takes a long swallow from his canteen. "Well then, maybe I don't need to know your name. But I'd like to call you somethin' besides 'girl.' So, who will you be then?"

Merit thinks he's mocking her. "This ain't a game. Given name's Merit, but that was the other baby's name. A Corporate name."

His smile spreads slow, thick and dark like molasses oozing across a plate. His nod is slow, too. "No, it's not a game. You start down this path, you best be prepared to dig many graves. Including one for yourself." He shrugs. "Fine, if it don't matter to you, I'll just call you 'girl.' We'll let those that come after, the ones who tell the legends, give you a name."

That doesn't sit right with her. So she snaps a contradiction. "Angel. It's what she—my mother—my *mothers*," she corrects, "called me."

33

The New Colossus

"WHERE'D YOU GET THIS?"

The embed reader fits in the palm of a hand, slightly longer than a deck of playing cards, and slim enough to slip into a shirt pocket. Its metal casing is pitted with dings and dents. A web of cracks stretches across the lower right corner of its permaglass screen. Battle-scarred but still viable, ready for the next foray, like a steadfast warrior.

"Question lacks precision," the old man taunts, wiping the screen with the tail of his shirt. "Do you mean where? Or how? Or from whom? Or what's its origin story?"

"All of the above, I guess," she replies.

"Less you know the better, for now. All you need to know is how to use it."

She's not used to having her questions dismissed with a verbal wave of the hand. The feeling crackles, like a shot of static.

"This'll get a hit on any embed within a twenty-five mile radius." He catches the roll of her eyes. "Yeah, it's a first-gen. You could tell that from the looks of it. Twenty-five miles is plenty for our purpose."

Our purpose. ***Our*** *purpose.*

"Tracks the embed's path. Won't give you its speed, but you can figure that out. Refreshes every two minutes. We've a couple of options. Sit and wait for them to stumble into our web," he says, tapping the cracked section of the screen, "or go hunting. What'll it be?" He pauses, appraising her. "Spider or wolf?"

Truth be told, she doesn't have a truly coherent thought, much less a plan. Just a feeling, deep, hot, guttering like a flame in a gust of wind. *They have to pay the price for what they've done. And that price can only be the highest. Death. They have to die.*

And how else can that be but by her own hand?

It doesn't seem like a plan. Is nothing like the carefully laid out instructions and schematics that she's followed in her Corporate-prescribed training. But hasn't she always balked at that? Hasn't she always found a way to improve the widget?

"Don't have a weapon," she mumbles. "You took my knife."

He rubs a finger across his chapped lips. The dry surface skin is pale, a dull pink, but in the cracks, the color is deeper, ruddier, closer to the color of life. He nods. "Guess I can return it. But I have something a little stronger you can use."

The sleeping bag provides no cushion against the unforgiving surface of the rock floor. She shifts and twists and turns throughout the night, jolting in and out of a sleep measured in minutes, not hours. But each time she rises up on her elbow, he is awake, propped against the round boulder that stands just left of center in the cavern. Angel wonders how it got there. There is no cracked depression in the ceiling from which it might have fallen. Did some ancient dwellers roll it in? And for what purpose?

The old man has dimmed the lantern, but she can see the pinpoint of its light reflected in his eyes. "Go back to sleep," he whispers. "Sleep that knits up the raveled sleeve of care, balm of hurt minds."

Instinct tells her the words did not have their origin in his mind. They sound like something that would come from Serafina's lips, rise out of her story.

"What's that? What you said. A story?" she asks, sitting up, ignoring the grind of her hipbones.

"Something lost," he mutters, shifting, his spine cracking. "No, thrown away."

"You want to sleep? I can do a watch."

He shakes his head, a shadow of a movement. "Macbeth does murder sleep. Macbeth shall sleep no more."

"But you—"

"Girl—Angel—lay yourself down. Rest. The path you're choosing is long and rocky. It'll be the hardest you ever walked. Best be prepared."

"I want my vocoder. My mother's voice, the story. It helps me sleep."

She knows he's listened a bit, without asking for an explanation. Now, he says nothing, but reaches into his pocket, and flips it to her. Angel presses the buds into her ears and resumes her tossing and turning, feeling the whispers in her belly ebb and flow as the night creeps toward morning.

"It was a time of machines. They ruled the land, shaped it. And molded the people. It was an age of ages. Steam, then electricity, and the black stream of oil. All was making and selling and getting and wanting. It was the age of invention. Of things and self. All of life marched to the rhythm and thrum of a piston.

"And the wonders that came forth out of the bellies of the machines, out of the furnaces that burned fire hot enough to melt rock, these were flights of fancy made real. The train, the automobile, the airplane. For the people must now always be in motion, never at rest. Joys and sorrows in the coming and going, the arrival and the departure.

"It was the age of captains of industry and robber barons, the giant men who became part of the machines and knit their bones with the iron skeletons of the machines. Their tendons became the belts that connected the gears and their joints the cogs. Men of monumental

*appetites who swallowed others whole. And the third divide, yet an-
other plague, split the land, as the fruits of the people's toil were
consumed by the colossus, by the machine men, who grew fatter and
fatter still, while so many others scraped by bone-thin.*

*"And the machines erected great structures of iron and steel and
glass, all materials born of fire, structures climbing to the sky, to touch
the clouds and go beyond. And the people climbed, too, always in motion, ever upward. To the blue bowl of heaven and beyond, piercing
the veil, traveling into a black unknown. A frontier, a new frontier,
having tamed the land and having been tamed by the machines, they
must go seek something new to subdue and bend to their will.*

*"And the machines gave birth to other wonders, new and
strange, year after year, time out of mind. Wonders of sound and
speech and vision and touch. And motion, ever motion. And still the
people believed. Believed that by the sweat of their labor, they, too,
would grow. That a man, any man, could transform from worker
bee to Hive ruler by dint of his efforts.*

*"And they believed the colossus goddess, the lady with the gold-
en lamp, who stood offshore and welcomed them, beckoned them to
cross oceans. Who boasted of the bounty beyond. Who proclaimed
give me your tired, your poor, your huddled masses yearning to
breathe free. And it proved true. For many. Though the streets were
not paved with gold, the air was free to breathe. And the opportunity was there. They rose. They rose. By sheer force of will, they rose.*

*"Oh Angel, can you believe this? Can you believe we were once
a race of giants?*

"Believe. And remake the world."

34

Scarecrow

THE FOREST ENVELOPS THE LAND in a stranglehold, rugged, dense, an embrace of jagged hollows and steep slopes threaded with jutting roots and chunks of sandstone. Angel stumbles over a slab of rock caught in the grasp of a gnarled tree root, half hidden in the leaf debris. Debs grabs her elbow, steadying her. Bends to sweep a scattering of curled leaves and humus from the rock's face. It has been touched by human hands before, chiseled by them. The lettering is faint, shallow, soft-edged. Effaced by the harsher touch of time and nature. Angel's hand is drawn to it, but even as her fingers trace the surface, she cannot read what once was written there.

"Gravestone." Somehow he knows without seeing her face that she doesn't understand. "Time was, when people died, they were usually buried in the earth. In places called cemeteries."

We buried her there. Took her deep into the forest.

"In forests?"

The old man barks a laugh. "No, the grounds were cleared, usually carefully landscaped, kept manicured. Not wilderness like this. These are from time out of mind. People who tried to tame this place. And failed." He rubs a thumb over the stone's edge. "Anyway, Corporate outlawed that quaint practice. 'Course, with severance, not many die here anyway. Those that do, well, who really knows what happens to their bodies?"

He presses on, but another oddity catches Angel's eye several yards away. The gray trunk of a tree carved from stone rises from a squat square pedestal. Moss drapes over the sides, a swath of sage green blending into the gray. The words carved into the scroll that ornaments the trunk are filled with moss of a darker shade, making this inscription easier to decipher.

FRANKLIN SYDES
BORN SEPT. 25, 1866
DIED FEB. 25, 1911

CAROLINE, HIS WIFE
DIED NOV. 1904

And below the scroll, a phrase: *"For there is hope of a tree if it be cut down, that it will sprout again, that the tender branches thereof will not cease."*

The old man moves on without comment, shoulders hunched, and Angel hurries to keep up, skirting the edges of other slabs askew in the woods, inscribed with other names long past remembering.

The cabin barely earns that title. Hardly more than a shed, it leans precariously to the left. The plank roof lets in pinpoints of light, looks like it would leak like a sieve in a good rainstorm. But the room is alive with good smells, the soft scents of pine and wood smoke underlaid with the sharp tang of lavender and rosemary. Sure enough, herb cuttings hang upside down from the rafters in a corner near the small, dust-streaked window, drying. In another corner a small sawed-off trunk of a tree serves as a table with an even smaller one nestled beside it as a stool. A sleeping bag is folded neatly along the far wall, under the eaves, away from those gaps in the roof. Angel spies a portable single burner stove, a duffel and a black box with the look of a 'tronic relic, all knobs and push buttons with a metallic mesh covering a circular opening bordering a small, cracked screen.

"How long have you lived like this?" Angel asks, as they stand at the water pump a hundred yards or so down a beaten path, splashing water over their faces and necks, washing away the trail dirt and sweat. Her sharp eyes discern the tiny fisted heart painted at the bottom of the pipe.

He shrugs. "Well, that's the thing. In the Shawnee, one doesn't note the passing of time same as out in the Occupation." He wipes his hands on a tattered towel, draws the embed reader out of his shirt pocket and thumbs it to life. Squints. "By this date, in Corporate time, forty five years, give or take a few months." He grins at the shocked expression that seizes her face. "You're sayin', 'couldn't he have fixed up the place in all that time?' This ain't my home. Just a place to hunker down from time to time."

"Where's your home?"

He shoots her a look, as if gauging her motives. "Don't really have one, I guess. Not in the physical sense."

"This is your life? Just hiding out? Wandering around the Shawnee? Waiting for someone, a goliath, to stumble into your territory, so you can slay him? And then go back to—this?" She waves a hand to encompass the whole of the hovel.

He slits his eyes, nods. "Put that way, I guess it sounds pretty aimless. Or maybe it's life stripped to the fundamentals. Shelter. The hunt. Food. Kill or be killed. S'all there is, ain't it?" Is there a twinkle of amusement in his eyes? He turns on his heel and ducks through the doorway. "Though sometimes it seems like we're all waiting for somethin'. Goin' to check my traps."

Later, after they've gnawed the last shreds of roasted meat from the rabbit carcass and are sucking on the bones, he says, casually, without looking at her across the dying fire. "I don't always live this way. There's a place up north I stay at from time to time.

People I trust. When our business is done here, maybe I'll take you there. When your time's near, you'll need someone to help."

"It's in human nature to strive toward perfection, Angel. You must believe that. Men and women put their hearts and minds on the line for this work, to perfect the union that was called America. Men and women died trying to achieve it.

"The struggle to erase the scars left by the original plagues upon the land was bloody, though the men and women who pushed forward did not take up arms. But violence was brought upon them. They clung together against the forces that would drive them apart. They rose up against the forces that would hold them down. They resisted, stood up, sat down, marched, sang, faced the ropes meant to hang them, the firehoses and the snarling dogs, the batons and the guns. In the face of the violence done upon their bodies, they made the change happen. They were the change.

"And these men and women, these warriors for change, were fearless. In the face of evil, they walked. They offered up their bodies to it, marched through the deepest, darkest valleys, keeping their feet to the path of righteousness. And change came, Angel. They brought it, carried it in their arms and on their backs.

"Because evil exists in the world. It is real, Angel. It lives and breathes as sure as you do. It struts down the street and looks you in the eye every day. Though you may not always recognize it because it fronts so well. As strength. As protection. Because evil's goal is not to make you do evil. It does that well enough on its own. No, Angel, evil's goal is to make you fear.

"In the words of one far more articulate than I, 'it was the best of times, it was the worst of times.' Life was beautiful. Life was ugly. Life was rich in promise. Life was an ever narrowing tunnel that led to a dark dead-end. People were kind. People were cruel. People reveled in each other. People despised each other. It was a time when the fewest hands held the most treasure. When the few who sat at

the table would barely condescend to sweep their crumbs to the floor for the rest to fall upon and fight over.

"The earth warmed in the hands of the people, fed by the heat of progress, the everlasting search for more and better and faster and cheaper. Weather changed and at the top and bottom of the earth where ice had once ruled for time out of mind, it began to give way and the oceans rose. Resources are precious. But we thought they were free-flowing, abundant and that wherever we looked, there we would find them, no matter the cost.

"But it wasn't to be. And our differences, the things that create hate and conflict, won out. The waters at our borders to the east and west no longer protected us from the tumult happening all over the world. Maybe we were never meant to be a global species, but to only live in our little like-minded tribes, ever-warring on the others who encroach upon our space.

"Angel, giants no longer walked the land. Only small men with grasping hands and stony hearts."

The scarecrow slouches in the middle of the garden plot, sourly eyeing the half-hearted growth of corn. Angel suspects he was shabby when newly-made, his head a threadbare pillow case stuffed with the guts of some decrepit chair cushion that had borne the weight of too many bodies for too many years. A crushed black fedora, shiny in the worn spots, tops his bald pate. It tilts precariously to the left, giving him the rakish look of a swag on the hunt for a pleasure girl. But below the neck, he is all Barter-town rat. Overalls bleached the color of a haze-softened sky, the plaid of his shirt faded to a uniform gray. He is a long-lost cousin to the strawman that Eben had staked, faceless, in the middle of their vegetable garden in summers past. Its blank visage had terrified the young Angel, so Serafina had dragged out the step stool and they had painted him an elaborate face: eyes and brows, nose, a cheery smile, dimples in his non-existent cheeks, a cleft in his non-existent chin. His carriage had been ramrod straight, thanks to the broomstick that formed his spine. This effigy leans with an air of uncertainty, like a man under the influence.

Yet it is surprisingly easy to pretend he's someone else. Someone real.

Pretending. That's what it's been all about for the past hour. Pretending not to be shocked when Debs opens a duffel bag he's pulled from under a loose plank in the shack's floor and hands her a pistol. Pretending to thrill to the chilly black weight of it in her palm, cupping the barrel, testing the grip, shifting the piece from one hand to the other. Pretending to be loose-limbed and eager to get on with the show, rather than stiff-kneed with dread, neck and shoulders aching.

"Antique," Debs mutters. "Salvaged from the security scrap-metal works, from back in the day when the brute squads and border guards still had to do a bit of work to kill a man—like aiming and pulling a trigger. Now they pack tracers equipped to hone in on an embed signal. One tap and they can fire as many rounds as it takes. With the head shot, that's usually just one. And just because you've no embed, don't think you're unstoppable. Just means they have to use the laser sight and take a second to aim."

Debs takes the pistol back and raises it up in his right hand and instantly a tiny bead of crimson glows on the grip and another, slightly larger dot of red appears on the scarecrow's forehead. As he adjusts his aim, moving his hand ever so slightly up or down, the laser pinpoints where the bullet will hit.

An explosion follows that shakes her to her bones, rattles the teeth in her jaws, splinters her eardrums. The charred air sears the insides of her nose and stings her eyes. But it is the old man's glare that leaves her cowed like a dog beat down by a once-loving master.

"Don't take this lightly. Understand? Don't pick up a weapon—any weapon—without a plan."

Angel nods solemnly, the shot still ringing in her ears.

"First rule, you shoot, shoot to kill. Don't shoot to injure or slow down your pursuer. That's like swatting a wasp. Just makes 'em mad and more determined to get you. Your goal when you pull the trigger is putting 'em down—permanently." Harsh words spoken in a harsh voice. "Goliaths don't usually wear armored gear, like the border patrol. Why would they? When's the last time you saw a worker bee totin' one of these?" He palms the pistol and gestures toward the scarecrow, who now has a ragged hole where his nose should be. "Try aiming and pulling the trigger."

The gun is an anchor holding her hand in place along her thigh, weighing down her arm, defying her silent command to rise.

"Two hands on the grip. There'll be a bit of kickback, but nothing you can't handle," Debs cautions. "Brace yourself and you'll be ready. Breathe. Hold it firm but don't choke the life out of it. And squeeze the trigger, don't jerk."

Pretend it's him—the shave-head devil and his goons. Raise your arm and steady your hand until the laser marks the spot and the red dot is the first drop of blood that will spill until it starts to flow like a river. How delicate the trigger feels under my finger... and now, just the slightest pressure...

Staggered by the recoil and the reverberating boom, Angel draws in and tightens up, solid through the core.

Debs nods his approval. "Good. Try this. Push forward with your firing hand as you pull back with your supporting hand. Equal pressure. Feel the tension? Good. Again."

Nine more rounds in rapid succession, barely pausing to draw breath or relax and retighten the muscles in her arms, finger pressing the slim trigger, firing on and on until she hears the hollow click of an empty magazine. Ten spent casings glitter at her feet like fool's gold and a wisp of smoke veils her sight like an unanswered question.

Inspecting the straw man, Debs grins. "Two to the head,

one more in the neck, one to the chest, one in the belly, one to the shoulder, only four complete misses. Not bad for a beginner. You'll do your share of damage."

As the heat from the pistol radiates through her hand, she feels her innards roil and churn. Fighting the urge to vomit, she thrusts the gun into Debs' hands, and makes a mad dash through the trees. Sputtering to a stop, she squirms through a gap between two boulders, away from the light of the sun-scorched afternoon, puking her guts onto the roots of a scraggly pine.

Debs finds her lying in the filtered shade of a shagbark hickory, where the air feels much cooler. She stares up into the sheltering umbrella of its foliage, pondering how it is that some people only ever said green to describe the color of its wondrous, lobed leaves, while others seem to know a different word for every variation in tone and tint: emerald, jade, moss, olive, chartreuse, holly, myrtle, pistachio, lime. Which is she? Does it even matter any more?

Debs paces the circumference of the circle of shade, as if waiting for some form of acknowledgement. He makes a noisy show of clearing his throat, acting like some old sweat nervously waiting on his performance review or a dog circling a favored resting spot, unable to commit itself to sleep.

"Stop already!" She scolds. "You're just stirring up the heat."

He hunkers down beside her, groaning under his breath as his knee joints pop with a loud crackle. "Angel, I know you think you can't do this but—"

"You're wrong. I'm not afraid I can't do it. What's truly scary is that I know I can."

Confusion on his face runs smack into her steady stare.

"In my mind, every single one of those bullets was going straight into someone's head. First it was the shave-head. Then one of his goliaths. And then the bastard with his hand on the water line. And the jerk who programs Iris and the swag—any swag—just because he was born a swag—and knows who his real parents are." Her voice is cold, clipped, though inside her head the words are flaming.

"Anger used in the service of a righteous cause is not evil," he says, eyeing her.

"Sounds like the voice of Galt."

Silence fills up the space between them like a fog, thick and chilly and unpleasant, swallowing up the things they might have said, should have said, until Debs reaches out and clasps Angel's hand.

"Time to try the rifle."

Afterwards, in the shack, he lays the pistol on the table and digs into the duffel bag. Working quickly, he stuffs a slim rectangle of black metal with a glimmer of brass into the grip, pulling the slide back and releasing it to chamber the first bullet. Then he pulls the clip out again and nestles one more cartridge atop the others.

"Thirteen. Yer lucky number," he says grimly.

35

The Valley of Elah

THE GREEN PING IS ADVANCING south by southeast. They've watched it for a day as it slowly but inexorably makes it way toward their position. When it first appeared on the screen, Angel felt a thrill crackle up her spine, sharp as an electric shock. She checked its progress on the hour. Now the thrill is muffled by a growing dread, a shifting burden heavy as a stone in her stomach. She checks every fifteen minutes, every five, her eyes fixed on the green dot, as if to either stop its movement or drive it onward at a faster pace, by the sheer force of her desire. She's a jitter of motions: feet tapping, knees jiggling, fingers digging at her ragged cuticles. Finally she jumps up from the log on which she's been perched.

"I can't sit here and wait for him to find us," she hisses.

Debs nods. "Wolf it is, then."

They travel light, the pistol tucked in its holster, strapped under the slight swell of her belly, the rifle slung across Debs' back, along with a rucksack stuffed with go fuel, Debs' nickname for their canteens and meal packets. They hike for a mile or so, hugging the ridgeline, until they reach a sloping glade dotted with purple coneflower. The drooping petals are sunbleached to a faded mauve, their once-coppery cores of ripening seeds burned

black under the scorching sun. Yet miraculously they stand, re-
silient in the face of drought, taproots sunk deep. Dots of yellow,
bright and drab, dip over the seed heads. Goldfinches, male and
female, feasting.

Angel starts forward, preparing to descend, but Debs grabs
her wrist.

"We keep to the high ground. Sit and wait," he says, gesturing to the boulders that jut from the crest of the hill.

She hasn't the old man's patience. Keeps pulling the embed
reader from her pocket to check the goliath's position, once,
twice, a third time in the span of less than ten minutes, until finally Debs plucks it from her hands and tucks it into his rucksack.

"Now we walk by sight, not by faith." He inclines his head
toward the woods spreading at the base of the slope. "That's
where your eyes should be."

Debs lifts the scope to his eyes, slowly scanning from left to
right. Shakes his head, holds it out for her to take. She brings it
to her eyes, but hands it back almost immediately. She doesn't
like the scope, feels it limits her vision. Dreads she'll miss something on the periphery. Like looking at the forest and seeing
only the trees.

Her legs start to cramp and her tailbone to ache. She senses
the shifting presence in her belly. She unfolds her legs and begins
to stand, when she feels his hand on her shoulder, forcing her
back down. He slowly extends his other arm, the one that ends
in that hideous claw sheathed in its black glove.

Nothing. She sees nothing but the trunks of trees. Then she
latches onto the movement. A black mass prowling in the midst
of the stationary grays and browns. Two of them. One tall, vertical. The other low, horizontal.

Debs sidles behind the slab of rock jutting from the ridge,
a makeshift sniper's nest. But Angel is frozen, even as she feels
that first hot trickle of alarm seep along her backbone. In that

instant, she realizes that she'll never be able to go through with this. Carry out the plan.

Let it roll me away. This tide of fear. And for a split-second she is gone, the great wave of panic crashing through her chest and carrying her off, in its tumbling, wild, white embrace. *Somewhere. Somewhere else.* Until she feels the very real earthbound tug of a hand on her wrist again, pulling her down and to the side, behind the very real barricade of the rock outcropping.

"I'll take the hound," Debs whispers, shouldering the rifle, resting its long barrel on the rock. "The goliath is yours."

I can't. Do the words rage only in her head or do they actually escape her lips? She turns her head away from the slope to face Debs, to make her confession that it's just not in her, the killer instinct, never was, never will be, it was just talk, wild thoughts conceived in loss and grief, born of fury. But he's focused on his target, eyes to the rifle scope, fingers curled on the trigger, so still and steady, a statue molded to one task and one task alone.

A shuddering blast, metallic, a whistle-rumble. A bass thrumming in her head, loud to the point of pain. And then an instantaneous muffling of all sound, shocking. Sparks of yellow flash, rising to the sky on the wings of the tiny goldfinches.

A second, crackling explosion.

Too fast, it's happening too fast. Yet she experiences it in half-time, too, when she shifts her gaze from the old man's profile, cheek and jowl to the rifle stock, back to the slope. A huge black form is charging, thigh-deep in the coneflowers, mowing the slender stalks down with each plunging, behemoth stride. The hound is gone, its body down somewhere in the field of flowers.

Another crack, a whistling. Debs is rolling away from her, rifle thudding to the ground, his gloved hand hovering over his right shoulder.

The dry stalks protest as they snap, but softly, in sighs and whispers and rustling moans. The goliath has dropped low now, slowed his movement, but his black mass is still advancing up the slope.

"Put him down!" Debs growls through clenched teeth.

The black mass is maybe fifty feet away. And her pistol is still in its holster.

"Put him down now!"

He will do this. He will do this for me.

"Now!" Debs shouts. He shifts behind her and jerks the gun out. The sleeve of his shirt along his upper arm is ripped, blotched bright red. He roughly takes her right hand and wraps it around the grip before falling back, his claw hand mashed to his right shoulder, where the red oozes through the ragged edges of torn fabric.

The black mass is low in the coneflower, thirty feet away. Another whistling crack.

"Take your shot!" Debs orders.

The mass comes on, low, zigging and zagging.

Not like the scarecrow, so still, so vulnerable. I can't. But her trembling finger finds the smooth curve of the trigger.

Twenty feet, maybe.

The black mass freezes. Long enough for the pinpoint of red to focus on its target. Her target. A pale blotch amidst the black. What she thinks is a cheek.

One squeeze. The boom crackle and kickback cause her to lose her balance, carom off the boulder. A breath of air afire. The black mass is still there, moving forward again. Fifteen feet, maybe.

Her finger curls again. The pinprick light locks. The pale swath again. A neck? Another squeeze. But this time she's braced for the recoil and the stench. Still the black mass comes. And she squeezes the trigger a third time.

The mass staggers, clutches at the crimson blossom that flowers at its neck and cheek. Sinks to its knees. Slumps to the right.

As Angel sags, leaning back against the boulder, turned away from the blood life seeping out only a few yards away, she finds herself acutely aware of a sound that is not natural . Not a *normal* sound. A fragile gurgling whistle. An intake. An exhalation. A sound of extremis.

She feels the rotation of the earth reclaiming her body, slowing her panting breath, draining the adrenaline from her muscles. Her shoulders go slack, her head lolls. She can't even keep her eyes open. As if death will claim her, too.

In time, the clammy sweat of fear becomes the everyday sweat of sitting under a relentless sun. She cuts her eyes toward the old man next to her, focuses on the scarlet stain that has set in across his ragged shirt sleeve.

Seeing her gaze, he shakes his head. "Just a nick. Stings like hell, but I've been dinged worse." He adjusts his arm, flinches, shrugs. Flinches again. "Can't take three shots to put your target down. You'll run outta ammo long before you run outta targets." He pauses, considering. "But still, you did it. Made it through your first. Some say it's the hardest. Not sure 'bout that. Guess it shouldn't ever get easy."

Angel turns her eyes back to the view before her: the ridge line, the tired greens of the grove of trees beyond, the swath of washed out blue above. In the turning of the earth, she sits, until the blood rush has slowed, until death has ceased its awful song and the sounds of the wild have replaced the noise of her own body. A bird call and its reply. The hum of insects. Burbles and hisses, tiny creaks. A great living noise, a blur of noise that obscures the pulse of her surging lifeblood, subdues it, tames it until she can utter aloud a sound of her own.

"How will we—bury—" She can't bring herself to look in either direction. Not towards the black mass. Not towards Debs. Just stares straight ahead and up, where a hawk is gliding, a dark arrow in the sky.

"We won't. He may be dead, but that embed's still transmitting. They'll come looking for him. And we'll be here to greet 'em."

36

All Warfare is Based on Deception

THE COORDINATES FOR THE EMBED PING haven't changed in twenty-four hours. No response on the comlink. Less than a week and Tanner's down two men. One presumed dead, the other just... gone. Vanished off the zoom as if erased from the system memory.

He has worried the shred of skin hanging from the side of his thumbnail until it seeps blood. Not something he's in the habit of doing. Not since he was a punk kid.

One side of his brain methodically recites the logical possibilities. The Shawnee is a wilderness strewn with danger. Trails that end abruptly, precariously, at the edge of twenty, thirty, sixty-foot drop offs, the sandstone rock fragile, brittle. One slip of a foot, a careless turn, and a man could be free-falling, plummeting to a surface that forgives no man his mistakes. That could explain the case of the one. But not the other. One might disappear into the Shawnee, but not disappear altogether.

And yet. The caves. Not true caves, but still. Get back far enough inside, far enough from the opening of one of those rock overhangs and the signal could conceivably be obstructed. And so, the question. What would cause his man to do that? Was he lying in wait for his quarry? Hiding from something? Cowering in fear? It is testimony to Tanner's mindset that the truth of the matter never even occurs to him. He resolves to send them out in pairs. True, they will cover less ground. But he gives a mental shrug. He has changed the order. *Bring the androg in. Alive.* He digs the edge of his fingernail into the sore flesh. Grins in the face of the sting, the burn.

It will take more time. But then, time—what was that he'd heard said of time? Oh so long ago, when he was just a boy in the Superior. Ten, eleven maybe. Cooped up in the house on a day when the rain descended in sheets like a liquid veil hiding the world. Roaming from room to room, from window to window, peering out like a caged beast, like the enormous spotted cat who paced back and forth behind its bars in the Hive's menagerie, the private zoo the corporate director kept for scientific purposes. Or perhaps his lady just liked to eye the creatures. Or revel in the accomplishment of assembling them. "My very own private ark," he'd heard her exclaim one day to a visitor, while he helped his father muck out the filth from the concrete floors of the cages.

How he'd loathed that. Refused to accept that was his fate in life. His track.

So on that rainy day, when he'd paced the small caretaker's house like the lady's prized jaguar and he'd stumbled upon his father reading the biblio, it hadn't been that difficult a decision. The bond was not, had never been, strong.

Why had he paused at the door to his father's bedroom in the first place? He wasn't in the habit of seeking him out, preferring the company of his mother. Where was she that day, that moment? Up at the big house, the manse, sweating over the blue flames of the industrial range, preparing yet another flamboyant, endless feast for the bushwazees, as she called them, the locusts from the Hive who swept in and out, devouring everything in their paths.

So why had he sought his father out that day, that moment? Tanner wasn't sure how he felt about the concept of fate, of destiny. But he knew it was this moment that had changed his life. That stormy afternoon when he put his eye up to the gap in the door that his father had left ajar. And why had his father done that, left it that way, instead of shutting it properly? Was he asking to be found out?

In the cool white light of the floorlamp, with the biblio open on his lap.

Maybe the answer was written on his father's face, with its taut skin stretched too thin over his fine bones. If Tanner had only been able to read it.

But his father had just smiled, like a man who has finally found the thing he's mislaid, discovers it's been sitting right where he'd thought he'd left it all along, and why has it taken him so very long to see it?

His father tapped the page. "Tomorrow and tomorrow and tomorrow, creeps in this petty pace from day to day, to the last syllable of recorded time, and all our yesterdays have lighted fools the way to dusty death." He closed the biblio with a snap. "Shakespeare. William. Your namesake."

Placing the biblio on the endtable next to his rocking chair, he stood and crossed the room to his closet. Pointed to the upended floorboard. To the hole next to it. Crouched, thrust his hand into the blackness, removed another black-covered volume.

"They thought we'd be the children of the revolution, but they didn't move quickly enough, didn't purge fast enough. And so..." He waggled the biblio, holding it out as if expecting the boy to take it. "Because it is written that man shall not live by bread alone. Nor by the feed."

No words passed between them. The boy Tanner had backed away slowly, as if to avoid startling a wild creature he'd stumbled upon in a clearing, feeding at the carcass of some dead thing, horrifying and fascinating at once. And two days later, he'd gone to the security guard who patrolled the grounds in his spit-shined black boots, leather bandolier strapped across his broad chest, and he'd set the severance into motion.

It did not creep in a petty pace.

His father was gone by the following morning.

The strategy is clear to Angel from the pattern on the embed reader. The goliaths are hunting in pairs now. Complicating, but not unanticipated. From the trajectory of the pings, it appears that two are heading for the slope where the body of their comrade lies, while the others are diverging in opposite directions, eventually dropping off the screen altogether.

Her stomach grumbles, but the chicken stew sits uneaten, congealing into a gooey glob in the open packet. *I can't sit here and wait.* She kicks a pebble, watches it tumble and come to rest again. Closes her eyes. Tilts her head, feels more than sees the orange glow of sunlight seeping through the thin layer of skin.

The hunger is there, gnawing at her innards, but not overwhelming, not yet. It is a goad, not a distraction. Drives her onward, on the trail of the deer, which move through the clearing tentatively, lifting and placing their delicate hooves, grey with travel dust, as if the hard-packed dirt will shatter with one wrong step. They've found grass to graze, at last, after an endless stretch of barrens, but they can't ease to the task, can't give in to their hunger. They sense the presence of something malevolent, just out of sight, just beyond the fringe of trees at the far end of the wispy meadow.

The she-wolf instinctively knows that the wide-open plain favors her prey. Full-grown and healthy, a deer can outrun the swiftest wolf. But in the dry riverbed that meanders along the western edge of the clearing, on the round stones strewn between its banks, the deer, pressed into a panic, will stumble.

And so she moves in, stealthily at first, belly to the ground, then assertively, darting back and forth, sowing confusion, preventing escape, zeroing in on the doe that lags behind, older, weaker, with ribs that ripple under a dry, patchy coat, the color of surrender. Black eyes flash liquid white as the agitation rises. White tails pricked in alarm, like flags, as the deer bound. The breath is ragged in the she-wolf's throat and nose. She cuts quickly, heads off the weak link, draws alongside and is struck by the sheer size of this prey. Senses something wrong. Falters in her stride, snarling in frustration. Doubts her ability to take down this behemoth thing, weakened as it may be. To bring it down by herself. Alone.

"You gonna eat that?"

Startled from her reverie, Angel blinks. Shakes her head.

"You need to eat some. If not for you, then for that baby there." The old man nudges the meal packet towards her. When she ignores it, he picks it up, takes her hand and wraps her fingers around it, like he'd done with the pistol.

"Eat," he order. "You'll be no good to the mission if you're fainting from hunger."

37

Fine Things

"I'm 'bout to faint from hunger. C'mon, chica, to the kitchen." *Em standing in the doorway, beckoning.* "C'mon."

The mujer's sleek kitchen was all black and gray and white, slick surfaced, metallic and forbidding, like anything you touched would turn your fingers to ice or slice them bloody. But we braved it anyway, opening the smooth paneled cabinets with quick tugs on the spotless chrome knobs. Everything we saw, we desired. Purplish black olives in a tall slender bottle, bobbing in a murky fluid, lush and salty. Intensely maroon cranberry chutney in a squat jar, sweetly tart licked from the tips of our fingers. Crackers thin as paper, their white surfaces blistered with brown, so crisp to the bite, yet so melting on our tongues. Hard cider, golden in long-necked bottles, bubbly in the nose, warm in the throat and belly, sending a frothy rush to our brains.

We didn't create a deliberate mess, not the debris of vandalism. Just the streaks and smears and crumbs and puddles that any feast would strew across a banquet hall. But after we'd eaten our fill, Em threw me a towel and we wiped it all down til it was slick and shiny and we could see our faces in the surfaces again.

We headed upstairs because Em needed to clean the mujer's bathroom. The Director and his wife didn't have a child so most of the rooms were empty, gaping holes. But their bedroom was lush, the *broad bed spilling pillows, fabrics tumbling from rods atop the windows, more fabrics underfoot. While Em sprayed and wiped and scrubbed, I idled and drifted. And there it was, on the dresser. The mujer's box. But a lift of the lid brought nothing but a frown. Guess she didn't trust her help, because there wasn't much glimmer nestling there. A pair of simple gold hoops, small, delicate. A plump silver heart on a fine chain. Tiny studs with glittering chips embedded in gold prongs. Maybe she had the rest locked up somewhere else.*

I popped open the closet's folding doors. A big walk-in, bigger than the biggest bedroom in a sweat's house. The mujer's clothes, mostly. And shoes! A wall full of little slots and each slot had a pair of swag kicks tucked in it. Every frackin' color you can imagine and some you can't. High heels, low heels, no heels. The mujer had kicks for every day of the frackin' year.

Back of the closet, there was a rackload of dresses, fancy swag gowns, hems brushing the floor. Oh, how they shone under the bright light. And sighed and murmured sweet memories under my hand as I drew it along the row. The rustle and swish.

"Try one on." Em, leaning against the doorframe. "Go on, ya know ya wanna." When she gestured to the dresses, the pungent smell of bleach wafted from her hand. I gave her the cray eye roll, but she strode past me and pushed a swath of dresses aside.

"This one, chica. It's screamin' your name," she purred, holding out the hanger to me.

The color was right, a warm peach shimmering with spangles across the bodice and billowing from the waist down in layers of filmy cloth, sheer as veils. Its length worked, but the cut was wrong, the pattern sized for the bruja's larger frame. It hung rather sadly from my shoulders, aching for a mistress to fill its generous seams.

"Maybe if you took that binding off. Let your girls go free," Em mused.

I cut her a look. "You know that can't happen." Then I turned back to the full-length mirror, frowning at the swath of beige that peeked out from the scooped neck of the bodice, and the bones that jutted above it and my too-long neck that stretched above the bones. At the wolf cap and its perky ears perched on the crown of my head. At the white respy sagging at my throat. At the agate stone that hung from its silver chain. At ridiculous me. That's when I noticed I'd forgotten to wear my talis.

"You done? I should get home," I muttered, reaching behind my back for the zipper.

"Oh, chica, you're no fun. Try another," Em cajoled.

I shook my head. "Dress-up's over. I'm not your life-sized doll."

She stuck out her tongue and pouted.

And then we heard the boots.

38

The Stars Over the Shawnee

THEY ARE SURPRISINGLY EASY TO KILL. After the panic of the first, the second and third go down with an ease, with a matter-of-factness that stuns her only later when she lays back, her body firmly anchored by rock and earth, her eyes fixed on the wash of stars spilling across the dead of night sky.

Slightly more economy this time. Two bullets for each. Debs again dispatching the hound.

"They're not men. Not human beings. If that's what gives you pause, makes your finger hesitate," the old man had said, as the green pings had moved inexorably toward their sniper's nest. "It's natural you should feel that way. That you can't bring yourself to take a life, no matter how despicable. But they're not humans, not in the sense we are." He had tapped the glass where the green dots pulsed. "They lost their humanity long ago. The day they left the womb, the day the embed was injected under their skulls."

Angel had wanted to argue that wasn't true. That she had known one of them. That he was a human being. A good boy. That he lived and breathed and walked and talked and felt, was caught up in the same wide web of emotions as she. And then it struck her. While she lived her life, her emotional life, ascending the peaks of mountains and tumbling into the deepest valleys,

Mars and the few other kids she knew seemed to reside on a broad flat plain that stretched on forever.

The walking grinbees.

Except for Suraj, who, sans embed, also growled and grinned his way along the heights and the depths that life threw in his path.

And Em.

Had the girl been another traveler who walked in the blur? The image of the child, the cruel red rose blossoming across her chest, overwhelms Angel and she blinks hard, once, twice, refocusing her stare on the great dark bowl upturned above her head.

A streak. A flash. There, then gone. She blinks again, head pounding. Another streak. It's not the zoom, which moves at a stately pace as it trolls the sky. Is this some new instrument of control?

She squints at the old man, just yards away. Is he awake? Did he see it, too? For once, he appears to be genuinely asleep, trusting her watch. She palms the embed reader, thumbs it to life. Its face glows gray. Blank. She should wake him now. Should try to get some sleep herself. A sharp bulge in the boulder digs into her back, into the tender spot near the kidney. She shifts. Feels the creature inside shift, too, take a jab at her ribcage, making its presence known. She puts her hand to her belly. Presses back, feeling the outer wall flex under the tiny pressure from within.

Who are you?

Out of the corner of her eye, she catches another line of light traced in a split-second over the sky, gone in the time it takes her to draw in a sharp breath, in the time it takes the creature to flex its will again. Staring fixedly now, willing her eyelids to stay open, the muscles in her neck crying out from the severe angle she holds, she keeps catching them, these streaks and flashes, but only in the periphery, never looking exactly in the right spot at the right time to catch them full on.

A nudge. She startles. Soundless he'd been, stealthy as a cat on the prowl.

She points up. "Something's happening."

The next streak comes, a long one ending in a white hot spark, like a far-off firework exploding.

"Meteors," says Debs, matter-of-factly, as if it was the least unusual thing in their long day. "August. It's the Perseids. Never seen a meteor? Guess your pop made you obey curfew." He chuckles. "Wasn't raisin' you to be a guevara, was he?"

Another streak.

"Some call 'em shootin' stars, but that's not accurate. They're just bits and pieces of space rubble. Debris from a comet. Earth passes through the orbit where dust and rock are trailing, the garbage dump. Scraps enter our atmosphere at incredibly high speeds. Burn up. Shatter. That energy's the glow, those trails of light. Funny thing is how tiny they really are. Size of a pea. Some, a grain of sand. Yet look at the show they make."

It's she who feels small in this moment. Infinitesimally small. *I know nothing. I'm s'posed to be a meme. Keep the knowledge, pass it on. And I know nothing.*

"How—how do you—know?" she whispers.

"Don't believe me?"

"It's not that. I just—how do you know? All that you know?"

She senses him shift his weight from one foot to the other, hears the scuffle of his booted foot in the dirt.

"I've seen. Read. Worked. Used my hands to make and measure things. I've lived a life." His voice takes on a brittle quality. "Why you think they dumped the memory? Burned the books? Incinerated the past? Why's the Hive so keen to get rid of people when they hit the magic age? It's not about the breakdown of the body. It's about accumulated knowledge. The passing of knowledge. That's dangerous to them. They want you to have only what they feed you."

A deep breath. A touch on her shoulder, barely there. "Get some sleep. Four more to go."

"Plus Tanner."

She thinks it might be the first time she's uttered that name.

But she doesn't fall asleep. Not immediately. Not in that moment of total exhaustion—body and mind and heart benumbed, bereft of feeling. In that moment, just beyond the veil of stars, Serafina's eyes glimmer. But when Angel silently cries out—*I'm coming*—the eyes narrow, darken.

Not yet, querida. Hasta siempre. Forever is not come. Will you leave your work undone?

But in the doing, what am I becoming?

The old man's words reverberate in her mind, as if echoing off the walls of a dark room. *They're not humans.* But they are, those men they call goliaths. Behind the epithet, lies the man, the flesh and blood human. And she's taken their lives. Cut them down in the chill of a moment without a thought of who they were, under the black uniform.

There has to be humanity left inside the skin, if only a shred, a scrap. There has to be. If not, then how would the world ever be remade? Who would be left to remake it?

Or is that just another slogan? Empty words tracing an empty dream.

The path she's walking is twisted and dark, like the trails of the Shawnee. It will take its toll. This she intuits. And she may well lose herself along it.

To kill another is to kill yourself. A little bit at a time.

"*Pain, it's mi amigo. A reminder that I'm still breathin'.*"

Ah, Em. Em.

So she draws the hunting knife from her pocket, its handle cool to the touch. The blade slips through the flesh of her forearm—once, twice, three times—meeting no resistance, as if parting a liquid curtain. Tally marks slashed on a body, rather than a bedroom wall.

In the pink-tinged light of dawn, the flies are a shimmering transparent black veil, wafting gossamer and silken, in the wake of an unfelt breeze. The rot smell, sick and sweet, is up in Angel's nose, heavy, tangible as snot. When Debs thrusts the last meal packet at her, some gellified mass of meat and noodles, she doesn't have time to turn away before she starts retching, bent at the waist. But it's a dry heave, nothing coming up but ache and fear and disgust.

"Didn't think to bring some Vapo with me," he says, without offering comfort. "Gives you something stronger to smell on." But he doesn't appear bothered by the ripening stench.

"I can't stay here!" she pants, stumbling up the slope toward the ridgeline.

"It's the surest way—"

"Wolf, not spider!" she gasps, as serrated pain knifes from the base of her spine down her right leg. Only his vise grip on her bicep steadies her as she falters, keeps her upright as she trips on the rocks.

"You can't bail now. You're swimming the river and you're midway between either bank. Makes no sense to turn back. You've already come so far. Got to keep going to the other side, because if you stay where you are, you can only tread water for so long. You'll drown."

"Can't stay here, with..." Finishes her thought with her eyes, the furtive, sliding glance over her shoulder, where the flies waver and scintillate, rising and falling and rising over the motionless black masses. But when she tries to step forward, that excruciating pain slides down her leg again. The wince gives it away.

"What hurts?"

She steps, gasps, gestures, pressing her hand to her tailbone. "Goes down my leg."

"Let's get you back to the cabin." He hesitates. "Have you checked the reader?"

She digs it out of her pocket, shoves it at him.

A quick glance, a nod. "Yeah, let's go. Here, lean on me," he says, slipping his arm, the one grazed by the bullet, with a wound that still seeps a little fresh blood when he moves too suddenly, around her waist. "The walking wounded," he chuckles. "You and me. We'll take it nice and easy."

In the shack, she lies on the cot, breathing in and out, slow and steady, trying to tamp down her nerves, to avoid any movement that might bring the pain screaming back. She watches the old man fumble about, attempting to clean his wound, blackish now, caked with dried blood. His claw hand is both too blunt and too sharp an instrument to do the delicate work, and as he swipes at it with a ragged gray cloth the scabs tear away, re-opening the small gash. Fresh blood trickles, scarlet bright.

"Stop," she huffs, swinging her legs over the edge of the cot, standing, wincing in anticipation of the pain. She hobbles to him, plucks the now-bloody rag from his claw, splashes it with fresh water from his canteen, wrings it out, douses it with peroxide from a dented plastic bottle. The liquid sizzles and foams. She daubs delicately at the wound. When he doesn't flinch, she pats more forcefully.

His muscles tense under her hand. He's feeling the sting, but refusing to acknowledge it. She wipes, squeezes anti-bac gel from its crinkled tube, spreads it with the tips of her fingers. The paper wrapper containing the bandage is yellowed, soft as tissue, but the gauze inside is still pristine white. She wraps it around the meat of his shoulder, secures it with tape from a battered roll, tape that is still, remarkably, sticky enough to hold. Surveys her handiwork. Nods.

"Thank you," he mutters, tugging on a denim shirt that has faded, over time and use, to a robin's egg blue. "Shoulda been on the nursing track."

She shrugs. "I fix things."

Later, after they've ravaged a pot of porridge, bland but fresh-tasting, free of the vague plastic taint of the pouched food, after they've scraped their bowls to savor every last morsel, she says, almost under her breath, "I can't go back there."

She tenses, waiting for him to argue, to cajole, to convince, to ask her to explain herself so that he can formulate a counterpoint. But he doesn't. Just nods. Takes the empty bowl from her hands.

"There's a place I want you to see."

39

In League with Stones

THREE BLIPS CONVERGENT at a single set of coordinates. Static. Silent.

Tanner has ordered the four with whom he still has contact to remain in the field overnight. To continue their pursuit. To avoid those coordinates.

He has never been an armchair commander, settling back in comfort to monitor the fray. Hanging to the rear while his men plunge into the danger zone. No, he has stalked the front lines of every action he has overseen. Every border skirmish and removal. Every surveillance and crush. Every sweep of every Bartertown and squatters' camp. He has hammered heads, crushed skulls, broken jaws and arms and legs. Left the bodies lie where they fall. Because he is a man. And a leader of men. And that is what a man and a leader does. And so he will see to it. Hike out to the coordinates. Come face to face with whatever is out there.

Gnarled faces jut from the rock wall, brows caught in perpetual furrow, mouth drawn in eternal frowns, like a cluster of giant men frozen in a spell cast by some sorceress of stone, a sister to the Gorgon Medusa. The sandstone contorts, perches precariously on the edge of hundred foot drops. Is slashed and creased and pockmarked with gouges, like the visages of men who have walked a rough road, thinking evil and doing worse, earning the faces they deserve. Ugly. Traces of blood and tears etched in the tracks and scars, the seams of red and brown. A warning to all who look upon them.

Live hard. Die harder.

Yet it is stunning, too, beautiful. Weird and wild and beautiful, this garden of stone at the top of the bluff, with its massive pillars and breath-taking overlook. A crumbling staircase and trail of cracked flagstone are the only signs that men, flesh and blood men, have ever lingered here, attempted in some small way to tame the untamable. To the east, the methane flares dot the scarred land of the gas mines, useless candles on a charred cake. To the west and north stretch acres of trees, alive, dead, dying of thirst, muted greens and browns and grays. And beyond them a horizon soft, washed with a filmy haze.

Debs nods at the gray smear in the sky. "Dust storm."

Still Angel imagines she can see forever and forever in the late summer twilight, a bluish world deepening to indigo around the edges.

When the full gloom has settled and they've consumed yet another meal packet, the old man lets her take the watch. But after the stretch of near sleepless nights, she finds her eyelids too heavy, sliding closed, resisting her efforts to keep focus on the gap in the rock where the trail meets the bluffs. They've seen the pings on the periphery. But the dots appear to be headed away from their location. A little disappointing. And yet...

The she-wolf slinks, nose to the trail, trotting with an effortless, gliding gait. When the deer halt, ears twisting, she halts, too, throwing up her head, regarding them steadily, nostrils flaring as she studies the scent. Her gaze is strangely wistful. It's not born of affection, but hunger, a hunger as cruel as her fangs, as merciless as a knife. Her fur ripples in the breeze, gray with an undercoat of cinnamon, the wind ruffling the hairs and then smoothing them, so that the vague hints of red appear and disappear. An illusion.

When Debs awakes with an urgent need to relieve himself, he glances over at Angel, sees she has fallen asleep on her watch. But seeing her face in the muted light of the lantern, he can't summon anger. In sleep, it's a child's face, unguarded, open, soft around the edges. He wants to check the embed reader, monitor those pings, see if they truly have retreated, but it's in her palm, resting against her belly and he can't bring himself to disturb her, wake her from this respite. He picks his way soundlessly over the rock and eases into the brush, moving like a cat in the night.

The she-wolf has singled out the chosen prey, the old female who staggers at the back of the herd. She lopes alongside, nipping at the slender legs, driving the doe away from the rest. The scent of it is up in her nose and throat, strong, full-blooded. She strains to keep her hunger-frenzy in check, to stay calculating, cunning, in control. She's close, so close. Ready to spring, to lunge, to grab at the vulnerable neck, to throttle and gash the petal-soft throat.

The pain is sudden, excruciating, the shock waves radiating out from the central blow, like sound shimmers out from the crash of a cymbal. The she-wolf staggers. The deer's hoof? Was that...

And then she's yanked to her feet, staggering like the wolf, like she's still in the dream, but that bolt of pain screams that this is the night and she's Angel and the hands gripping her arms are savage, a tight vise clutch that bends them behind her back, straining her shoulder bones until they feel as if they will pop from their sockets. Another stinging slap rakes her cheek.

"Stop. He said alive."

"Didn't say undamaged."

"Don't chance it."

Guttural, those voices. Harsh in the throat and the ear, like the grit of sandpaper against fingers.

Goliaths.

Her fingers tighten around the embed scanner, but it slides

in the sweat suddenly soaking her palm. A metallic clink. The weight of a steel bracelet clamps onto her right wrist. A jerk wrenches her other to a painful angle. Struggling, twisting, stomping, snarling through bared teeth, the she-wolf rampant. But in this useless resistance, she loses her grip on the reader, feels it slip from her fingers, hears the crack as it hits the unforgiving face of the stone. Sees the faint glint of the lantern light on its glass face as it skids, caroming off the boots of the goliath who'd slugged her, the one who now is turning toward another sound that pierces the night, an urgent sawtooth whistle.

As he turns, there comes a crackling boom and then he's twisting, falling away, another black mass thudding to the ground.

"Frack!" Her captor abandons his efforts to bind her. Wraps his tremendous forearm around her chest, clutching her directly in front of him, a flesh and bone shield. "Who's out there?" His breath sears her ear, the whisper rough and ragged with fear.

Mute, the she-wolf's thoughts are tumbling, banging up against each other, flashing like jagged blue-white bolts of lightning. Not coherent, yet leading to something. Scattered like pieces of a puzzle that she can't quite fit together, but she must, she must. To see the big picture.

To survive.

"Who's out there?" the goliath rasps again, squeezing her chest, the pressure such that she is sure the cage of her ribs must collapse, crushing her vitals.

Useless. Useless to claw at that massive muscled arm, solid as a steel coil. The other arm is extended and she knows without seeing that it ends in a gun. So she lets her arms relax, dangle at her sides, the weight of the metal cuffs anchoring her right wrist.

With the fingers of her other hand, she traces the savior sheathed in her cargo pocket, solid against her outer thigh. The edge of the handle, the sharp curve of the bolster, the straight edge of the spine, around to the thumb clip that will expose the blade.

"Bitch, you better tell me."

At least that's what she thinks he starts to growl, but his voice catches mid-vowel and sputters to a soft "oof" and a gasping "uuuhh," clenched surprise mixed with pain.

Because the she-wolf has bared her fang and sunk its five inches of high carbon steel into his flank.

40

Dying is an Art

AS HE WATCHES THE ORB SPIDER methodically weave its lace-like spiral web across the branches of the pine, its beautiful death-bringer, Mars remembers her squeamishness. How she loathed the creeping, crawling things of the earth. The things with multiple sets of legs. Things that crunched and oozed under foot. He can't picture her in this wilderness, making a bed in the humus, hunkering down amidst centipedes and pillbugs, clawing her way through the underbrush where webs hang like curtains, gossamer yet tenacious. It must be breaking her. Killing her. Slowly.

Or maybe she's toughened up out of necessity. Maybe the constant exposure has driven the fear out, made her immune. Knowing Merit, that seemed more likely.

Knowing Merit.

He's trying to think, to remember as much about her as he can, what he knows with any degree of certainty, before the pain kicks in, before the vise starts squeezing his skull. So much is gone, drained away, like water through a sieve. What remains are fragments: her long, slender, square-tipped fingers gripping a chess piece, the crown of the black queen, swinging it idly, to and fro, over the squares of the board. But he knows her mind is not idle. That she's plotting her move, a sly smile stretching her lips. Once she learned the game, she had been relentless. Beat him every time. And he'd loved it. Loved sacrificing himself to her triumphant gleam. Loved the shine of her.

Those lips, unexpectedly dry and chapped, in the twilight's purple gloom, skin bluish under the solar light on her porch, the evening he brushed them with his own, just to feel them. And the way she startled, stepping back from him, brushing her hand across her face, as if his lips were some foreign thing she'd stumbled into, a cobweb strung from rafter to rail.

He'd always known she was more girl than boy, not a true androg. Knew it in the way his body responded to her. Knew it in the way he longed to lower his head and bury his face in the hollow of her throat and simply breathe her in. Knew it way before the moment in the barn when he had cut his hand and hers and bound them in blood and unwound the veils that shrouded the mystery of her. The mystery that was Merit.

But now the pain comes clutching and his brain starts to explode a little, with white stars and ghost flares and all the colors shimmering at the corners.

It's time to hunt.

She has spent the small hours of the night watching the man die. A curious thing, death. A process, not a singular event. Here and now, a gradual one. Beginning with disbelief and denial in the flailing, useless, disjointed movement that only inflicts more harm, as the expansion and contraction of muscle accelerates the pounding of the heart, the rush of blood through arteries and veins, the spurt and seep of it through the gash in the vitals. At first, an active struggle against the inevitable, like a fish flopping on the end of a line. But blood loss weakens the will and so the fight becomes passive. The limbs quiet, but the eyes still blaze.

Debs had wanted to hasten the process, to put the man out of his slow misery, like you'd put down a sick or wounded animal, but Angel had stayed his hand.

The goliath has given over to acceptance now. She recognizes this as she lies beside the man, just beyond his reach, the lantern between them, casting a somber glow on his face, glinting in the whites of his eyes. His massive hand, which has been pressed to his stomach, as if to stanch the bleeding, slips a little, slides away in the slick of gore.

His is the face of a man neither young nor old. A face with broad planes and sharp angles. A face that belies the bones beneath the skin. A question spreads there, across that chiseled face, pooling in the eyes, blue eyes that hold her gaze. Not why. That is known. How, maybe? How had he come to this? How does anyone come to this?

Or maybe it's just the shadows cast by the lantern.

Through the time—minutes, hours—in which she watches life ebb from the body, she feels it grow in hers. Not the creature. Its shifts are subtle. Something else.

Eben had once tried to explain why he loved being a medic, why he pursued it with a passion. *"I won't deny there's a power to it. That feeling of having power over death. Of course, it's just an illusion, but it's a mighty one. Knowing you have the skill to ward it off with your own hands, with the decisions you make. People once prayed to gods, Merit, prayed for deliverance from sickness and pain and evil. And, in a way, I can do that. Be the deliverer. And it's no small thing."* He had shaken his head. *"My pride and my shame all mixed together. A strange feeling."*

Strange indeed. To stare at those eyes and see the light dimming, the life ebbing, the lips moving soundlessly, growing pale and paler still, like the flesh of something that lives hidden from the sun. To watch the essence of the man, the thing that made him who he was, drain out. To witness this diminishment, from goliath to man to body to shell. And to know she was the one who set it in motion. Holds dominion over it.

When the eyes are fixed, the pupils black even as she brings the lantern close, when the strong jaw softens and the lips go slack, when she reaches, with trembling fingers, to pinch the strangely cool flesh of the cheek, she feels the swell, something filling her, cool, thrilling, like the first swallow of icy water on a dust-choked day. A powerful feeling.

And she likes it.

Another slash of the knife across the forearm. Another tally mark to join the three scabs already crusted there.

The embed scanner is gone. Dawn reveals nothing but its loss.

"Probably at the bottom of the bluff. No sense looking. It's a tough mother, survived a lot, but a drop like that to a stone floor? Nothin's gonna put that humpty together again." Debs shrugs. "Two goliaths left? Plus Tanner. It's practically an even fight." He gives a tired grin. "Hell, I'd hate to be them."

They'd woke to muffled whines, hiked down toward the noise coming from below the bluff to the south, and found the pithound muzzled and roped to a maple.

"Too hard to get it up the bluff," Debs speculates. "Not climbers."

The only thing Angel regrets is that she has to waste a bullet to put it down. Debs' rifle is empty and by her calculations, she's already used eight of her thirteen bullets. The goliath's blood has dried on her shirt, leaving it stiff, prickly against the skin of her back. In the light, her eyes avoid the black masses. Instead, they skitter from boulder to horizon to tree line to merciless sky, pale in the sun's slanted glare. She picks at the dirt wedged under her fingernails, grown long. Wishes for her clippers to trim them. A random thought of the showerhead back home. The last time she'd stood under it, face to its warm, stinging spray, letting the water blast away the grime of the day. How wonderful it felt. How she took it for granted. The very act of it. Not realizing the wonder of it, the biological and physical miracle of it. The feat of engineering genius that brought it to her. She had just stood there, letting it do its work.

Coming clean.

She wants to vow, should she come out of this and find the way back to a life, that she'll never take it for granted, the simple act of showering, the simple act of turning on a tap and pouring a glass of water, clean and clear and cold. Wants to pledge this to whatever is out there, pledge to that something larger than herself. But she knows it would be a hollow pledge, a vow meant to be broken.

Because in her gut, she knows a sip of water *should* be something taken for granted. Not a miracle. Just a low-level need fulfilled, so that one can focus on something else, something bigger, something above and beyond mere survival.

The creature kicks at a tender spot just under her lowest rib.

And Angel realizes she is starving.

If death is a process, what happens after is as well. Far from being dead, a rotting corpse teems with life. Decomposition begins minutes after death and follows in stages. After the heart ceases its rhythmic beating, blood circulation and respiration stop, depriving cells of oxygen and the ability to remove waste. Carbon dioxide, the toxic by-product of chemical reactions, builds, causing an acidic environment. Enzymes eat through cell membranes, beginning with the liver and the brain. Eventually other tissue and organs begin to break down.

As the body slowly digests itself.

Weather, temperature, and moisture can hasten or delay the process. But in the end, the process will win out. Damaged blood cells spill from broken vessels, discoloring the skin. Body temperature plummets. Rigor mortis, the stiffness of death, sets in, starting in the eyelids, jaws and neck, working its way into the trunk and the limbs.

Inside the work continues, driven by bacteria. Enzymes produce gases that can bloat the body to twice its normal size. The peculiar, memorable smell of death is the product of these complex chemical reactions, a cocktail of acids, sulfurs, alcohols, nitros, aldehydes, ketones, aromatics. Combinations and quantities change as a cadaver goes through the stages of decomposition, from autolysis to bloat to decay to skeletonization.

As the body is stripped to the bone.

Tanner is ignorant of this science. What he knows is he has three men down, one missing and two more non-responsive on the comlink. His gut tells him he's lost all six. That all six are gone. Permanently gone. And that something is loose in this wilderness.

A sudden gust lifts the bandanna from his nose and carries that rotting flesh smell, sweet and sick at once, up the slope to him, rustling through the prairie grass, rattling over the dry heads of the coneflower, crackling through the leaves, with a sound like the spitting and snapping of flames.

And he can't believe he has not thought of this sooner.

41

At the Canyon's End

WITHOUT THE EMBED SCANNER, they are wandering, following a dry creek bed as it cuts its way through a steep-walled canyon. Another dying place that once teemed with life. A great forest now a graveyard. Gray trunks, some massive, some slender, rise and rise above the bulbous spread of roots. A desolate place, desolate beyond all reason, where beauty has been bled out, all the colors washed away, leaving gray upon gray upon gray. Sad. Obscure. Grim in its lack of birdsong. Even the warning screech of a jay is muted and far away. Up ahead, a smudge of fog hovers, strange in the sere air, and Angel imagines how cool the mist will feel on her skin.

Until the smell hits. And the realization. It's not fog.

The fire is a living, breathing entity. Malevolent. Ravenous. It roils, a turbulent orange ocean, the flames a hot, buoyant fluid washing over the land, consuming as its waves crash. Its furious hunger gives a deafening roar as flames lick at the parched bark, mouth the brittle grasses, tongue the sapless needles and leaves, which dissolve instantly to black ash. Its accomplice, the thuggish wind, carries the flame from treetop to treetop while it drives the conflagration along the ground, one bully goading another.

Get out! We need to get out of the canyon! The scream inside stops her in her tracks. Instinct cautions that, for now, the river bed, even dry, is the safest place. It lacks the fuel the flames crave, the desiccated vegetation the fire is greedily consuming.

Debs strips off his threadbare bandanna and douses it with precious water from his canteen. Shoves it up in Angel's face.

"Breathe through it, but not too deep," he chokes out, coughing as the heavy smoke seeps around them, filling the canyon. He wets the collar of his shirt and tugs it up over his nose and mouth. Then they are jogging again, stumbling over the loose stones of the creek bed, fleeing the flames.

The heat sears all. Skin, eyes, the insides of mouth and nostrils, throat, lungs. But the smoke is soft and harsh at once, stifling, suffocating one minute, jagged, knife-like the next. Every breath feels the opposite of life, and Debs knows that whichever way the fire is driving them, it is meant to end at a single destination.

Death.

Mars targets the column of smoke long before word of the fire comes over the comlink. In fact, by the time Tanner's squawks come through, the distant white flume is now an iron-gray wall, a wall that's moving, whipped by the strong breeze that blows from the southwest. Driven by that wind, the conflagration will, in turn, drive their quarry towards where Mars and his partner lie in wait.

Or so Tanner seems to think. What he calculates. If he's wrong, the fire will simply consume the target like every bone-dry stick, twig, leave, and blade of grass in its path. The Shawnee is acre upon acre of tinder, fuel for the flames.

Flee or die. Or die in flight.

For Tanner has changed his mind yet again. *Put the target down.*

Barnes, a veteran with a face and voice as flat and empty as the fields that stretch across Illiana, crouches slightly to the fore, wedged between two boulders, rifle propped at the ready, scope covering his eyes as he scans the canyon opening from right to left. Mars hangs back, hunkered down in the driver's seat of the overland. They'll need it to outrun the wildfire. A sense of heat presses up against the skin of his cheeks, heat that has nothing to do with the slant of the sunlight. The hound, quivering in the shotgun seat, sniffs and whines through its muzzle.

The movements all happen at once, or so it seems, simultaneous, not sequential. As if not governed by the laws of cause and effect. Barnes flips the viewscope up, lifts the rifle to his cheek, presses his eye to its lasersight. Two figures slip through the stand of spindly trees on the edge of the dry creek, in sight, then hidden by the slender gray trunks. In sight, then hidden again, by the wafting gray smoke, thick and thin. Flashes of orange spurt behind them, high and low.

The crackling booms are not simultaneous. They are distinct, and differ in intensity: one shot, followed rapidly by a second and then, a third. The figures in the trees freeze, then drop and disappear, bodies blending in with the thick layer of humus covering the forest floor. When the hound whines again and follows that with a clenched growl, Mars calmly puts a bullet in its brain. Vaulting out of the overland, he strides to Barnes, now slumped forward over the boulder, a crimson splotch spreading across his back. He tugs the scope from around the man's head and brings it to his eyes. Through the lens, Mars can see the figures amidst the smoke as they slither toward the thicker undergrowth, like sidewinding snakes. When one pauses and the head lifts, he thinks its face belongs to Merit. Thinks he recognizes its contours even through the smears of black soot and under the wild tangle of matted hair. Her nose, her mouth. Cheekbones, forehead and jaw. And yet, something is different.

The eyes. The look of them. In them. Feral. Almost savage.

And the stretch of her lips. The bite of the teeth. Almost vulpine.

Something stirs in his belly. Some strange dread, hollow yet thick, shrinking, expanding. He calls out her name, the one she no longer recognizes, no longer accepts. But she cocks her head at the voice, familiar in a once-upon-a-time sort of way.

And so he approaches, each step hesitant, a tentative progress, ever the man who's not sure he wants to get where he's going. Hands raised, empty, the gun tucked back in its holster. Coming in the posture of surrender. It's what he wants. What he feels in the tender parts of his body. To be soft against the body of this hard girl.

And so he calls her name again, the Corporate name, because it's the only one he knows.

"Stop." Not a shout. Just a clipped command, the voice curt but full-bodied. Undergirded with authority.

And Mars obeys. He's maybe twenty feet away.

The girl he knows as Merit pushes herself to her knees, a hand cradling her belly.

He marvels at the swelling there, can't place the significance of it immediately, this sight he's never seen before. And so his eyes are drawn to it, fixated on it.

"Merit." Statement, question, declaration, exclamation.

No time. There's no time. The fire snaps its jaws, opens its maw. The sharp crackle has become a roar, a beast unchained, growing more insatiable by the minute. The smoke drives them forward, coughing. Merit and an ancient being who propels her, arm wrapped around her shoulder, eyes white and wild in a soot-stained face.

"The overland. We can get to the road."

Mars is thinking this, but the words come out of the old man's parched and wrinkled mouth, in a guttural croak. He wants to wrap his own arm around her, but the look she slings, when he raises it, freezes the limb in mid-motion, sends it drooping to his side again, where it feels useless, almost detached, a phantom.

They scuttle past the black mass that once was Barnes. At the overland, the old man grabs the pithound by the collar and drags its lifeless bulk off the seat, letting it thud to the ground.

"Angel, here," the old man rasps, as he wastes precious time swiping at the blood spatters on the shotgun seat with the ragged sleeve of his shirt.

She trusts this decrepit bastard. Mars sees this, in the way she takes his hand, lets him assist her into the transport, fingers in a grip, skin stretched tight, paler splotches visible through the layer of filth, stark against the black gloved hand beneath it.

Who is this man?

But his question is not about identity, only affinity, what this man means to the girl. Though he tries to be stealthy and swift, his sheer size, his tightly-bound bulk, betrays him. Too slow. Ever the molasses boy, the thunder to her lightning. Because, as always, in one sleek motion, the girl he knows as Merit, the girl the old man called Angel, has a burner trained on him. Those black holes where her eyes should be, impenetrable. His only hope, the slight tremor quaking her hand.

That's what he counts on as he draws his Galt-issued weapon, the one they called the handcannon in boot camp. The one he, boastful, callow youth, nicknamed Fate. It's what he counts on as he lifts his own burner. And draws a bead on the old man's head.

It's the last mistake he makes.

42

Word as Like a Fire

IT'S ALL A COLD FLASH white hot sweat-soaked dry mouth crystal clear blur. All red white blood and bone fragments. The explosion caught in time, the frozen frame of life. There before her. Something she can't even blink away, because when she closes her eyes, for a split-second or an eternity, it's there, etched on the backs of her eyelids. The work of her hand. What can she tell herself to make the vision depart? To erase it? The work of her hand.

She stares at it. Folded in her lap. Outstretched, grasping at nothing. Clutching the door handle as the overland hits a cavernous pothole and the jounce sends her briefly airborne. When they reach a smoother track of paved road, she stares at it hanging casually from the arm now resting on the doorframe, elbow jutting. She knows she's looking at her hand, but all she sees is the spray of red and white, blood and bonechips.

She'd aimed for his right arm. Knows she aimed for his arm. Is certain she aimed for it. Thinks she aimed for it. Believes she aimed for it. And yet.

Leans forward to vomit, but there's nothing. Just retching. Painful dry heaves from the core of her. And a clutching there, as if another hand is clawing her from the inside, gripping, squeezing, twisting, battering. It's then she feels the ooze, the wet heat of it, between her legs. When she reaches down to probe, the fabric of her cargoes feels slick.

And the faint smear of blood on her hand is very real.

The overland is built for brute force, not for speed, but on the flat, smooth, well-maintained asphalt of the Southern Road, it's a serviceable steed. But they can't ride it forever. It's low on biofuel and its embed will be a focus of the zoom. Alongside the pavement runs the great trench where the water pipes are buried, the massive conduit from the lakes of the north. Does it still course with its life-giving fluid? Or has this pipe been shuttered, too? The land gives the answer, stretching to the horizons unplanted, gray barrens broken here and there by faded yellow, where withered stalks of foolhardy weeds dared to raise their heads to the hostile, unforgiving sky.

They have been trundling along for two hours, maybe three, and the sun should be settling in the belly of the west, but where its orange glow should suffuse the horizon, instead, a storm-colored wall billows. But these are not the anvil-shaped bringers of lightning and rain. And then it becomes a race to find shelter. The overland balks at sixty miles an hour, but Debs keeps the pedal to the floorboard, scanning left and right, searching for any structure, however dilapidated. But this sector has been swept years ago, the homes and barns and silos of the old independent farms bull-dozed, eradicated like vermin. Wayside fuel stations lie uprooted amidst the rubble of pulverized concrete. Shards of a past life. A hardscrabble landscape.

Sensing the futility, Debs steers the overland off the pavement and into the fallow fields, heading northwest, perpendicular to the dust storm, hoping to outrun its width. Keeping his clawhand on the wheel, he flips open the storage box between the seats, paws through it, comes up with a pair of wrap-around black-outs, pokes them at Angel.

"Put 'em on, now!" he shouts over the competing roars of the motor and the wind. He tugs at the bandanna that hangs limp from her neck. "Cover up!"

Barely a minute passes and they are swept into darkness as the wind screams in their ears, spewing a razor-edged stream of fine sand in their faces. The landscape is gone, swallowed by the tempest. Nothing exists but dust. They are consumed by it, twisting in its roiling belly. Grit scours the skin of his cheeks, grinds in his eyes and up his nose. Though his mouth is clamped shut, he tastes the fine grains on his tongue.

The engine of the overland sputters and chokes as it dies. It rolls along for a bit, carried by sheer momentum. When it comes to a stop, Debs pushes Angel out, settles her on the leeward side, down low behind the wheel well. Blind in the maelstrom, he feels his way around the transport to the cargo hold. Rummages through it, grasps the slick surface of a huge rain poncho. Fighting the gale, he drapes it over her, tucking it under her legs, between her back and the tire, then clambers underneath it, huddling next to her, holding firm as the wind yanks and tugs at the poncho, mad to carry it off, to expose them to its fury.

It's a morning. She knows that much. After an overnight rain. Which means she is young. Five, maybe six. She holds a hand. Is it Eben's? No, from the look of it, bronze, sturdy, long-fingered, it belongs to Serafina. The path they walk is paved with bluestone. Tiny pools of water linger in the low places on the uneven surface of the slabs.

"Spring is a wonder. A miracle," Serafina murmurs.

Where there had been nothing barely a week ago, now there is green, in the freshest shades of lime and chartreuse and apple, arching, stretching, reaching. Leaves, fronds, stems. An explosion of green.

"Every year. There's no growing immune to it. Every year. The astonishment of it." Serafina crouches and tugs Merit down beside her.

The leaf is rounded, delicately pleated and scalloped along its edges, like some fancy swag saucer, olive-green and velvety soft. Along its skin, the water drops cling and roll, sparkling in the slanted rays of the sun. Liquid diamonds.

"Lady's mantle. Alchemilla mollis. She cups her hand to hold

the morning dew."

She remembers extending a finger to one of the raindrops, piercing the surface tension that holds the bead in its perfect dome, lifting it to her lips, licking the wetness.

The taste was... green.

Angel holds tight to that, the taste, the spectrum of green, clings to it throughout the fearsome roar of wind and the rattle of dirt buffeting the makeshift tarp that lies over her, clings to the memory as fiercely as she clings to Debs' hand, the good hand, the hand that is malleable in her own, easing and tightening its own grip in return, the bones like liquid in her fingers.

In time—Minutes? Hours? Did the length of it really matter now, did anything?—the storm passes, the howl easing to a hum and then the hum to a hiss, the shifting of fine grains over a smooth surface.

"Wait," he says with a staying motion of his hand, as he slowly slips out from under the poncho. The slice of light she sees is gray, filmy, alive.

When he lifts the poncho again, the lower half of his face is hidden behind a white respy and blackout wrappers cover his eyes and he's holding another respy, gently slipping it over her head, fitting it carefully over her nose and mouth, delicately adjusting the band.

Shapeless, shifting. A mist-shrouded world, but dry as an ancient bone.

"Have to put some distance between us and this overland, before the zoom makes a hit. Find a new ride. Can you walk?"

As if she has any other choice? She nods.

The compass shows him north in this world without visible landmarks. And they move on with tentative steps, like new-walking toddlers testing their balance, arms outstretched, fearful of letting go of one support before grasping the surety of another, fearful of being marooned between landmarks and lifelines, with nowhere to go but down.

43

Madonna of the Trail

THE GIGANTIC WOMAN SPRAWLED in the waist-high weeds, half-buried in storm-driven dust, looks twice the height of an ordinary woman. Half the woman's stone face is hidden by the brim of a sunbonnet, the other by the shifted soil. A child clings to her skirts, pink face pressed to the swell of her broad hip. Small feet rest under the curve of her breast, but the body from which they spring is obscured under the dune of dirt.

With a sweep of his hand across her flank, Debs removes one layer of dust, and then another. As he works at her head, the rough rosy face, stolid, sad-eyed, yet resolute, emerges. As Angel shifts more dirt away, she discovers that the feet resting in the woman's massive hand belong to a babe cradled in the crook of her arm. Her other hand grips the barrel of a rifle. Debs brushes along the statue's toppled base and letters begin to appear, engraved in the stone block beneath the woman's booted feet.

MADONNA OF THE TRAIL

Debs hikes a foot up on the woman's ham-sized calf and clambers atop the statue's overturned pedestal. He brushes away the grit piled there, then sits back on his heels. "At Vandalia, Abraham Lincoln, member of the Illinois legislature first formulated those basic high principles of freedom and justice which gave the slaves a liberator, the union a savior," he says, reading the inscription.

Odd name. Has Angel heard it, somewhere in time, perhaps in Serafina's voice? In one of her stories? A man's name on the statue of a woman. Madonna of the trail.

"What's it mean?" Her voice is paper-thin and just as fragile, as she runs a finger over the coarse-grained cheek of the child, uses a fingernail to trace the groove that separate the locks of his stone hair. "Madonna?"

From his perch atop the monument, Debs scans the remains of the settlement surrounding them. "In the old beliefs, the Madonna was the mother figure." He eases himself back down to the ground.

"This?"

He shakes his head. "A metaphor." He digs at the front of the pedestal. "Honoring the pioneer women," he adds, pointing out the lettering. "Those who helped settle this land in the early days of the old Republic. Maybe Corporate sent a crew to dismantle it, but they didn't get around to blasting it to bits, like they've done to so many other monuments of the old nation. Or maybe it was vandalized by locals. When there were still some around."

He's already turning his attention elsewhere. To the shells of buildings, the hollowed-out remnants of an existence. Brick corners rising to nothing, supporting nothing but air. Skull-like storefronts, windowless, roofless, gaping holes, dirt forming dunes in the debris.

"Stay here," he says. "Goin' to scout around. See if there's something rideable."

Inside her, the creature squirms. She doesn't want to be alone. "No, I'll go with you."

The mansion, with its sharp, gabled roof and lacy ornamental spindles, must have been beautiful back in the day, fanciful and flamboyant as a gingerbread house. A round turret juts from the left side of its façade. A dirt-crusted bay window, bisected by a jagged crack dominates the right. Paint peels from the siding like giant shreds of pale blue skin and the wide porch hangs off the front of the house in a perilous slouch, a nail pop or two away from collapse. The tip of a tree stretches through a gaping hole in the roof.

"Wonder how the 'dozers missed this one," Debs mutters, eyeing the rotting stairs. But his focus shifts to the rickety shed squatting at the far edge of the property, caught in the stranglehold embrace of spindly tree branches, grey and leafless, skeletal fingers clutching through the years of neglect.

The door is shackled with a rusted padlock, but one good yank pulls it off its hinges. It gives a screech of protest as it reveals the dim innards strung with wispy cobwebs and littered with relics of days past. To Debs, it's a goldmine. There in the corner lean a pair of decrepit bicycles.

When the old man hauls them out from under the shroud of sticky webs, one is missing its front wheel. The other looks to be in fairly decent shape, considering its age. The tires are flat and the rubber feels dry and brittle when Angel gives them a squeeze. Slivers of cracks mar the sidewalls.

"Dry rot. Won't last long," she says.

"Don't need 'em to last long. Can get where we're goin' in a day."

She eyes him. But he's already turned away, scanning the shed.

"Where we goin'?"

"Old friends."

"But we—I—still have work to do. To finish."

"Yeah, but first we need to rest up. Regroup. No shame in that."

His eyes light on a compact, two-wheeled pod upturned in the other corner. A bike trailer for hauling children. They use a rust-scarred but operable hand pump to inflate the tires to the extent they dare. Angel cringes with each push of the handle, anticipating a blowout.

When the old man fumbles with the hitch, she brushes his hands aside, murmuring, "I got this." But by the time she mounts the trailer to the rear axle and has the bike and trailer in working order, dusk is settling with the last of the dust.

"We'll camp here. Head out at dawn," Debs says, eyeing the growing gloom.

They forego a fire and hunch inside the circle of wan light spread by the lantern, its battery slowly weakening. They scarf down a couple of protein bars, silence cloaking them, until Angel breaks it.

"I been thinkin' 'bout what you said."

"Said a lot. What in particular?"

"About where the orders came from. For the—" She's about to say 'removal,' but stops short and uses the real word. "The murders. I want the man who turned off the water. And the swag who gave him the order to do it."

His eyes are fixed on the lantern. "And so on and so on, until you reach the origin."

"Yeah, that's right."

He shrugs. "It's good to have ambition. To have big dreams." She can't tell if he's being sarcastic.

Then he shifts. Tugs at the zipper of his backpack. Angel tips the lantern towards him to illuminate the pack's interior, but he waves it away. He knows exactly what he's hunting and where it's located.

He draws out a small rectangle coated in plastic film. Dog-eared at the corners, crinkled along the edges, smudged all over, it's seen hard use and the touch of many hands. But the image is still clear enough. An image of a tall tower, curiously sinuous, its facade a billow of inward and outward curves, golden bronze in the stark sunlight glinting off its glass curtain.

Debs taps the image, holding it out to Angel. "You want the man who turned off the water, this is where you'll find him." He flips the picture over. On the other side is an image of a fortress-like building squatting against the backdrop of a swath of blue.

"Chicago. That's where the engineers are. Sit up in this tower," he turns quickly back to the first image, "and run this building, the waterworks," he says, flipping it over again, "for Lake Michigan and the Illiana aquifers and rivers."

Angel takes the card. Examines the Y-shaped tower with its three jutting prongs.

Debs taps the image again. "These are the men who follow the Hive orders."

"Then that's where I want to go," Angel says, holding the image out to him.

Debs nods, a little grin playing around the corners of his lips. He slips the card from between her fingers, tucks it back into its place in the backpack.

"You carry that with you? Wherever you go?"

He tucks his chin in the barest semblance of a nod.

"Why?"

"One can learn more from failure than success. Providin' you remember it. Let's get some sleep."

"D'you know his name? The water man?"

"Been years since I had that kind of intel. But where we're goin' we might be able to sniff it out." The bitterness that stretches the man's grimace is deepened by the shadows the lantern casts. "Sleep."

But sleep doesn't come. The knife digs deeper into her forearm this time, and twists, to bring the the bite, the spasm that should have seized the body in the moment of the killing, but did not. There is blood. And then there is blood. And she has spilled that which she once mingled with her own. Even as the blood seeps down into the crook of her elbow, she fingers the veins that pulses at her wrist and neck. Where the skin is especially thin and delicate. How easy it would be.

Serafina, I'm coming.

Querida, what you killed was not what you loved. Hasta siempre. Forever has not come. Will you leave your work undone?

The house beckons her to approach, sentinel silent in the night still thick with dust. She feels the specks float past her, settle on her forehead, kiss her cheeks above the respy, cling to her eyelashes. Mounts the porch steps cautiously, placing each foot lightly, testing its mettle under her weight before she commits. The boards sigh and chirp as they sag. When she leans back against a post, it creaks in protest, but ultimately holds.

Looking for comfort, she fits the buds in her ears and thumbs the vocoder to life.

"We are the hollow men. We are the stuffed men, leaning together, headpieces filled with straw. Alas, our dried voices, when we whisper together are quiet and meaningless as wind in dry grass or rats' feet over broken glass in our dry cellars... that's from a biblio. So many years ago I read it and it was written so many years before that. And still true. Angel, it was laid to waste. Laid to waste.

"Bonds broken. When those who had so very much still came to believe they didn't have enough. So afraid of losing what they had. When the possessive became mine, instead of ours. That's when it fell apart. When those for whom every day was a feast could not be moved to sweep even the crumbs from their table for the rest. Then it fell apart. When people turned to leaders who could not lead, weak men who hid behind a facade of strong words, a facade that splintered at its brittle seam, men and women with voices that incited resentment and fear and hatred, voices that pitted people, one against the other. For hatred, like fire, will burn and burn until it consumes everything in its path.

"And the storms raged. And the heat built. And the ice melted. And the oceans rose. And they did nothing. And the anger burned and boiled over and scorched the earth. That's how civilizations end. Fighting your brother for crumbs. Not with a bang, but with a whimper."

A sudden pop explodes in her head as the buds are yanked from her ears, but her gasp of pain is silenced by the hand that clamps over her mouth, that forces the fabric of the respy between her parted lips. Before she can claw at it, another hand grips her right wrist, twisting and wrenching it behind her back.

"Got a taste for trespassing, don'tcha?"

It's fire in her ear, hot flame singeing her skin.

Yet she struggles, gouging the flesh on the back of that restraining hand with her jagged fingernails, until her captor wrestles and shoves her across the narrow porch, slams her full-length into the façade of the house.

A tremendous crack bursts in her head with sparkle and shimmer, like the boom and beauty of fireworks. It's all aglimmer then, the light inside, behind her eyes, the pain radiating through her jaw into her teeth. The world is gleaming and aglow, as her knuckles grind against the coarse grain of rotting wood as she squirms to free her hand from under the crush of his, still clamped on her mouth. Her temple, her ear are flat against that weathered wood, her captor's cheek pressing upon hers, intimate as a lover's. A hand traverses the small hemisphere of her belly.

A grunt, a little sigh of—pleasure? Anticipation?

"To kill two Birds with one stone." His lips brush her ear, the skin chapped and cracked. "But then I'd never know which one died first."

A pinpoint. A prick. A sharp intake of breath.

Hers.

His.

It's Em who gasps, hearing the boots. But she's also quicker on her feet, thinking-wise. All a sudden everything is whack and we have to bounce. There's a slow drumbeat of steps on the floor below and I'm 'bout to crap my pants cuz I'm still wearing the ridiculous dress, but she shoves me behind that curtain of gowns, hissing, "¡Cál-late! I can make this right!" and sprints out of the closet. I start to follow her, but that's a fail. The boots are close, on the stairs, maybe. I don't hear Em, don't know where she's gone. All I know is I'm not gonna make it, but I ease back behind the dresses anyway and suck it up tight, trying not to breathe. Muffled footfalls, the swish of boots on carpet, and then I can see him in the slit of space between a white gown and a black one—a shave-head devil. He takes a quick scan around the bedroom. Then he comes into the closet. And I'm frozen behind the dresses, and there's this odor hanging there, a combo of body odor and foot stink and something flowery but stale, worn out. And my nose starts itching and twitching and I'm for sure gonna sneeze or cough or both. He perimeters the closet and stops right in front of the damn dress rack, so close I can smell the sweat stench comin' off him and I'm rat-shit freaked he can smell me, too, but I swallow it, and feel the hope burning in my brain that the foot smell is stronger. And close down my body cuz I'm sure I'm gonna crap or pee, when all of a sudden Em calls out "got it!" What is she doing? She needs to just run.

Then the world ends. Not with a whimper, but with a bang.

The she-wolf lopes while the terrain heaves and shifts under her. Blood. The taste of it on her lolling tongue. The scent of it up in her flaring nostrils. She's running in a landscape drained of all color, reduced to shades of white, leaning to gray. A hushed world squeezed dry of sound, but for her own panting breath and the scrape of her paws over the hard-packed soil. She senses more than feels the heat of the sun. Senses more than sees its knife-sharp glare. Stumbles over a loose stone. Trips over a clod of dirt. Steadies herself. Runs on.

PART THREE

At Zion's Door

That I may show forth all thy praise
in the gates of the daughter of Zion,
I may rejoice in thy salvation.

Psalm 9:14

44

The Color of Life

GREEN. SHE'S SWATHED IN IT. Softly at peace in it. Bathed. Lifted. Absorbed in it. Shadows hover. Voices drift, dim as the light. Something cool and floating. Green and light on her skin. Soft and rough, sliding slickness, wet and liquid and soft and rough, melting on her, melting her.

"Just a child, really."

Cool and liquid. Green. Beyond the flutter and fringe of her eyelashes, shadows waft. Out of focus. In a blur. Green. Overwhelming green. A green to sink into. The murmurs fading in and out.

"Five months? Six, maybe?"

Pressure on her belly, floating in the cool, the slick. But gentle. Green. Hands, maybe. Sliding, probing, cupping.

"Yes, at least six. She's a long tall drink of water. Hides it well. Not like me."

Tinkling, like glass on glass. No, softer, more whispery, more like... green. Laughter. The laughter of women. But gentle, not mocking. Green.

A tsking, a sighing exhalation of breath. A hand lifting her arm, lightly tracing a path between the crook of her elbow and her wrist.

"Five scabs festering. What could've caused them?"

Silence. A cluck. A tugging. At her head. The pain is orange, sharp, unpleasant.

"Won't be able to save this. Too many tangles. Have to cut them out."

"Shame. But the better to see that lovely face, yeah?"

Drifting. As if on a cushioned raft in the middle of a slow-moving river, languid under the mid-day sun. Green and drifting, til the dark swallows the light.

Green.

A warm scent in its midst. Yeast? Rich, enveloping. Butter? A scent to sink into, wallow in. Her mouth is watering from it, for it. A hole where her stomach should be. Gaping. Arms flailing at the restraining sheets, she sits bolt upright, crying out at the pain that slices up her side.

"Oh, here, lovie, no need for that."

Hands, gentle but forceful, attempt to press her back down, but she resists, twists away.

"All right then, you must be feelin' better. There's a strong girl."

Where the woman's voice is lush, soft, thick around the middle, her body is rail-thin, hard-muscled and compact as a boy's. Her face is all flat planes and sharp angles, except the lips, which are plump and full and plum-colored, and look as if they know their way around a smile.

"Look what I've brought you."

The platter she places on the bed next to Angel overflows with all the colors of the rainbow. The reds of tiny, bite-sized tomatoes, the orange and yellows of thin strips of peppers, the velvet green of lettuce and kale, the purplish indigo of round grapes ready to burst their skins. Brown chunks of bread smeared with something thick and white.

"Go on. That bread there is especially tasty right from the oven."

Still, she hesitates, forgetting what it means to trust. And yet, the smell of it. That scent calling her to dive into its rich, enveloping, bottomless pool.

The first bite makes her groan.

"What? Don't you like it? I could bring some without the cheese."

But when she devours the rest of the slab in two enormous bites, the woman chuckles. "Knew you'd like that. Go on, polish it off. Plenty more where that came from."

She feels wolfish in the way she tears through the food, half expecting a snarl to escape through her teeth. But there's no room for manners in her hunger and the woman watches with seeming approval as she lays waste to the bounty on the platter.

The woman holds out a glass. Her hand is one accustomed to manual labor from the looks of it, the nails clipped short, cuticles dry and overgrown, greenish veins ropy and thick, snaking under the surface of the tanned skin. As Angel reaches for the tumbler, a clutching pain grips her along the ribcage. She gasps, freezes, winces.

"You took a bad one there. Took some stitching to close it up. But you were lucky. A little higher, a little lower and I can't say for sure you'd be sitting here, eating Kuba's brown bread. But the human body's an amazing machine, the parts of it put together just so. There's a reason so many vitals are tucked inside our ribcage."

The water has a mineral taste, not unpleasant.

But the effort involved in sitting up, eating, drinking, is exhausting. She's embarrassed by her weakness, but the callused hand on her forehead gives her silent permission to ease back into the green world that is part sleep, part fever dream.

The room is austere, but pleasant enough. Sparsely furnished, with the small bed, a dresser over which hangs an oval mirror, and a nightstand, all painted a creamy white, a fresh contrast to the soothing sage green of the walls. She suspects the quilt that covers her is handmade, though the stitching is so fine and precise she can't be certain. An enormous single star spreads across it, with a magnificent mosaic of red, white and blue diamonds radiating out from its center. Her fingers trace the piecing.

"It's the morning star," the woman called Vida says one evening as she sets the tray with Angel's dinner on the nightstand. "An old pattern with a story. All the patterns tell a story. Just before the sun rises, there's a star standing alone, shining in the east. It announces the coming of light to the earth. Heralds the dawn. The gift of a new day."

She's let Angel be. Not asked questions of her, not prodded her to talk, to reply. Let her be mute in the face of kindness. Let her wonder in silence. About Debs. About this room. The bounty of food. The women who've attended her. The person who bakes the bread, the one called Kuba. But she's kept it all inside.

The woman, this Vida, isn't much of a talker herself. She always give a cheery greeting upon entering the room. A hello, a good morning, a how's my lovie doing? She doesn't bustle, no one as lean and compact as she is can bustle, but she does move quickly and efficiently, quietly tidying, smoothing sheets, removing plates without clatter, chasing dust with a quick sweep of a cloth.

Yet, in the midst of all this, a fear takes hold in Angel. Unreasonable, perhaps. Yet she can't stop its growing, just as she can't stop the growth of the creature inside her. Is she a prisoner, here in this cool green place? Well-fed and tended, cooed over. And yet...

But when she hoists herself out of the narrow bed, cringing at the sharpness that seizes her right flank, and shuffles to the door, enjoying the feel of the cool, solid wood under the soles of her bare feet, the knob turns easily in her hand. She pulls the heavy door open a slash, just enough to bring her eye to the slender empty space. A hallway. Dim in the late afternoon. From down the length of it, past where an opening looms and light puddles on the floor, she hears sounds. The clatter of metal. Pots and pans, maybe. A thrumming. A murmur that might be voices. But not talking. Singing?

Back to bed. Go back, the fear warns. Safe. You're safe there. So far.

For the first time in weeks, she has no weapon at hand, clad only in a shapeless shift that balloons over her belly, the fabric a random pattern of tiny pink flowers. She feels naked. Worse than naked. Helpless.

Then, clarity. A voice louder, present.

"War, children, it's just a shot away." Young. Male. Slightly off-key, perhaps.

Like a siren song, it draws her. One foot in front of the other, down the corridor, past doors open and closed, until she reaches that opening of light, an arched entryway. Beyond is a kitchen, brightly lit, spacious. Over an island counter, skillets and pots hang from a wrought iron rack, along with bunches of drying herbs tied with twine. Music rumbles while flour and the tang of onions hangs in the air like dust at a construction site. In the midst of what seems like chaos after the calm, cool green room stands a boy, kneading a swelling ball of dough with his knuckles.

How he senses her presence in the doorway is a mystery, amidst the noise and his focus on pummeling the dough, but his awareness of her comes just seconds after she steps foot there. He's not startled, or so it appears. As if he's been expecting her.

He nods, as if in greeting. "You s'posed to be out of bed?" His voice, not quite boy, but not yet man, is slow, like it's coated in honey. Oozy. A female voice cries out in the music's frenzy and the boy reaches out to the black metal box at the other end of the counter and twists a dial, lowering the volume.

"Too loud? Wake you?"

She can't tell if he sounds apologetic, concerned. She shakes her head.

"Kuba," the boys says.

Can't say for sure you'd be sitting up here, eating Kuba's brown bread...

She nods.

The baker is a copy of the woman who's been tending her, strong-jawed, doe-eyed, small, compact and tight muscled, but instead of her auburn hair, his is a fierce black, sleek to his head, caught back in a short pony tail at the base of his neck. Do his eyes, curious and slightly wary, rest on that mound of flesh under the nightgown? She shifts from one foot to the other.

"You should sit down. Look like you're gonna lose it," he says.

She shakes her head, but too quickly and then she does feel faint, white lights crowding out the colors and the buzz firing out fuzz through her skull.

"C'mon." In two steps, he has her, strong hands supporting her arms, guiding her to a stool behind the counter. Now her biceps are dusted with flour.

"Sorry," he says, grabbing a dishtowel and daubing at the residue. He peers at her, his gaze focusing first on the gauze bandage encasing her left arm from elbow to wrist, then back on her face. Waits a beat, before adding, "Talk much?"

Is there a sarcastic edge to his voice now? But something inside her is glad he's not treating her like some fragile china cup.

He takes a jug from the refrigerator, pours a tall glass of something blackish red and shoves it across the counter. The fear comes crawling back like some loathesome beast, slinking through her pores, scuttling along her guts and up her spine, slithering through the synapses of her brain, swimming along the canals of her bloodstream. Fear casts her eyes to the periphery, tightens her muscles, heightens her sense of smell. Brings the light glinting off the steel blade of the chopping knife into sharp focus. It rests on the cutting board next to a small mound of onions. Within the reach of her long right arm. And then, in a snaking second, she is brandishing it, chest high, though she is instantly seized with regret.

Debs' admonishment. *Don't pick up a weapon, any weapon, without a plan.*

She has no plan.

"Whoa, girl." The boy's hands are up, palms outward, the universal gesture of surrender, appeasement.

"Where's Debs? The old man? Where is he? Take me to him!" The questions come tumbling, a breathless spurt tinged with the panic in her throat, the vise that's constricting her chest.

"Whoa! Sure, sure, I'll take you to him! Just—whoa. Lose the knife. You don't need that. All you had to do was ask." He cocks his head, taking in the wild skittering of her eyes. "What? You think it's poison? Drugged?" He raises the glass of liquid ruby to his mouth and takes a generous swallow. Licks his lips, lovely, plump, bow-like.

Lights pop and flash around her head again, in the corners of her eyes and she grips the rounded edge of the counter with her left hand, feeling the cool of it against her burning fingertips, but all the while keeping the knife raised in her right. She knows he can see the tremor, the waver of the blade.

"I'm not taking you to him til you've had a drink, though. Need some sugar in your blood before you face-plant on this floor. Ain't the most comfortable place to fall. Tile's hard as CQO Zinni's heart." He smirks, but his eyes are trained on the blade.

When she brings the glass to her mouth and takes a sip, the fluid coats her tongue in velvet and a tang that makes her lips pucker. "Tart cherry?" she finally ventures, after waiting for him to speak, feeling completely ludicrous—wielding a weapon, drinking fruit juice, sensing the whispery movements of the being inside her. "It's—good."

He nods. In the midst of his silence, she feels obligated to take another sip. Realizes other people know how to play the game. "Angel," she says, draining the glass. Another nod. "Of the Shawnee," she adds, pushing the glass back across the counter.

"That's about as uncorporate as it gets," he says, digging his knuckles deep into the dough, but keeping those deep-set eyes on her and the knife. "So, Angel of the Shawnee, what's your plan?"

Someone's taught him the same lesson. But she knows how to throw him off-guard. Stares right back.

"To remake the world."

45

In the House of Isa

DEBS BURSTS INTO A SHAKY, GURGLING GUFFAW that trails off into a throaty coughing fit when the boy steps out the kitchen door and saunters across the flagstone patio, with Angel close behind, still clutching the knife chest high, aimed somewhere between his shoulder blades.

"What the hell?!" he sputters when he finally gets control of his spasms. "Put that blade down!" He flings a gesture at the small round table beside him fashioned from the trunk of a tree.

Angel lowers the knife but keeps it firm in her hand.

The pergola that stretches above them is a sturdy-looking structure of vertical pillars and crossbeams fashioned from repurposed PVC pipe. A network of leafy vines drapes, blanket-like, from the open lattice of wood laid across the top, sheltering the space from the light and heat of the day. Debs reclines in a wooden chair that looks too small for his frame, his long legs stretched out before him. His eyes are hidden by black shades, but by the way his body settles back in the chair, relaxes into the slant of it, Angel thinks he looks at home, at ease, as much at ease as she's ever seen him in the short time she's known him.

He glances up at her. "You s'posed to be out of bed?"

Angel sighs in exasperation, gives Debs a sidelong glance,

signaling for him to dismiss the boy, to engage in a private conversation. But Debs just gestures to another of the slant back chairs. "Take a load off. And put that thing down." His voice is jocular, but thinnish, like it takes a lot of effort for him to speak.

Angel tosses the knife to the table. It lands with a thud. "What's going on? Why are we here?"

Debs shrugs. "We're here for you to heal up. And from the look and sound of it, I guess you are."

"Kuba?" The voice is jagged, serrated, but not unpleasant. A voice that, like Debs', sounds like it doesn't get much use. "Kuba?"

Turning toward the sound, which wafts from the far corner of the pergola, where the shadows lie deep and green, Angel makes out a figure seated in a wicker rocker. But for the utterance, Angel would have presumed the woman is asleep, so still does she sit, white head, hair fine as floss, drooping onto her chest. But with the boy's first scuffling footfalls towards her, the chin lifts.

"Gray-gray," the boy murmurs.

"Early for supper. Sun's barely got 'round the corner. Air is still cool on my face."

"Not supper. I've brought someone to meet you." The boy beckons for Angel to approach. When she hesitates, he inclines his head with an insistent set to his mouth, eyebrows raised for emphasis. Angel takes a couple of steps, but not enough for the boy, who takes her hand and pulls her in front of the woman, whose head slowly tilts upward.

If Debs is old, then this dried-out husk of a woman is ancient. Wisps of hair halo a mottled face that is all bone and wrinkled skin, pale between the brown splotches, and blue eyes unseeing under a milky film. Her hands curl claw-like around the arms of the rocking chair, her lower body shrouded under a star-patterned quilt identical to the one on Angel's bed. Only the tips of her slippered feet peek out from the bottom hem like shy mice.

"Gray-gray, this is Angel... of the Shawnee," Kuba says, gesturing.

Perhaps the woman can still discern the shadows of movement for her head turns. "Ah, yes," she croaks. "The commotion in my home."

"Angel, this is my great-great grandmother, Isa."

"And?" The woman nods. "I've heard—some, but not from her lips."

"She's come to..." He trails off, then nudges Angel. "You tell her."

Angel looks at the boy, confused.

"What you said to me. In the kitchen."

Angel shakes her head, embarrassed, but Kuba just nods. "Tell her. Your plan."

She implores him with her eyes, but he's impassive. The crone, too.

Finally, she spits it out, like a poison she's ingested. "To remake—the world."

It sounds so stupid, so ridiculous, saying this while standing in front of this decrepit woman, in the manner of an introduction. Flames spread across Angel's cheeks.

The woman remains slumped in her chair. But then, with apparent effort, she raises her hands from the arms of the rocker, and stretches them out before her. Tremors quake the gnarled fingers.

"Your face, please."

No, I won't be touched—can't be touched by this—

But the outstretched hands draw her face to them, as if by some magnetic force, the pull of the crone's personal gravity bending her, reeling her into her orbit. Just before the fingers alight on her cheeks, she dreads that they will be dry and rough, and rasp like sandpaper over her skin, but when the moment of contact arrives, she's shocked to find them soft, cool, and oh so gentle. The fingers seem to read the contours of her face, the angles of her cheekbones, the plane of her forehead, the strength of her jaw, the sweep of her nose from its narrow start to its flaring tip. They trace her wild eyebrows, the curve of her lips, the arcs of her ears. The geometry of her visage.

"Where did you learn those words?" The woman finally asks, letting her hands come to rest, her palms cupping Angel's cheeks.

Suraj's voice echoes in her mind. *And the people will know us by our words.*

"From my—from the man who raised me."

"Who was...?"

"Eben Bird."

"And where did he learn that phrase?"

"I don't know. Maybe from the man who brought me here. Debs. He knew him."

"Ah. And where did *he* learn them?"

"I don't know. Ask him. I don't even really know what they mean. I just—"

"You say them without knowing their meaning?"

"I..." Angel, at a loss, trails off.

"Well, you're not alone in that. Bad habit, though." Isa pauses, cocks her head a little to the side. "This young man is notorious for it."

"*Was*," Kuba corrects. "*Was* notorious for it." He smiles, shrugging, unflustered, unembarrassed by the chiding.

"Okay, I won't quibble about the tense of the verb." The old woman pauses, takes a breath, as if the act of conversation is wearying. "I learned those words from my father," she continues. "When I was a little girl, ninety-some years ago. When he was the President of the United States of America. The *last* president of the United States."

The phrase provokes a twinge in Angel, like the echo of an ache that has been kept at bay, but pulses a painful reminder when one moves a certain way, lifts or twists a limb just so.

The words. She can hear Eben's voice. Hear the words. See the atlas. The map. The letter splayed across the broad expanse of landmass, the quilt of colors binding the shapes together, never the same color bordering itself, orange and pink and yellow and green, some of the shapes seemingly random until she looked closer and saw the blue lines weaving through, the rivers that create the boundaries.

"Yes, I am that old. You know nothing of that country, that nation. But I remember it as if it were yesterday."

She releases her hold on Angel's face, but as the girl straightens, the hands caress the curve of her belly. As the old woman feels the ripple that runs under the fabric of the nightgown, under the skin, the flex of a tiny foot or the jab of a tiny hand, she smiles.

"And so this will be another child of the revolution, a child of a different revolution, perhaps." She gestures to the wicker armchair to her right. "Sit with me, Angel—of the Shawnee. Kuba, some tea, please. Raspberry leaf for Angel, nettle for me."

The boy hustles off, sandals slapping his heels. They sit in silence for a minute or two before Angel feels the sudden overwhelming urge to speak.

"We—my family—we had a biblio. Full of maps. And I can picture the map of the old nation. Eben taught me the names of the lakes from it."

Isa responds with the slightest of nods, as if conserving energy.

"My mother—my assigned mother—was a meme, a knowledge keeper."

"And did she tell you about that country?"

"She left me a vocoder with—a story."

They lapse into silence again.

When the boy arrives with two steaming mugs, he sets them on the small wicker table between their chairs and makes to settle himself on the three-legged stool in the far corner of the patio, but Isa dismisses him with a flick of her finger, like she's shooing a gnat. He frowns, opens his mouth to protest, then shuts it again and stalks away, pulling the screen door closed behind him with just this side of a slam.

"Impetuous, that one," she chuckles. "Gets it from me. Though it skipped a few generations, thank goodness." She cocks her head.

Angel takes a tiny sip of the tea, the bitter and sweet of it colliding on her tongue, honey and earth amingled. "What is this place? How many of you live here?"

Isa squints into the middle distance, across the flagstone in the direction of Debs at the opposite end of the pergola. "You didn't tell her a thing, did you, old man?" she says, her voice raised to carry across the distance.

"I was a little busy," he replies, swatting at a fly buzzing near his head.

"Busy?" Isa echoes, a hint of disbelief in the two syllables.

"Busy," Debs huffs. "Busy as a one-legged man in an ass-kicking contest."

"You always were a vulgar rogue." Isa sighs. "It's what I love about you."

Angel's gaze shifts from the one ancient to the other. "You know each other?"

"Toldja she was quick on the uptake," barks Debs.

"Oh, stop, go back to sleep, old man," Isa chides. "This place is our home," she says to Angel. "Been our home, my home, for, oh, eighty-some years now. My father sent us, my brother and me, away from the capitol six months before the coup. The Potomac Virus was ravaging what was left of the coastal populations. The perfect weapon. Kept its hosts alive just long enough to infect dozens, hundreds more, whoever they came in contact with. So Papa sent us inland, first to Ohio, to my grandmother. But she was elderly, frail. When she died a year later, by then both my mother and my father were dead, executed by the rabble. A cousin spirited us off in the night. And he brought us here, to this land, this farm."

Angel wants to speak, but bites the words back, wary, still not certain how far she can trust this woman, these people. Yes, Debs seems to have a relationship. Yes, they've been unfailingly kind, the women of the green room with their strong but gentle hands, bearing sustenance and relief. And yet...

And yet, she plunges onward, into the unknown. "How are you still here? In the Protectorate? You should have been severanced—ages ago."

Isa's wine-colored lips turn upward at the corners, deepening the creases etched across her face. "Ha, you've noticed," she cackles, pointing a bony finger, the nail at the tip ridged, slightly yellowed. "Debs, you weren't kidding. She is a clever little vixen. So, what's your theory on that, dearie?"

"You're off the grid. The boy, too. And the women in the green room."

"All, yes, all of us. Fifteen? Twenty, maybe. I can't even remember how many of us there are nowadays. Funny, some of my memories are so clear, especially those long ago ones. And then again, I can't recall what I had for breakfast. And whether this one or that is my great or my great-great grandchild. At a certain point, it all blends together, you know? Well, no, of course you don't, young thing that you are. But most of them that are here are from me, out of me, ultimately. My descendants." Her scrawny shoulders lift and fall. Her mice-like feet stir in their slippers.

"It's rather like Genesis. Isa begat Amaranth who begat Vida who begat Layla who begat—Jakub. There the matriarchy falls apart. Because the next one she popped out was also a boy. And her cousin Bethsaida, too. All males. Handy in a pinch, though not more so than the female of the species." Her eyelid flutters, perhaps in a wink.

"How have you lived off the grid for so long?" Angel asks.

"I might ask you the same question," Isa replies, cocking her head.

Angel's hand automatically goes to her neck, reaching for the talis that no longer hangs there. "I had an embed. From a baby who—died. Wore it on a chain around my neck. Kept it hidden."

"A clever idea, that. Sort of *on* the grid, but not *of* it. We've managed the old-fashioned way. Laid low. Been self-sustaining. Asked nothing of the Protectorate. Sought nothing. Grown our own food. Purified our own water. Generated our own power. Lived simply, quietly. Unobtrusively. And—" Here she smirks, "in the pinch of necessity, engaged in a bribe or two, all manner of persuasion, pretty or not. And, when called for, a certain—violence." She utters the word carefully, as if not certain she enjoys the taste of it on her tongue.

With effort, she raises her arm and gestures to the vista beyond the pillars of the pergola. "Have you been out? Walked the grounds?"

Angel shakes her head, takes another sip of tea.

"Have Kuba take you around." Isa's arm drifts back to her lap. "For now, I'll rest, like my good friend Debs." With a glimmer of a smile, she inclines her head toward the now-dozing man. "We'll talk later. You can tell me what you think of our place."

And then she folds into herself in the manner of a cat, seems to shrink and Angel thinks she's fallen asleep that quickly. But when the girl bends to take Isa's mug on her way back to the kitchen, the old woman reaches a hand to stay her.

"Leave it. I'll sip on it. And ask Vida for some regular clothes. My eyes are not completely gone yet, and Angel you may be, but not of the heavenly kind, even in that white shroud, not yet."

46

The Tender Land

"DON'T HAVE TO BE CRAZY to farm bottomland, but it helps."

Angel, Kuba, and the border collie, Vato, stand on the edge of a stretch of soybeans ready for harvesting, the bean pods plump and lush under their cover of brownish fuzz, the leaves of the plants a luscious amber. The boy stoops, picks up a clod of soil and pulverizes it between his palms. It's a rich black, pliable with nutrients, the bounty of the river's endless cycle of give and take.

"Long as that river gets out its banks every three years or so, we don't have to fertilize it."

"Did it flood this year?" Angel asks. "Down region, we raised nothing but dust the past couple of years."

He nods. "River ain't flooded in four years. We've had just enough rain here to make do. When we need to, we run water from the river."

Beyond the field, the river slinks, brown and lethargic. They move on, slow as the water, Kuba pointing out the systems that keep the farm independent: the water purification ring with its concentric circles of nested concrete sifter drums, the array of solar panels with their perfect grids, a sapphire contrast to the greens and golds of the surrounding fields.

"We've got millet and sorghum over there, a small field of rye, a little wheat and corn, mostly for feed and biofuel," Kuba explains, pointing out the plots.

They turn down a dirt lane where stunted trees are lined up two by two like soldiers in parade formation. "Got tart cherry and green apple in this orchard here, and over there, we've got some grape vines. Cherries don't do so well now, Grey-Grey says. It's the lack of cold in the winter. Cherries like a bit of chill that we don't get much anymore. Apples, too. Now the melons," he continues, pointing to a fenced-in plot just off the lane. "They're thrivin'."

They pause to admire the fruits weighing down the rambling vines. The oblong watermelons, green-headed and white-bellied, the canteloupes with their heavily netted tan rinds, the smooth pale green honeydews, the casabas with their wrinkled yellow skin. Angel's mouth waters at the thought of the secret juicy flesh hidden beneath it.

They follow the turn of the lane as it heads back toward the main house. Two generous-sized cabins sit on either side of a stand of hickories.

"Casa Aguilar. Over there's where the cousins live. Bethsaida's brood's in the one and we're in the other. It's a little tight with the four of us, so when I need some space, I pitch a tent out by the river."

An aged, two-wheeled motor scooter leans up against a shed where two boys scrape blistered paint from weathered siding. Angel can tell they are watching her, even though their eyes are hidden behind blackout shades.

"Ignore 'em. Just my primos." He calls out to the pair. "Paws off my ride, güey!"

"So, we should just paint over it, culero?" The taller of the two yells back.

Kuba flips them the bird. "Thinks he's a badass, but he knows what's comin' if he touches it," he grumbles, though Angel senses his irritation is mostly swagger.

The kitchen garden is laid out in eight small sections separated by weathered railroad ties. Cukes, string beans, brussel sprouts, a rainbow of pepper plants in varying states of ripeness. Kuba's pride is unmistakable when he points to a scarlet tomato hanging from a vine, its skin stretched to bursting, barely able to contain its juice. He plucks it with delicacy and presents it to Angel on an outstretched palm.

"Go on," he urges. "You won't taste nothin' better'n that."

She sinks her teeth into the ripe fruit. Skin pierced, the sweet-tart juice explodes in a torrent, spattering her cheeks, dribbling down her chin, trickling along her neck. Her squeal is one of shock and joy as she chews the delicious flesh, reveling as its liquid heart drips through her fingers.

Kuba snorts. "Go ahead. You can wipe up with that shirt, it's one step from the rag bin." He pauses. "No offense, but we don't have a lot of spare clothes. Live pretty close to the bone."

Angel nods, polishing off the last bite of tomato, wiping her hands on the threadbare smock that floats out over her belly, lifting its edge to wipe her mouth.

"It's how we keep Corporate hands outta our business. Do for ourselves. Barter when we need to. Grey-grey was younger'n me when she was brought here. Up til then, she'd lived a very coddled life. She'll tell you if she's in the mood to talk. Things given to her, provided for her, with the snap of her fingers. But that changed quicker than a dog can lick a dish." He bends and chucks the dog under its white chin. "She grew up quick and adapted to a new life. Hell, a new world. Toughened up. If there'd been more like her, maybe the old Republic would've survived. But too many were soft, needed to be cared for, wanted to be cared for. Took the easy way out."

The boy nudges a random stone from the center of the lane back into place along its border. "The minute you start lookin' for a handout, start takin' their assistance, that's when the trouble starts," he continues, the timbre of his voice intensifying. "That's when they sink their hooks in. Start to own you. And once they own you, they own you. Totally. That's how it all got started. People not doing for themselves, thinking they were owed something. People filled up with fear, wanting to be protected, givin' up their freedom for a little safety." He hocks back and spits in the dirt as if to add emphasis to his words.

"You've never had a b-squad of goliaths come through here?" Angel asks.

Kuba shoots her a quick hard arrow of a look. "Didn't say that." He hikes up his jeans, which have slipped down his narrow hips. "But those who stray into the eagles' lair don't emerge—intact."

She ponders the cryptic remark. It's hard to separate the truth of the possible from the boast of youthful bravado, but the set of his mouth adds weight to his words. She blinks and turns away, remembering her own deeds of the past weeks, actions she would have once thought impossible, suddenly made real. She scans the ripening fields, row upon carefully plotted row, and wonders where the bodies are buried.

Then the image of a face rises in her mind, heart-shaped with its delicate pointed chin and flaring forehead, wild tendrils from a mane of black hair curling around the ears, cheeks flushed in vivid life. And then another, this one finely sculpted and fine-skinned with an ever-present smile that puts the rising sun to shame, ruddy in laughter.

"Words are easy," she says, turning back to the boy. "But you were born lucky. Born free. What about those who are born into it, that slavery? The ones who get embeds injected in their brains before they get a chance to let out a good wailing breath. Shipped off to whoever the Hive deems worthy of being parents. Born just because a few swags decide there's a need for fruit pickers in Agsector Three. Or another hulking ass-kicker for a brute squad. Or another body in the Service track pipeline. You don't know until you've lived it. So maybe save your self-righteous crap for late at night when you're talkin' to your mirror."

She pivots and stalks back down the path, shocked at the out-
burst of bitter-soaked truth that has just spewed from her lips.

Later, she tries to avoid the boy's eyes when they all sit
around the long communal table, a thick slab of hickory into
which the hieroglyphics of much love and use have been etched.
But he sits directly across from her, making that a difficult task.

Isa's clan is eager to meet this girl who was brought into the
midst of their harvest and she has to endure a round of introductions. But with the smiling faces all so similar, the deep-set eyes,
the tumble of dark curls, strong teeth and strong jaws, the names
pass in and out without sticking. The matriarch herself is not at
the table, taking supper in the quiet of her room, but another
very—though not quite so—old woman sits at the head of the
table. Ama-something? Amaranth? Was that what Isa called her
daughter? A man sits at the corner beside her, plowing through
his chicken and root vegetables the way Angel suspects he plows
his fields, like a man who values efficiency in all things. Four of
the diners don't fit the mold. Angel gathers they are the hus-
bands and wives somehow drawn into the family. And there are
three boys younger than Kuba, who inhale their food in between
sidelong glances in her direction. She's perched in the middle of
it all, between Vida and Vida's daughter, Layla, whose whispery
voice she recognizes from the green room.

At first, in the midst of the introductions, Angel felt self-
conscious, awkward with all eyes on her, but now, amid the jingle
and scrape of forks and knives, the chewing of food, the jibes
and laughter and side conversations, she feels comfortably anonymous. Vida and Layla talk around her and over her, not in a
rude way, but in a way that says she is one of them. Only Kuba's
probing eyes disturb and make her squirm.

"You see the pumpkins? I hope you're prepared to put up in
a few weeks. Cuz they're just about ready and it's a motherlode,"

Vida says to Layla over Angel's back, spreading a generous slab of butter across her slice of bread.

"I'll be ready. You can?" Layla asks in Angel's direction.

Angel, expecting the woman to continue, waits, chewing her bite of chicken, but the woman does not elaborate and seems to be looking for an answer. "Can what?" Angel finally asks, and sees the quizzical expression in Layla's eyes turn to amusement.

"Can. Can food. Fruit? Veggies? Sauces? The process."

Angel feels the heat of embarrassment on her cheeks as realization dawns. "Oh—no, I don't have skills in the kitchen. But I know my way around a toolbox."

"Really? Well, we could use a handyman—or woman. Someone who knows one end of a hammer from the other." She nods in Kuba's direction. "The boy can prepare a feast, but Mr. Fixit, he's not. Can't abide the slaughtering or hunting, either. No chicken or venison on that plate. But that's okay, s'long as he finds someone else who can abide it, he'll be just fine. That's what life's about, yeah, finding someone to fill your gaps."

Angel forks a piece of carrot and chews it slowly, carefully, so she doesn't need to reply. She leans forward so she can see Debs, seated at the far end of the table. She expects his plate to be clean, but it's still full of food, mostly untouched. He pushes at a roasted sprout, gleaming in its coat of oil, spears it with the tines of his fork, but doesn't bring it to his mouth. Sets the fork back down. She tries to catch his eye, but his gaze seems to be traveling a fixed path, from his plate to the now-depleted bounty laid along the center of the table, the platters with remnants of roasted chicken, the bowls where the carrots and brussel sprouts had been heaped, the plates with crumbs where the bread had been laid, the half-empty bottles of wine and hard cider and cherry juice. His gaze does not pause for long, but moves ever onward until it comes to rest on the face of the woman who sits at the opposite end of the table.

Angel recognizes the man's expression, has seen a semblance

of it before, in quiet moments around the kitchen table when she'd catch a glimpse of Eben staring at Serafina, as if pondering her. But Eben's gaze had been awash in pleasure, a reverie of what was. In the melancholy that hangs from the corners of Debs' eyes, melancholy that seems more than just a trick of the dimmed lights, it strikes her that the old man's stare is more a rumination on what was, once upon a time, and what might have been.

The gears click in Angel's head. It makes sense. They look of an age, the man and the woman. And the woman, Amaranth, does not avoid the man's gaze, the way Angel has been avoiding Kuba's. She meets it frankly, as if to say "and there it is."

Later, Angel seeks him out, under the pergola, lolling in the same slantback chair, a long leg draped casually over one of its arms, head back, eyes closed to the stars that teem and pulse in the late September sky.

"How do you know these people?" she asks, dragging another chair close to his.

He says nothing. Idly scratches his knee.

She waits. He waits. They play the waiting game until he finally shifts in his chair, swings his leg off the arm, stretches and flexes it in front of him, his ankle joint popping with a soft crackle.

"Have a history with this place."

Silence stretches like a patient cat. Angel breaks first. "You were in love with her," she jousts. "The silver-haired one who hardly said a word at supper. Amaranth."

He sucks in the night air through his nostrils, breathes it out through his mouth, a deep, calming breath. "She was in love with me. Or thought she was. But that was a very long time ago."

"Don't bullshit me. I saw it from across the table. Saw it in your eyes."

"Ah, yes, windows to the soul," he mutters, an edge of sarcasm cutting through. "And what if I was?" he continues, crossing his arms across his chest. "So be it. Met her the summer I worked over in the wildlife refuge, the Chautauqua, when it was still a refuge, still being cared for. Bordered this place. Summer between my first and second years at the university in Champaign. Things happen with a pretty girl. But I knew better'n to take her with me, ask her to live like I already knew I was gonna live, even then. Wasn't right to ask her to take on that burden."

"Isn't that what life's about? Finding someone to help you carry the burden? That's what Serafina said. And Eben."

"Maybe. I couldn't do that to her. Because I already knew the weight would be too heavy."

"You didn't even give her a chance to try."

Debs waves her off. "And I don't think I was wrong. She was Isa's only child. And I knew *this* life, this isolation, wasn't the path for me. I needed resistance, an active resistance, not disengagement. I went off to plant the seeds for a rebellion. She stayed here and gave birth to her daughter and her son, fathered by a good man, far as I know."

"How romantic," Angel drawled. "And your rebellion withered and died. But her children live."

"If you call this livin'," Debs retorts.

"They seem happy. And you came here, brought me here."

"Any port in a storm."

"You don't really believe that, old man."

He sits, mulling a reply. Finally it comes as a low mumble. "You got me there. You do."

Angel stands, stretching tentatively, wincing at the pain that nips along her flank, running a hand under the edge of the bandage wrapped around her middle. "All that being said, when do we move on?"

"Keep turnin' on a dime, you gonna get whiplash. We'll go when you're healed up. Though you might think about hunkering down 'til you whelp that pup," Debs drawls.

"Where's my pack," Angel asks, ignoring his suggestion.

"I got it. Don't fret, everything's still in there. You want it, go get it. It's hanging on the back of the door to my room."

She wants to think that she trusts him, after all they have endured. But once back in her own room, she still feels the need to unzip the filthy backpack and paw through it, to verify that the pistol and the knife are where she last left them, to close a hand around the grip of each. To greet them as old frenemies. Her knuckles bump up against another metallic presence. Her fingers encircle the round form, trace the picture engraved across it, the raised figure of the ancient train. Suraj's pocketwatch. Hers now. She tugs the zipper closed even as it hisses in protest and shoves the pack into the corner of her closet, a dark place to hide secrets.

47

Land of Milk and Honey

THERE IS A RHYTHM TO LIFE on the farm, a predictability that Angel falls into step with, sinks into like an old comfy chair, a sameness that she relishes after the chaos of the past months. Although the women have made it clear she is to rest, to recover from her wound, to avoid strain that might harm the life growing inside her, she is a doer. A tinkerer unable to sit still for any length of time. So she channels the enforced repose into a posture of learning.

As the sun breaches the horizon to the east, she's trailing Lylah to the shed for the morning milking. Three goats huddle around the corner of their pen, nosing the gate, jockeying for position. Salt, the largest and boldest, gets to a station first, shoving her angular head through the open catch, sinking her long Roman nose into the feed bucket, where a breakfast of grain awaits. Her pendulous ears, bell-shaped and soft as heaven, lop over her wise brown eyes, her horizontal irises casting an exotic spell. Seated on her stool, Lylah gives the doe's udder a thorough wash with a soft rag dipped in sudsy water. When she's satisfied that she's removed every speck of dirt and debris, she grabs her strip cup, a little black mug, and coaxes a couple of squirts from each teat. She examines the milk, swishing the white fluid around, checking for blood specks or clumps that might indicate mastitis or other problems.

"The first couple of squirts also carry the most bacteria and dirt," she's warned Angel. "Doin' this clears that out before you milk into your good pail."

She sets the deep steel cookpot under Salt and gently grasps a teat. Using her thumb and forefinger, she closes off the top of the teat and use her other sturdy, square-tipped fingers to expel the milk.

"Don't pull on it," Lylah explained the first time Angel accompanied her to the shed. "If you do, your goat'll let you know she's not fond of your technique with a swift kick to the bucket and there goes your hard work, soaking the straw."

Lylah works swiftly and efficiently, with both hands. When Salt's udder is empty, she rubs on balm that smells of calendula and lavender, a pungent and earthy scent of tree resin and cut hay. Then she repeats the process twice more before hustling the pots of milk to the main house. In the small wash room off the kitchen, she filters the milk through a canning funnel and a fine mesh strainer into a row of glass jars, seals them, and then pops them into the dairy cooler.

By then the hens in the coop are cackling, demanding attention. Released into the pen, they pick and scratch at the black oil sunflower seeds Lylah has scattered, while the women gather the treasures left behind in the nest boxes. White, brown, green, and speckled—Angel is amazed at the variety. She helps Lylah clean the nests, replacing soiled hay and wood shavings with fresh, filling bins and bowls with feed and water.

By then, Angel's stomach is grumbling and she's grateful when they pause to eat their own breakfast, plates of eggs that Kuba has scrambled with chunks of pepper and onion, with hunks of day-old bread toasted and slathered with jam on the side. Then it's on to harvesting, the rest of the morning spent in the gardens. In the plot nearest the main house, Lylah hands Angel a basket and points to the pole beans.

"Less bending," she says.

The vines are lovely, straight and tall, as taller or taller than Angel, their tendrils wrapped in a stranglehold around supporting stakes, lush with leaves shaped like arrowheads. She stands perplexed, the basket in her hands, seeing nothing but leaves.

"Push 'em back," Lylah encourages. "Those beans are hiding on you."

Sure enough, when Angel brushes a clump of leaves aside, the beans hang there, waiting, a vibrant green, longer than a finger, fatter than a pencil, curving gently to pointed, needle-like tips. It takes a tug and a pinch with the thumb to snap the recalcitrant pods off the vine. Just when she thinks she's found all the beans ready for picking, she spots another cluster dangling behind a curtain of leaves. She fills one basket and Lylah nods at her to take another. The older woman has been working the tomato cages. Her bushel is heaped with egg-shaped plum tomatoes.

"Here's your chance to learn to can, if you're interested," Lylah says, hefting the bushel onto her jutting hip.

Angel nods. She'd never had much interest in Serafina's small garden, beyond running the old tiller to turn the soil every spring and mending the chickenwire fences that kept the rabbits out. That garden never flourished like this one, cursed as it was by the vagaries of the weather, some years drenched in rain to the point of rot and mildew, and then parched into shriveled submission by the lack of it.

They stop to rest and stretch and drink deeply from their canteens, wiping the sweat that clings to their foreheads under their wide-brimmed hats. Lylah cleans her blackout shades with the hem of her shirt.

"You're a hard worker," Lylah says, staring at Angel, speculation in her eyes. "Glad we got this done this morning." She cuts her eyes to the western horizon, where anvil clouds are growing. Then she gestures towards the house. "Let's get these to the wash room and clean 'em up. While we're there, we can peek into the kitchen and see what's for lunch." She winks. "Get our share before the human locusts descend."

In the afternoon, Lylah crafts cheese from the surplus milk. She heats a gallon of it in a stock pot on the stove until gentle bubbles form and its surface is foamy. She's plucked three small lemons from the tree that grows in a bucket just outside the kitchen door and now she squeezes them to produce a cup of juice. She turns off the heat, pours the juice into the pot and gives a quick stir with a wooden spoon.

"We'll let that sit a spell and you watch what happens."

Angel's impatience is that of a child anticipating a magic trick. She peers over the rim of the pot. No change. She draws back. Aches to stir it, stretches her fingers toward the spoon.

"Nope, let it be," Lylah admonishes.

"Yep, steer clear of that pot. When it comes to her cheese, she'll buzz you like a red-wing blackbird protecting its nest." Kuba's just stepped in through the kitchen door with a basket full of cuttings from the herb garden. "Here, busy yourself. You can help me bundle these for drying."

The proximity to him, to the smooth and rough of him, makes her skin prickly, itchy. They've exchanged mere words and phrases since she rounded on him in the garden and Angel supposes that's part of the problem. Too much time has passed to set things right. But when he holds out several sprigs of rosemary, she takes them from his hand.

He snips a short piece of string and ties the bundle with a sliding knot that tightens as he pulls. "Stems shrink as they dry. You want to be able to tighten the bundles before your herbs fall all over the place."

She nods, but her fingers seem swollen and useless when she attempts to tie the same knot to her bundle. Out the corner of her eye, she scans his face for the first sign of derision or mockery, but he's a patient teacher and just nods encouragement.

"Took me a time or two to get it right."

She waits for him to pick up the string and tie the knot, but he taps the stems. "I'll talk you through it, but it's best if you do it. Get the steps in your fingers."

The nearness of his fingers heightens the twitchiness that starts at the back of her neck and worms its way down and around to her groin. The tips brush her knuckles as they guide her through the double loop. The sting is electric and she flinches. If he notices, he pretends not, and points out where to secure the loops with a pass through.

"There you go, a poacher's knot. Slip it over the ends of your sprigs, pull and you've got your first bundle down."

The loop slides easily to secure the stems.

"Okay, again," he says, pushing stems of thyme her way and gathering a spray of oregano for himself.

She manages to tie the knot, though her fingers fumble a bit under his gaze.

"You got it. I'll leave you to it." He grins and heads back out the kitchen door.

Angel stares at the pile of stems still left to be bundled. A soft chuckle makes her turn. Lylah is scraping what looks like lumpy oatmeal into a colander lined with gauzy white fabric.

"Looks like you have an official chore now," she says, tapping the spoon on the colander's rim. "Make him hang 'em, though. I don't want you climbin' the stepstool."

"I'll be fine," Angel replies, her feelings all in a mix, disgruntled that he's left and glad at the same time. She steps over to the counter and peers into the strainer.

"Separatin' curds from the whey, the liquid." Lylah gathers the ends of the cloth up around the mush, ties them neatly around the handle of a wooden spoon and sets the spoon across the top of a jar, the bundle hanging inside. "We'll let that drain. In the meantime, I'm gonna go turn the compost heap." She winks. "Happy bundling."

In the quiet, small sounds are magnified. The drip of the creamy white whey into a deepening pool at the bottom of the jar. The tick of the archaic pendulum clock that hangs on the far wall. The hum of the refrigerator in the corner. The swish of leaves across the wood block counter as she pulls stems together. And in the quiet under the sounds, the tiny being inside of her flexes. A foot? An elbow? Some part motioning to remind her of its presence. A twist. A roll.

These secret communiqués, she's slowly coming to appreciate them, to enjoy the feeling of connection they spark. The intimacy of being the only one who knows, the only one receiving these cryptic dispatches. The language may be foreign to her, but she feels that she knows, by instinct or intuition, what it's trying to convey. A smile, as small and quiet as the sounds that lurk in the kitchen, softens the set of her lips. She remembers a feeling from long ago.

A curled-up, soft feeling. On the sofa, nestled in the crook of Eben's arm, listening to Serafina strum the guitar. Softly. As Eben hums along to the tune, she feels the thrumming vibration along her cheek, through the flannel of his shirt. The candles winking in the twilight of early autumn. Soft. Soft and hushed. Subdued. Warm.

To name that feeling. This feeling. This small feeling. She wonders if it is contentment. Something even close to joy.

Or merely the absence of fear.

Lost in the activity, the movement of her fingers, the bursts of fragrance from the herbs, the nubby texture of the string, caught in the flow of the work of tying knots, the joy of losing herself in the task, she doesn't hear the patter at first. And when she does, she can't quite place the sound.

It's been so long.

But finally the insistent tapping, strident and sibilant at once, forces her to turn her head toward the window across the room. The glass is spattered.

Rain.

The others, caught in the sudden squall, are scurrying for shelter under the sheds and in the barn. From their makeshift havens, they stare out, amazed, at the girl who dashes out the kitchen door into the midst of the deluge and turns her face to the downpour, lifting her arms to the sky as if to embrace it.

48

From the Hive

As September gives way to October and the angle of sunlight becomes more pronounced, the days remain warm and dry, perfect for the harvest, while the nights linger cool, lengthening and deepening.

"A good season, a good year for us," Vida says, "though hard for so many others," she adds, scanning Angel's face.

By now they have heard the story from her own lips. Or part of it. Sat in silence while she's told of the mass murder of an entire sector. They are careful not to tread upon her still-raw grief, though she's covered it over, fashioned a scab out of the flow of the moment, the busyness of her hands. Their eyes occasionally stray to the real scars on her left arm, where the skin stretches pink in five fierce lines.

The women stand on the edge of the squash garden, admiring the sheer variety, the diversity of the pumpkin universe. Blue-gray skinned pumpkins cozy up to smallish pink-skinned ones pocked with rough growths that have the look and feel of peanut shells. Pear-shaped pumpkins with crimson-orange skin blaze next to their paler cousins, creamy beige pie pumpkins. Miniature sugar pumpkins peek out of the shadows of the tall upright ones called Howdens. Luminas are ghostly white amidst the greens and oranges.

Vida has set the four boys to picking and hoisting, forbidding Angel from bending and lifting, although her bleeding stopped long ago and the wound at her rib cage has healed to an angry red scar. The boys commenced the work diligent and sincere, but have succumbed to the call of foolishness and braggadocio. Uriel, Kuba's younger brother, juggles three of the mini pumpkins, passing them from hand to hand, over his head, under a bent leg. One falls to the ground and Vida is quick to scold.

"That's our barter you're toying with!"

The boy, lithe and dark-eyed, retrieves the pumpkin and scoots off to add it to his bushel, but not before doing one more quick juggling pass, as if to set his error right.

Vida shakes her head, but a smile tugs at her lips.

Raphael, Bethsaida's younger boy, not to be outdone, attempts to juggle three of the larger pie pumpkins and fails miserably when two go flying and hit the ground with dull thuds.

"They'll be bruised," Vida warns. "Put them aside so I'll remember to use 'em quick. And stop your foolin'!"

The words are barely out of her mouth when Gabriel, Raphael's older brother, turns around. His t-shirt is stretched across his grossly distended belly. One hand supports the underside, the other rests along the top, in a pose familiar to Angel, one she is striking at this very moment. At the frayed hem of the boy's shirt, a sliver of orange peeks out, starkly bright against the faded blue of the fabric.

She bursts out laughing. Hard and long and lung-bursting, until she is breathless, in a squealing wheeze that seizes at the windpipe and throat. Laughing at the boy and at herself, til tears seep out the corners of her eyes and her sides strain in a stitch. Laughing because she can't remember the last time she's laughed. Like this. Or at all.

Kuba, catching sight of Gabriel's mockery, moves to swat him, but stops and pivots when he hears the raucous music of her laughter. He follows through with the swat, but it's gentler than it might have been, accompanied by a shake of his head and a roll of his eyes over the lowered rims of his shades.

"She carries it better'n you, frackhole."

"Course she does, she's a breeder."

Kuba punches him hard now, in the bicep, so the boy's hand slides off the top of the hidden pumpkin and it starts to slip out from under his shirt. "Don't never call her that!" Kuba hisses between clenched teeth, under his breath.

"It's what she is," replies Gabriel, laying the pumpkin in the wheelbarrow, rubbing his arm gingerly.

"No, she's not."

"Well, what is she then? She obviously ain't one of them androgs and she don't look like no guevara."

"She's a girl. A woman. A free woman who's free to go wherever she pleases."

He stares at Angel from behind the cover of his blackout shades. She's taken off her own sunglasses and is wiping the lenses with the hem of her smock, her face still alight with a wide smile. In this moment, her cheeks flushed with the exertion of her laughter, her eyes liquid and soft, she is beautiful.

And he knows he wants to follow her, wherever she goes.

Molten gold sags from the edge of the spoon, forming a strand of sweet pure joy that seeps down toward the surface of the pale brown tea. When it finally collides with the steaming liquid, it pools in a lazy spiral at the bottom of the mug, needing encouragement from the spoon to melt and meld with the tea.

Alone in the kitchen in the middle of the morning, Angel is still surreptitious as she digs the spoon into the canning jar a second time and brings it, honey-laden, to her lips, the sweetness slick and thick, cementing her tongue to the roof of her mouth.

"That the wildflower? It's especially fine this year."

She hastily removes the spoon from her mouth and plunges it into her mug, stirring with a gusto born of guilt.

Sensing her embarrassment, Kuba shrugs. "Eat some more, if you like. I'm not partial to honey straight up myself, but Grandma Vi swears by a spoon or two a day." He notes the doubt hanging from the corners of Angel's eyes and lips. "No one's gonna chide you. Plenty more where that came from."

His arms cradle several butternut squash, which he sets on the counter. "Ever see a beehive?"

Angel takes a sip of tea to help melt the honey in her mouth. "Only from a distance."

"Well, come on then." Kuba starts for the kitchen door.

Angel clutches the mug, chasing the chill from her fingers. "I don't really like— insects," she admits.

"You? 'fraid of bugs?"

She takes it as an accusation. "Everyone's afraid of something," she blurts.

Kuba cocks his head, considering. "I guess," he finally agrees. "I have some problems with blood, rather not see it." He gestures to the canning jar. "But you know, if you eat stolen goods, you should pay homage to the one you stole from."

"I didn't steal it! You just said take as much—"

Kuba smirks. "I meant the bees. Come on," he coaxes. "I promise it's safe."

The hives are a short stroll down the path to the south, just past a small utility shed where they stop to don broad-brimmed white hats hung round with gauzy veils. Kuba shows her how to wrap the strings under her armpits and around her chest and tie them securely.

"Don't want a bee in your bonnet," he jokes. "These girls are pretty docile, but it's autumn, the robbing season, and they're on the lookout for intruders, with wings or without."

The mesh of the veil is fine and surprisingly easy to see

through, tinting the world with a hint of gray. But the fear sweat is already beading on Angel's forehead. A drop trickles and pools in the corner of her eye.

Even after all you've done...

"Word to remember is calm. If you're calm and stay calm, the bees will be calm, too," Kuba says, tugging on a pair of form-fitting leather gloves. "Bees can smell fear, just like any animal. It oozes out our pores and they sense it."

The hives are long rectangular boxes with peaked roof covers set atop cross-legged platforms. To avoid encountering guard bees, they approach from the back. Kuba carefully lifts the angled cover and cocks his head.

"You can tell a lot just by listening. A loud buzz means they feel threatened."

The hum is quiet, restrained.

"You can't see anything if you're so far away. Come closer," Kuba says. His movements are gentle, graceful, slow but not hesitant. He fishes his multitool out of his pocket and bends out a short flathead screwdriver, then carefully pries up the end of one of the wood bars that hang across the width of the box. Slowly lifts it to reveal a golden u-shaped swath of honeycomb, crawling with brown bees.

Oh, how her feet want to flee, but Angel forces herself to stay rooted, although she feels herself leaning back and away.

Kuba lightly taps the bar on the edge of the box and most of the bees fall back into the hive. When he hoists the bar again, the pattern of cells is clearly visible.

"Bees ain't just hard workers. They're smart, too."

"Why?" Angel forces her body forward, leaning in rather than away.

"The hexagons. The way they fit together without wasting space. A circle, a cylinder, would hold a bit more liquid, but when you line 'em up in a row, the curves leave gaps. The bees would have to make more wax to hold the hive together and have less time for making honey. The hexagon solves the problem."

"No gaps, no overlaps," Angel observes.

"Right. It's late in the year. I won't be harvesting any more honey," Kuba says, resting the bar upside down across the others. "They'll need some to get through the winter. Though Gray-Gray says it's not nearly as harsh as it used to be. It snowed just a couple of times last year. Temperatures barely dropped below freezing. But that's still pretty cold for a bee. They eat the honey to keep their energy up, keep warm. Though that don't help the drones," he adds, pointing. In the dirt under the hive lie the carcasses of several largish bees.

"What happened?"

Kuba grins. "Drones have one purpose. To mate with the queen. But any one of 'em has about a one in a thousand chance of actually doing that. And if they're successful, they die. If they're not successful, well, they just eventually become a burden on the colony. The workers let 'em hang around in the summer, even though they don't do a lick of work. But when the chill hits and the flowers are gone and the bees have to survive on what they got stored, drones are just one more lazy-ass mouth to feed. So the workers round 'em up and kick 'em out. Drones don't have a stinger to fight back. So they croak, either from the cold or starvation."

"The bees' version of severance."

Kuba nods. "Yeah. But when you've got thousands and thousands of mouths to feed..." His voice trails off. A bee is crawling on his gloved hand. He nudges it off gently. "Somebody's got to make the tough decisions."

"Who decides?"

"A hive's definitely got a pecking order. The queen's on top. Her job is to make more bees. So she pretty much determines whether the hive is a success or a fail. She's the one who decides the kind of lives her babies will lead. Some of the eggs she lays will be fertilized and some won't. The ones that ain't come up drones. The ones that are will be workers or maybe even another queen."

Kuba pries another bar loose and draws it up out of the box. The comb hanging from it is much larger than the first, with areas that are waxy white, dark bronze and butter yellow. He points to a pair of cells near the top at the far end of the comb. They resemble peanut shells.

"Queen cells. The eggs inside these will get the royal jelly treatment by the nurse bees. Those are the eggs that can grow into queens."

"But there can be only one queen, right? Why would they raise more?"

"At some point, they have to requeen the hive. As the queen ages, she starts to slow down, lays fewer eggs," Kuba says, turning the bar to examine the cells on the other side. "The workers are the ones who decide when they need a new queen. So they'll raise a few. Most'll leave to start new colonies."

"What happens to the old queen?"

"If she doesn't die on her own, the workers will smother her." He replaces the bar in the box, pressing down to secure it. "Life's tough for everyone, even the queen. She can't do her job anymore, she's out. The colony does what it needs to do to survive."

"That's why they call it The Hive," Angel muses, half to herself.

"What?"

"Corporate. Galt. That's what the bees, the workers, call it. The Hive. The bees are the backbone, but there's a handful of swags making the decisions, who gets born, what they'll grow up to be. Everyone knows their place and does their job. But it's not really the same, because in the Protectorate, the workers never get to smother the queen."

A bee spurts out of the empty space, humming gentle and low. It hovers just above Angel's hand resting on the edge of the hivebox. She so very much wants to swat at it, to turn and run, to let out a shriek and pull her hand away.

"Calm," Kuba reminds her.

"A worker?" she asks.

Kuba nods. "The smallest, but, in some ways, the mightiest."

The bee comes to rest on the back of Angel's knuckle, where the bone rises, a hill above the valley through which the blue-green vein, the river of blood, runs. The lightest of caresses, the tickle and stick of its six legs.

Still, be still. Only the movement of blood through the body.

She is shocked to realize that she longs to touch the tiny furred body, the iridescent wings. The bee rears up, cleaning an antenna, pulling it under a foreleg from one end to the other. It repeats the process with the other, then suddenly rises into the air again and zips back down through the gap into the dark of the hive's interior.

"I'll make my way there some day."

"The Hive?"

"Yeah," she nods.

"That's where you're headed?"

Angel shakes her head. "First, I have to go to Chicago."

"What's in Chicago?"

Angel eyes the slashes on her forearm from under lowered lashes. "Unfinished business."

49

Radio TCT

Perched on the bottom step of the front porch, Angel revels in the contrast between the cool of the breeze and the warmth of the late afternoon sun on her forehead. She's worked up a sweat wrestling with the farm's oldest generator, which has been out of commission since spring. The men want to scrap it, but Angel recognizes the squat form when she sees it in the corner of the barn, where it's been banished, silent and sulky, like a miscreant child in permanent disgrace. It looks a lot like Mr. Oceguera's. The one she's repaired a half dozen times.

Kuba and Debs stride up the bluestone path with Vato at their heels. The boy dismisses the generator with a smirk.

"What's that hunkajunk doin' out the barn?"

Helping keep your lights on this winter, Angel thinks as she works away at a bolt, rusted and recalcitrant.

Debs hunkers down on the middle step, then stretches his legs out before him with a sigh. Kuba flings himself down on the top step of the porch, patting the boards with the palm of hand. Vato bounds up and stands at attention. The boy begins an inspection, running his hands over the collie's body, checking under his collar, using his fingers like the teeth of a comb. He pokes in the dark hidden places where ticks are likely to burrow. Between the toes. Under the tail. Near the groin. Behind the front legs. He examines the pert ears thoroughly, inside and out, then takes a brush from a hook on the porch post and runs it through the glossy fur.

"No bloodsuckers here," Kuba states, hanging the brush back up and giving the dog a scratch behind the ears.

A pool of quiet settles around them, not awkward, but not quite comfortable. Angel works with a wrench and a screwdriver, loosening nuts and bolts, prying off parts, eyeballing them, cleaning off the accumulated gunk with rags soaked in vinegar.

"Shouldn't you take a look at yourself?" she finally murmurs.

Debs gives her a sidelong glance, skepticism oozing into the creases around his eyes. "After livin' in the Shawnee, I think I can make my way around a sorghum field without picking up critters."

"You can give me the once over," Kuba offers and though she has her back to him, she can hear the wink in his voice.

"Bring it, then," she replies. *I'll play your silly game.* Plotting to be matter-of-fact, like he's just another obstinate bolt in need of a good twist of the wrench.

But when he's standing there before her at the bottom of the stairs, her fingers are tentative in their touch, hesitant and shy as they lift the curls from the back of his neck and pull the collar of his shirt away from his damp skin that is strangely soft and rough at once, furred, like velvet.

Enough of this nonsense! With her thumb and forefinger she gives a quick flick to the fleshy curve of his right ear. "Nada," she snaps, easing herself back down to the step and picking up the wrench.

"Owww," he fake-whines, cupping his ear with his hand. "Vicious. Just for that, no pie for you. I baked a pumpkin this morning. But don't come sniffin' around for a slice." He winks and bounds up the steps, snapping his fingers. "Vamonos."

Vato is on his feet, trailing his master into the house.

Angel wrinkles her nose at his retreating back and then bends to her task again, encountering a particularly stubborn bolt. She positions and re-positions the wrench, leans into it, leveraging the weight of her entire body, but it refuses to budge. She douses it with a little oil. Tries again. Same result.

"Might need to let that set. Here, lemme give it a go." Debs holds out his hand.

Angel reluctantly gives way, swipes impatiently at the sweat that has popped up along her hairline. *Where's the damn breeze now?*

When the old man scoots down to the bottom step and crouches forward, working the wrench, she spies the thing on the back of his neck, just at the hairline where the salt and pepper wisps curl. An engorged tick, body swollen to the size of a small bean.

"You got one on you, and from the look of it, it's been feeding awhile."

"Shit," Debs mutters. He fishes in his pants pocket and pulls out his multi-tool.

"Pair of tweezers on that," he says, handing it over to Angel. "Dig it out."

Angel brushes the hairs aside and works the tweezers with delicacy, grasping the tick at the surface of the old man's skin, pale under the hair, a stark contrast to his ruddy neck. Her fingers want to quiver but she steels them to pull upward with steady, even pressure. *Don't twist or jerk.* Eben's voice as he guided her in removing her childhood ticks. *Don't want the mouthparts to break off and remain under the skin because then you'll just have to keep fishing for them. Nice and steady, pull.*

The tick comes out cleanly and with an ease that suggests it was ready to detach itself, full with blood.

"Got it," Angel says, depositing the beast in a discarded bottle cap she finds in the tool chest. She douses it with rubbing alcohol from her supply of cleaning solvents.

She splashes the bite area with more alcohol. "You should shower, old man. You might be harboring a few more of those in places where the sun don't shine."

He scowls, adjusting the collar of his shirt.

"Keep an eye on that wound. Tell someone if you start to feel feverish." She hears the scold in her voice. And something else, the beginnings of a drawl, not unlike that of the men and women of the farm.

Debs bends back to the obstinate bolt. "Been bit by them buggers before. Been fine by some and made sick by others." A grunt escapes him as the bolt finally surrenders. "Always made it back on my feet, alive and kickin', which is more'n I can say for your chances to revive this piece of crap."

She extends her hand for the wrench. "Don't recognize a survivor when you see one?"

He plops the tool in her palm. Regards her for a moment. "I see you." A crooked grin, small and wry stretches across his face. "I see you." The grin fades. "Put out some feelers for that name yer lookin' for."

Angel blinks, turns the wrench, squeezes it tight. "And?"

"Give it a couple days."

"How—"

He shakes his head, flicks his hand toward the generator. "Finish yer business."

The eyes staring at her are round and weak, fixed in an expression of perpetual surprise. The nose is barely more than two slits in the chubby face, the mouth a grimace of sharp crooked teeth. The visage of the jack-o'-lantern is a disconcerting mix of passivity and menace.

This carving ritual is foreign to Angel. She's enjoying a rest in one of the slantback chairs when the three youngest of the clan each lug a large pumpkin onto the pergola and stab them with their utility knives. They slice in a circle and, using the stems as handles, lift off the round tops they've created. Plunging their hands inside, they pull out fistfuls of guts, stringy innards flush with gray seeds. They plop some of the mess into pans. The rest of it, they fling at each other with abandon. A long strand of it lands on Angel's cheek, where it clings with the slimy tenacity of a leech.

"What are you doing?" she asks, peeling the pale orange webbing from her face.

The boys pause to look over, shrug, mumble their apologies without a shred of true regret and then return to their gruesome work with renewed gusto.

"No, I mean it, what are you doing?" Angel repeats, watching Uriel cut a precise triangle out of the rind.

Raphael finishes cutting a circle in his, sits back on his heels and cocks his head at her. "Making a jack-o'-lantern," he says, pausing a beat to emphasize each word. He stabs the pumpkin again and slices out another circle a few inches apart from the first.

Gabriel turns to squint at her. "Ain't you never made one?"

She shakes her head.

"Go get yourself one. Not the pie kind. Those ain't for carving," the boy continues with the authority of one who knows. "Get you a big one."

Uriel motions for her to stay put. "I'll get it. Gram wouldn't want you haulin' it."

"Why are you making them?"

All three boys stare at her, disbelief lifting their brows.

"Uhmmm, it's Halloween," Uriel snickers.

"She wouldn't know about Halloween. Corporate outlawed it before Year 5." The thin but sharp voice catches them all off guard.

"Grey-grey!" Raphael shouts, skipping over to the stoop just outside the kitchen door. He takes Isa's outstretched hand, steadying her frail body as she steps down onto the pergola's stone floor. He guides her shuffling path to a chair and helps her settle in, before returning to his pumpkin.

"Tried to wipe the whole slate clean. Did their damnedest.

The federal holidays went first, of course," Isa says, rubbing her fingers along the arms of the chair, tracing the grooves carved by time and use. "Anything that celebrated the republic. And then the religious holidays. There was no religion beyond the corporate religion, the belief in the Protectorate. They squeezed out the traditional, the secular, too. Why would you celebrate your mother and father when all beneficence flowed from the Corporate Hive? Why honor love?"

Gabriel puts down his knife and, taking his finished creation in his arms, carries it over to Isa. She inspects its evil face.

"Hmmm, a grimace this year," Isa muses, following the downward curve of the jagged mouth with her fingers.

"The better to ward off evil spirits," he says with hoodoo snark in his voice and an arched eyebrow.

Uriel sets a pumpkin down in front of Angel. Lusciously round, its skin is an unblemished, earthy orange, its grey-green stem the curving neck of a swan. "Go on," he urges, offering her his knife, carefully extending its handle. "You know you want to."

She accepts the knife, lets it rest in her palm, appreciating its heft, the way the grain of the wooden handle feels against her skin. But appreciation morphs into something else when she grips it and places the tip against the pumpkin's skin. That's when the memories seep in, conflated, stark yet shrouded, elusive, filling the space between thought and action. How the piercing of human flesh is a silent business. How it is not the skin itself that cries out or lets slip a moan. How little resistance it offers to the shank as it slides through fat and muscle, like a hand through water. Mute. Passive. Until the blade hits bone.

She passes the knife back to Uriel. Caresses the pumpkin's curve and lets her finger trace a groove that arcs along it, a line of longitude marking its body.

"Not this one. Not today. This is the one that got away."

The sun sets before the extended family gathers for dinner at the communal table. The boys light beeswax candles inside the hollowed out pumpkins and the jack-o'-lanterns flicker to life. Jagged music in a minor key thrums from the disc player. A serrated violin screeches a triton. Zig, zag, zig. Laughter. Reminiscences of times past when the boys were little. Of improvised costumes. Of trick-or-treating at the goat shed, the barn. Of home-made candy corn.

Raphael, just ten, sighs. "Yeah, it was awesome to be a kid."

The adults drift away. After the dishes are washed and the kitchen set to right, the boys carry the pumpkins out to the front porch and line them up on the broad railing, largest to smallest. Tumble down the steps like overeager puppies and admire their handiwork, the eerie faces glowering at them. A glance passes between them, furtive, conspiratorial, and they slip out of the porchlight's glowing circle and into the gloom.

"Early for them to be heading to bed," Angel says to Kuba, as they stand on the top step.

"Not heading to bed."

"Well, I figured that, from that look they traded. What's up? Pranking?"

Kuba shakes his head, shifts from side to side, like he's weighing a decision. "If I ask if you can keep a secret, that means I have doubts you can." His eyes slide to the side, then back, as he regards her with the utmost seriousness. "Come on." He heads down the stairs.

"Where we going?"

"I should blindfold you, but considering it's pitch black out here, just come on."

With the growth of her belly, the tempo of her strides has slowed, become more stately, the progress of a queen. Her deliberate pace forces the boy to match his strides with hers. In the dark of the path, she places her feet with extra care. Where the path forks, he takes the lead and her hand.

"It's tricky here, gravel's loose," he says.

Amidst the night chill, the warmth of his skin against hers feels good.

They walk on, much further than Angel expects, past the outbuildings and up a gentle rise into a drift of trees. Fallen leaves rustle under their feet. The rustle becomes a murmur, the murmur, a voice.

A light flickers up ahead from somewhere above, shining in the midst of the leaves that still cling tenaciously to a magnificent old oak. Kuba lets a low whistle slip between his teeth, three mellow notes, and then again, rising and falling. A response comes from above. Along with a rope ladder.

Looking up, Angel spies a crude construction, a platform crafted of old boards.

"Go on, it's safe. I'll be right behind."

Angel, skeptical, grabs hold of the rope and gives a tug.

"Don't worry. That thing's not comin' loose any time soon. Tied the knots myself."

When Angel's head tops the gap in the board that serves as a doorway, she finds herself greeted by the interrogatory glare of a flashlight.

"You fit through that hole?" It's Raphael's voice.

A snicker bursts from the shadows, and then another.

It is a tight squeeze, but she makes it through, boosting herself with her arms and then scoot-waddling back from the opening. Kuba follows quickly.

The treehouse is a classic design executed with middling skills. Boards rise to form chest-high walls along three sides, with the fourth open to an enormous branch. The boys have furnished this hideaway with a ratty, paint-stained blanket to give them a soft landing and reduce the threat of splinters. An upturned plastic crate serves as a table with a few mouldering cushions for seating.

"Why'd you bring her?" Gabriel snipes, redirecting the flashlight beam to his cousin's face.

"It's slick, güey," Kuba replies. "Get that thing outta my face."

Angel hunkers down cross-legged in the unoccupied corner. "Not slick, güey. You should've asked," Gabriel shoots back. "Just turn the damn radio on before I smack you upside the head," Kuba says without real menace, settling himself next to Angel. The beam of light skims across the treehouse floor to spotlight a battered black 'tronic box. Its face is studded with grimy chrome buttons and knobs and a tiny screen that glows orange, illuminating a series of black numbers as Gabriel turns the largest dial. Crackles of static spurt in and out as the boy turns the knob.

"Shortwave," Kuba says. "Ever seen one?"

Angel nods as recognition surfaces. The 'tronic box Debs had in his cabin.

"Outlawed." Kuba continues, a bit of brag in his voice.

"Exactly," Gabriel cuts in. "So you need to keep your mouth shut about this."

Angel just stares at him through the sharp edges of shadow and light.

"Come on, Gabe, she don't have diarrhea of the mouth, unlike some people I know. Tune it and turn it up. We didn't come here to listen to your gash," Uriel gripes.

With a shrug of his shoulders, as if shedding the burden of responsibility, Gabriel turns back to the radio and gives the dial a disgruntled twist.

Static, a vibrating whine, and then the whine is cut short by the throaty bark of a saxophone, the notes brutish and beautiful, curdled honks connected by sinuous curving moans, and just under those moans, the right-angled plinks and thrums of an electric guitar, and supporting it all, a squared-off bottom of bass and drums. A voice cuts across the plane of this musical geometry, doggedly minor key, tight with a restraint that seethes a barely hidden venom.

You don't own me, I'm not just one of your many toys...

A thin veil of buzz hangs over the music, but it only

intensifies the performance. The voice swoops from defiance to declaration, from minor to major.

I'm young and I love to be young, I'm free and I love to be free...

Fervor non-stop, pushing through upwards and outwards, breaking some invisible boundary, the saxophone and the voice in a feverish call-and-response. Triumphant. The music reaches the edge of a cliff and takes a leap, falling in one last dive of the sax and twist of the guitar and roll of the drums.

"Thank you," comes a man's voice out of the crackling undertow. "Found that one on a vinyl scored from a basement in the Erie Region. Yeah-uh, what used to be O-HI-O. Mads worked out the chords and Jeffers did the arranging. Original had some violins, but we don't go for that, do we? Though, if we had a couple, we'd would, yeah-uh?"

Another voice cuts in, slightly garbled. "Violins or violence?"

A harsh "haw" of a laugh. "Well, I'll 'fess to engagin' in a bit o'the latter every now and then, what?"

More sniggers.

"Right then, enough of the comics. We're not here for shits and grins. Oh, wait, Mads tells me we are."

"¡Venga ya!"

"¡Venga! Uno, dos, tres, cuatro..."

The bass starts pumping out a riff.

"You're tuned in to Radio TCT, Three Chords and the Truth."

Song after song spews forth from the radio's speaker, each more rancorous than the last. Then, just when the malevolence is at its height, silence settles again, like dust after the whirlwind. And then it's just an acoustic guitar picking out a simply melody. The voice, once a growl, is now a purr, plaintive, seductive. A sigh, a whisper, taking the listener into its confidence.

My country, tis of thee... An exhalation. *Sweet land of liberty...* A breath, audible. *Of thee I sing...* A pause. *Land where my fathers died, land of the pilgrims' pride...* A sigh. *From every mountainside...* A quiet exhortation. *Let freedom ring.*

The sizzle of static.

Gabriel turns the radio off with a snap of his wrist. Throughout the transmission, he's been hunched into a coiled ball of potential energy, but now he stretches out on his back, face toward the canopy of branches that arch and twist above the treehouse.

"They were on fire tonight," he snarls.

"Kickin' it," echoes Uriel.

Raphael, on the edge of the light thrown by the flashlight's beam, looks dazed.

"It's time we got back," Kuba says, taking charge.

"Awww, man, can't we just bunk out here?" Uriel whines.

"No."

"But—"

"No," Kuba repeats firmly. "Get your ass down the ladder."

On the walk back, Kuba and Angel put some distance between them and the boys, who dawdle, stopping to relieve themselves against trees and examine every semi-interesting rock and pebble they spy with the flashlight beam, like alpha dogs inspecting and marking their territory, even though they've trod it a hundred times before.

Kuba's silence tells her he's not going to volunteer any information, so she's forced to ask. "What was that? Did you tap into the Corporate feed?"

"Frack no! That sound Corporate?" He swings the flashlight to illuminate the path. "Outlier all the way. At least I think they're Outlier. Band called Damn Otis."

Angel looks at him sharply and stumbles as a loose piece of gravel skitters away under her shoe. Only Kuba's quick grip on her bicep keeps her upright.

"It's—real?"

"Frack, yeah. They only shortwave now and then. Cuz it's obviously all on the downlow. Halloween is one of their regulars.

You've never heard 'em before?"

"Heard them? No. Heard *of* them, yeah. Although I didn't really believe it. That they actually existed."

Suraj and his t-shirt and his brag. Saw 'em live and in person.

"It's more than music," Kuba says.

"What d'you mean?"

"They're not just shortwaving to play some kickass music. Got some type of messaging goin' on."

Angel stops walking. "Like a code?"

"Yeah. Just wish I knew the cipher to crack it."

"I heard they break into the Feed sometimes."

Kuba nods. "Sounds like something they'd do. You can't spill this to anyone," he continues, nudging her back into motion. "Debs set us up with it. He uses it when he's up here. Contacts his old guevaras, I guess. Grandma Vi would blow up if she knew we were listening."

"Why, if it's not from Corporate?"

"It's still all wrapped up with it. I might not be able to crack the code, but I can read between the lines. They're lookin' to bring it."

"Bring what?" Angel asks, feeling stupid for having to ask.

"Instigate."

"A protest? Against Corporate?"

Kuba bristles at the skepticism in her voice. "A rising, a riot, a rebellion... a frackin' revolution. Gotta start somewhere. It's gonna happen, sooner or later. Maybe it has. Yesterday, for all we know. When it does, there's not gonna be a neutral ground. Grandma doesn't get that. She thinks if we just keep to ourselves, stop up our ears and blindfold our eyes and keep our mouths shut, we'll just ride out whatever storm comes our way. But we've just been lucky. At some point our luck's gonna run out."

The lights are out in the main house, except for the solar lanterns mounted on the posts of the pergola out back. They round the bend and reach the fork where the path diverges, one branch to the cabins and one to the house. In the dim blue glow, Angel spies a figure slouched in a slantback chair, long legs splayed in front. Kuba sees it, too.

"Not a word," he reminds her.

She nods and they part, Kuba making his way toward the cabins, Angel to the pergola. She assumes Debs is asleep from the way his head lolls to the side, but at the scrape of her shoes across the stone, he turns toward the sound. "Who's that?"

"Me," Angel whispers, settling into the chair next to his.

"Late. Where you been?"

"Out walkin'."

Silence settles again, but there have been things on Angel's mind, questions she's wanted to ask, but never seemed to find a good time for asking. Now, alone, in the blue light and shadows, after the sudden reminder of the world that exists outside the farm's sturdy fences, the time seems right.

"Somethin's been weighin' on me. I've been tryin' not to think about it, but I can't shake loose of it." Her hand creeps to her side, the one where the scar stretches like a seam. "Did you kill him? At the farmhouse?" And there it is, blunt as can be.

A long moment passes. He shifts, tugs the collar of his jacket a little higher on his neck. "Getting' chilly, now. Do believe a frost is near." The words sound slurred, as if he's speaking through a mouthful of cotton.

Drunk is her first thought, but she knows he barely touched his glass at dinner and a quick scan reveals no bottle on the flagstones under and around his chair.

"You don't know, do you?"

His head moves from side to side, just barely.

"Was it..." but her voice trails off because, in her gut, she already knows the answer. So she asks a different question. "Can he find us here?"

The old man's shoulders rise and fall, just barely. "When it's time to go, we'll double back, cover our tracks, keep these people out of the loop. Leave a different trail for him to follow."

"You should've made sure he was dead," she spits, anger flaring.

"I had to make sure you and that baby would survive," he tries to spit back, but his anger sounds frail, wavery, muffled.

"A murderer's child."

"And I let go of askin' you about that. The father. None of my business, I thought. But maybe that was the wrong thing to do." It seems to cost him much effort to speak those few words. Too much effort.

"You feelin' okay?" She wishes for more light beyond the weak solar flare near the doorway. When he doesn't answer, she leans forward and boldly places the back of her hand against his forehead. "You're burnin' up," she snaps, pulling her hand away from his scorching skin. "How long you been like this?"

When he still doesn't reply, she takes hold of his chin, its stubble raspy under her fingers, and turns his face to hers. "You fool, whyn't you say somethin'? I'm getting Vida."

"Nothin to do... nothin'," he grunts through that mouth full of cotton.

"You're the one don't know nothin', old man."

"Oh, I know somethin'."

"Fool."

But when she releases his chin, Debs grips her hand, tugs her close. "His name. The waterman."

Her cheek is so close to his, she can feel the fever radiating.

"Rivers. Apropos, no?"

50

The Medic

SOMETHING VIRULENT HAS THE OLD MAN IN ITS GRIP. The poultices and the fever teas of yarrow and elderflower are useless against the onslaught. He sweats, but the furnace within only burns hotter. The shakes come and go. His right hand swats and scrapes, flails in the air, as if chasing phantom flies. Vida, with the patience of a woman who has spent many hours with a rod and reel in her hand, sits at his bedside, spooning broth into his mouth in those rare moments of quiet and lucidity. But he's wasting away, what little spare flesh he has dropping from his frame with each passing day. She tries to keep Angel out of the sickroom, for fear of contagion, but Angel, a medic's child and beyond the lies once told to keep her safe, bulls her way in.

"It's past the point of infection, and if not, I don't really care." When she sees his sunken cheeks, her breath slips sharply between her teeth. "He needs a medic," she says, watching a shudder roll through his limbs.

"That's not our way," replies Vida, dipping a washcloth in a bowl of water on the nightstand. She wrings it out and applies it to the old man's grey-skinned forehead. "We don't deal with the sector clinic."

"It's time to start," Angel insists, watching convulsions pulse through Debs' body.

Vida shakes her head. "That's inviting trouble to our door."

"Medics take a vow to help people in need. My father was a medic and he—"

"No doubt he was a fine man," Vida cuts her off. "Honorable. But you can't assume every other medic is fashioned in his mold. We don't truck with Corporates."

That's the last Angel needs to hear. She bolts from the sick room, ducks into her own just long enough to grab her backpack from the corner of the closet where she's stashed it. She finds the boy squatting in the herb garden just outside the kitchen, snipping the last of the basil.

"I need to borrow your scooter. Where d'you keep the key?"

Kuba squints up at her, finding her face dark, unreadable, haloed by the sun.

"What? Where you goin'?" he asks.

Angel toes the wood beam that corrals the soil of the raised bed. Considers a lie, then shakes it off. "Get a medic for Debs." Kuba starts to speak, but she cuts him off. "I'm getting him. Her. Whoever. What Vida's doing is not helping. Where's the key?"

Kuba stands. "You don't even know the way to town."

"I'll find it."

"Get there faster if I take you."

She weighs the offer. "Fine," she snaps. "But we have to leave now and it's your skin those women'll flay when they find out."

It's a tight fit, the two of them on the shortish seat, and the thrumming shudder of the engine rattles her, making her feel as if her bones will slip their sockets. The long driveway spits gravels out from under the fat tires. The drive opens onto the cracked and pitted bed of an ancient road. Every jolt seems aimed straight for her pelvis.

"Ain't the smoothest route, but it's the quickest. Fact, it's the only," Kuba shouts over the engine's sputtering groan.

A dip in and out of a cavernous pothole sends them airborne

and Angel, who's been holding a mere fistful of the boy's shirt, wraps her arms around his chest, her belly snug against his back. He grins at her over his shoulder.

"Keep your eyes on the frackin' road!" she shouts back, squeezing her own shut tight. When next she forces them open, it is due to a rhythmic bump-bump-bump under the tires and the pull of gravity on her face. The engine chugs and whines under the strain of descending a steep hill in low gear on a street paved with time-worn red bricks.

The town has somehow escaped the Corporate bulldozer. Relics line the cobblestone street, from time past, from time out of mind, the time before the Protectorate, before the collapse. A few of the houses look habitable, some even inhabited. The rest sag under the weight of all that time, unloved and uncherished.

After this decayed beauty, the clinic is stark, ugly, a squat white rectangle. Fusty gray splotches crawl up the siding where wind-blown dust clings, where the sweeps failed to do a thorough job of powerwashing. Or maybe the cleaning squads don't even come through here. Here, in this forgotten place, maybe even those on the grid are off.

Kuba points out a large plywood board that is nailed across a window opening toward the back of the building. "Place got broken into awhile back—or so I heard down in the Chautauqua. In Dealer Alley. Thieves made off with sweeties, lethe juice. And anti-bac, which is worth more'n the other two combined. Heard it might've been an inside job. Cuz no brute squad rolled through to shag the place. Mostly migs 'round here anyways. Field workers. They ship 'em in and out," he says, setting the kickstand.

"You know a lot for not havin' any truck with Corporate." Angel says.

"Hah! I might not truck with 'em, but I keep my eyes and ears open."

Inside the squat building, a bulldog of a woman in floral-patterned scrubs hunches behind a small window cut into a tall counter, shoulders up, head down. When she looks up from her tablet and her eyes take in the small mound that juts out in front of her, her furry eyebrows arch like caterpillars in mid crawl.

Still, she manages to cough out a few syllables. "Do you have an appointment?"

Kuba shakes his head. "This ain't about us. We need the medic out to our place."

The receptionist's bulging hazel eyes, froggish, scan back and forth, from Kuba's earnest face to Angel's forthright belly and back again. She swipes at the mop of mousey brown waves that have escaped her black fabric headband.

"What place is that? Dr. Robie was just at Ag—" She pauses, squints, eyes skimming something behind the counter. "26 and 27 yesterday. You from 28?"

Kuba shakes his head again. "We're across the river."

The woman consults the schedule again. "He's due over to 28 and 29 tomorrow."

Angel bristles at this frittering away of precious time. "No, they're independents. Someone at their farm needs a medic. Now."

The froggy eyes bug out. "I'm not sure what you mean by 'independents.'"

It's apparent the receptionist is not sure how affronted she can afford to be, faced with this obviously pregnant girl. In this woman's known world, there are only two classes of fems permitted to be in this condition. Those belonging to the first class are secured and secluded away from the prying eyes of the general population. She's never set eyes on the any of the mystical ovas, the breeders. She's heard stories of friends of friends who knew someone who lived up in the Superior for a time and that someone knew a woman who had the honor of joining the facility as a mid-wife. From whence sprang the legends, handed-down stories of how stunning these breeder fems are.

The receptionist lets her eyes travel down the girl's lanky body and back up again to rest on her face. She has the height that breeders' supposedly do. And this girl might be considered striking, although that's being kind. She's not beautiful in the Corporate sense of the word. Maybe it's the cropped hair.

As far as contact with the swag class, she'd glimpsed a couple of fems during her training days in Champaign. The golden-haired, warm-skinned director's wife, who had stalked the campus in her heeled shoes, usually dressed in her preferred yellows and oranges, and her black-haired protégé, who appeared and disappeared at regular intervals and whose purpose, other than to look beautiful, was not apparent. This girl does not resemble those women, either. Elegant is not a word she calls to mind with her fingernails bitten to the quick. Her unruly eyebrows. Chewed lips.

Suddenly, the girl presses her largish hands to the swelling, fingers spread wide, and lets out a keening gasp. The woman's training kicks into gear, overcoming her suspicions. She darts up from her chair, sending it rolling backwards and jabs the green button on the side of her counter with a stubby thumb.

"Have a seat there," she calls out as she makes her way around the counter.

In three breaths, the medic bursts through the door that separates the reception area from the exam rooms. He is a narrow man who looks accustomed to squeezing in and out of tight situations. Tall, of middling age, blonde hair buzzed close to the scalp to hide its rapid loss. A man with a long, narrow face and the long, purposeful stride of the doer. But the sight of Angel, that protrusion, trips him up, pulls him to the side like a horse reined in from an easy lope, like he is suddenly confronting a situation too confined for even him to slip through.

"What's going on?" Not a small question. It looms big in his blue eyes, eyes that are not unkind, though the color, reminiscent of frost on rooftops, makes Angel shiver.

It's a risk, but a calculated one, so Angel takes it, though it rankles to the bone to play the weak kitten. But she can and she does, to perfection. Tears well, the full lower lip trembles, a supplicant hand falls light as a windblown leaf upon the medic's forearm. From what hidden well she draws the story she cannot be sure, but draw it she does and it flows. How it flows, like a swelling stream tumbling to join a river. A tale of a journey south from the Hive itself, of an inspection tour of agsector after agsector, of a walk in a field of sorghum, a swollen tick, of a husband, no, not just a husband, a man who sat at the right hand of the CEO himself, a vital man sick to near death, of a child who will be left fatherless... unless...

By the end, she's hunched over in the hard plastic waiting room chair, hands clutching her belly, eyes fixed on the floor, panting, close to hyperventilating, feeling the baby roil, feeling like she's got an ocean, barely contained, in her womb.

He'll either call the goliaths or...

Those frost-colored eyes, wondering, weighing, considering, but not unkind.

"I'll get my keys."

Before they leave, he insists on taking her vitals, although she guesses he has no specific training in the concerns and cares of pregnancy. Why would he need that here where women are empty vessels? And when he sees their mode of transportation, he insists Angel ride with him in his transport, while Kuba leads the way on the scooter.

As a barrier to awkward conversation that will just lead to more lies and to having to remember what lies she has said before so she can repeat them and repeat them until they fashion themselves into an alternative truth, she covers herself in the façade of weakness again, while questions run through her mind. What would an elite fem do? How would she hold her body? Place her hands? Her downcast eyes focus on those hands. Those worker's hands, with split skin and chewed nails. She folds them into fists, tucks them away in the pockets of her jacket, a farmer's jacket, too big in the shoulders and long in the arms, a hand-me-down from Amaranth's dead husband.

He knows it was all a lie. He has to know. So why is he doing this?

The darkest of dark thoughts seep in under her lowered but not quite shut eyelids. Eyes cutting to the side, the better to watch his every move.

Is it too much to believe he is a good man?

Like Eben?

51

The Path of the Good Man

MOST OF THE FAMILY MEMBERS are out and about, doing autumn work, repairing fences, prepping the algal ponds for the coming chill, cleaning the solar panels, digging potatoes. Only the three elderly women are at the main house when Angel and Kuba arrive with the medic in tow.

He has fashioned a poker face to wear when dealing with both his patients and his Corporate overlords, but he can't don the mask quick enough to hide the ripple of consternation that wrinkles his forehead and sags his jaw when he sees them. And why shouldn't he be amazed at the sight of the living fossil in the rocking chair by the stone fireplace, swaddled in a star quilt, filmy eyes staring but not quite seeing as she listens to the relic in the armchair beside her reciting in a fluid, expressive voice, that fem's eyes focused on a biblio that rests in one hand as the bony fingers of her other turn its pages?

As she looks up to greet them, Amaranth's smile melts away. Kuba's left hand flicks a warning as Angel again places her own gentle, pleading hand on the medic's forearm to distract him, to guide him to the sick room down the hall where his patient waits. But he's taking it all in, the people, the room, the furnishings, using his carefully honed skills of observation and inference. It could go either way. Angel sees that now. The placement of trust. Yet it's too late to turn back. Only forward to the room where Debs lies dying.

Oh, he sees it all, for sure. The women who should have been severanced decades ago. The shock in Vida's face when he come bursting into the midst of her ministrations, her hand stopped in mid-wipe across the old man's brow, a shock which hardens into anger when Angel strides in behind him, anger which melts into fear when she sees the medic staring at the stump that nestles amidst the wrinkled sheets. Staring at the place where the old man's left hand should be. At the place where the claw had been strapped until Vida removed it three nights ago when Debs, in the grip of convulsions, thrashed and flailed, hitting himself and her, leaving purple bruises on both their cheeks.

It now sits on the small dresser next to the black glove that had covered it, and the medic observes this, too. And while he can't be absolutely sure, he feels a sense of recognition at its skeletal form. Is that a hand wrought in metal, welded from common household tools?

He asks precise questions in a clipped tone and Vida adopts that same tone in her replies, very business-like. He, too, is business-like in the way he examines the old man, checking vitals, lifting the closed eyelids, shining a minuscule flashlight into the pupils, waiting for a response, for the contraction of the irises against the bright stimuli. He lifts the arms and legs, checking for movement and reflex. Presses hard on the jaw and the nail beds of the fingers, looking for a response to this pain stimuli.

Skulking in the far corner, sliding her hands in the crease where the two walls meet, the hollow space in the small of her back, shoulders slumping under the backpack, which suddenly feels filled with boulders, Angel can see, even from this distance, that it's too late. The old man is doll-like in the medic's hands, limp, bending at will without resistance or reaction. Though his heart may still beat, he is already gone.

When the medic turns from the body on the bed, it is Angel he seeks, ignoring Vida, who sits rigid in the chair next to the bed, and Kuba, who stands beside her, arm encircling the old woman's shoulders.

"There's nothing I can do for this man," he says, fixing Angel with his cool eyes.

His eyes. They're not—not unkind. They're not.

He takes her by the elbow, the grip of his hand firm, but not rough, and ushers her out of the corner, out of the bedroom, and down the hall.

"How much longer does he—" Angel can't get the rest of the words out.

"Hours. Days, maybe. My guess is encephalitis, a swelling of the brain. Without tests, I can't confirm that, but I saw the radial rash along his neck, where you found the tick. It's most dangerous to the very young and the very old. And he is—of a very advanced age. I'm sorry."

When they are out of the house, off the porch, standing under the sullen sky weighted with slabs of clouds that look heavy as granite, he takes her by the shoulders, a curiously intimate gesture.

"Is this your family?"

She shakes her head.

"How long have you been here?"

She stands mute. He is barely taller than she, and she feels the awkwardness of being face to face, eye to eye with this stranger. A man she is not sure she can trust, especially when he leans in, as if to kiss her. But instead, his words bite.

"I don't know how you came to be here, or how you are connected to these people, but you should leave." A squeeze of her shoulders. "Now."

She longs to close her eyes, to squeeze them shut and wish him away, all the while realizing this is the folly of a child playing peekaboo. And she can't afford to be a child.

So she fixes her eyes on his. *They're not—unkind.*

"You can come with me," he says, gesturing toward his transport parked beyond the bend in the path. When she doesn't answer, not even with her eyes, he glances around quickly. "Isn't there somewhere else you should be? Other—" his gaze drops to her belly, "people you should be with?"

Up against the wall of her silence, he surrenders, releases his grip on her shoulders. "Look, whatever that old man really is to you, I don't want to know. I haven't been in this sector very long. I'm just looking to do my job to the best of my ability, to aid my fellow men and women, to assist the Protectorate in its mission to create a safe and sustainable future for all, and to live—"

"By the Corporate Way," Angel finishes the mantra along with him.

"Galt provides," he invokes.

In that moment of communion, Angel knows what she has to do.

There is a word for the set of the man's shoulders as he turns and makes his way along the path back to his van. A word for the manner in which he strides. The way he holds his head level. The way his momentum sets his arms into motion, the way his fingers curve into not-quite fists. He's a man on a mission.

Resolute.

And so, not taking her eyes from the medic's retreating back, she reaches into the backpack still drooping from her shoulder and curls her fingers around the grip of the pistol that's been nestled there, awaiting her touch. Its cross-hatched texture prickles the skin of her palm, like a rash. In the instant she pulls it out and lifts it shoulder high to draw a bead on the medic's narrow back, a large enough target, though a moving one, she feels that rash spread up her arm, a crawling, creeping mass of burn and sting and needle prick and itch. To fight against it, to struggle to overcome it, is to spread the toxin faster and deeper, until her whole arm is shaking with both the sensation and the effort to resist it. She still has the bead, but just. Still has the bead, but now it's a blur, for the itch has reached her eyes, a liquid sting. Still, she can just make out the red pinpoint and amid the tingling, her finger feels the curve of the trigger.

It is the sudden weight of the gun that drags her hand down, its ponderous heft. Or so she tells herself as she feels it drifting, drifting down, a tremor at its core, radiating out to her fingertips, the skin on the back of her knuckles, her wrists. It is an anchor holding her in place as the medic retreats further and further into the distance, around the bend in the path. She can just make out his blue scrubs through the tangle of branches that stretch from the shrubs bordering the gravel.

It is the unbearable weight of the gun.

Not the man's kind eyes.

52

A Walk Through the Valley

TANNER HAS NOT BEEN A COOPERATIVE PATIENT.

The medic named Emmerich has dutifully recorded this in his notes more than once. *Dismissive of the severity of skull fracture. Initial refusal of pain medication. Verbally abusive to the nurses.*

Now that he is past the critical stage, Tanner regrets flipping on the comlink and radioing for help. At the time, he thought he might actually be dying and he absolutely refused to accept that outcome. With his embed removed, he was off the grid, out of the focus and hell knew when someone would stumble across that ancient farmstead to which the pithound had tracked the girl. And so, sprawled on that rotting porch, with what felt like a white hot knife slicing through the back of his head, radiating pain in all directions, fluid trickling from his ears and nose, he had squinted to see beyond the grey veil that floated before his eyes and jabbed a shaky finger at the connect button.

He suffered through the ministrations of the medic and the nurses, endured the indignities of the cleansing, the examination by strange hands, the prodding and poking and scanning. After they proclaimed that he required surgery and he'd tried to walk out, they'd sedated him with lethe juice and held him in thrall with its powerful drip, drip, drip. Under its influence, he relived the nightmare of losing the trail and the triumph of finding it again. Felt the scorch of the blaze on his cheeks, tasted the granules of soot on his tongue, choked on the smoke in his throat, thick and solid as a wad of gum. Perseverated on the thoughts roiling in his mind and belly. Knowing in his gut that even as the forest was consumed, as it died in the onslaught of the flames, even as he witnessed its destruction with his eyes, that she still lived.

Finding the stolen overland, even half-buried in the drifts of dust, was cake, thanks to its embed signal. Finding the girl took a bit longer in that grit-covered world that shifted on the whims of the wind. But once the pithound got hold of the scent, he clung to it like he was grappling with a bone. And when the wreck of the farmhouse loomed up suddenly in the shrouded gray light of the gibbous moon, Tanner had patted the beast's head and passed it a chunk of kibble as a reward, before muzzling it up tight and chaining it to a rust-gnawed post at the far end of the crumbled drive. He'd hunkered down there for awhile, at the edge of the drive, where a stand of parched weeds provided a bit of cover, reconnoitering with his eyes, strategizing.

And then it had been so simple. She'd just appeared around the corner of the house, mounted the dilapidated steps and stood there, leaning up against the rail. Just standing there, free for the taking.

His own weakness had precipitated the failure. That need to feel her in his grasp. Under his hands. That curvature. That swelling and its astonishing solidity, its firmness, had thrown him for a moment. He could admit to that. It was only a moment's lapse. But that moment was long enough to do its damage.

Not knowing the form or shape of her savior, height, weight, age, the statistics of identification, puts Tanner at a disadvantage. But it is a challenge. And a challenge is what's been lacking. Or so he tells himself.

By his reckoning, he's lost well over a month in this agsector clinic. And he has been a specimen upon which the staff plied and honed their skills. They don't get much practice on head injuries. Migs are expendable. Not worth the cost of treatment. Bashed skull? Put 'em on the train. There's always another one in the pipeline, ready to go.

However, he recognizes that belligerence is not the card to play on this table. He knows they've reported his status to Cent-Com up north, which in turn would have flagged that one of its assets has been out of the zoom for over nine months. They will have observed the reason noted, fertility application, and seen it cross-referenced with his wife. They will have run another cross-check to see if a pregnancy has been registered in their name. The system will turn up nothing. The data clerk will duly record that the asset has three months remaining before the application expires, at which time the embeds of both are due to be re-installed.

He pushes that thought aside, sweeps it off the table of his mind. His current mission is clear. Best not to muddy the waters with other issues.

So he plays docile and lets the medic run through the procedures of treating a brain injury and gives the nurses no trouble, no trouble at all, so they begin to wean him off the subduer and the painkiller, decreasing the dosage day by day. Sometimes the nurses forget that he's no longer in a deep lethe sleep. Breaths rolling even and regular, playing possum, he lies so still that they forget he's even there as they bustle about his cubicle or congregate at their station in the hall, just beyond his curtain wall. They seem to come in pairs, like socks, but mismatched. During the day, a lean, tough-muscled blonde of indeterminate age works in tandem with a brunette not long out of training who, despite CQO Zinni's metrics and admonitions, is on the softer side, pillowy even. During the night, a willowy youngish woman with auburn hair cropped short and an array of freckles spanning the bridge of her sharp nose and flat cheeks partners with a squarish woman approaching severance, with grayish frizz riding her temples and grayish eyes that always seem to regard him with suspicion.

This woman, regardless of those suspicious eyes, is prone to gossip and has a voice with a volume control of loud and louder. At first it was as annoying as hell, but now, on this night, Tanner appreciates her oral gusto.

"You remember when they ran off that colony of squatters in the old town—Vandalia? Before the sweepers bulldozed it? No, you probably don't. Too young."

The redhead, bird-like, cheeps. "I'm not from around here. Grew up in Huron."

"Well, there was this little tribe of freeloaders set up camp there. Off the grid. 'Course no one knew they were off the grid, for awhile anyhow. Kept to themselves, grew their own. Bartered. I only saw a couple of the women, in passing. Had that mig look, you know? And they got away with it, 'til the numerators came around."

Another cheep. "What's the point of numerators anyway? You'd think the embeds would be enough to keep track of everybody."

"I know, right? But for awhile there, refugees were streaming in, 'til the border walls were up and secured. Once they were in, they bred like rats. So down here, that's what caught 'em, the numbers men sweeping through, readers blazin'. Brute squad rounded up every last squat and deported 'em. Sent 'em back to the Outlier."

"Serves 'em right."

"Well, here's the thing," Gray Eyes continues, lowering her volume a decibel or two. "Apparently, there's another group like that, livin' up in Ag 29."

"That's north of here, right?"

"Uhmm-hmm."

A pause in the conversation. Then Gray Eyes starts up again. "Here, see. By that river. I'm tight with the head nurse at the clinic there. Go way back, did our clinicals together. She voxes me the other day. Two kids come in off the street with this wild story 'bout needing to fetch the medic. And get this—" Dramatic pause. "The girl is pregnant."

"Swags?"

"Well, that was the story, but no, not from the looks of 'em, Alba says. And they weren't from anywhere around that sector or the next, as far as she can tell. She says when the medic got back, he was really tight-lipped about the whole thing. Of course, she has access to his patient logs, so she looked and there was nothing." Another pause for dramatic effect. "Nothing. Not a thing recorded for the time he was gone. No embed reads, no names to cross-check, no treatment information."

"Weird."

"More than weird. When was the last time you saw a pregnant woman traipsing around down here in the back of beyond?"

A little chasm opens in the conversation. Tanner pictures the redhead pretending to wrack her brain, the skin of her nose wrinkling under its dusting of freckles.

"That's right," Gray Eyes confirms in her stout voice. "Never."

Tanner wrestles with the part of him that wants to haul ass out of the bed and bully his way out of the clinic that very minute in the middle of the night. The cool, clear-eyed strategic thinker struggles with the hothead, the one who wants to move now, and at two hundred miles per hour. Foolishness lies down that path. Raise a ruckus and hurt something or someone on his way out the door, it will get reported. This is all in his data file now. Perhaps command has even tried to make inquiries to his wife. One can only remain incommunicado for so long.

And of course, they have his weapons locked away.

The nurses move on to other topics. At some point, they lapse into silence as they settle into their duty routine. All the while, Tanner lies in wait for dawn.

In the morning, it's all very civil. The medic says it is against his better judgment to release Tanner, even though he's made remarkable progress. Tanner pulls rank and as Director of Special Services for the Illiana Region, Lower District, approves his own release. The medic rattles off a list of symptoms that Tanner should watch for: spasticity, ataxia, executive dysfunction, post-traumatic stress disorder, aphasia. Tanner pretends to attend to this one-sided conversation, but his mind is elsewhere. The medic waits for a response at the end of his spiel. Tanner dutifully affirms that he will seek medical attention if he feels impaired in any of his functions. The medic nods.

And then it is Tanner's turn to wait. The two men stand there, having run out of script. It is a tad awkward. Finally Tanner breaks the impasse. "My—personal belongings?"

"Ah." The medic leaves. A minute or two later, the day nurse, the roomy, pillow-soft one, sweeps in through the curtain, places a couple of plastic bins on the bed, eyes him like a bird eyes a sitting cat, retreats behind the cubicle curtain.

The tang of detergent and something citrusy wafts up from the top bin as he opens it. His uniform has been laundered and neatly folded, the odors of smoke and sweat banished, the wrinkles ironed into crispness. When he lifts the lid on the second bin, the reek of fire and metal seep out. Inside he finds his gear. Tactical vest, soot- and sweat-stained from his march through the blaze, blackout shades tucked into a pocket, lenses smeared with his fingerprints. Duty weapon. Multi-tool. The fish gutter with its curved blade. Comlink. Mobile focus. Swinging the vest around to slip it over his shoulders, the sudden movement catches him off-guard and sends him staggering. He clutches the bed rail, steadies himself. Waits for the buzz in his head to subside.

The sector garrison is just another hideous construction of cinderblocks and plywood. Clinic, company store and, at the far end, the local b-squad barracks. Parked out back of the low-slung, nearly windowless building is a single overland. The squader at the front desk is barely more than a boy, still pimply at the chin, cheeks flush with baby-fat. But he has the requisite bulk in the shoulders and a neck of a pithound. He jolts to attention when Tanner pushes through the entryway, though it is unclear whether he recognizes the man himself or just the high rank.

"I'm taking that overland you got back there," Tanner says in lieu of introduction. The man-boy nods, as if unsure of what to do or say. Tanner shakes his head. *This is what we harvest on Security Track these days.* Holds out his hand. "Keys."

"Yes, sir, Director Tanner, sir."

So he does know. Tanner digs into his vest pocket, slaps the 'tronic key to the overland that he abandoned on the counter. "Use the mobile zoom to locate that one. In fact, you'll find two, north end of Sector 23, south of the old Vandalia rubble. Both are assigned to Sector 21. See that they get—" He stops himself. There is no point in sending anything back there. That sector is gone. "Cancel that. Retrieve 'em and keep 'em here."

The boy fumbles to open a drawer behind the counter. Holds out his hand, respectably large, but with a slight tremor. Tanner takes the 'tronic key from him.

"Do you need a wingman, sir?" asks the boy, with surprising boldness, even as he trains his eyes to avoid staring at the angry red scar running up the side of Tanner's skull.

"Well, that would require you to abandon your post, Officer—" Tanner squints at the name tag sewn across the boy's uniform shirt pocket. "Blankenship. Is that what your superior officer has taught you?"

The squader shakes his head with vigor. "No, sir, I—" He stops, thinks better of whatever explanation he had been about to offer. "No, sir."

"Carry on," Tanner commands as he turns on his heel. Another buzz zips around inside his skull like a hovering bee, bringing with it a fleeting vertigo, a spinning of black and white into gray. Shuts his eyes, darts a hand to the round edge of the counter. When he opens his eyes again, the boy is blinking at him.

"You okay, sir?"

A breath, deep in the lungs, head-clearing. A question right back at him. "You like your job, boy?"

The squader nods, adam's apple bobbing in agreement.

"Then shut your mouth and do it."

53

The Blood of Patriots

CONDEMNATION IS THICK AND ACRID in the dining room, like smoke from a wildfire. It hangs in the air, chokes out the usual conversations so that the only sounds are the scrape of knives, the clink of forks, the muffled noises of chewing and swallowing. Looks pass between the men and the women same as the plates and the bowls, with the utmost care so that nothing is spilled and no meaning is lost.

Angel sits in her usual place between Lylah and Vida, defiant, eating with a gusto that she doesn't really feel, consuming her stew without tasting it, pondering which of her sins is worse in their eyes. Bringing the medic here in the first place or not killing him when she had the chance. She knows she has to leave. Debs will pass, perhaps overnight, perhaps within the hour. She will be with him when it happens and she will see him buried. And then she will go.

She sits with him in the light of a low-burning candle, chair drawn up close beside the bed, her hand clasping his, the flesh cool and loose, the shell of a shrunken man. Mostly she is silent, talking to him in her head. In some mad, pitch-black hour, she hears the click of the door opening and closing again, a shuffling of soft soles along the wood floor. But her bleary eyes, sore when she blinks, as if filled with grit, remain fixed on Debs' face, on his chest, following its rise and fall with each shallow, infrequent breath. The figure that sidles into the circumference of the candle's light is tall and spare, ghostly in its filmy cotton shift and wild spray of silvery hair. She steps to the other side of the bed, the side where there is no hand to hold. She lets her gnarled fingers drift down to cover the stump, like a shroud of skin and bone.

"We all do what we can to save what we love, some by holding on and some by letting go." Amaranth's voice is as threadbare as her nightgown.

Angel pushes herself to her feet, offering the chair, but the old woman shakes her head. "Stay. Now and here. With us. I know your mind is on leaving. But that will only hurt everyone. You, your child, and yes, this family. This man is almost gone. And Isa will leave soon. Nothing lives forever, not even indomitable old crones." A wry smile twists her pale lips. "And not long after she goes, I will follow. Because I've never been as tenacious as my mother. But you. You are one of that breed. Relentless."

Angel shakes her head, mute, but Amaranth nods. "Oh, yes. I've seen the scars. And I know what they mean. And still you persist. And we need that."

"They'll never let this stand," Angel whispers, hand sweeping, gesturing to the four walls, encompassing all that stretches beyond. "This farm, this life. Now that I—now that they know."

Amaranth's chuckle is low and husky, tinged with wood smoke and homebrew. "Girl, they have known since the beginning. Year Zero. We've dealt with numerators and ag inspectors and goliaths. Done our share of nasty deeds. Righteous deeds. As a giant of the Old Republic said, 'the tree of liberty must be refreshed from time to time with the blood of patriots and tyrants.' And here we are." She strokes the stump one last time and then tucks it under the bedsheet. "The tree also needs new branches. Stay."

"There's a man—who may be looking for me. Hunting me,"

Angel whispers, and speaking it makes it so.

The graying brows rise with the bony shoulders. "And? So? Let him come." The woman glides around to stand beside Angel, presses something soft, wraith-like into the girl's hand.

The ragged red bandanna, pale as a ghost.

Amaranth's whisper is a dagger. "The tree could use some water."

Debs passes sometime in the night. When Angel wakes in the bleak smear of light that marks the arrival of dawn, groggy, achy and stiff-necked, angry at herself for falling asleep, she reaches for his hand and finds it not cool, but cold, the fingers stiff.

They bury him quickly under the heavy November sky. The boys dig a deep hole in the northwest corner of the compound, where Isa's and Amaranth's and Vida's men are buried near a stand of hickory trees. Eyes are dry as the boys shovel the earth back into the grave, the clods landing with solemn thuds on the sheet-wrapped body.

When the last shovel of dirt has been flung back into place and the soil raked smooth and the grave marked by four small boulders, one at each corner, then the sky lets go of its burden and the rain falls, light at first, as the family makes its way back to shelter, and then in a torrent.

Now that the burying's done, Amaranth's eyes are welling as she eases herself into her rocking chair. But Angel's remain as dry as the empty sockets of a skull. She'll let the sky cry for her.

In the nights after the old man's death, sleep is an elusive quarry. Part of it is the cumbersome weight she bears, the impossibility of finding a comfortable position. On her back, her womb oppresses like a boulder pinning her to the mattress, leaving her nauseated, dizzy and short of breath. On her side, her hips cry out with every turn. She feels as if her body is slowly coming apart, the joints loosening, the bones refusing to fit together as they once did.

But dread also shares her bed, a supple, sinister presence that keeps her in a twilight state in which every creak of the eaves or yawning of the wind jolts her awake, that keeps her from settling into the deep sleep that refreshes and repairs.

The days are shades of gray. Steel-colored at her bleary waking. A milky gloom in the morning as the sunlight strains through a filter of flat ash-colored clouds. Mottled at noon, with darker lilac jutting up against platinum. Monotonous in the late afternoon, when the weight of water finally breaks the backs of the clouds and the rain comes down, sometimes as a fine mist that beads diamonds and pearls on Angel's hair, sometimes as a tumult, liquid curtains that obscure the world.

Now, as she walks, she wonders if it's raining down in the Shawnee.

The dawn brought fog as the chill from the northwest settles over the still-warmish land. The mist, thick in the bottomland, clings to her eyelashes, beads on the brown tarp that she has fashioned into a rain poncho. She regrets taking it without permission, but that would entail too many complications, entreaties, delay, when she knows the best way to repay these people for their kindness is to put as much distance as possible between her and them. She's left the way she came, without salutations. It's better that way.

She's taken the threadbare bandanna and the mechanoid hand, though she cannot fathom why. She just knows she has to have them with her, as much as she needs Serafina's vocoder and Eben's armored vest and Suraj's pocketwatch. And the plastic-covered image of the Chicago tower where the man she must kill sits and waits.

When she trudges up to the glass doors of the clinic, by a quick glance at Suraj's pocketwatch, she's been walking for an hour and a half already. But she can't think about what that means for the journey ahead. She squares her shoulders.

Stop. Breathe. Focus. Think.

The same nurse is on duty this morning. And she sees the instant recognition in that square-jawed face.

Well, of course, she'd recognize this belly anywhere. Even hidden under a tent-like tarp. *Smile pretty for the lady.* Oh, a broad smile it is, full of teeth, the smile of a she-wolf in sheep's clothing. And the walk, too. Walk pretty, like a good gentle swagsheep. It is practically a waddle, the way she makes her way to the counter, pelvis jutting forward, shoulders sloping, bellycentric.

"I want to thank you for the assistance that you and the doctor provided." She slips the totesack off her shoulder and sets it on the counter.

Oh, the suspicion studded with curiosity, spiced with a pinch of alarm. The nurse still hasn't uttered a word.

"So I brought you these." Angel lifts one canning jar and then another out of the tote and places them before the nurse. She partially unwinds the strip of cloth she has wrapped around the glass to cushion them on their journey. Strips she has torn from her battle-scarred t-shirt. That she has worn and slept in for the past three days and purposely left unwashed.

The honey radiates a golden glow, like a slice of the sun is hidden amidst its thick sweet ooze. Angel taps the lid of the jar. "Black locust. A very rare honey. The tree only produces blossoms every couple of years. Or so I'm told." She twists the lid off and inhales the fruity aroma, admires the amber hue, tilts the jar toward the nurse, encouraging her to take a sniff.

A stare. The woman is uncertain. Weighing the situation.

Angel shrugs, replaces the lid and unwraps the top of the second jar to reveal its rich dark nut-brown contents. "Perhaps you favor buckwheat? Strong as molasses." She carefully rewraps the jars and pushes them across the counter. "Please, I know it's not much. But it's what I have to give, with my gratitude."

Which is, of course, not true. The jars are not hers to give, considering she swiped them from the farm pantry. And what she feels is not gratitude.

The woman has spilled something to someone. Her eyes give that away, the fast-twitch blinks that set her eyelashes aflutter. Maybe not through official channels. But she is a gossip, no doubt about it. The medic? Closed mouth, like a corpse. Angel is sure of it, or as sure as she can be. If he'd reported it, Corporate would have sent an inquisitor squad down quicker than the nurse's nervous eye tic.

"I'm on my way to the Chicago garrison. To see someone who's very important to me." Forcing another smile. "You ever been to Chicago?"

The nurse shakes her head, blinking the whole time. A tight little faux smile stretches her lips. "No," she offers. "I've never been north of Sector 45." A pause and then a probe. "You goin' alone?"

Yes, ask me questions, so I can answer them. Leave a trail to follow. So when the shave-head devil comes, you can spill your guts to him before he slices them open.

Angel lets her own smile shift and fade. She doesn't have to fake the look that replaces it. "Yes, I'm alone now." Looks down. Wishes she could squeeze out a tear, but the rage that's simmering behind her eyes is dry, like fire. "Well, not really alone." She lays a hand where the tarp swells. "But I do need to hit the road. Long way to go before nightfall. Again, thank you for all you've done."

The honey jars will sit on the counter until the medic returns from his rounds. He'll comment on them, the jars wrapped in strips of faded green cloth. If he notices. If he doesn't, the nurse may mention them and the visit from the pregnant girl. She'll venture that she should throw them away. She won't use the word 'poison.' Contamination, perhaps. He will scoff, mumble about 'good people,' tell her to leave them be. He'll take them if she doesn't want them. But in the busyness of his life, he'll forget. And the jars will sit there.

And the next day, the nurse will leave them on the counter, but push them to the side, still wrapped in the old t-shirt. She'll vow to toss them if he doesn't take them by the end of the week. And there they will sit, liquid gold and amber, the industriousness and hard labor of the bees going to waste.

Until the morning the glass doors part and through them strides Tanner.

PART FOUR

By the Rivers of Babylon

How shall we sing the Lord's song in a strange land?
Psalm 137

"Vengeance is in my heart, death in my hand,
Blood and revenge are hammering in my head."
William Shakespeare, *Titus Andronicus*

54

A Brother Born

THE LAND ALONG THE RIVER is like a pleasure woman's body, swelling and dipping, sinuously curved. Hiking the rises and falls strains the calves and the back. From the old map, Angel knows she can follow the river north to the place where it meets another, and then follow that waterway all the way into the Chicago garrison. The roads might not still exist, but the river surely does. Although the rain holds to a drizzle, as morning slides into afternoon, and the light shifts from east to west, she feels like a rag in need of a wringing. Her shoes squelch thick and oozy sounds on the broken pavement of the abandoned road. Just weeks ago she lifted her face to receive the water's blessing. Now its weight feels like a curse.

Another weight rests at the bottom of her pelvis. Everything has shifted, has sunk into that cavity cradled by loosening bones. Her belly seems to have dropped. The pull of gravity, of the earth, seems stronger than ever. All she desires is to lie down and sleep. Pull the tarp over her head and let the whispery patter of the raindrops lull her into slumber. But she keeps to her feet, slogging forward.

A buzz in her head, low yet annoying. Grows louder, whinier, an engine straining. Envelopes her until she can no longer endure it, but must clap her hands over her ears. Then it's beside her on the rubble of asphalt, farting and puttering, until it suddenly cuts off, but still she keeps her hands clamped over her ears as she trudges on, until a restraining hand on her arm, a voice yelling just behind her head, jolts her to a stop.

"Angel, what the hell?!"

Shoulders hunched, as if in anticipation of a blow, head tucked, eyes squinched shut, the stance of a victim, not a warrior.

"Angel."

Hands over hers, drawing them away and down, cupping her chin, lifting it. Thumbs and fingers brushing over her eyelids, down her temples, smoothing out the lines of tension, easing the clench of her jaw.

"Didja think I'd let you ghost me? Frack that. I'm goin' with you. Wherever. Chicago, the Hive, North, the Outlier. Wherever."

Angel shakes her head, but her eyes betray her.

"Don't ask me—don't tell me—to go back," the boy snarls. "Wherever you're going, there I am. Your enemy is mine. That's the way it is. The way it's gonna be. Even if it brings me nothing but pain."

Or death? But that is best left unspoken.

And so silence is her reply. For he would be noble, in the way of young men stoked on passion for a cause, a cause that both was and wasn't his. He wouldn't be dissuaded. This brother born for adversity. A manchild to replace the one she lost when she aimed her burner at Mars Lund. And yet, how much help can this boy, who shies from the slaughter, the hunt for game, be? When the time comes will he be willing and able to do what needs doing? Yet she says nothing, just nods her acceptance. But before she mounts the scooter, Angel palms a piece of fabric from her pocket, yet another strip torn from her t-shirt, balls it up and drops it into a cleft in the cratered pavement.

The scooter carries them to the outskirts of a garrison before it runs out of biofuel, sputtering to a stop amidst the residue of a removal left incomplete. Hillocks of concrete rubble shed rivulets of rainwater. A rusting razor wire fence surrounds a graveyard of ancient vehicles, guzzlers of old fossil fuels. The metal carcasses, lined in rows, rot from the outside in, the ghosts of lettering haunting their flanks.

Kuba suggests sheltering in one of the hulking orange transports for the night, to get out of the persistent mist. He has brought provisions in his saddlebags and backpack, enough to last several days. Added to what Angel has stashed in hers, they can eat for perhaps a week if they conserve, if they subsist on a single meal a day, with a snack to fill the empty corners in between.

The interior of the transport stinks of abandonment, underscored with the faintest residual whiff of burnt carbon. Dust furs the backs of seats, fills the crannies of the window frames, the grooves of the rotting rubber floor mats. But it's a dry place to eat the small green apples that crackle with a crunch both tart and sweet and the hunks of brown bread scraped over with a tiny dollop of goat cheese.

The garrison, what's left of the Old Republic city of Peoria, lies across the river. The blue glow of its solar lights is muted, diffused through the rain spatters and film of dust on the transport windows. At the appointed hour, the voice of the Protectorate resounds, but at this remove, it, like the light, is attenuated, blurry. Just an annoying blare of random sound without meaning, like the whining buzz of a mosquito in the ear.

"First time I heard the nightly, I thought the voice was talking just to me. I was maybe seven. So puffed up cuz I got to go with my dad to Dealer Alley. First time ever. So many firsts that day. First time across the river. First time I saw a 'tronic board. And that face. Twenty, thirty feet high. She was so..." Kuba pauses, fishing for words. "Stunning, so beautiful. Never seen skin so white. And when she spoke, her voice sounded so kind. Cruel and kind at the same time. Impossible, but that's how I remember it. Gray-Gray called it benevolent malice. Or malicious benevolence. That voice made me feel so ashamed. Cuz I knew no matter what I did, I'd never live up to what she was askin'. And I was grateful I didn't have to."

"CQO Zinni. The queen of the hive," Angel says, picturing the swoop of ice blonde hair across the sapphire eye.

"Dad just rolled his eyes and kept on walking, but I stood there and stared and stared, 'til he was so far ahead and around a bend in the road that I lost sight of him and had to haul ass just to catch up. Running so fast that by the time I caught him, it felt like a pair of iron hands was trying to crush my lungs. When we got home and Gray-Gray asked me how I liked the Deal, all I could really remember was the face, that beautiful, horrible face and the wonderful, terrible voice and not even the words, just the way they made me feel. Gray-Gray told me to forget it. Said to drain it like pus from a wound. But I never really could. It's there. Faded but still there. Like a scar."

Hers is a hardly a walk, more a waddle. She seethes, yearning to reclaim her old body, the one that could easily do whatever she asked of it, a body lithe and supple and close to the bone. This one is alien, with its bulk, its changing center of gravity. A body that keeps her slightly off-kilter. Yet the reptilian brain has taken over. The instinctive behaviors that drive survival. The automatic response to seeing a transport on the far side of the river is to dart for cover behind the leafless shrubs. To hide their scat and bury their food scraps. To communicate with gestures and looks, winks and nods and finger signals. They can stomach their own stink.

That instinct drives her to press on, to walk another mile or two or three before they break and pitch the semblance of a camp each night. The rain has let up, but the sky remains leaden, the slate clouds oppressive, like a ceiling that's too low. The river bends toward the east and the terrain shifts under their feet, hints at secret meanderings through layered rock and shadowed recesses where relentless water trickles and excavates. Removals have cleared the hamlets and towns that once littered the area on the old map. But traces of existence remain. A spur of railroad track that dead ends in a field of withered corn stalks. A row of wooden poles from some obsolete communication system. A stand of wind turbines, rotor blades idle, that rises like a crop of forlorn three-petaled flowers from a barren plain.

They've inched their way like tightrope walkers across rotting beams barnacled with rust, the remains of crumbling bridges that spanned the swollen creeks and narrow rivers that feed into the old Illinois. Where the bridges have collapsed into and been swallowed by these streams, they've waded through knee and thigh and hip deep water, treading cautiously to avoid hidden debris. In shallower channels where concrete and rebar breach the surface and the water eddies and swirls, parting for the intrusion, they use them as stepping stones to cross from one bank to the other.

They have lapsed into a silence that feels crusted over. He has asked questions that she has refused to answer. Letting them hang in the air. Clouds of words that drift along forever on the wind, round and round in little cyclones, going nowhere and everywhere. They eat. They sleep fitfully, in shifts, both always in a twilight state, neither one sure that the other will keep them safe.

55

Tender Mercies

THE PITHOUND IS KEEN. Off the trail while his master recovered, he signals his joy, his eagerness to be back on the hunt with his tail and his alert head and eyes. Olfaction is his special sense, a thousand times more sensitive than that of his master. A nose cool and moist, prime conditions for capturing scents. The hound sniffs, a series of rapid, short inhalations and exhalations. Its nasal cavity is perfectly designed to collect lingering odors. From there, nerve impulses are transmitted to the brain, to the complex olfactory lobe, the incredible machine that allows the dog to recognize a scent and follow a trail. Moisture plays a key role in this process. Which means the dog's sense of smell is even better during rainy weather. On this day, in the light drizzle, the scent particles absorb the moisture and expand, making them easier for the dog to follow.

And follow it does, reveling in its work. Relentless from birth, the ancient way of the predator is embedded in its genes. Scents waft and hang, waft and hang. The musk of deer. The heavy, skulking reek of skunk. The rambling odor of raccoon. The scuttling scent of field mice. The cloying aromas of damp soil and rotting leaves. So much on the mist of this morning. Pungent, sour, tart, rank. The dog sees the complex world with its nose, all of nature an olfactory circus, bombarding the hound with a spectacle of scent.

Nose low, it hones in on the trail of an opossum that has idled in the brush on the near side of the crumbled pavement. The dog hesitates, raises its head, body quivering, preparing to follow this new trail. Here is where the discipline of its training at the hands of humans takes over. For the instinctual canid response is to follow the freshest trail, to seek the quickest way to prey. But his handler recognizes the hound's distraction in its body language. He is as well-trained as the dog.

"Leave it!" Tanner commands and that's all he needs to say.

The hound lowers his nose, snuffling. There it is, the original trail, a much older trail, faint but still identifiable. Still traceable. The one he is committed to tracking.

Dead. Tree. Stump. Rotting in the woods. That's what I am. Angel, the fixer of things. Cannot fix herself. The ache stretches across her body, pinning her to the ground like a phantom wrestler. Through half-closed eyes sticky with the residue of sleep, she catches a flicker of movement to her side. Turning her head sends a shiver of pain around her neck and across her shoulders. She can just make out Kuba's silhouette beyond the tent flap, bent over a low-burning fire. She boosts herself up on her elbows. Her hands feel like claws, fixed in a permanent curl. *Get up. Just get your butt up and shake it off.* Frowns at the plate of fried panfish that Kuba offers.

"Fresh caught," he cajoles.

Instead she nibbles from the pouch of granola kibble, cocks her head, listening to the jibberjabber of birds as they go about their morning business of hunting insects, seeds and grain, dwindling resources in late November. It's a Bartertown of winged creatures advising, warning, threatening: *Here's a deal, there's a scam, stay outta my way, hands off that, it's mine!* Under the birdsong, another sound pulses in the fresh air, a churning hiss that goes on and on, unchanging, unceasing, a forever kind of sound.

Kuba catches the tilt of her head, the narrowing of her eyes. "Think I've found a way to cross this thing."

With night closing in, they had stumbled upon the banks of what Angel thinks is the old Vermilion River. Storm-fed, it looks too high for a wade-through. All that remains of a bridge that once spanned the water is a concrete abutment, pockmarked and riddled with cracks. Short hikes upstream and down proved disappointing. So they had pitched camp with the thought of trying to find better luck further upstream.

Now Kuba stands, beckoning her to join him. "It's just a short hike. Ready to hit the trail?" He holds out his hand.

Angel eyes it, and, feeling contrary, boosts herself up, ignoring the spasm that runs from the tops of her thighs to her ankles, a whiny child of an ache that will plague until it gets its way. *Not with me, not today.*

They break camp, packing the tent, scattering the remnants of the fire in all directions. A good effort to erase their presence. Not perfect. But then Angel doesn't want it to be. She carefully drapes another strip of fabric over a low branch of a shrub.

The churning sound expands as they follow an overgrown trail, steep and root-laced, that skirts the river. Cedars and conifers have shed their needles across the path, laying a fragrant carpet that crackles and whispers under their shoes, a sound soft and prickly. The hardwoods atop the bluffs on the far side still glow with their autumn glory of oranges and reds and yellows. The path curves and then, suddenly, through the curtain of trees, Angel sees the churning whitewater of a river awakened, angered. It gathers speed as it dodges grey slabs of sandstone that sprawl in its way. Tumbles over a dark, wide rim of ancient rock, fractured into boulders, its rapids roiling in a white spray, its hiss building to a roar.

"Looks scaresome, but those boulders are just steps apart. They'll get us across. If you're game." Kuba eyes her and she knows exactly what he's eyeing. "Otherwise, we—"

"I'm game," she says, repositioning the backpack on her shoulders.

This body will do what I tell it to do.

He nods, continues up the path a few yards and takes a fork that leads down to the water. The trees are so thick Angel loses sight of the rapids for a time, though its tumult is ever-present. Gravity propels them down the trail in a quickstep and they lean back to resist the inexorable pushpull that threatens to send them tumbling head over heels. Then, again so suddenly it takes her breath away, the path opens and they are standing on the bank, confronting the liquid onslaught. The river crashes and plummets over and around the broken wall of boulders, spraying white plumes. One enormous slab, the color of ash, rises like an isle of calm in the middle of a sea of reckless motion.

"Rockslide, maybe," Kuba speculates, gesturing to the deep cut sandstone and the clefts in the bluffs on the opposite bank. "Boulders in the water are stable. I tested 'em."

With the devilish grin of a boy who has rarely thought twice about anything, he springs from the river bank to a large flat boulder just offshore, then continues on, bounding from one slab to the next until he reaches the island-like boulder. Arms stretched wide, he embraces the whitewater spray that pelts his chest and face.

"Whooo, runs cold here!" he shouts. "This'll knock the sleep out of you!"

Angel hesitates, eyeing the distance between the slabs, calculating her chances. Kuba is compact, a small bundle of muscle and energy, with an athlete's edge and sense of balance. *And what've I got? Long legs, a big belly... and fear.*

Not anymore.

One step back. Two. A swallow of breath. And then forward with a burst of speed and a strong thrust with her right foot off the river bank, flinging herself into the air, flush with momentary panic and a giddy thrill, the feeling that comes from being temporarily unbound from the earth. Free from the clutch of gravity. *Like a bird.*

She two-foots the landing and, feeling her heel slip on the slick surface of the rock, brings her arms up to steady herself. Then, teeth in a clench, she leaps again and again until she stands beside him, halfway between either shore, in the midst of the tumult, the nerve starting to drain away, wash down her spine, like water down a pipe.

"This is crazy!" shouts Kuba over the rushing roar. "Nothing like the river back home. But water will go where it wants. And get riled if you try to stop it."

Four more boulders to pass over. Surefooted as a goat, the boy makes the trek look easy, capering from one to the next. She navigates them slowly, negotiating one at a time, stepping tentatively, securing her footing, before looking ahead to the next. Her eyes are down, scanning for a flat landing spot on the second to last stone, when she hears a skittering, rustling snap and then a grunting "owww." With a quick glance up, she sees Kuba on the shore, bent over, rubbing his ankle.

"You okay?" she calls, still moving forward. The distance between the boulders here is longer, requiring a jump.

"Yeah, just put a foot wrong. Stone skipped out from under my foot. No damage," Kuba calls back.

Angel flings her body into the void and lands two-footed, but just a hair short of the flat top. The spot she hits is rounded and slick. First her right foot and then her left slips and she finds herself in the air yet again, this time flying spread-eagled, out of control.

Grab something there's nothing to grab too close too close to the edge

The icy clutch of the roiling water squeezes the breath out of her in one short, guttering gasp. Cold like the pain of a thousand needles jabbing her flesh, cold like a sucker punch to the belly. Before she can even formulate a thought beyond PAIN, the angry rush of the current sweeps her out of reach of the rocks. The weight of it stuns her, the liquid heft of it. The way it drags her down and carries her along at the same time. The way it swallows up sound except for its own deafening gush. A beast has consumed her whole and she is trapped inside its frigid, fluid maw.

The impulse spreads through her like poison seeping into the bloodstream from a snakebite. *Stop fighting it. Just let go. It's the one way back to her. There she is, do you see her? There, ahead of you, her black hair twisting in the current. There's her hand. Take it.* But the face admonishes, rather than welcomes. And the voice is harsh, not imploring. *Hasta siempre. But not yet. Forever has not arrived.*

Bursting out the beast's mouth, gasping, dizzy, she squints through the blur, trying to see—something, anything—to latch onto.

"Grab hold!" Kuba's voice sounds far away, distorted, rumbly. "To your right!"

And then she sees it, the branch extending over the river, dead, the bark gray and moss-caked, the end of the limb thin and brittle-looking, as if it will snap under the slightest pressure.

But it's a lifeline—the only one you have—

She thrusts her arms out of the water and clutches at it with both hands. Under the claw of her left hand, the thinnish end of the branch snaps. But under the grip of her right, the thicker section of the limb holds.

"Steady!" Kuba shouts, pulling the branch in, hand over hand. Like a fisherman cautiously reeling in his catch, fearful of losing it, he hauls her out of the current and onto the rock-strewn riverbank.

He expects her to break. Gasping, dripping, heaving, spitting. He expects the next liquid to be flowing from her eyes. He's seen his mother fret and rail, over hailstorms, the loss of crops, the deaths of beloved chickens, the monumental burden of bearing a child. He's seen her tears and Grandma Vi's, too. So he's prepared for it, wraps his arm around her shoulder to steady her in the inevitable turmoil that will come. Is coming.

That does not come.

Pulling ragged, shallow breaths at first, she closes her eyes, breathes deep and holds, holds, then lets it out. In through her nose, out through her mouth, a long, slow exhalation. Again and again, until her shoulders have ceased shaking, until the tremors of trauma have stilled, and it's just shivering from the chill that racks her body. But no tears. No tears. The only water that drips is from the hem of her jacket, water she wrings from the fabric with strong, steady, capable hands until not a drop remains to splash the sandstone over which she stands.

Rooting in her sodden backpack, she pulls out a handful of fabric that is only slightly damp. She unfolds it across the boulder. In the center of the bundle rests a black pistol. She rips a strip of the fabric, what looks to Kuba like a well-worn t-shirt, plods over to the stone at the end of the bridge of boulders and shoves one end of the cloth into a crevice that splits the rock face. She lifts a black holster from the pack and buckles it under her belly. Shoves the gun inside, picks up her coat to slip back into it. Kuba grabs the sleeve. Strips off his jacket and extends it.

"It's dry." His eyes are on hers, but she knows he's seeing the burner.

"I'm going to Chicago to kill a man," she states, voice firm, emotionless. "Maybe two. If I don't kill the one who's trailing me before I get there." She pushes the sleeve of the outsized flannel shirt up her left forearm, exposing the five scars engraved there. "There's plenty of room left."

Relief. Trepidation. There on his face, exposed. He is not one to mask his emotions, wear the game face, tangled up in the reality of finally knowing what he both wanted and didn't want to know. He can't help staring at the notches. So much he wants to ask, but doesn't, because he knows she won't speak of it. That much he understands about this strange girl-woman. But he's heard her muttering in the midst of sleep, in the dreams that twist and turn her body. *Hasta siempre. Undone. Still undone.*

The map tells them they have less than a hundred miles to go before they reach the garrison at Chicago. They have not seen another human being since they passed Peoria. He is the furthest he has ever been from the only home he has ever known. He knows it is too late to turn back.

But only dread dogs his steps going forward.

56

Cocytus

THE PITHOUND WHINES AND CIRCLES, whines and circles, until the man finishes doing his business. The small clearing in a thicket of scrub just a ways down from the rocky bank of a river is laden with the special scent, redolent with it. Fresher than it has been. The quarry took pains to hide its stay, sweeping away the ashes of its fire, scuffling dirt tamped down by sleeping bodies. But its presence lingers in the smallest particles of odors. Unwashed bodies. Smoke. Fish. And the strip of cloth dangling from the branch of a spindly buckthorn, feather light, but so heavy with the aroma of the prey. The dog's been trained not to seize hold with his teeth until given the command. But he bares them nonetheless, snarling, canines dripping with slaver.

The man strides over, takes the fabric between his gloved fingers.

What is the bitch doing? Marking her trail? What endgame is she playing?

"There it is, boy," he mutters, shedding his gloves to untie the strip from the limb, shoving the cloth under the hound's nose. "It was here. But where has it gone?"

The man gives the dog its lead. Over the years he's learned to let go, in this and only this. Let go of the need to control. He can determine the tactics to employ and the speed of the hunt, but he can never be sure with any degree of certainty where the scent is or in what concentration. That's the hound's job. And he has learned to let the hound work it. To stop pushing, prodding. To read the animal's body language. To slow down. To be quiet. To not become a distraction. To enjoy the hunt, the journey as well as the destination. So he offers the latest iteration of the scent. And then he lets the dog do its job. While he quietly does his own. Pondering the question.

Why does the girl want to be found?

They could be back in the Shawnee. A moment of dread floods Angel. Have they been walking in the wrong direction? That's impossible. She's consulted the map and the compass. They've gone north and east. But the lay of the land, the bend and swell and curve of it, the blunt rise of rockwalls, is eerily reminiscent of the cleft earth that she roamed with Debs.

Walking a bygone trail of pitted cement, they've skirted the edge of a small canyon. The forest here is thick and many of its leaves still cling, slow to drop in the absence of a killing frost. The boy yearns to scramble down the layered cliffside to the bottom of the gorge. But Angel's days of descending the steep, treacherous slopes are over. With a shake of her head, she kills his buzz and he petulantly kicks a loose stone over the edge. As it ricochets off the sandstone, the crackle is as stark and loud as a gunshot. Hearing it shames him and he steals a guilty glance at her belly.

In her palm, the compass feels like a talisman. Its red and white needle wavers and then points true north. The way back to the main river, the old Illinois, the way they need to follow. Her gut tells her that this east-heading path they are on will not lead them there, but the narrow ribbon of hard-packed gray dirt winding through the undergrowth might. Squinting, she wades in through the brush, gritting her teeth as slimy leaves slap her cheeks and twigs catch in her hair. Ten yards in, the course becomes easier to discern and navigate. They press through the thicket in silence until they reach a tiny clearing where the path forks. Angel breathes deep.

Stop. Breathe. Focus. Think.

With a flick of her thumb, she veers to the right.

Pine needles the color of weak tea crunch softly under their feet and the air smells tart. The path slopes downward in loose switchbacks where slabs of gray sandstone poke through the darker soil.

"I can always smell it before I see it," Angel murmurs, thinking aloud, sensing the deep, wet odor as only one who has had the mournful stink of dust and decay up in her nose truly can.

Then in a bold, green-gray instant, the river is crawling before them, wide and impassive. A scanty stream trickles down the slope, the water churning to white foam as it roils over and around rocks that hunker like smirking bullies trying to block its path to the river. But the water always slips through and, in time, will wear away the blockade altogether. Such is the way of water, be it a trickle or a torrent.

Tanner ponders why he didn't kill her when he had the chance. That first time, not so many months ago, although it seems like a lifetime. What was it that stayed his hands?

He has the taste for it. The taking of lives. The taking of particular lives. The dispatch of the anonymous soul is too easy. Unsatisfying. An empty act that signifies nothing. Removals are Corporate acts, whether en masse or individual. No animus there, just a job to be done. Anyone with grit and a gun can do it. True, it takes a certain mindset. And a modicum of behavior modification and training, but he's been killing since he was a young boy, pulling the wings off flies.

He hadn't planned to kill his wife. The plan had been to create life, not take it. But if he was honest with himself—and he believes that he is always honest with himself, no self-deception here—he accepts that the plan, the goal, was hers and hers alone.

It is a shit world, one so totally broken that it will never recover. He knows this because he is a man who also understands that it has been something very different before. He knows about Eden and Zion and Canaan and the Promised Land and the New World and Pax Americana. He found his father's hidden stash of biblios that eluded the goliaths. Read them, one by one, before setting them ablaze. All that history eaten alive by fire, page after page, until all that remained was a pile of ash and the odor of smoke clinging to his clothes and hair. He'd shaved his head then. To rid himself of it. All of it.

But this world? This Protectorate? It is a dung heap upon which beetles crawl and feed. Why bring a child into it?

But he had agreed to it. Acquiesced to her strenuous desires. Made the trip to the Hive. Thwarted the psychologicals, the interviews. Achieved the permissions. Let himself be put under for the extraction procedure. Woke up without an embed, feeling freer than he'd ever felt in his life.

He has long suspected the Hive has altered and expanded the embed functions beyond tracking and population control. Has seen it in his trainees, who come in smiling and aw-shucksey and in the span of a few short weeks turn as grim-faced and relentless as the hound hot on the trail ahead of him. He doesn't flatter himself that it is all due to his drill methods, the conditioning that trains inductees to submerge their individuality for the good of the unit. The recruits are bred for that, placed on the Security Track for that trait, among others.

No, there is brainwashing... and then there is Brainwashing.

Yet, what may brutalize the other recruits had actually tempered him, kept his rage at a simmer, a useful simmer, a controllable simmer. Once that control was gone, removed, the flames leapt higher and the simmer rose to a boil.

Boiling water resists its container. And has only two ways to escape: by transforming into something else, rising as steam from the pot. Or to roil and leap out, spattering whatever is in its way. Unpredictable. Uncontrollable.

She had fought him. Hard. It astonished him at the time. She was a swag, a daughter of elites, tall and lithe and healthy as only the Morametrics could prescribe, but still it surprised him. She was a woman who wanted what she wanted and was used to getting it immediately. Acutely aware of the limited amount of time allotted for these machinations. And when it didn't happen, immediately, when her plan did not progress in the way she envisioned, it was, of course, his fault. He couldn't remember the flash point. The precise words of accusation. The look. She had so many. But it happened. And she had struggled mightily under his grip. Scraping and clawing at his face and neck. His arms and the backs of his hands. Struggled mightily to remain in this shithole.

Perhaps that was the difference. The difference between death for the one and life for the other.

The girl had not struggled at all.

57

The Vanishing Point

THE FORESTED BLUFFS along the river give way to flat plains with only occasional pockets of trees, planted as windbreaks amidst the furrowed fields of an agsector. They had spent an uneasy night in one such thicket, too wary and restless to pitch the tent or light a fire, sensing they are nearing a human presence. Angel passes the dark hours hunched against the trunk of a middling oak, wrapped in a sleeping bag, drifting in a nether world between sleep and true wakefulness, a state in which it is difficult to distinguish between the real and the imagined. She dreams of birth. Of monstrous creatures emerging from her womb. Hairless rats with razor teeth. White worms. A swarm of furious bees.

Now, staring at the strange yellow sign, faded and rust-eaten, bolted to a double-layer chain link fence that rises fifteen feet or so to triple coils of razor wire, she feels a push up against her ribcage. A warning? A black trefoil, resembling the blades of a fan captured in motion, dominates the metal triangle. Beyond the fence, cement barracks cluster around an odd dome-shaped structure and what appear to be two tall smokestacks, ringed in red and white.

"Rail bridge. That's our only play," states Kuba, like he's calling an audible in a game of gladiator ball. "Or we can keep walking and hope to find another place to cross."

Angel shakes her head. They stand at the confluence of

two rivers. The map shows one, the old Kankakee, breaks south, the other, the Des Plaines, north. They must cross to keep on the path toward Chicago. The crossover for the bullet trains is about one hundred yards west of the garrison. The bridge is low, stretching mere yards above the water, upstream from the lock and dam controlling the river's flow. They've been crouching in a copse of buckthorn for an hour or so and have spied no human movement around the garrison, just a drone tracing the perimeter of the grounds, skimming above the barbed wire as it patrols. Now they will have to move into the open, across a stretch of bare field. The early dusk will provide cover in this color-bled world, their gray jackets camouflaged by the gray light and the gray mist and the gray river. But Angel's focus is not on how many three hundred pound trolls might be lurking under the bridge or within the barracks beyond the fences. It's on the monster that could come hurtling out of the murk on the far side of the river.

Bullet trains don't run on a set schedule. They don't run every other day or even every week. They run when there's a need. When the controlling minds of the Hive require their services. There's no way of knowing when one will barrel in and blast on by and be gone again into the distance, just a blur of sight and sound, a silver flash to dazzle the eye, a piercing whistle to puncture the ear, a gale force wind to knock the unsuspecting, the unprepared, to his knees.

How the tracks trick the eye, the mind. She knows the rails are parallel, set precisely the same number of feet apart from here to their origin point, wherever that may be. Somewhere in the North, maybe. Perhaps even the Hive itself. Yet, as they recede into the distance, they appear to converge and vanish, even before the mist swallows them whole. Everything ends at the horizon.

Then it's a good thing you never get there.

Without a word, she rises from the crouch, thighs and knee joints sighing and crackling in relief, and begins to walk. She hears him behind her, the crisp brush of his boots through the shriveled weeds. Once on the tracks, she matches her strides to the concrete ties, treading carefully, as much as she longs to run. And as much as she longs to cast a glance toward the garrison, to get a handle on the drone's location, she keeps her focus forward. A vaporous curtain hangs before them, behind them. A sheer wall, fine, wet, yards and yards and yards wide and thick, leaving traces of their passage on their faces, their hair, the sleeves of their jackets.

A memory comes unbidden. From a time when joy was still present in her small world. The joy of a child with long legs, loping. With Mars Lund running just behind. No, not running—bounding, so gleeful was he at that moment. A moment beyond the feed, beyond the monotonous drone of the Corporate voice, the voice that punctuated the dawn, the day, the evening. Beyond, for a slender slice of time, the reach of the Hive mind and the clutch of the Corporate hand. A pause to catch their breaths. Then, a clamber up the gravel slope. Kicking off her shoes, teetering on the rail, pirouetting like a gymnast on a balance beam. Clutching the edge of the steel rail, warm from the summer sun, with her toes as she steadies herself after the spin. The curious vibration crawling under the soles of her feet.

When she'd looked at Mars, wonder in her eyes, somehow he had guessed. And taken it as a dare. *The culvert,* he'd shouted, pointing to the man-sized pipe that channeled the creek bed under the track. *We can beat it.* Crazy. Vibrations stronger now. *Can't be sure what direction it's coming from. So when in doubt, go forward!*

No, you don't run toward a bullet train. And yet he does. Because when he takes off, she stays put and scans the horizon and discerns the movement. Or thinks she does.

And when it came, hurtling, suddenly, into view, she had leaped and landed in a rolling ball on the gravel, skinning her knees and shins. So she never saw whether he'd beaten it or not.

Really beaten it. She had to take the word of the slow, molasses boy that he'd jumped into the creek bed just in time. No evidence to support his claim. No mud on his shoes, no water splashing his ankles or thighs. The creek was dry and hard as stone. Yet she couldn't remember a time when he'd lied to her. So it must be true.

But memory itself could be false, as malleable and moveable as the line on the horizon. The vanishing point. And yet... When they reach the railway bridge, she hikes her foot up on the rail and bends awkwardly to remove her boot.

"What're you doin'?" Kuba asks, eyes dark, deep and quizzical against the wet sheen of his cheeks and forehead.

She ties the laces of her boots together and slings them around her neck. They droop over her shoulders, yet another weight anchoring her to the earth. This time as she steps up onto the rail, it is cold and slick under her bare feet.

"Vibrations. You can feel them long before you hear or see the bullet," she says.

But she's not the lithe, sure-footed girl who spun in one swift pirouette. Her bulk has saddled her with a sense of vertigo, a fear of falling. She takes a tentative step, feels the dizzy sensation and thrusts out her arms for balance. Feels his hand grab hers, the clasp of his fingers bringing an instant sense of steadiness, of security, of safety.

The bridge spans to forever, or so it seems, with high side walls of solid steel, no openings to slip through to escape an oncoming train. A deathtrap. And even if openings existed, the plunge to the water holds a maximum of danger. They can't be sure how deep the river really is. Hitting a rocky bottom would mean broken bones. Or worse.

With his hand to grasp, how quickly she treads the rail beam, how smoothly she navigates the narrow path and keeps her body moving forward. The mist is thickest over the river.

Neverending veils of it. Part one and you are confronted by another, on and on and on. Soon they are lost in it, unsure of how far they've come and how much farther they have to go. And then she feels it, the barest tingling along the sole of her left foot as she brings it down, like the sweep of a feather along the skin, but not here and gone again. No, this is steady. Persistent.

"One's coming."

What she needs is time and vision and she has neither. So she relies on the memory. A memory that might be a lie. And she begins to run. Forward.

"What're you—" But the rest of Kuba's words are lost. There's only Mars' voice in her head: *When in doubt, go forward.*

The concrete ties sting the pads of the she-wolf's paws and the gravel flies up and pelts her belly, but she's glad of the pain, rejoices in it. Keeps her focused. Reminds her she's still alive, even as she hears the whisper of an artificial wind. Miles in front of her. Miles and yards and feet and inches. When in doubt, go forward. The horizon, the vanishing point. It's all an illusion. But just ahead is a landmark, a goal to reach. Cross beams that signal the end of the bridge. The she-wolf digs in, though the pain snaps from the base of her spine down through her leg and makes her leap and plunge to take the burden off sinew and nerves, to defy the ache of gravity for just a moment, even as she hears the wind rush that begins as a whoosh and peaks in a whine and ends in a gushing exhalation, the death rattle of a sleek monster traveling two hundred miles per hour.

Falling forward, eyes squeezed shut, hands instinctively clutching her belly, she's preparing for impact, when, out of the gray void, an arm wraps around her chest in a grip that feels like it will go on forever. And instead of gravel, a body and a grunt cushions her fall. In the sudden quiet, between the fringe of her lashes, the curtains of mist swirl and waft, all astir, thrust apart by the bullet, frayed by its casual violence, until at last they settle again, betraying nothing.

Kuba is still, too still, underneath her, his arm still clasping her. But the rise and fall of his chest radiates through the fabric of her coat, pulsing all the way down to her skin and through it, into the bones of her spine and ribs and shoulders.

"Why the hell did we do that?" he finally croaks.

Sitting up, shaky, bone-shattered, he presses his hand to the back of his head, tentatively. It comes away bloody. Angel bends to him, parting the thicket of wet hair. The gash is long but thankfully narrow. She hacks away a chunk of his tangled mane with her knife, spreads what's left of the anti-bac gel in the wound, and plasters the last bandage over it.

"Thank you," she murmurs.

He shrugs, wincing at the pain that slices along his shoulder blades. A heavier damage that can't be fixed with a poultice and a gauze strip.

At the rail, she bends at the knee, as if genuflecting to the trail of the beast that nearly slaughtered them. Touches the steel beam, a curious gesture, and then rises, slowly, wearily.

And then they set out again. Heading north and east.

To the old Chicago.

58

Ozymandias

THE SCENT IS STRONG at the remains of the power plant, where the nuclear waste is buried deep and its underground mausoleum is guarded continuously by human surveillance and the unblinking eye of the zoom. The mist has risen and the sun is a milky disc behind thinning clouds. Across the railway bridge, the hound zeroes in on the strip of cloth tucked along the steel beam, while Tanner stoops to inspect an odd black clump, stark against the pale gravel. A hank of hair. Human hair. And that brownish smear? His fingers hover over it. Blood. He knows that. It's almost a duplicate of a smear that flits in and out of his mind's eye, seemingly with a will of its own. Blood will out. Will haunt. Or so he realizes. In hindsight. Always 20/20. Nine months later.

He knew there were two. The foolish one, barely more than a child from the sound of the voice, gave that away. So much evidence. The work of inexperienced criminals. Muddy footprints leading to the front door, streaks of it on the mat. Drips of water on the tile floor. Damp marks on the cushions of the sofa and the kitchen stools. A blotch on the counter that was normally pristine. But the smear on the wall at the foot of the stairs was older. Reddish brown. Set at just about the height of the forehead of a tallish woman.

He'd forgotten to clean that. Or was the oversight intentional?

To mark the spot of the kill. A trophy.

He never saw the young bitch. Heard the shout, recognized it as a signal, pretended a retreat. Left the closet, exited the bedroom. Faked a march down the sweeping staircase. That's when the older one came barreling out of the bedroom, shouting "run!" Wearing some ludicrous—mask—hat—pulled down low and a white respy tugged high, so all that glowed in between were a pair of feral, fear-sprung eyes.

But he was there, waiting.

Strong, quick, that feral thing was. Agile enough to slip from his grasp and plunge headlong down the stairs. Agile enough to stay on its feet, with a lightning flash reflex to stretch out its arms in time to cushion the impact with that wall.

That infamous wall. And its brownish red smear.

It was a tall one, as tall or taller than his wife. His dead wife. And he knew it saw the smear. And something about it, something about that smear threw the feral thing's timing off for a split-second, compelling it to freeze and stare. Just long enough for him to wrap a hand around the back of its long elegant neck and pin it to that wall, like some exotic insect specimen pinned to a display.

A rational man would have wrestled it into a pair of cuffs and read its embed. A rational man would have jerked it to face him. Yanked off its absurd cap. But a bottle of oblivion does strange things to a man. Out the corner of his eye, he caught a movement even as he felt the wallop of a heavy blunt object strike the back of his head and, an instant later, heard the crystalline screech of glass shattering as the object landed on the unforgiving surface of the tile. Even with its throat in his grip, the thing managed to choke out a command to the small one just in the periphery of his vision.

"Run!"

And the small thing did, but not before flinging another of his dead wife's crystal candlesticks, which hit him in the shoulder, leaving a bruise that would last for several weeks. The memory of what happened next would last much longer.

Now, kneeling on the gravel slope just below the span of the tracks, he marvels at whatever frenzy had him in its grip then, beyond the liquor's madness. In retrospect, he can reflect on it as a moment of irrationality. View it dispassionately, from a distance. Standing outside himself.

If asked, he wouldn't be able to talk about it in anything but disjointed sentences and fragments of thoughts.

The need to control. To possess, yes. The need to know.

Know what?

Something about the boyish hips, and what lay above, but of that he wasn't sure. That was an ache.

Thrusting his hand roughly up under the black t-shirt, ignoring the smooth sweep of the flat belly until his fingers brushed up against the pebbled texture of the bandage. The winding fabric that kept the thing's secret. Her secret.

That. Yes. He recalls the feel of the fabric on the skin of his fingertips. The way it fell away, layer by layer. And the way the wisps of hair curled out from underneath the knit cap. That, yes. And the glint of the delicate metal links at the back of her neck. And the oddest thought. That a gold chain would have complemented the warm tones of her skin so much better than the silver.

Now, he runs a finger over the smear of blood on the stone and shudders away the memory.

Once a great metropolis loomed. Now there are only ruins. Nature is reclaiming the land here, though traces of civilization linger. Up through the cracks in the concrete and asphalt, cracks gaping and narrow, plant life stretches toward the sky. Tree-of-heaven, musk thistle, spurge. Milkweed pods, exploded, seeds scattered, to which a few bedraggled shreds of floss still cling, fine and white as the hair on Isa's scalp. Towering Joe Pye weed bent under the weight of its now-dried but still massive blossoms. On the edge of winter, they are brown, withered, crooked under the burden of life near its end. At the height of summer, the growing stalks would have obscured the gray slabs molded and laid down with machines guided by human hands. Even now, the pavement, what's left of it, is difficult to discern. Hard to define the shape and limits of it, its curves and bends, the intersections in the network of roads that once divided the land into orderly grids.

The structures, what's left of them, slouch as if under a great weight. Stripped of anything portable, anything barterable, they resemble the pumpkins that the boys carved on the farm: hollowed out of all that sustains life, gutted with black empty holes, rotting along the cut edges, the skin and rind shrinking, curling in on itself as the juice of life dissipates, exuding the odor of decay, of death.

The ruins extend for miles upon miles. They pause to gobble down the last of their apples, perching on the cracked concrete stoop of the last derelict house on a winding street half asphalt, half weed. A spindly tree reaches for the light through a massive hole where part of the moss-caked roof has caved in. Others sprout from the shingles.

"So many people. There had to be, with all this." Kuba's gesture encompasses the acres upon acres they've passed and the miles still ahead. "Where'd they all go?"

Angel just pushes herself to her swollen feet, which ache and press angrily against the confines of her boots.

Time to move on.

It doesn't mean the child is his.

A part of him is adamant that it is not. That insists the slut could have easily been with dozens of men before him and after, border jumpers and Bartertown junkers. But another part is equally insistent that she had been his and his alone, a singular event. And another part ponders how she could have masqueraded for so long, hiding in plain sight. And how he could have been so blind. But then he never mingled with the bees, kept himself apart, so that when he had to bring the hammer down, there was no possibility of entanglement to stir up feelings.

That day, when he was spent, his anger and his seed, he'd staggered back from her, momentarily overwhelmed, head fogged, oblivion-soaked, vision blurred, and the girl had lit off running, out the front door. Instead of giving chase, he'd watched her go, splashing through the standing water and the muck, leaving only the bandage behind on the tile, where he'd let it fall from his fingers. And a shoe that he'd find later, sunk in the mud. He can't explain it. Realizes he has a price to pay for his weakness. Knows that before he puts her down like a she-wolf that's been ravaging his flock, he has to look upon her face. In the flesh. Fully. For the first time. And then be man enough to do it.

In the small dark hours, he squats in the guts of some once monumental structure that is rotting from the inside out. Exhausted, yet unable to sleep, his mind roils with fractured thoughts. Thoughts of her. He can't remember her eyes, the image he displayed at that roll call. Ages ago. Pairs of eyes flit through his imagination, like images projected in rapid succession on a screen. The first time he'd truly beheld her face. The day he had called for her death.

He wanders the remains of the building as his mind wanders the ruins of his life. The long hall of small, cell-like rooms, walls shedding strips of paint, the peelings hanging like the molted skin of a snake. Iron bolts jutting from the concrete and cinderblock, where doors had once been mounted. He comes to recognize it. A place where, in the old Republic, criminals were caged, warehoused. What did they call them? Prisons? Penitentiaries? A place where those who had broken the law could rethink their lives, pay their debt to society. Perform a penance. Be penitent.

Shakes his head. He's read of the old system. Courts. Judges.

Juries of peers. Sentences of detention. A waste. Of space and time and treasure. So much cleaner now. So much more efficient. Removal. The gas. Or the water. Painless. Quick. Society freed of the burden of these beasts instantly and forever. And now the next-Gen embeds controlling, taking away the very impulses that drove the aberrant behaviors.

As the black night morphs into the gray of approaching dawn, he looks up and considers the limestone towers, castle-like, the barbican of this once mighty, forbidding fortress. When the strain in the muscles of his neck overwhelms, he looks down again and sees the letters etched in the stone beneath his feet. Brushes away the dirt that's settled in the creases, that obscures the meaning. Even as the words emerge, they jumble in his mind, forming, re-forming, twisting into a semblance of sense.

IT'S NEVER TOO LATE TO MEND.

And he falls to his knees.

And weeps.

59

To Know Even as I Am Known

THE BARTER TOWN ENCAMPMENT takes them by surprise in the waning afternoon as they push through a ragged strip of forest along the river. Sounds and smells hover in the damp air. A bark of laughter. The murmur of conversation. The sharp tang of smoke and cooking meat. Through breaks in the thicket, they spy tents pitched around the curve of a strange building. Circular, broad and low-slung, windowless. The outer walls may have once been white, but now they are plagued with swaths of grey and rust-colored stains and choked with the ever-spreading arms of creeper vines.

A half dozen or so campsites cluster around a main fire, over which a gaggle of men and women are roasting smallish carcasses. Squirrels, maybe. Other rodents that offer a few decent bites of flesh. And there, amidst the small circle of rabble, squats the bike man, Mr. Cain, still sporting his ragged-ass old cap.

She presses her way through the tangle of branches, even as Kuba hisses, "What're you doin'?"

"I know him." And she knows with a surety in her gut that this is the right thing to do. In the time it takes to trundle across the weed-choked concrete to the cluster of tents, she ponders whether he'll even recognize her, hair matted and wild, face and body bold without respy and tunic.

Like a murder of crows, the vagrants are up, jackets and

shirts and blankets aflutter, weapons glinting in the firelight, knives, crowbars, a vicious length of heavy chain. Kuba darts in front of her, drops in a defensive crouch.

"Get back!" he shouts, his hand slipping to extricate his own knife from backpocket. She clamps a restraining hand on his wrist and steps around him.

"Mr. Cain." She says it warmly, as if greeting an old friend.

The old man doesn't respond. Displays not a hint of recognition. Not immediately. Not in the instant. But the hands of the bartertown vagrants freeze in varying degrees of threat.

The belly. It draws all twenty eyes. Causes more than one jaw to sink, revealing gaps amidst corrugated, yellow-stained teeth. But instead of feeling awkward, conspicuous, Angel feels a power slipping up her spine and through her shoulders, drawing them straight and square. She is a flag unfurled, proud.

And then it's there in his watery, pale eyes. The swelling rise of memory, like a swimmer surfacing from below the water. He brings his forearm to his mouth, wipes the grease from his lips with the frayed sleeve of his flannel shirt. Grins crookedly.

"Miss Stillwater, I presume."

Later, after Angel inhales chunks of the mystery meat proffered on skewers improvised from the spokes of old bike wheels, and Kuba polishes off a wrinkled apple, they are bombarded with questions. But Cain shushes his compadres.

"Miss Stillwater don't talk much. As for the other, he don't look old enough to know much."

Amidst the cackles, Angel senses Kuba bridling at the insult. She nudges his knee with hers and gives him a side-eye to keep it zipped good and tight.

"Actually, Mr. Cain, I've changed," she says, her voice all silk and satin. "Am changing," she corrects. "Finding my voice."

He nods approvingly.

She gives them the bare bones of her journey. Cain nods, affirms his own witness to the removal. The junkers chime in, adding accents and grace notes to her tale. Rumors heard. Persecutions endured. Raids that have left so many of their colleagues dead.

"Happenin' all over the southern regions. 'Stead of lettin' the displaced head north, flee the drought, they're just killin' 'em off," mutters a woman whose face is bisected with a long white scar running from eyebrow to chin.

"Cullin' the herd," adds a man with a mangled, misshapen hand.

But the one question, the main question in all the minds, just hangs in the air with the smoke from the cookfire, until the other junkers have drifted away to their tents. Cain's taking the first watch and Angel sits with him around the winking embers. Kuba lingers, too, eyeing the old man warily, until Angel shoos him off.

"Get some sleep. I'll just toss and turn anyway."

He retreats, but not far, spreading his sleeping bag with a disgruntled shake just beyond the edge of the concrete rubble, where a swath of fallen leaves provides some cushioning. She senses that he's lying on his side, keeping an eye on them.

She stands to stretch as the life inside pushes against the walls that confine it. Does it seek an escape hatch? The time for that must be fast approaching. Her belly is at Cain's eye level and he startles her by placing a hand on it. She grabs his shoulder to steady herself.

"Behold the handmaid," the old man mumbles, hand fixed on her belly. "How'd this come to pass?" And then he answers himself. "Don't got an embed, do ya?"

Angel shakes her head.

"His?" Cain shrugs toward the boy.

She shakes her head again.

"Where's that voice?" The old man rasps.

"It's a murderer's child." She wants to sit back down on the boulder of broken cement, but his hand has her feeling immobile, captured in the moment.

"Ah, the iniquity of the fathers visited on the children, unto the third and fourth generation." He shakes his head. "But the biblio was all very muddled in the end. About that. Fathers and children and sin. Each prophet sayin' a different thing."

It is all mumbling nonsense, but the span of his fingers remains firm on her belly.

"I gave up preachin' the word a lifetime ago." He sighs. "Your time is near. What'll you do?"

"When the time comes, I'll do what I have to."

"A free born child is almost a miracle," Cain whispers, half to himself. Angel feels the heat radiating from the palm of his hand.

"I don't know what that is," she replies.

He nods. "Why would ya?" The baby kicks and he feels it, even through the layers of fabric. He smiles. "Feisty thing. Where you headed?"

"Chicago."

"What for?"

She shrugs. "Business."

Skepticism seeps onto his face, oozing along the deep wrinkles that frame his down-turned lips. "Ain't much there but rubble and waste. Some factory zones. Some squats. A garrison 'round the water plant." His hand slides from her belly, moves to her wrist, drawing her down onto the boulder.

"I ken what ya mean to do. I was there with Debs, with Eben, with all the guevaras, burnin' with the fire of youth." He digs under the collar of his shirt, pulls out the ends of a tattered bandanna, a sad washed-out red. "I wore it well." He leans in, so close she can smell the rot of his teeth. "And I tell ya, no. Go far as ya can in the opposite direction. Or back to that corn-fed boy's bunker."

"No, Mr. Cain, I'm going to Chicago. I'm gonna finish what I started. It's what I've been taught to do. And if the shave-head devil comes lookin', I want you to tell him that. You hear me? Promise me."

She holds him in the vise of her stare until he nods. Only then do her eyes flit to the cluster of bicycles chained to the thin trunk of a sapling maple.

"My dogs are barkin'." She hefts a foot onto the smaller rock in front of her, bends to unlace her boot. Wrestles it off, tugs her sock down, to reveal the raw blister at her heel and the red crease running along her instep. "I could use another form of transportation." She tilts her head in the direction of the bikes.

The bike man nods. "And I say unto you, rise and thresh, oh daughter of Zion, for I will give you horns of iron and I will give you hooves of bronze, and you will break to pieces many nations."

"Only one," she replies. "Just one."

When Tanner strides into the junkers' campsite, the sun's been up an hour and the girl and her companion are gone. He gets nothing out of the rats hunkered around the fire. Not whimpers. Not sidelong glances. No tells of the eyes or hands. No pleas of ignorance, no offers of deals, no bargaining.

Nothing.

Just a sullen silence, a wall of it that stands solid, even in the face of his fulminations. And the muffled snarls of the muzzled pithound. And his pistol.

He's losing his grip on the ledge. A ledge he never dreamed he'd be slipping from. A ledge for which he has no name. But slipping he is. Trying to dig his fingers into intransigent stone.

Before, he would have been the silent one. The still one. The unwavering. The unblinking. Watching as the subject of his interrogation split at the seams. Now he rants at this pack of barely humans. And these junker vermin just slouch and slump. Pick their noses with a blithe indifference. Shove their pinkie fingers into their ears and mine for wax. Scratch at the fleas nipping their asses and armpits.

What is happening here? What is happening? To him?

In the end, it's the yawn that fractures the world. Or so he convinces himself. Because it—the yawn—was not spontaneous. Of that he is sure. He thinks. No, it was conspicuously studied, that yawn. Completely calculated. An opening of the mouth, a dropping of the jaw, a stretching of the chapped lips achieved by a careful and deliberate effort, accompanied by a lazy, rumbling crescendo, the universal sound of infinite boredom, rippling from between the gaps in the old bastard's teeth.

The four companions Tanner dispatches quickly, efficiently. A bullet to the brain. Nearly instantaneous. Or so they say. But the old bastard must pay for his disrespect. For the collective disrespect. And so one in the knee for maximum pain. And one in the gut for the gradual, agonizing ebbing away. The exquisite, excruciating knowledge that one is slowly dying.

But then, isn't that all of life itself? Just a slow dying?

The hound gnaws at the rabbit and rodent carcasses that had been the intended breakfast of these derelicts. Tanner sniffs the murky contents of a cookpot while he listens to the staggered rasps burst and seep from the old man. Takes a swig and spits out the bitter swill that barely passes for coffee. Hears something that sounds like a word. Crouches near, grips a hank of frosted hair, brings the man's mouth closer to his ear.

The syllables are drawn out by the excruciating paroxysms that slice through the man's innards. But recognizable.

Chicago.

Tanner lets the man's head fall back to the concrete. Sees the curious imprints in the muddy basin where the strip of broken cement ends.

The narrow tracks of a bicycle tire.

60

The Garrison

HURT. A world of it. One giant, sprawling mass of it. That is the state of Angel's body. But she tries to ignore it as she stares at the raised bridge, feeling the blood rush heat flooding her belly.

The garrison here is a grim, gray, hard fist that the Protectorate brandishes in the face of all who dare to even think about going where they shouldn't. Quadrangles of single-story, cement block barracks surround a central tower that rises in several stories of concrete and steel, with the narrowest of slits for windows. It hunkers at the confluence of the north and east forks of the river. Across the waterway runs a massive concrete wall out of which rise steel spikes threaded with razor wire. Here, on the west bank, a greenbelt, drab now in the late autumn, stretches just beyond the last cluster of buildings. A paved path carves a black stream through it. A wide landscaped berm borders the greenbelt at the river bank and curves inland around the cluster of buildings. A massive sliding cantilever gate bars the path of the single road into the facility. Most of the far perimeter of the garrison is protected only by chainlink fencing. While forbidding razor wire spools along its top edge, some sections of the lower fence are corroded. These rust-eaten links, after some effort, give way to the wire cutters on Kuba's multi-tool. Squeezing through, Angel nicks the back of her hand on a sharp edge. A scarlet bead oozes and she sucks at the wound.

The two crouch on the backside of the sloping wall of earth, peering over its ridge, surveying the layout of the garrison, the river and beyond, weighing their options.

On the south side of the river, a forest of concrete and steel is surrendering to time and the elements. The remains of a ravaged settlement lies lifeless on its banks, the brittle outer husks of buildings crumbling under the glare of the sun and the sting and the slap of the rain and the wind, flanks mottled with mold and moss.

What happened to this place? In this place? What happened to the people who once lived and worked in these buildings? Angel ponders, eyes scanning.

Throughout the trek, she has sensed more than seen evidence of human life in the present, the now. A vague form flitting around the corner of a tumbledown house. Smoke curling from the odd chimney. A structure where openings that used to be windows have been carefully boarded up with thinnish sheets of salvaged wood. They have seen garden plots, raised beds bordered with half-rotted railroad ties, surrounded by rusting chickenwire, littered with the residue of a year's harvest. Withered stalks of corn, the sprawling scrawny arms of cucumber and squash vines. In one attic window where an unbroken pane of glass still fit the frame, Angel swore she saw a woman's face, but as she stared, the vision faded slowly from view, as if the woman was backing away from the opening.

Or perhaps it was just an apparition, a trick of the longing mind.

"This was a great metropolis once," says Kuba at one point, awe in his voice. "That's what Grey-Grey called it. Ten million people lived here, clustered around a lake. She'd lived here as a child, somewhere here." He swings his arm in a vague, encompassing arc. "She has a memory of crowds, masses of people, buildings looming around them, except to the east, where the lake stretched."

They have traversed the skeleton of a civilization. Flesh eaten away, rotted, corroded, melted. Gone. Leaving only bones. Scattered, piled, picked clean.

A vertical life. Unimaginable. And the tightness of it. All of it packed into such a small space. Life stacked on top of life. One box after another, rising, rising, making the sky seem low, small, mere patches of blue. Claustrophobic. A pressing weight instead of the comforting wide arc over the Shawnee.

It makes her skin feel too tight.

But the skin of these lives, these buildings, is gone, the glass gone, and the wind whines and moans and whistles through the skeletons, the ribcages of iron and steel, bones gnawed by time and rust.

On the far side of the river, beyond the wall, the buildings, while weather and time-beaten, look occupied. They line the streets, forming deep canyons. And then, there it is, looming in the near distance, its y-shaped, curving facade undulating, scraping at the sullen clouds that skulk just above its uppermost stories. The water man's lair. She is sure of it, but still she draws the laminated card from the pocket of her backpack and scans it, eyes shifting back and forth, from the facsimile to the reality.

"That's the building?" Kuba says, peering over her shoulder.

Angel nods.

He sighs. "So another fracking bridge to cross."

Angel's eyes return to the simpler structure that lies close at hand. A small concrete turret with a glass-enclosed observation deck and control room rises on the riverbank, in the swath of cement in front of the bridge, one designed solely for transports.

"At least it's not a fracking bullet bridge," she mutters, flattening herself as best she can against the grassy slope as a pair of beefy runners, goliaths from the size of their biceps and thighs, jog by on the trail below.

They've cased the north fork of the river for other crossings, without luck. Evidence of bridges exists, bridge-tender houses, crumbling concrete abutments and massive cracked counter-weights, but the spans are gone.

"We could go further north, see if there's another way. May-be a boat docked," Kuba suggests, knowing it's barely a longshot.

Angel doesn't even shake her head, just gives him a side eye. Now that she has the water building in sight, she won't risk losing it.

The transport crossings probably run on a schedule. But in the two hours they've watched, there haven't been many signs of life and activity.

But I bet security does a thrice daily inspection. That's part of the Morametrics. Follow procedures without fail. Do everything the same way twenty-four seven three hundred sixty-five. Security squaders are bred for that. It's in their genes.

Kuba studies her face. "I can't hear what's in your head."

"There'll be an inspection. That's how they roll. Inspection goes down, that's when we cross."

How can I even be sure the inspector will lower the bridge? Maybe he just does a sweep of the controls. Eyeballs it.

She huffs a short sigh to dismiss the inner voice, the critic. But out loud she admits, "Can't be sure they'll lower the bridge as part of the routine."

"Then I make 'em lower it."

Angel's eyes shoot a look skyward. *Yeah, right. Gonna creep up on the guy and give him the ol' one-two—and lights out, down he goes?* She keeps that in her head, but he catches the look.

"Got a better idea, spit it out," Kuba continues. "I'm here to get the job done, whatever it takes. If it means using some less than friendly persuasion, I'm all in. Runs in my family."

So says the boy who shuns the slaughterhouse. Angel studies the tower and the bridge, her face a mask of contradictions. Brittle fear. Supple speculation. *A night crossing would be smarter. Cover of darkness and all that... Maybe. But how'd you get the bridge lowered then? That's the trickiest part. Look at the side walls. Way high enough to provide cover for the day crossing.*

High enough to cover our bodies, maybe. Not our heads.

Kuba tears out a handful of thatch and flings it in frustration. "Look—"

"You're right. It's crazy dangerous and I wish there was another way. But there isn't. So we have to—" She catches herself before she uses the word 'try.' Trying will not suffice. But there is that contradiction on her face again. Determination propping up the corners of her lips, while doubt weighs down her eyes.

"Game plan?" Kuba asks.

"Inspections at the agsector and the clinic were done at the beginning of a shift. I'm guessing it's the same here."

"How many men you think are in there?" Kuba claws at another fistful of thatch.

"Tower? I doubt more'n one. That'd be a waste of resources. At the agsector, goliaths worked six-hour shifts, trained for another four."

"So, new guard relieves current guard. Inspector pops in and does his thing. I bust in and do my thing," Kuba says, popping his fist into his palm for emphasis. "Bridge lowers, you haul it across and I burn some rubber bringing up the rear."

Angel stares at the boy. "You won't live to cross that bridge unless you make the kill. Understand?"

The boy stares back. Swallows. Nods.

"And know this. When you kill something, someone, you kill a little piece of yourself, too." She drags her eyes from his open face, his too-readable face. She plunges a hand into her backpack, fishes Suraj's watch out of its pocket. Flips it open, eyes its face. "Almost noon. Where do you want me?"

A moment's hesitation before Kuba replies, pointing. "That

stand of trees down near the end of the berm. Sit tight there and when you see the bridge start to lower, put your kicks to the pedals and go. And don't look back."

A nod, serious, almost somber. And something else. The way her eyes meet his and then skitter away.

"What? No kiss for luck?" Kuba jokes, nerves sharpening the edge of his voice.

Angel's reply is a fist pressed to her chest. "To remake the world." She thrusts it forward. And they seal the deal solemnly, bone on bone.

Crazynutjobwhack. They scramble down the backside of the berm to the shrubs where they've stashed the bikes. She awkwardly straddles hers for the short ride through the grass to her hiding place in the pines. Kuba pushes his back up the berm, then hunkers down to wait for the changing of the guard. The gloom of the thicket accentuates the chill, but Angel's brain is broiling. *Sure fail.* Peering through her scope, she keeps her eyes on the control tower, but her inner voice is a blade brandished in the face of her doubt.

Stop. Breathe. Focus. Think.

A steady distant hum throbs from the stubby, round generators that jut from the flat roofs of the barracks. It undercuts the whiny voice inside her head that refuses to stay mum, warning her that something here will end badly.

Through the scope, Angel watches two men clad in drab camouflage fatigues stride toward the turret. One is tall, burly, an engineered goliath. The other, of a smaller and lighter build, has to be the inspector. Bred for brains and submission to authority. She shifts the scope to scan the crest of the berm. No sign of Kuba.

The men reach the tower and pause at the armored steel door. The taller man eyeballs the scanner and swipes his fingers as the other waits for the biometrics to clear security and release the lock. Then the goliath pulls the door open and the two disappear inside the tower as the door slowly closes behind them.

A swooping movement on her left. Kuba, coasting down the berm, pulling up to the right of the door and ditching his bike there, so that when the door opens again, he'll be hidden by its bulk. Crouching, waiting, body tense and coiled, a snake ready to strike.

Movement again, up and to the right. Behind the large window in the control room, three men stand together, hands gesturing, heads cocking and nodding. Engaged in greetings and end-of-shift bantering and the typical macho changing of the guard chest thumping. Pretending it all hadn't been hours of mind-numbing boredom.

Go on. Cut the bull session. Get on with it.

As if by her command, one guard moves out of view. Seconds later, the turret door swings open.

He never sees it coming. Probably barely even feels it, so swift is the movement of the arm that swings around and throttles his neck, so pure and sharp is the knife that slits his throat. And then the guard is on the ground, his life a gush of crimson pooling around his head. And Kuba is through the door.

Red, so very red against the gray of the concrete.

She swings her scope up and to the right, just in time to see the glint of a knife as it arcs under the blue-white lights inside the control tower. And then it is all garble. Garble and twang.

I'm swaying—like there's a hand on my head, and a drill boring into my skull, and it's pushing me over and down and there's no air and too much light...

Then it's as if a hand is tugging her up off the ground. And a voice jabs like a cattle-prod, not her inner voice, a gruff voice, raspy from lack of use, a voice she has not heard for awhile...

No time to pull a fem act! Get up! He's got it comin' down. Get on the frackin' bike and ride!

See the bridge look at the bridge it's coming down get on the

*bike get your legs moving don't think about anything else—about—
no, don't think about it see the bridge look at the bridge don't think
about it just ride the bridge look at the bridge don't think about anything but the bridge don't think about the possibility of a transport
barreling out of the canyon of towers beyond that bridge just ride...*

Down the berm she hurtles, and then up the rise, grinding
over the packed gravel, feeling it in her bones, her muscles, up
along her spine, through the cradle of her pelvis, until she rears
up over the curb and reaches the smooth cement of the bridge.

*Keep riding just ride a third of the way don't think about it
halfway mark don't think about it just follow the rail don't think
about what's behind don't think about what's ahead just ride...*

A whoosh and a ping. The ack-ack-ack of an automatic rifle.

Get low! The voice screams and she tries to shrink down near
the frame of her bike, but her bulk makes it impossible.

*Where's it coming from back there or up ahead don't think just
ride... and don't look back...there it is the end of the bridge see the
steel plate once you're over it you're on the other side on your way to
the water man...*

But something is wrong. The teeth of the plate are separating from their mates on the other side. Angel sees the small gap
as she passes over it and feels the thump as her rear tire drops a
few inches.

*It's opening it's rising again don't look back don't look back
don't look back...*

But she has to, grabbing the hand brakes and pulling up
so sharply that she almost takes a header over the handle bars,
craning her neck just in time to see a bike and its rider vault from
the edge of the swiftly rising span into the air.

There's nothing there to hold him...

Nothing but sheer momentum to guide the arc of his flight.
Yet there he hangs as if suspended by invisible wires. Hanging,
flying, floating. Just there in the air. Until gravity finally snares

him and hauls him back to the earth. Kuba tries to land on his back tire, but the bike tips forward and spins away underneath, throwing him sideways. He lands on his back in the gravel. Instantly motionless.

Angel flings her bike away and races to the boy. Kneels awkwardly beside him, bending low as she can, ignoring the wide swath of blood that stains the front of his jacket, grabbing his limp hand, squeezing tight.

"Kuba? Kuba!" She runs her fingers gently across his sweat-soaked cheek, afraid of jostling his head.

His eyelids flutter and he moans. But when he opens his eyes, they are fierce, accusatory. "Told you not to look back," he croaks. "Get on that bike and ride. Gotta get distance between us and them."

"I'm not leaving without—"

"Then help me up."

She clasps his extended hand, stills its tremor in her grip, and gives a heave.

And they are off again, hearts in mouths, head rush of pure adrenaline pulsing in their temples, pedaling madly down the asphalt street into the canyon between the skyrisers, swerving around transports parked along the curbs, leaning into a sharp turn that takes them down a side street out of the line of fire. And suddenly they are in the midst of more people than Angel has seen in months. A cluster of bees at a mobile kiosk gives them a look en masse as they whiz past.

Time to ditch. They'll be looking for two on bikes.

A mobile approaches, huge and green, like a giant, irradiated caterpillar. It slides up to the kiosk, its electric heart purring softly, blocking them from the view of the queue.

Angel signals to Kuba, turns down another street, then jams on her brakes and skids to a stop. "On foot. Now."

In the steel and glass-walled canyons, the light is dim and it's impossible to keep the skyriser, their destination, in sight. Sirens echo to the west. The streets ooze with sweats headed home from their shifts. They elbow their way onto and out of packed mobiles, into the sour, damp air, looking tired and snappish, buds dangling over drooping shoulders as they seek a momentary respite from the constant barrage of the feed, wanting to hear only the simple peace and relative quiet of the commute. The low thrum of the mobile's electric heart. The hushed scrape of shoes trudging on the pavement. The rasp of voices muttering greetings and farewells.

They cast sidelong glances at Angel and Kuba, at their filthy jackets and disheveled hair and red, strained faces, but if they have suspicions, they shrug them off. Just another pair of sweats shuffling back to the shelter Galt provides for them, where they would cook and eat their meals, with their Protectorate-pre-scribed ingredients and Protectorate-regulated calorie count.

The girl and boy blend into the stream of workers as it flows around another corner. Swags, in personal transports, emerge from the dark mouth of one building, and wave their left hands in front of the sensors, or, if they are the most elite, merely stare at the optic reader. The gates to the facility swing open and they speed through, pulling out into the street. Sweats file slowly through the side tunnels, past embed sensors and through body scanners that check them, with a soft electric murmur, for contraband.

Rounding a corner, they encounter CQO Zinni staring down at them from the side of a towering edifice, her milky skin stretching in digital glory, her perfect plum lips, uncreased, plump, parting and closing in rhythm. Kuba blinks, recognizing the face from the 'tronic sign. "It's her!"

"What did you accomplish today? What did you do to de-serve your place in this society? These are the questions you must ask yourself every single day of your life. What I have done to contribute to the well-being of my fellow workers? What did I do to make this a better place for all? Did I strive toward perfection? Did I seek achievement for myself alone or did I make those around me better, too? If you are not asking yourself these crucial questions, then you are failing. Failing yourself and failing those around you, and failing the Protectorate. Galt provides."

The richness of that voice. The perfection of its tone and timbre. In its absence, Angel has forgotten its seductive qualities. But not the resentments it breeds, bubbling up amidst the induced calm. On Kuba's face, she sees the guilt staining his cheeks, the enormity of what he's just done. He is transfixed, by the face and the voice, that voice from the 'tronic sign and the shortwave pickups, the clandestine sessions with his brothers huddled around the radio in the dark. He rubs the palms of his hands against his thighs, as if wiping something away.

"Don't look, Kuba." But in that moment, she sees the afterimage of the goliath at the bridge tower, the glint of the knife as it arcs through the air, the spray of a red fountain. The boy's innocent hand bent to her own vengeful will. Drenched in her venom. And she shudders.

Kuba gapes at the looming image, a brittleness glazing his features. As if he will shatter with a flick of her finger.

Averting her eyes, Angel hurries past the 'tronic board and its pretty poisons. Glances up. The waterman's skyriser is gone again. North and east is all she knows, sensing its location somewhere in the canyons. North and east. Down a crowded sidewalk. But now she's catching looks. Fighting the current of sweats. It parts for her, but the eyes—she's melting the glaze over them. Her belly's melting the glaze. Some even stop and stare, mouths a little slack, not quite gaping, but almost. When she glances over her shoulder, they're standing motionless, watching her retreating figure.

They plow onward. Around the next corner, the crowd of sweats thins and the flow of transports ebbs. Daylight is ebbing, too. A deep gloom settles into the city canyons and with it a chill mist. The solar lights brighten, casting their violet glow, as the lights within the buildings dim. Angel catches sight of the tower again, bands of bright light encircling its upper floors like a be-jeweled ring on a finger. Or a beacon signaling to her.

Out of breath, she pauses, leans against a light pole, its surface clammy under her palm. Only then does she notice it. The yawning pain expanding below her belly.

61

Reckoning

FUNNY HOW THINGS SOMETIMES COME INTO CLARITY in an instant. It astonishes Tanner, the suddenness of his realization.

She's going for the water plant.

With the tip of his boot, he toes the thin layer of shiny rime crusted on the dull grass. He's passed the night eyeing the maelstrom of activity churning through the garrison. It was the spiraling yellow lights of the mobile medic transport arcing through the mist that attracted him in the first place. Drew him in.

He doesn't have to show his credentials. The men of the unit know him by sight. But he flashes them anyway to command the captain's attention. And his deference.

An ambush. At least two perps, possibly more. One man dead. Another critically injured. Perp used a knife. Does not appear to be armed with a burner. Or, at least, did not return fire after being fired upon. Crossed the bridge on bikes, which they abandoned almost immediately. Description sorely lacking in detail. Inspector so severely wounded about the throat that he is unable to communicate at this time. Perps wearing black jackets. No, grey jackets. Perhaps brown. Mist hampered view as they fled. Motive unknown.

Damn shame. Dead man was an amazing physical specimen.

It is then, when he has absorbed the pertinent information and tuned out the squad leader's recitation of the dead goliath's attributes, that Tanner scans the land beyond the river, the forest of skyrisers, and catches sight of the tower. The weak sun struggles to penetrate the film of clouds and its rays fall half-heartedly on the black steel and glass, but they still spark a glimmer off the imposing facade.

And then he just... knows.

She would—wouldn't she? In tracking her these many days, he thinks he has come to know her. In a way. Like one comes to know the habits of the quarry. The way the hunted deer darts and dashes, then pauses abruptly to sniff the breeze, turn its head to the side, and take in the lay of the land with its huge liquid brown eye.

The morning's air is frosty, carrying with it a freshening smell, the possibility of snow.

A voice comes to him, unbidden. His father. Keeper of knowledge. Singing. Even as the brute squad led him away.

"One more river to cross..."

"You need to stop lookin' at me like I'm a pile of crap you just stepped in. You've done the same. Hell, it's the reason you're heading for that skyriser, ain't it?"

Angel keeps her eyes fixed on the east, where she's longing to see a sliver of sun break the horizon, longing to see the clouds streaked the sherbet colors of orange and pink. She understands, deep in the gut, that it's not any look of hers, but his own feelings of guilt that are gnawing at his innards like some ravenous beast, as he tries to convince himself of the righteousness of his actions. Tries to surmount a wall of doubt.

Don't expect me to thank you. She seethes inside, the beast gnawing at her as well. For the knowledge of what the boy did. For her. In her name. In the night she has cut two more notches along her forearm—one for the goliath and one for the boy. The boy who could not bring himself to slaughter a chicken or take down a deer. For *that* boy, now gone.

They had passed the night huddled in a narrow alley alongside a rusted composting dumpster that stinks of wet and rot. When Kuba hefted the heavy lid to ditch his bloodstained jacket inside, the stench broke over them in a wave. He insisted on taking the first watch, but sleep eluded Angel as the tide of pain ebbed and flowed across her belly. He'd tried to engage her throughout the black hours, but she had turned away, cradling herself, fear creeping up her spine with each swell that swept across her body like a seiche barreling across a lake.

Now the boy pushes himself up and stalks away, headed toward the street.

"Where you goin'?"

"It talks," he mutters, but keeps walking.

Angel grabs hold of a handle on the dumpster. The chill of it, and the slime, resists her grip, but she pulls herself to her feet. "I said, where you goin'?"

"To take a piss, d'ya mind?"

"I'm not lookin' at you like you're shit. That's what you're thinkin' 'bout yourself." She didn't mean to let that escape her lips.

He rounds on her, grabs her roughly by the shoulders, pulling her in so that his face looms just inches from hers. And then something changes. In the gloom, Angel can hardly make out his expression, but she feels the change in his hands still gripping her shoulders. An ease in the press of his fingers. Less anger, more of something else. She turns her face away before his lips can meet her own. They briefly graze her cheek and instantly he releases her, his hands falling helplessly to his sides.

"I'm sorry," he croaks, the syllables caught in his throat. And he stumbles off into the shadows of the alley, leaving Angel alone with the dying night and a jumble of feelings to pick through, fumbling around like clumsy fingers trying to untangle a knotted skein of yarn.

Stop. Breathe. Focus. Think.

The wave of pain rolls through again, deep in her belly. In the face of its assault, she falls back, finds support in the brick wall against which they've been sheltering. Feels a gentle thump on her breastbone. Reaches up under her jacket, digs beneath her flannel smock. Fingers close around the smooth oval stone. It's surprisingly warm, even in the night chill, absorbing heat from her skin.

Its firm but gentle contours under the tips of her fingers conjure a face beloved. A face whose planes and angles, bones and flesh are engraved in her memory as indelibly as an inscription carved in stone. *Hasta siempre. I will see you with my heart until I see you with my eyes. But forever has not come.*

The tide of pain recedes. She breathes. Runs a finger once more along the arc of the stone.

When Kuba trudges back down the alley, skirting puddles and potholes, his needless shame a yoke upon his shoulders, he is vacillating between apologizing yet again or going the silent route, letting it all just sink or blow over. By the time he reaches the dumpster, he's swung back to offering an apology. But there's no one to accept it. Their backpacks lean up against the building as before. But Angel's is gaping open, the flap lolling like a monstrous tongue.

The girl and the gun are gone.

It is a living, breathing organism. Sighing, swelling as it fills its vast lungs. Lapping, shifting, insistent. Potential brutality lurks within the surge of every wave, small and large. A savage energy hides under the surface of its liquid skin. It stretches and yawns, a drowsy beast. Growls and hisses, snarls and purrs by turns. Impetuous, contemptuous of the human hand attempting to tame it. As if to say, take what you can, if you can, for as long as you can, but I will win in the end. I will endure long after you have returned to the muck out of which you crawled.

The wind out of the northeast, traveling the full bore of the beast, slaps her cheek, disturbing her reverie, shoves like a back-alley bully against her shoulder. She drags her hood up over her head, pulls it low to ward off the assault. In the rush of the white-capped waves against the concrete abutments, she hears a guttural laugh.

She has never seen so much water in all her life. And she is mesmerized.

The skyriser, too, is mesmerizing, in its own way. Its facade, a curtain of bronze-tinted glass and black aluminum, has withstood rain, sleet, and the snow of the long-ago Midwestern winters. The sun and scorching heat and monsoon-like storms of the present. But what strikes Angel as she stands at the base of the tower and stares straight up are the lines and curves of the architecture. They resemble paths to an unknown destination. The vertical paths straight and true, rising, forging onward, the shortest distance between two points. The curving paths undulate, like the swoop of the waves on the lake, on the horizontal, along the circumference of the building with its unique triad shape. Not unlike the roads of life. The choices involved. Whether to take the fastest path or the slower, careening one, with the opportunity to see more along the way.

The needle-like pricking at the base of her neck and the dizzying whirl of vertigo forces her gaze to level out again. A guard in the lightweight gear of building security, a navy blue jacket emblazoned with the Galt logo, is eyeing her with professional curiosity, strolling towards her, his manner casual with an undertone of officious courtesy.

It all comes rushing at her. The madness of it. What purpose does she have for standing here at the base of Galt's Water Quality Calumet Number One? She's thought none of this through, really, although it's been on the burner of her mind for months now, simmering. What can she say to this man to convince him to let her in? And even if she manages to breach those forbidding glass doors, she has no idea how many sweats and swags work in this immense building. Of those, can she really be sure who she's hunting? All she has is a name.

The waterman. Rivers.

A cramp grips and churns her belly, like a hand squeezing a sponge. She wills her fists to stay in the pockets of her coat, to not clutch at herself, but the strain of the contraction pinches her face, purses her lips. Draws the guard to her side.

"Ma'am?" He ventures cautiously, using the old-school swag term of respect, although he cannot truly believe that she is one of them, given her dirt-streaked face and matted hair and filthy jacket and the human reek of her. Can he?

"My—father's in there. I need to see him."

How quickly the lie is conceived and birthed, sliding out between her lips. He shouldn't believe it. The deceit is there in plain sight, laid bare by the shambles of her appearance. But something in the telling, in her voice, makes him accept the false as true. At least momentarily.

Maybe the way she keeps her eyes fixed on his, instead of letting them slip to the side as she searches for words to shore up the falsehood. The way she presents the facade of sincerity. Or maybe it is the pain so obvious in the grim set of her jaw, the wince that wrinkles the corners of her eyes and knits her brow. Maybe it is the modicum of humanity that remains in this young man, a residue of compassion not yet fried by the Galt embed, a trace of benevolence that still pulses through the synapses.

On the chill gust that huffs in from the lake, a few minute white flakes drift. Land on her cheeks. Brief icy kisses. The first snow of the season.

The guard is hesitating, the first seeds of doubt germinating in his mind. She can't let them sprout. Her hand, stiff with the cold, slips out of the pocket of her jacket. Hovers a moment.

Comes to rest on his wrist as he's reaching across his body for his comlink.

"Help me. Please."

A lie well-told often passes for the truth. Enhanced by a look, a gesture, it becomes the actuality.

The guard, Steelman according to the tag above his badge, is a lost boy, not yet completely dominated by the hive mind. He misses his mother, maybe, or a girl back in his home region. Perhaps this is his first posting and he thought it would be different. The Chicago Garrison. *Such an honor. To be the guardian at the great Calumet, supplier of life to the Illiana.* But the reality does not live up to his imagined scenario. Kicking around in front of the cold monolith, catching his lonely reflection in the windows. All the dull moments spent pacing the colonnade at the base of the tower, leaning against its imposing black pillars. Tracing and re-tracing his steps around the perimeter of the transport garage. Reconnoitering its subterranean depths. Wandering the stone path in the green space planted above. Making the rounds of the bunker-like water plant just to the north of the tower. Nothing ever happens. The sweats and swags come and go, shuffling, striding, ignoring him. He means no more to them than the steel bollards that line the curb, anchored in concrete.

Maybe it's her words. Maybe the tone of her voice. Maybe the fraught weight of her hand on his wrist, a unkempt hand, skin red and chapped, fingernails black with dirt, but a hand, the human touch of it, imploring, recognizing him as a fellow traveler. His need makes him gullible to her ragged persuasion. The girl's eyes, the genuine fear—terror, even—the gasping trepidation in her voice as she confides her tale of the evil trailing her, tracking her, relentless, insidious. Those eyes, even more than the words, haunt him. Bring him to the realization that he is indeed the bollard, the stalwart defense that will stand between her and this menace.

"He wants to kill the baby. This child of Galt."

He insists on notifying the chief engineer in advance of his visitor. To ensure he's available to receive her. And he's so fixed on completing his mission, on getting this poor waif to her father that he doesn't notice her eyes slide to the side and her hand slip into her pocket.

He doesn't know how close he comes to death.

The lobby is empty. There is no reception desk, no receptionist. There is no need for one. No one comes without having an explicit reason to be there. No random visitors. Hence there are no witnesses. No one to interfere. But something stays the girl's hand from curling its fingers around the burner's grip.

After the guard conveys the message through his comlink, tells the waterman that his daughter has come to see him, Angel can't hear the waterman's reply, but it causes the guard to eye her, not necessarily with suspicion, but as if preparing himself for a barrage of questions. He says yes and yes and yes, again. And then, "She believes someone's trying to hurt her so I think you should let her come to you instead, sir."

When the assent comes, how it thrills this man-child to have his advice taken. From the astonishment in the chief engineer's voice, the guard senses this will be a momentous reunion. He flashes forward, seeing the commendation letter added to his digital portfolio. He yearns to accompany her to the shrine, the sanctum inside the water plant where the waterman begins his day. The guard has seen only glimpses. Slices of the bronze mural as the door swings shut. A menacing creature arcing from a russet wave. A fish writhing in the grip of coppery talons. But he knows his place in the world. Knows that his duty is merely to accompany her through the greenspace that stretches between the tower and the purification plant. To allow the entry scanner to read his embed. To watch as the gap between the doors slowly narrows, until she is just a sliver of a disheveled young woman, and then she is gone.

He rocks heel to toe, heel to toe, his body mimicking the sense of elation that floods over him. But how quickly it ebbs and he's struck by the emptiness in his gut now that she is no longer by his side.

The muffled clump of heavy boots on the concrete walkway startles him. He's seen this man before, this tall, shaven-head man, somewhere, sometime in his training, a man of import. Who? His brain tells him one thing even as his gut tells him another. That this is the evil stalking the girl. And then the lies spill from him, as he knows with certainty that her life and the life of the child depend on them. Even as he realizes that his own life depends on the truth. Or maybe it doesn't matter what he says, as the feeling creeps up his spine, vertebra to vertebra, like a thousand-legger inching its way along an arduous trail. Reaching his throat, it traps the words, the words that no longer matter.

Because the face into which he's staring is Death.

The thuds of the backpacks against his ribcage, twin assaults from the front and the rear, hinder his forward progress. But Kuba can't bring himself to jettison either of them. That would imply a finality. That there is nothing beyond the tower. That the skyriser is the end of the road. And he can't accept that. Won't accept it. Chases all thoughts of that from his mind. But they keep creeping back, slinking into the corners, glowing like the eyes of animals in the dark when caught in a stark beam of light.

Sweats and swags are starting to dribble into the early morning streets, exiting mobiles. He dodges and darts amidst the plodders, who seem in no hurry to get to their destinations. Several curse as he jostles past and he's automatically mumbling apologies, until a sharp voice in his head tells him to not waste his breath or time.

The colonnade plaza at the base of the tower is deserted. Through the glass doors, Kuba can see a few swags crisscrossing the lobby. But the entryway with its prominent embed reader is closed to him, unyielding, immovable. He paces, circling the skyriser, restless in the gathering gray light of another cloud-muffled dawn.

A sharp crack pierces the gloom. It comes from the direction of the low-slung building just to the north. Without thinking, he breaks into a run, the lug soles of his shoes thudding on the cement. Stops abruptly when he sees the sliding door of the entryway in motion. But the motion is repetitive. Constant. Sliding open, sliding closed. Not quite closed. Blocking the door's progress is one black-booted foot.

The soft edges of the guard's face signal he's been on this earth just a few year longer than Kuba and now he's leaving it, his existence seeping out onto the gray marble tile beneath his head as Kuba drags him just beyond the entryway, allowing the door to close with a whisper. Only the movement of his fingers remains as they spread over the holster at his hips, where his pistol still rests. Along with a few mumbled words.

"He's going to kill her."

62

The Waterman

"WHO ARE YOU?"

The waterman is not as she imagined. She's pictured him tall and solidly built, with a heft apropos to a man with such control over life and death. Envisioned him dark-visaged, heavy-browed. Instead, he is slender, stoop-shouldered, head about level with her own. Thinning hair, the color of wheat chaff, clipped short. Pale eyes blinking amidst the creases and sags of aging skin. A man as weightless and inconsequential as the curl of steam rising from the mug sitting beside him on the bench. Dwarfed by the monumental sculpture that consumes the wall behind him. Reduced to insignificance by the roiling glory of life that teems through the figures wrought in metal.

To see him in the flesh, so average, so indistinct is disconcerting. Disappointing. Of all the men she has killed, she wanted him to be the colossus, the gargantuan. Befitting his place as the last man she'll ever kill.

"Who are you?" The man repeats. Even his voice has an everyday monotony to it. Ephemeral. That of a man who could be here one minute and gone the next and no one would miss him very much, if at all. "You're not my daughter. Steelman said—but—"

She aches to accuse, to threaten, to rage. And then give him time to beg for his life. Aches for the trappings of revenge. But there is no time for that. There is only time for the doing. The grip of the gun feels so very familiar as she clutches it, still inside her pocket. The eye of the whale glares at her from the mural. She meets the fiery gaze of the hawk, talons clenched around its victim.

So finish it and be done. Quickly. And there's an end to it. Because there is no living after this.

Serafina awaits. She catches glimpses of her, she thinks, somewhere in the mist that hovers over the lake, just beyond the wall of windows. Beckoning. And so she draws the burner from her pocket and takes aim. By now, her finger fits the curve of the trigger as if it had been molded to it.

Disbelief transforms the waterman's face. Widens the eyes, the mouth. Shock freezes them. And then a shuddering boom. The sanctuary's steel door slamming back against the wall. The shave-head devil in the void.

Serafina, I am coming. Hasta siempre. Forever is now.

Even as she pivots to train the pistol on Tanner, she knows she doesn't have time to adjust. He won't give her the time. He is not the hesitating kind.

And so as the thoughts race through, some a blur, some piercingly clear, she thinks she must already be dead. That this is death, instantaneous. And now she has all kinds of time, an eternity, to ponder the past. *Is that what the dead do?* And then the rolling wave of a contraction washes over her, prying her open, the excruciating pain reminding her that she is still very much alive, refocusing her thoughts on the men before her. And her task. *How many? How many bullets left?*

The weight of the gun reveals nothing. It feels as heavy as the first time she hefted it with a trembling hand back in the Shawnee. When the old man had re-loaded with a grim joke.

"*Thirteen. Yer lucky number.*"

How many are left? Three? Two? One? Enough to finish the work? *Never leave your work undone, lest it unravel like a thread unknotted.* So who will it be? The one who administered death from afar, with the push of a small button? Or the one who wielded it at close range, who looked it in the face?

Blood-stained hands. Both.

Time freezes then. But her senses sharpen until they cut like the fine-honed blade of a knife. The steely bang of the door once more against the paneled wall. The explosive crack of her gun and the stuttering jolt to her arm. The cannon-like boom of another. The fraught metal reek of gunpowder burning the inside of her nostrils. The swollen thud of a head hitting ceramic tile. A fountain spray of red, the beads of it hanging in the air, or so it seems in that forever moment. The weight, the weight dragging on her. So heavy, so monumentally heavy. Hauling her down until she feels that gush of life ready to depart her body. And with it, the incredible need to expel it. To let it go. To give it up. To go.

Serafina. I'm coming. Forever is now.

From miles away, gasps, but muffled, wavering, as if they are coming from eons ago, like light from the stars. From near, the chill of the tile on her thigh as a hand peels her leggings down, easing her knees up. A raw snarl, but the hand under her head feels gentle. Something soft wedged underneath to cushion her skull. A shadow hovers over her and then it is gone again.

The eyes of the green man of the mural, molded soft in the hard metal, regard her from amidst the wild burst of hair, like the mane of a lion. His enormous hands reaching, lifting the figure from the water. A birth from the sea.

Parched. Her throat aches. *Water. All around and none to drink.* And then a hand under her head again, lifting. "Have a sip."

But even as her lips feel the smooth rim of the waterman's ritual glass, the overwhelming need to push, to bear down, grips her. A hand folds over hers as it scratches for purchase along the tile, nails scraping.

"Hold onto me."

And she squeezes, the urge to bellow swelling inside her chest and throat. But she bites down on her lips, shredding the ragged skin there, tasting blood, but holding the scream inside, using its energy to fuel yet another push. And suddenly a vast emptiness, a void, a cessation. A sighing relief, like the exhalation of a long-held breath. A ball of wet heat on her bare thighs. Fire and ice. A smaller wave, another tight squeeze, but the vice grip not so strong this time, and more heat seeps between her thighs.

"Gray-gray, what do I do now? What now what now what now!" A plea. Voice panic-drenched. Imploring. As if the ancient could hear him a million miles away.

She wants the hand again, but it's gone. So she flounders and scrabbles for something else to hold. And feels the piece of metal on the floor beside her. Light. Oh, it feels so light now. Practically weightless in her hand. Liquid almost, like water, taking its shape from her grip. She knows in her gut that there's one bullet left. There must be.

"Beautiful, so beautiful."

The boy is not looking at her. He's preoccupied with the hot and bloody little treasure in his hands, wiping its face with the tail of his shirt, turning the tiny body over to give a tentative thump on its blood-streaked back.

For all the pistol's weightlessness, the muzzle feels solid against her temple. Warm and dry amidst the sweat beaded there. And yet suddenly the trigger feels so very heavy to pull, an immoveable object against the insubstantial flesh of her finger, now weak, drained of its power.

"It's a girl. You have a beautiful little girl." So amazed, so full of wonder is that voice, half man, half boy, tears there. Awe.

The shadow of him turning toward her. A cry. Two cries. One a gurgling squawk, the other loud and sharp, as the shadow lurches over her body, one hand clutching the baby to his chest, the other stretching out to ram the barrel of the gun, sending it spinning out of her hand and skidding across the floor.

"What're you doing?" Shadow no longer, he's solid flesh, his hand raised, pulled back as if poised to slap her. But it's frozen there, time stopping yet again, and when it restarts, he brings it down slowly and lays it across her cheek.

"You have a daughter." A whisper amidst the tumult, the bedlam of battering.

A child of a murderer.

"Your child."

Yes, my child.

And now the wet heat is flowing from her eyes, scorching tears, long held.

"Look at her."

Angel turns her head away, but Kuba lays his fingers along her chin, gently but insistently pushes it back. "Look at her."

Through the wet blur, she sees the squashed red face looming above her, the eyes slits of liquid pooling amidst the puffy folds of skin, the nose a pugged flare of nostrils, the mouth pursed and pink and wet, waxy flakes peeling from the mottled skin of the bulbous forehead and cheeks. A slick of black hair clotted with blood.

And in that face she sees the visage of another. But it can't be. Because she understands in a rudimentary way that it is impossible without the ties of blood.

She drags her hands across her eyes, wiping the tears, trying to focus, expecting the visage to clarify into something else. Something more true.

But still she sees. And she knows.

It is Serafina.

Come back to her.

At last.

They have fed from the waterman's bounteous trough. Drank from his flowing fountains and bathed there, too. Washed the filth from their bodies. And the blood. Though some stains are permanently embedded within their flesh, impossible to scrub away with soap and water.

She appreciates the waterman's lack of stature now that she is wearing his clothes. Appreciates his swag taste for soft furnishings when Kuba slashes an exquisite blanket from the man's closet and fashions it into a sling. When he cuts the luxurious towels into diapers and bandages. The boy has talked and talked and talked, an incessant spew of information, as if he's wielding the words like a sword and shield, weapons to keep something at bay. Rambling on about the needs of a newborn. The work of a mother. Safe places he's heard tell of in eavesdropped conversations amongst the old women at the farm and amidst the junkers down in Dealer's Alley. Only once does he mention going back. And when he does, Angel fixes him with her eyes. He blinks, but doesn't look away. He's known all along, in his gut, in his heart, where the seeds of all such knowledge germinate.

There is no going back.

Under his chatter, the morning feed from the Hive drones from the vox on the waterman's kitchen counter. Storms over the Superior Region promising snow. The schedule for intake crib renovation and reconstruction. A change in the regional water quality conference's location.

Angel simply breathes. Holds the infant against her chest until their heartbeats meld into one.

She feels the preciousness of time. The guard's shift will end soon and then the reckoning will come. There is no space for weakness, for the sensation of fragility that floods her body in a moment of stillness. The walls are collapsing, within and without, and there is only one path. Forward. Now.

On the way out, she stoops to pluck the shave-head devil's

blackout shades from the pocket of his jacket. Wipes the finger-prints and grime from the lenses with his shirttail. Avoids look-ing into those strange, staring eyes, the ring of amber vivid in the blue iris. Places the sunglasses over her own eyes. Studies the view of the world through the sudden gray veil.

Another memento mori.

They will follow the water. With the future bound to her breast and the past slung across her back, she will head North. Without a backward glance.

Only a whispered *hasta siempre.* To remake the world.

Acknowledgments

Love to fill the Great Lakes to my husband, Larry Pincsak, and my daughters, Cecily and Simone, who somehow endure the trials and tribulations of living in close proximity to a writer, which may occasionally—perhaps more than occasionally—feel as if one if living life on a rollercoaster.

Rivers of thanks to Debi Workman, Sallee Brossard and Nancy Headen, who read early versions and gave valuable feedback and encouragement.

Streams of gratitude to the original members of the Soon to be Famous Author Project™ committee, including Dee Brennan, Liz Clemmons, Julie Stam, Sue Wilsey, Nikki Zimmermann, Denise Raleigh, and Cris Cigler, along with the public libraries in Illinois and across the country that welcomed me onto their shelves and into their presentation rooms. Winning your award validated me as a writer and gave me the determination to keep going. Thanks for plucking me from the field and adding me to the bouquet!

Heaven truly is an open book and a library to wander in.

About the Author

Joanne Zienty was born in Chicago, Illinois. She is the winner of the 2014 Soon to Be Famous Illinois Author Project™ Award for her debut novel, *The Things We Save*, for which she was also named a semi-finalist in the *Publisher's Weekly* BookLife Prize for Fiction. She studied English Language and Literature at the University of Chicago, earned her teaching certification at Roosevelt University, and her Master's in Library and Information Science at Dominican University. When she's not writing, she uses her position and influence as a teacher/librarian to help her young students grow as readers and find their voices as writers. She lives in Wheaton, Illinois with her husband and a very ornery cat.

www.ingramcontent.com/pod-product-compliance
Lightning Source LLC
Chambersburg PA
CBHW021340110726
47900CB00005B/1553